AZERBAIJANIAN PROSE

AN ANTHOLOGY

Edited by Mirza Ibragimov

PROGRESS PUBLISHERS
MOSCOW

Compiled by *Ismail Shikhuly* and *Isi Melikzade*

Designed by *Nazim Babayev*

ПРОЗА АЗЕРБАЙДЖАНА

Антология

На английском языке

70500-493
A —————— 76-76
014(01)-77

Contents

A few words on
Azerbaijanian literature*

Literature brings us together, creating a spiritual kinship among peoples. I repeat these thoughts without fear that I might lapse into banalities because the literary tradition of my people, represented in this book, has always been a humanistic tradition. And this is not a matter of chance.

Since olden times Azerbaijan has been called "Odlar Yurdu" — Land of Fires. To this day in the village of Ramany near Baku one can still find the ancient temples of the fire-worshippers.

An unextinguishable flame burns eternally in our people's spirit as well. Even in pre-revolutionary times when the great majority of Azerbaijanians were illiterate it was difficult to find a ploughman or shepherd, not to mention a person working in the city, who did not know a great number of verses, fables, and *bayati* songs (quatrains and proverbs). Yes, since olden times Azerbaijan has also been called "Sheir Yurdu" — Land of Poetry.

I share the conviction of many historians that the Azerbaijanians are descended from the ancient Medes and that their poetry has ancient roots. The people's first literary creations are myths and legends. The most famous of these is the legend of King Astiag and his general who betrayed his motherland out of a desire for personal revenge. Recounted by the "father of history" Herodotus, this legend is retold in almost all anthologies of Azerbaijanian literature.

From the 4th to 9th centuries A.D. Azerbaijanians created heroic legends about the fearless Babek who led a popular uprising against the Arabian Caliphate and local feudal lords, against the Islam, a religion being spread at the time by fire and sword. At the same time other forms were being developed in the national literary tradition: tales, proverbs, sayings, and the marvellous *bayati*, that unique, pithy, formally rich quatrains of oral folk poetry. During the rule of the Azerbaijanian dynasty of the Shirvan-shahs in the 12th century, on the basis of oral folk art the classical poetry of Azerbaijan came into bloom; its leading representatives were Mekhseti-Khanum, Khagani and Nizami Ganjevi. The works of these remarkable Azerbaijanian poets have brought them great renown in the Near and Middle East, representing a vivid page in the book of the humanistic, progressive poetry of mankind. Nizami's famed *Quintuple: Seven Beauties, Khosrau and Shirin,* and *Iskandarnama* as well as *Tokhfatul-iragein (Gifts of Iraq)* and *Khabsije (The Book of a Slave)* are a well of wisdom and noble human feelings.

In the 13th and 14th centuries the poetry of Azerbaijan was enriched by the work of Nasimi Imadeddin, a great poet and pantheist who boldly attacked the lifeless dogma of Islam and religious bigotry. For this he was condemned by a

* © Издательство «Прогресс», 1976

© Translation into English. Progress Publishers 1976

religious court to be skinned alive in broad daylight at the bazaar in the town of Khaleb. He courageously endured the fearful tortures of the medieval Moslem inquisitors and breathed his last without renouncing his convictions.

In the 16th century there was a new flowering of poetry in Azerbaijan. At this time the great Fizuli created his world-renowned philosophical and lyrical ghazals and poems. Fizuli's poetry was imbued with the spirit of a profound humanism; it reflected the discontent of the masses with feudal rule and demonstrated a progressive political position for the times. Fizuli developed the finest traditions of his forerunners. He came out against the dogmatism of Islam contrasting mysticism and superstition with the true, human feelings of this world.

For Fizuli, the harmonious combination of a man's material and spiritual needs was the moral, philosophical, and ethical standard by which one should live.

In the same epoch, the well-known Shah-Ismail Khatai, next to Fizuli the leading figure of the era, wrote remarkable short and long poems.

The 16th century was characterised by the rapid growth of folk poetry. Many *dastans* (heroic or lyrical folk tales) were created during this period, among them the immortal epos *Keroglu*. The poetry of Azerbaijanian bards, the Ashugs, was also highly developed.

In the second half of the 18th century, Vagif and Vidadi closed the medieval era and began a new Azerbaijanian poetic tradition. The work of both, particularly the *goshma*—the amorous philosophical verses of Vagif—was vividly realistic and reflected human emotions.

The 19th century marked a new page in the history, life and literature of the Azerbaijanian people. At this time close, brotherly ties developed between the Azerbaijanian and Russian peoples. Through the Russian language and culture Azerbaijanians came into contact with the progressive revolutionary thought and literature of Europe. The ideas of the Russian Decembrists, of Russian revolutionary democrats, of Radishchev, Belinsky, Dobrolyubov and Herzen came to Azerbaijan, Pushkin, Lermontov, Gogol, Tolstoy, Nekrasov and Turgenev were read. The progressive members of the Azerbaijanian intelligentsia became acquainted with the ideas of the French Enlightenment and the works of Voltaire, Diderot and Helvetius.

In the 19th century profound developments occurred in Azerbaijanian society; the people began to strive for progress, civilisation and freedom. These grandiose changes and tendencies in the people's life found reflection in the work of a great pleiad of realists led by M. F. Akhundov. This school included, among others, such distinguished writers as Zakir, Mirza Shafi, Seid Azim Shirvani. Naturally each of these men had his own artistic style, devices and convictions. Some largely adhered to the ideas of enlightenment, others to democratic ideals, but together they all reflected a new period in Azerbaijanian literature. The colossal figure of Akhundov towered over all other writers and cultural figures of Azerbaijan in the 19th century. Akhundov brought Azerbaijanian realism to its highest stage of development—critical realism. He had an all-round education, absorbing the best of Eastern and European literature, culture and philosophy. He laid the foundations for Azerbaijanian drama and prose. And his works are classics as regards form and content. His comedies *Hadja Kara* and *Molla Ibragim the Alchemist*, his novella *The Stars Were Deceived*, and his philosophical treatise *The Letters of Two Princes* are classed among the greatest achievements of Azerbaijanian realistic democratic literature.

In the late 19th and early 20th centuries, Azerbaijanian literature witnessed the advent of a distinctive, colourful pleiad of writers of the revolutionary-realist bend. Critical realism reached its apex in their works. Djalil Mamedkulizade, Sabir, Narimanov, Akhverdov and Vezirov, among others, depicted the revolutionary struggle of the Azerbaijanian people and the entire East awakening under the influence of the Russian revolution of 1905 and the Great October Revolution of 1917 to struggle, as Lenin put it, for their elementary right, for democracy and freedom. With the triumph of Soviet power in Azerbaijan on April 20, 1920, a new era began for the people. This also entailed the flowering of the artistic intelligentsia. Azerbaijanian Soviet literature, whose seeds were sown to a certain degree before Soviet power by such major writers as Narimanov, Sabir, Ordubady, and Mamedkulizade, was able to achieve full development. During the first ten years of socialist construction, there was a struggle to bring literature in closer touch with the people's life, to reflect the great changes in people's lives and psychology. Writers strove, in other words, to master the methods of socialist realism. In the process developed the major writer Djafar Djabarly who founded Azerbaijanian Soviet dramaturgy. His plays *Seville*, *Almas*, and *Yashar*, among others, chronicle the struggle of the Azerbaijanian people for a new life, for a socialist transformation of reality during the first decade of Soviet power. Other major Azerbaijanian Soviet poets and writers who began their careers in those years include Suleiman Rustam, Samed Vurgun, Mikhail Mushfik, Rasul Rza, Mekhti Gussein, A. Abulgasan, S. Ragimov, Ali Veliev, Akhmed Djamil, Sabit Rakhman, Mir Djalal, and Enver Mamedkhanly. Today the works of these outstanding writers are not only published in all the languages of the peoples of the Soviet Union, but in many other languages as well. Samed Vurgun's poetry is exceptionally popular because it is imbued with the great ideas of socialist humanism and because it depicts the noble spiritual qualities of Soviet man, defender of peace and builder of a new life. Samed Vurgun's realism is inspired with romantic ideas; his work has a powerful idealistic and artistic impact. His colourful poetry has universal appeal, because of its distinctive national features and its vivid descriptive qualities. Poetic thought for Vurgun is inseparable from the poetic traditions of his people.

The themes of internationalism and friendship among peoples are predominant in contemporary Azerbaijanian literature. This is natural enough. Our people struggle for peace and they love peaceful labour which brings happiness to all men on this earth. The heroes of our writers' works are the peaceful workers who create all the boons of the earth.

It is my profound hope and belief that this anthology will not only give the reader some notion of the literature of our ancient country, but will promote friendship and co-operation among all peoples of the earth.

Mirza Ibragimov,
People's Writer of Azerbaijan

16th-early 20th century prose

Fizuli

I am a sovereign supported by armies of words,
The thunder-bearing word brings me victory.
Each word of mine is a giant whose strength comes from
truth,
Should the word will it, land and sea will submit to it.

Ghazal

**Mirza Fatali
Akhundov**

O, Iranian people! If only you had tasted the sweetness of freedom, if only you had been versed in the rights of mankind, you would never have consented to such a shameful enslavement and to submissiveness.

...Your numbers and resources are a hundred times greater than those of the despot and tyrants; you lack only the unity of thought and spirit to forge a revolution and free yourself from slavery.

1862

Mamedkulizade *O, my brother Moslems! If my words strike you as funny and you grin from ear to ear and howl with laughter,... don't think that you are laughing at Molla-Nasreddin. O, my brother Moslems! If you want to know whom to laugh at, hold up a mirror and look well at your own reflection....*

Molla-Nasreddin, 1906

Abduragim bek Akhverdov

An educated man should be of benefit to others. Educated people should be eyes for the blind and lanterns for those who live in darkness. We especially need educated men, for our people are ignorant and helpless.

1900

Letters from Hell

**Nariman
Narimanov**

On one side is capital, which buys and sells all things — faith, humanity and conscience; for it is the same capital that provokes bloody conflicts between peoples. On the other side is labour, reinforcing brotherhood among peoples, elevating man's spiritual world, preparing him to struggle with the elements and opening the hidden treasures of nature to him. We want to inaugurate an era where labour truly is triumphant. Only those who themselves labour shall reap the blessings of that labour.

1919

From the article *The Slogans We Bring to the Caucasus*

Mukhammed Fizuli
(1498-1556)

This great poet, master of the lyrical ghazal and author of the classic poem "Laila and Majnun", left posterity only one short prose piece, "A Complaint". This is reason enough to establish M. Fizuli as the founder of Azerbaijanian prose fiction.

True, more than two centuries before Fizuli, in the 12th century the poet Khabani Shirvani wrote a series of letters which some scholars regard as the first models of Azerbaijanian epistolary prose. But Fizuli's work is so original and perfect that it is far more deserving of the right to occupy the leading place in this anthology.

"A Complaint" is a clever satire on the feudal regime of those times, on the customs instituted by despotic rulers. Fizuli's satirical short story is almost entirely written in rhythmic prose and some lines are rhymed.

Despite Fizuli's great poetic gift, his entire life was spent in poverty. He died of cholera and was buried in Iraq, in the town of Kerbela not far from Baghdad.

In 1956, the USSR marked the 400th anniversary of this great Azerbaijanian poet's death. A monument has been erected to Fizuli in Baku.

A Complaint

To His Excellency Nishanchi Pasha.

The lord who adorned the world, wise sovereign of nations, bestowed good land for men to live upon and entrusted the distribution of the blessings of life to just kings, merciful rulers. For each needy man, caught in the grip of poverty, he reserved a share from his mysterious coffers.

May your musk-dispensing pen be the key to the gates of the treasure-house of life's blessings, and your words, fragrant as ambergris, fortifying the foundations of the kingdom, be a torch for perspicacious eyes.

After offerings of gratitude and salutations:

I, a lowly slave, a man who has no worth,
Distant from life's freedom, from her joys and mirth,
Long accustomed to my lonely, wretched state,
I, who never have rebelled against my fate,
Suddenly began to dream of wealth and fame;
Wishing to be great, to have men speak my name.
And I wished for such success in all my ways
That I might be worthy of our ruler's praise;
But I did not realise that day and night
I would always feel men's jealousy and spite;
Soon I learned the evil that results from greed;
Man becomes a fool, a slave who can't be freed.

21

If a man does not submit to heaven's will
He will know misfortune and all earthly ills.
And his dreams and hopes however high they be,
Always will be prey to pain and misery.

To be brief, when the crown of content adorned my head and my body was clothed in solitude and I preferred to try to understand the spiritual world rather than to master the material world, when I was the sovereign of the land of unconcern and disdain, the ruler of the valley of poverty and non-existence, the pearl of my nature wished to rise, for the sense of intoxication had gone from my life. I heard the voice of an angel who addressed me from the world of benevolence. "O foolish one," he said. "The material world is the expression of divine attributes, the source of rays of unlimited pleasures. The earthly kingdom is inseparable from the heavenly kingdom. People who have not enjoyed earthly blessings will not be granted heavenly blessings. One must address the rulers of this earth to obtain the desired reward. The king's favour is the path to obtaining one's goal.

For truly does the *khadis** say that "the emperor is God's shadow on earth". The man who scorns this errs. There is another well known saying: "With the exception of prophets and angels, there is no higher state than that of a king." To ignore this is sinful. It would be particularly sinful to ignore our sovereign whose kingdom is the throne of the caliph and whose throne is the post of imam.

Sultan Suleiman is king of land and sea
And the sultan's rule is a government of right.
Allah! May the sultan rule eternally
For his rule of wisdom is the land's delight.

In a word, fascinated by such thoughts I begged for a share from the highest throne and had the good fortune to receive it. I, who had scorned the nine heavens, was told that I must be satisfied with a grant of nine *akcha*** from a *vagfa.**** Wishing to receive a transfer of this sum, I sent the document to His Imperial Majesty and waited for an answer. When the proper amount of time had expired, and my hopes and expectations of a favourable answer had been raised by pleasing communications, I received the answer to my petition. I was awarded a state *barat*,**** adorned with the garb of knowledge and enlightenment. Black lines, the colour of ambergris, appeared: "the flower of nocturnal darkness";***** in the places that had been left white, the colour of camphor, reflected "the clarity of dawn"; the lines arranged on the page shed their life-giving moisture like a layer of clouds; the periods set in these lines glimmered like stars in the heavens. The letter, which had been handed to me with great respect, was full of expressions strung together like priceless pearls thrown on the shore by the waves of bounty; it was as full of musk as the navel of a deer from Khotan.*) Its title

---

* Tales and legends about the maxims of Mohammed or his imams (apostles).—*Ed.*
** *Akcha*—a monetary unit.— *Ed.*
*** *Vagfa*—willed property.— *Ed.*
**** *Barat*—an order or document.— *Ed.*
***** A verse from the Koran.— *Ed.*
*) Musk is obtained from a gland under the tail of a deer native to the plains of Khotan, in China.— *Ed.*

22

read: "So be it"; the contents recalled the saying: "God's perfection is expressed in his readiness to give each man what he wishes for. God is our benefactor."

The end read: "This is from Suleiman in the name of Allah, the all-gracious and merciful." *

> *Respect and glory elevate man's soul,*
> *A man rejoices in a lovely scroll*
> *That is as full and ample as the moon.*
> *A scroll is like a key that will release*
> *Great treasures, like a heart that knows no crease,*
> *And like the scent of musk and ambergris.*

And truly the gracious epistle filled me with a joy that cannot be described by lips or pen. When this scroll, the herald of happiness and prosperity was given to me, my sorrowful soul was seized with a joy so great that I have not the power to describe it.

> *I am filled with consolation*
> *In the dead of night I cry,*
> *"God, do you bestow salvation*
> *On this creature who must die?"*

To be brief, I rose involuntarily and set off to present this order to the administrator of *vagfas*. True it was not given me to contemplate him, my imploring arms did not reach him; but I went to his office which is well known among the people. And since I arrived at the most unhappy hour, I saw a group of evil-tongued people there. I noticed not the slightest trace of honour or truth in them. Here was a group of rogues spreading their nets. They were beasts, the most rapacious of beasts. Their depraved manners seemed to saw at one's heart like files; evil, vicious, insulting words thundered like the waves of a flood that destroys all in its path.

I greeted them. But they did not take note of my greeting, saying that "Salam" is not a bribe. I showed them my decree, but they ignored it since it did them no good. Although they expressed a superficial readiness to obey it, in fact they answered differently to all my questions.

I asked: "Gentlemen, what is this lawlessness? Why all the frowning faces?"

They answered: "It is a custom of long standing."

I said: "But it was decided to help me. I was given a decree for a pension so that I would be able to use it always on account of a *vagfa* and would be able to pray for our padishah in peace."

They answered: "O miserable one! They have occasioned you a great evil and doomed you to a life of litigation. You will be eternally involved in a lawsuit and eternally obliged to gaze upon evil faces and hear abusive words."

I said: "Why should not the *barat* be carried out?"

They answered: "Because the sum must be allotted from surplus funds and it is impossible to obtain them."

* All excerpts in quotes are taken from the Koran.— *Ed.*

23

I said: "Surely there must be a surplus with the large revenue you receive."

They answered: "Should something remain after sacred expenses, then it will not slip past our hands."

I said: "It is sinful to appropriate money from a *vagfa*."

They answered: "We bought the money with our *akcha*; we are permitted to do this."

I said: "What if you are called upon to answer for your crimes and these are exposed?"

They answered: "That will be in the other world on Judgement Day."

I said: "You know that people must answer for their crimes in this world as well."

They answered: "No, we are not afraid of that for the secretaries have also been satisfied."

I saw that they were answering my questions with empty words and had no intention of seeing to my needs. What could I do but cease to argue and sorrowfully return to my cell. I took umbrage at these insults to my *barat*; but it had shamed me by subjecting me to so many difficulties. Like a cancelled cheque it had lost its power, and I, like a slave who had been deceived, had lost all hope.

> *I am the one who wishes it ill — it is misfortune to me.*
> *I am beneath its contempt — it is the fire that burns me.*
> *I bring it sorrow and toil — it brings me toil and grief.*
> *That is the reason I spurn him. That is the reason it spurns me.*

Finally when my despair had reached its limits and the sea of astonishment overflowed its shores, a thought crept into my heart: black clouds cannot hide the sun of grace ascending from the horizon of bounties; the transparent water streaming from the sources of goodness cannot be clouded by sand raised by an evil hurricane. Soon all this must come to an end and the barriers will be removed.

> *Lord, may the caliph's rule not prove*
> *A tissue of lies and deception.*
> *Lord, may the shah's decree not prove*
> *A dragon to honorable men.*

O, my sovereign, let it be no secret to you that the state *barat* cannot be executed because there is a discrepancy between its contents and the notification. And in truth if the word "surplus" implies that only after all expenditures connected with payment of employees and workers, with the grants of pensioners, the purchase of feed for animals and other constructive and destructive endeavours have been effected will there remain a share for me, then the great court should have made a notation to this effect: "Although the wretched, criminal slave Fizuli lays claim to our grace and considers himself more worthy than others of help, we, expressing the sovereign's will and grace, have given him that generous *barat* so that from this day on he might know his place and consider himself lowest of the low, lower than animals, stones and sand and should not importune our employees to the payment of that *barat*."

In truth I do no regret the difficulties and losses I have suffered, only the labours undertaken in vain. What can be done? How can I show my gratitude to you for this? Such is fate.

> O sovereign! The heavens will not lend
> Me aid in trying times like a true friend.
> The tree may bring forth countless buds in spring
> But few of us will taste the fruit they bring.
> Although I've suffered endless grief and pain
> Things satisfy me. I do not complain.
> The source of all my ills is my own fate.
> I've seen much pain, but I do not berate
> The shah. I glorify his throne, and may
> He stand unshaken on the Judgement Day.
> May all our rulers know prosperity
> And wisdom reign unto eternity.

Mirza Fatali Akhundov (1812-1878)

This prominent Azerbaijanian enlightener and realistic writer was born in 1812 in the town of Nukha.

His parents prepared the youth Fatali for a career in the priesthood, but the young man was attracted to literature.

His acquaintance and friendship with the exiled Decembrists A. A. Bestuzhev-Marlinsky, A. Odoevsky, with poet Ja. P. Polonsky and others and conversations about Russian literature and the Decembrist movement played a large part in the formation of Akhundov's political views.

He began his literary career as a youth and his first poetic efforts are composed in traditional genres. Later Akhundov devotes much of his efforts to publicistic writing and prose. He writes philosophical works and socio-political essays. He is particularly famed for his plays which constitute an epoch in the history of Azerbaijanian culture.

M. F. Akhundov's story "The Stars were Deceived" (1857), rich in ideas about the liberation of Azerbaijan from feudal despotism, laid the foundations for Azerbaijanian realistic prose.

The Stars Were Deceived

When the Safawid dynasty came to power in 1501 Kazvin was the capital of Iran. The events described herein took place in the seventh year of the reign of Shah Abbas I.

At three o'clock in the afternoon on the third day following the New Year, which falls in the spring, Shah Abbas was talking to his favourite wife Salmi-Khatun when Khoja Mubarek, the chief eunuch, entered. He bowed low and said:

"The chief astrologer wishes to be received by Your Highness in connection with a very important matter."

Shah Abbas told his wife to return to the harem and ordered the eunuch to usher in the astrologer. The latter entered, bowed low, then clasped his hands in the ritual manner and said a prayer for the glory of his ruler.

"Well, what is it?"

"Almighty God preserve the life of the ruler of the Universe! The movements of the heavenly bodies indicate that fifteen days after the New Year the planet Mars will pass the constellation known as the Scorpion. As a result, in the Eastern lands and, namely, in Iran, a terrible blow lies in store for the supreme ruler. That is why, being a devoted slave to Your Highness, I felt it my duty to warn you of the impending catastrophe."

The Shah was only twenty-two at the time, an age at which life is sweet and dear to every mortal, and especially to one who stood on the top rung of well-being, enthroned as a shah. That was why the young shah became so distraught at the astrologer's words. He became as

27

pale as a ghost and seemed more like a corpse than a living being. A moment later he raised his head and dismissed the astrologer, who bowed low and exited.

When Shah Abbas was alone again he mused in silence for half an hour, then called to the eunuch and said: "Send the guards to summon the grand vizier, the commander of the troops, the treasurer and the chief mullah!"

They all appeared shortly after.

"I have summoned you to discuss an important matter and hear your opinions. You may all be seated," he said.

When the assembly learned of the astrologer's warning, they were astonished and confused. After a moment's silence the grand vizier spoke:

"Everyone knows of your humble servant's devotion to Your Highness. Our great king of kings may recall that the Treasury was in a terrible state in former times, when the Shah's noble ancestors, being of inestimable kindness, appointed as viziers men who were extremely near-sighted and limited. As soon as your humble servant learned that the Treasury was empty, I tried to find some means of replenishing it and devised the following method for doing so. Whenever a courtier received a new appointment, or was endowed with new power, he was to bestow a gift upon the Treasury commensurate with his appointment or rank. Besides, whenever any of the above were graced with Your Highness' personal attention or a visit to his home, he was to repay this grace by offering a certain sum of money and lining his doorstep with precious gems and carpets, which then became the property of Your Highness. In this manner, though a full seven years have not yet passed since the great king of kings has ascended the throne, the Treasury is brimming over, praise be to Allah! Your humble servant has always helped the state in every possible way and has never yet been amiss, but I must confess that I am at a loss as to how to influence the movements of the stars."

The general spoke next. "The beard of your faithful servant has turned grey in the service of our great country. Thus, ten years ago a Turkish force consisting of seventy thousand soldiers invaded Iran. Our revered Shah's great father then put me in charge of all Iranian forces. Although they were not inferior to the Turkish forces, I was afraid our noble warriors might be defeated by the infidels and so ordered the entire area along the Turkish border, which is Azerbaijan, to be turned into rubble, with the crops destroyed, the cattle driven off, the roads ploughed up and the bridges demolished. Thus, when the Turks crossed our border they met no opposition. However, the roads were so bad that their heavy artillery was immobilised, and only after great hardship was the infantry and cavalry force able to reach Tabriz. Then the Turkish raiders dispatched troops to the countryside to find provisions for their army. Not a single ear of grain, not a single cow or bull did they find. The hungry, exhausted Turks fled from Tabriz on the third day, having become the laughing-stock of all the world. Thus was the Iranian nation saved from foreign invasion. Moreover, ruining the roads and bridges had been such a wise move that our government found it preferable to leave them thus as a guarantee that no invaders would ever dare cross our border again. In this way our victorious armies were out of danger and well-cared for throughout the campaign, and not even a single drop of blood was shed. In any similar situation this old watchdog of Your Highness' Court is always able to act with wile, but ... my mind is incapable of inventing any thing to stop the movements of the planets."

Fear gripped the Shah's heart more strongly than before when the general finished speaking. Now it was the treasurer's turn.

"Your insignificant servant, who is a kinsman of the grand vizier and has been brought up by him and given his present post through his intercession, has always been most faithful and honest. The lower ranks and warriors are paid from the Treasury in accordance with an order which it has been my duty to sign. When it became apparent that the Treasury was empty, as the grand vizier has already mentioned, I was distraught. Though I continued signing all the orders for paying the soldiers, these orders were sent to the various districts only to sustain the authority of the Shah. Besides, I always sent the district rulers special orders which informed them that on no condition were they to pay out any money despite what the first orders I had signed said. Instead, they were to await further orders. Thus, the Treasury was soon full again. As for the troops and the officials who were not receiving their salaries, due to the peace and quiet reigning in the land and the fantastically low prices of everything, they did not feel in any way constrained. My brain is quite able to cope with such emergencies, but I cannot think of anything that might influence the heavenly bodies."

It was now the chief mullah's turn. After a flourishing introduction he said: "When your great father made me the chief mullah, half of the inhabitants of Iran, including those who lived in the capital city of Kazvin, were Sunnis, but through fervent sermons, on the one hand, and threats, on the other, I succeeded in converting all those who held to the Sunni creed to the one true doctrine of Shi'ah. Now, praise be to Allah, there are not a dozen Sunnis left in all of Iran. I would also like to mention the fact that all the former Sunnis revoked the creed of their ancestors at a single word from me. I wanted to convert the Armenians and Jews as well, but wise men advised against it, saying that there were other nations wherein small numbers of Armenians and Jews resided who were left to practice their own faiths.

"Now, at a time when Your Highness' life is in danger, your faithful servant's heart is rent by grief, it is like a fish out of water, while my insignificant brain tells me that that accursed astrologer is the only person who can find a way out. He is truly a scheming traitor, for he has told you what the stars have in store, but has concealed the means to avoid the impending disaster. I am positive that he has something up his sleeve, for I cannot imagine that, having told you of the poison, he does not know of the antidote. I think you should summon him and order him to find a way to avoid the danger that threatens the king of kings. If he refuses, off with his head!"

The chief mullah and the astrologer were bitter enemies. Now conditions seemed propitious for doing away with all astrologers, including the Shah's personal astrologer. It had been very foolish of him to tell the Shah the terrible news, thus plunging their ruler into despair and endangering his own life. In later times he was often held responsible for this, but he invariably replied:

"I hurried to tell the Shah the news, because I feared that some other astrologer might do it and then the Shah would consider me an ignorant ass and remove me from office."

Be that as it may, after hearing the news, the Shah began to hate him, and after what the chief mullah said he became so enraged he called to his chief eunuch and told him to send a guard for the chief astrologer immediately.

29

In less than an hour's time the man was brought before the Shah. Shah Abbas was like an enraged lion as he rose up from the carpet on his knees and roared: "How dare you son of a dog threaten me with danger hidden in the stars and not tell me of a way to avert it! Executioner!"

The executioner appeared instantly. He had a sabre stuck into his belt and was holding a length of rope. The astrologer had turned as white as a sheet and was shaking visibly.

"Take him away and cut off his head!" the Shah commanded.

Although his general was a brave soldier, he was kind-hearted and so began pleading with the Shah to pardon the astrologer. "Who will come to our aid if the dog loses his head? I beg Your Highness not to act hastily. Order him to find a means of averting the danger that threatens your life. If he cannot, then have the executioner cut off the worthless slave's head."

The Shah heeded his words, dismissed the executioner and addressed the astrologer, saying: "Despicable slave! Find a way out immediately!"

The poor man had no idea of what to do, but in the face of imminent death he tried to conceal this, saying: "I venture to say that there is a way out, but I must have at least an hour in which to consult Ulug Bek's *zeij*, known as the Book of Stars, and see what it advises in such cases." Naturally, there could be no such advice in the book, but this was the only way he could gain time and consult his teacher, Movlana-Jamal-ed-Din, whom he believed to be the most learned of all astrologers.

The Shah agreed, but before the astrologer had a chance to leave the room, the chief eunuch entered and announced that Movlana-Jamal-ed-Din requested an audience. The Shah consented and told his astrologer to remain in the palace. Movlana entered, bowed low, sank to the cushion indicated and said:

"May the Almighty extend your days, O Ruler of the World! The unpropitious location of the stars has made me disregard the weight of my years and appear before you, Your Highness. Fifteen days after the New Year the planet Mars will pass near the constellation known as the Scorpion. This will bring terrible misfortune to our most noble ruler. Your humble servant felt it his duty to warn Your Highness of the impending danger and also to advise you on how to avert it, since the younger, less experienced astrologers might not have noted the signs."

"That is exactly what we are discussing," the Shah said. "I would like to hear your suggestions."

"All during these coming days of darkness, meaning the fifteen days after the New Year, Your Highness must vanish from sight, having renounced all power and abdicated. During this time some criminal deserving of death will be enthroned. Then destiny's terrible blow will fall upon the sinner who will at the time be the accepted ruler of Iran. After the false ruler is smitten, Your Highness will reappear, be enthroned again, and will reign on in perfect health and happiness, thus glorifying our mighty nation. However, all this must be done in great secrecy, and not a single one of your subjects must know that you have been forced by circumstances to abdicate for a short while. They must all believe the criminal is the true ruler of Iran. All the marriage contracts Your Highness has signed must be annulled. Your wives can then be offered in marriage to Abbas Muhammed ogly, no longer the Shah of Iran, but a plain commoner. Those who consent will be married to Your Highness again, while those who refuse will be divorced."

The chief astrologer had had a narrow escape. The Shah no longer seemed frightened. The colour returned to his cheeks. Everyone praised the wisdom of Movlana. Then the beaming Shah asked the chief mullah whether he knew of a likely criminal and sinner.

"A shiftless sinner named Yusuf has recently come to live in our fair city of Kazvin, Your Highness," the chief mullah replied. "By trade he is a saddle-maker, and no one knows where he came from. However, he has gathered all the dregs of society around him and does nothing but hurl impertinent and angry words at the highly-esteemed scholars and selfless clergy. This accursed man openly preaches to his followers, saying that the highly-esteemed clergy is deceiving the people. He says that any holy war is detrimental to the country, and that modern scholars intentionally criticise the opinions of their predecessors in order to elevate themselves and confuse the people. He also criticises the authorities, saying that all officials, from the village elder to the Shah himself, are thieves and tyrants who do the country no good and who grow rich by levying untold and unjust taxes upon the people, trampling the tenets of justice and honour. There has also been talk that he belongs to some infidel sect that preaches the transference of the soul. I believe this accursed rabble-rouser would be a fine candidate for the role. The stars will wreck their vengeance on him, and he will find a befitting end in the hell-fires!"

The members of the royal council were unanimous in conceding that that dog of a saddle-maker, Yusuf, deserved to be punished by the heavens and deserved to die.

"I agree," said the Shah. "May it be so. Everything shall be accomplished tomorrow."

The members of the royal council dispersed.

If the reader doubts any of the above, I would suggest he look into the pages of a history book devoted to the seventh year of the reign of Shah Abbas.

I would now like to introduce the reader to the saddle-maker Yusuf.

Yusuf was born in a village near Kazvin. His father, a peasant, was a very religious and pious man who dreamed of his son becoming a mullah and thus being able one day to join the educated circle of scholars. To this end he took Yusuf to Kazvin and entered him in a religious school. When Yusuf came of age he wished to broaden his knowledge of theology and so set out first to Isfahan and then to the sacred city of Kerbala, where he studied under the venerable theologians.

During the long years of study that followed, Yusuf came to know the spiritual fathers and theologians closely. Seeing that they were hypocrites and liars, he became disgusted and was averse to joining this brotherhood. From Kerbala he moved to Khamadan.

At the age of forty Yusuf learned the trade of a saddle-maker and returned to the capital city of Kazvin, where it was easier to earn a living than elsewhere. Here he married and opened a shop. However, seeing the hypocrisy of the mullahs and the unsavoury machinations of the corrupt officials, this honest and honourable man felt he had to unmask .them publicly. His truthfulness and boldness won him many faithful friends, though in the end they brought on his death.

At ten o'clock in the morning of the following day the Shah commanded that all his ministers, courtiers, officials and mullahs, from the grand vizier to the last street elder, gather in the palace. Each had taken his place, and now they all anxiously awaited the appearance of the Shah. Finally, the Shah appeared in all his glory. There was a glittering crown on his head, a golden sceptre studded with gems in his hand, and his jewelled sword, the symbol of his might, hung from his belt.

The Shah ascended the throne and addressed his subjects as follows:

"For six years, by the will of the Almighty, I have ruled over you. As far as possible, I have shown mercy towards each of you, and am pleased with every one of you since, being completely devoted to the Safawid dynasty, you have never been lacking of true sincerity and devotion. Now, due to circumstances which I do not find it necessary to reveal to you, I must abdicate and appoint in my place one who is more worthy and experienced in matters of state than I. This man will be named by the members of the royal council. You must then go to him and escort him to the palace with all pomp and circumstance. Once having enthroned him, you must accept him as your sovereign and carry out his every wish. Misfortune will come to him who dares disobey my order and shows the slightest trace of insubordination towards the new Shah." At this the Shah removed his crown and placed it on the throne. He then unbuckled his sword and took off his bejewelled raiments. Having changed into ordinary clothes, he said: "From now on I am a subject like any other, a poor man named Abbas Muhammed ogly, and you shall see me no more. Farewell, and may the Almighty protect you!" He stepped down from the throne and headed towards his harem.

His faithful subjects were dazed and confused.

At the Shah's order all his wives were assembled and awaited him. When they saw him dressed as a commoner, the beauties had a hard time trying not to laugh, but his stern countenance and angry eyes quickly suppressed their smiles. The chief eunuch was told to bring in the mullah and two of his aides. They, too, had been forewarned and waited outside the harem door. After they had entered and been seated at the Shah's command, he spoke to his wives.

"My dear companions, it is with a heavy heart that I am forced to tell you of a most unfortunate occurrence. From this day forward I will no longer be the ruler of Iran. I no longer possess my grand palaces, a treasury or other riches that would let me clothe you in silk and brocade and keep you in splendour. From now on I will be a common man of Iran, one who possesses nothing and is of no importance. That is why I shall be forced to divorce you. You will then be free to choose new husbands." He ordered the mullah to perform the divorce ceremony, which the latter did. When the words were spoken, the mullah tore up all the marriage contracts.

The beauties of the harem realised that something terrible was happening and were stunned, for they knew nothing of the reason for this sudden change.

Now the Shah said to them: "If any of you still wish to marry me, despite the fact that I have become a commoner and will be a poor man, the mullah will remarry us."

Since he was young and handsome, all but two of the women agreed to remarry him. Besides, they were certain that this was all part of some joke and could not believe that he would suddenly become a commoner, for reasons unknown.

The two women who refused were two beauties who had been sent to the harem against their will. They said that though they had never been ill-treated by the Shah, they wished to receive their freedom. This was immediately granted to them.

One of the two was a Georgian girl who had been sent to the Shah as a gift from the ruler of Georgia. She quickly packed her jewels, clothing and gold trinkets and set out for home the very next day, escorted by a cousin. When she arrived, no one would believe her story. She was accused of having escaped from the harem. There was even talk of returning her by force, but eventually everyone forgot about her and she quietly married a young Georgian.

The other was the daughter of a rich merchant from Kazvin who had been engaged to a handsome young man. When the Shah's servants had heard of her great beauty they had hurried to tell the Shah about her. Soon after she was taken from her father's house and installed in the harem. She was now taking advantage of this rare chance to return home and soon married her betrothed.

After the other wives had been remarried to Abbas Muhammed ogly, the chief eunuch escorted them to a house on the outskirts. He then returned to the palace. Abbas Muhammed ogly was the last to leave the harem. He disappeared shortly after.

The saddle-maker's shop was located on the east side of the mosque square. It was three o'clock in the afternoon. Yusuf was busy making a harness which had been ordered for that day. Two of his friends sat nearby, listening intently as he spoke to them of the high prices that had ruined the poor that difficult year. He said that the previous year's drought and the lack of water in Kazvin had killed most of the crops. This, in turn, had caused prices to soar. "I'm amazed at the government," he said. "It's had so many opportunities to bring water to the city, but isn't in the least concerned about such an important thing."

At that point a cloud of dust appeared on the west side of the square. Yusuf, needle in hand, raised his head to look out. He could see a solemn procession. Naturally, he had no way of knowing it was heading towards his shop. Twelve of the Shah's servants in bright uniforms and four-cornered hats led the procession. Following were twelve standard-bearers. Then came a crowd of palace servants, one of whom was carrying a large round tray on his head. Then came guards armed with poles and escorting the head groom, who was leading a high-spirited steed. The fine saddle and saddle-cloth were studded with gems, the chest-piece was embroidered with gold, the nose-piece was studded with pearls and a tassel of emeralds hung from its neck.

Next came the chief mullah, the commander of the troops, the grand vizier, the treasurer, the chief astrologer and his teacher, and all the rest of the Shah's courtiers, with mounted soldiers and soldiers on foot bringing up the rear. The grand procession came to a stop outside the saddle-maker's shop.

The chief mullah and the general stepped forward and bowed low to Yusuf. He was startled, but returned their greeting. The chief mullah was the first to speak. "It is written in the stars, Yusuf, that from this day forward you are to be our ruler. Shah Abbas is no longer the Shah of Iran. Have mercy on us and come to the palace, where you will be enthroned."

Yusuf the saddle-maker was stunned beyond words. He could not understand what had happened to have brought all the Shah's ministers to his doorstep. After a long pause he replied:

"Most esteemed mullah! I have always regarded you as one of the most sensible and influential men in Iran, but now... Are you sure you are in your right mind? Perhaps you've smoked hashish, and it is making you speak so strangely. I'm a simple tradesman. The idea of accepting the crown has never entered my mind, for a great chasm lies between the throne and me. As Allah is my witness, I don't know what you are getting at. I would greatly appreciate it if you left me alone and did not mock at me further."

The general was the next to come forth. "At present, Yusuf, you have been appointed ruler of Iran, and we are all your servants, the slaves of your most blessed court. It is unbefitting of you to *ask* us to do anything, for you are now our master. We are all in our right minds, and the will of the heavens is absolute. From this day on, you will be the Shah of Iran. That is why, as the chief mullah has had the pleasure of saying, we beg you to come to the palace in order that the coronation ceremony may be performed." He then turned to four of the palace servants and said: "Bring the Shah's raiments and help our ruler into them!"

They carried in the tray on which the vestments were folded and set it on the floor. It was useless to resist, and so Yusuf gave himself up to them. They took off his worn artisan's clothing and dressed him in the rich robes of the Shah. Then the head groom led the fine steed up and Yusuf was helped into the saddle, at which the entire procession turned and headed back to the palace, with the guards shouting loudly every so often, making the people move aside, for every living soul was now out in the streets, hanging out of their windows or clustering on their rooftops, gazing raptly at the grand procession, at a loss to understand what was happening.

When they reached the palace the servants helped Yusuf to dismount, the chief mullah and the commander of the Shah's troops escorted him to the Grand Throne Room with all due pomp, while the courtiers, scholars, high officials and the rest of the glittering court stood before him, their arms crossed on their chests, in respectful expectation, waiting for him to speak.

The chief mullah said a prayer, placed the crown on the saddle-maker's head, buckled on his sword, slipped on his gem-studded cuffs and handed him the royal sceptre. Then he said another prayer and turned to the court, saying they were now to hail the new Shah.

The shouts and cries of "Glory to him!" echoed and reechoed through the endless halls and chambers of the great palace. The musicians played a solemn anthem. Fireworks lit up the sky, and one hundred and ten salvoes were fired to commemorate the occasion.

Although Persian poetry went into decline after the demise of the great poets Sa'adi and Hafiz, for the work of the later poets was mostly an empty and flitting agglomeration of words, there were poets who came forth on this propitious day to recite beautiful odes in honour of Shah Yusuf. The rare qualities of the new Shah were extolled, and he was compared in wisdom to Solomon, in generosity to Khatem, in courage to Rustam and in might to the elements. The poets spoke of his ascension to the throne, saying:

> Yusuf was not a king of handsome men,
> He was the Shah of the Iranian nation.

When the ceremony was over, the chief mullah told the gathering they were free to disperse. The courtiers immediately left the palace. Shah Yusuf remained on the throne, while the chief eunuch, several lesser eunuchs, the major domo and several lesser servants waited obediently by his side. Members of the Shah's guard could be seen in the palace yard.

Yusuf was certain he was dreaming. He was silent for some time, then asked the chief eunuch who he and all the others were.

"We are your faithful servants, the eunuchs of the Shah's harem. I am the chief eunuch, and these are my helpers."

The same conversation was repeated when Shah Yusuf asked the servants who they were. He was also told that the guards outside were waiting for his command. At this, Shah Yusuf said: "I wish you all to leave, everyone except the chief eunuch."

When they had all gone, he called the chief eunuch over and said: "I can see by your expression that you are an honest man. Please tell me what this is all about. I can't believe that you don't know the reason for all of this, since you live in the palace."

Indeed, the chief eunuch was a simple, honest person, and so he decided to tell the new Shah all he knew. Since he had always stood in waiting outside Shah Abbas' door, he knew all of his sovereign's secrets and could now recount the events of the afternoon in detail to Shah Yusuf.

"Where is Shah Abbas now?"

"He changed into a commoner's clothes and vanished. No one knows where he is."

Shah Yusuf was an intelligent man. He had never believed in the prophecy of the stars, but this unexpected rise to power frightened him. In the end, however, and since he had been crowned by the ruling classes, he could not resign and was thus forced by circumstances to take over the management of the government.

He began by summoning the head of the guard. "Take twelve soldiers, go to the city and arrest the chief mullah, the commander of the troops, the grand vizier, the treasurer, the chief astrologer and his teacher and put them all in the prison in Arik. Report back to me when you have carried out my order."

The head of the guard bowed low and exited.

Shah Yusuf then summoned the major domo, told him he had not eaten in hours and was hungry, at which the man replied that all the cooks and chefs were busy preparing His Highness' dinner.

Shah Yusuf then said he would like to inspect the palace, the harem and his own bedroom.

The chief eunuch and the major domo led the way. The first hall was richly carpeted. The ceiling and walls were covered with paintings of birds, flowers and grasses. In the second hall, which was also richly carpeted, the walls were hung with portraits of former Shahs of the Safawid dynasty and princes of the blood who had gained fame in the arts. The third hall held a collection of portraits of famous Shahs of former dynasties. The walls of the fourth were covered with frescoes depicting scenes from the *Shah-name* in which Iranian warriors of yore battled the horned and tailed divs of Mazenderan. The paintings in the next hall depicted the campaigns of Shah Ismail. The walls of the harem rooms were covered with paintings of youths and maidens. The youths were shown offering the maidens bouquets, as the maidens held out gold cups of wine to them. There was a sumptuous bed in each of the harem rooms.

Shah Yusuf chose one of these rooms as his bedroom. Then he asked the chief eunuch where the clothes and jewels of the former Shah's wives were kept and was told that they were all locked up in a special room and that the only Keeper of the Chests had the key to it. He was immediately summoned and told to unlock the great room. Chests both large and small stood along the walls. Shah Yusuf was shown the beautiful clothes, the cashmere shawls, the silks, brocades, gold, filigree bouquets and diadems of semi-precious stones, the diamond earrings, rings, pearls and many other luxuries.

Shah Yusuf had three daughters and two sons. His eldest daughter was fourteen, the next was twelve and the youngest was eight, while his sons were six and four. He chose a golden bouquet, a ring, a necklace, a pair of earrings, a fine Byzantine shawl and a lovely gown for each of his daughters. He chose a shawl and gown for his wife, and then handed every thing over to the chief eunuch, telling him to take everything to his house in the city and give it to his wife. Shah Yusuf also told him to calm his wife's fears concerning his own whereabouts, and that she was to send his sons to the palace the following day.

The chief eunuch left, accompanied by two servants who carried the gifts.

The sun would soon be setting. The major domo asked the Shah to return to the first hall, where candles set in gold candle-sticks had been lit and the Shah's dinner would be served. The Shah performed the evening ablution and prayer and sat down. Servants carried in the various dishes. After he had eaten, the cloth was removed. He washed his hands over a small basin with water poured from a pitcher, and then coffee was served. After that a hookah was set before him.

As he was smoking, the head of the palace guard entered to report that the Shah's orders had been carried out. Then the chief eunuch entered to report that the gifts had been received with great excitement and that his family was no longer worried about him.

The Shah then asked them about matters of interest to him. Night had fallen. He finally went off to his bedroom, telling the head of the guard to station the palace guards as they had always been stationed. He soon fell asleep. The major domo and the chief eunuch both departed for their own chambers.

The following day Shah Yusuf summoned his faithful friends to the palace and appointed them chief mullah, commander of the troops, grand vizier and treasurer, respectively. He abolished the post of the chief astrologer as being detrimental to the people and the nation.

The Shah decreed that all provincial rulers were to receive orders to discontinue taxing the population unjustly, to stop demanding bribes from the populace under threat of legal punishment, to stop executing and torturing them by gouging out their eyes or cutting off their ears and noses. He then appointed his own trusted men as government officials in every district. They were to collect data on the state of affairs in each given district, on the needs of the populace and report back to him.

Shah Yusuf summoned these newly-appointed official overseers to the palace and addressed them as follows: "Speaking in my name, tell the rulers of the provinces to fear the Almighty, mete out justice fairly and not plunder the people by means of unlawful taxation and extortion. Impress upon them the fact that such conduct will bring about their own downfall and perhaps even death. They know from experience that those who become rich at the expense of others often end their days as paupers, or by being beheaded. No single tribe of Ariana ever retained treasures acquired through unjust taxation or outright robbery. Each official that became wealthy in the government service was sooner or later brought to justice by the Iranian rulers, who confiscated this wealth and either executed the offenders by some ghastly means or else doomed them to penury for the rest of their natural lives. In this way the rulers of the provinces are like leeches that have become bloated from the blood they have sucked, but then lose everything when they are torn away. Many of the leeches perish, while the remainder are weak and helpless. If the rulers of the provinces reduce their demands and are content to live within the limits of their legal salaries, their futures will be guaranteed, the people will respect them, they will receive promotions, increase their fortunes and be known as just men." He then dismissed the gathering.

The Shah decreed that the palace expenses be cut; that the roads and bridges be repaired; that caravan-serais be built along the roads between towns and large settlements; that schools and hospitals be built in each district; that canals be dug and water brought to areas suffering from drought; that widows, orphans, the crippled and the blind all receive pensions.

Shah Yusuf then decreed that all good-for-nothings be banned from joining the ranks of the clergy and that each man who wished to attain this office receive special permission from the chief mullah; that the number of mullahs conform to the needs of the population; that the clergy henceforth be given salaries from the treasury, thus making dependent upon the government and thus silencing the mullahs who claimed that all government officials who received salaries were parasites.

Then he set up special courts of law to handle all cases pertaining to the government, and to take them away from the jurisdiction of the clergy. In this way he wanted the people to feel independent of the clergy in matters concerning lawsuits and not have to seek the advice of the mullahs in settling their controversies, but appeal to the state courts.

He decreed that donations to charity and other money collected for the poor be handed over to the four most honest citizens of the city. They were to distribute the funds in accordance with the needs of the various poor families and were then to present an annual report on the sums spent. In this way the Shah wished to distribute the public funds fairly among the needy.

He abolished the custom of every person contributing one-fifth of his income towards the support of the clergy and the *sayyids,* the descendants of the Prophet, in order that said descendants at last gave up their life of alms-collecting and begin to work honestly like the rest of the population. Much-respected mullahs found corresponding references in the Koran, and this tax was abolished on the basis of their findings.

The Shah decreed that the following order be read out in all the provinces: henceforth, no one was to dare offer gifts to him or to any of his dignitaries or officials, nor to try to obtain any office for himself by means of gifts, since all posts were to go to men who had proven their honesty and ability in matters of government.

All state income from the provinces was to go to the Treasury and be under the jurisdiction of trusted officials in the districts. All the classes, including the clergy, were to pay a tenth of their income to the Treasury if they lived in the town, and one-twentieth if they lived in the country. All soldiers and officials were to receive their salaries regularly.

Shah Yusuf learned that when the head groom took the Treasury horses to the mountain pastures each year he lorded it over the local population and extracted a tithe from them; that the commander of the artillery troops appropriated the salaries of all the cannoneers; that the director of the Treasury passed out counterfeit coins among the population; that the chief of police of Kazvin accepted bribes; that the tax collectors hounded the poor and were extremely lenient towards the rich; that the street elders did not look after the cleanliness of the streets.

The Shah ordered all the above officials to be dismissed, and honest, hard-working men to be appointed to their posts.

The imprisoned chief mullah was told by his jailer that his worst enemy, Molla Ramazan, had been appointed chief mullah. He could not take the blow and died of a heart attack.

Shah Yusuf ordered the streets of Kazvin to be widened and the ruts and pot-holes to be filled in so that the people would no longer break their bones during falls. At the Shah's order the city poor were issued grain from the state granaries, for there had been a terrible drought and starvation threatened. A council was set up to work out a plan for bringing water to the city.

There was a small Dutch colony near the Persian Gulf, and an ambassador and his retinue had arrived in Kazvin at the time described to sign a trade agreement with Iran. Shah Yusuf received the ambassador and signed the agreement. The Dutchmen left with rich gifts from the Shah. They were amazed at his hospitality, intelligence, far-sightedness and royal bearing.

A week had now passed since Yusuf had ascended the throne. Each day was marked by new decrees, all of which were beneficial to the people. A new golden era had come to Iran. Unfortunately, however, man never values that which is truly precious and advantageous. For instance, what did Adam and Eve lack in the Garden of Eden? Yet, they disobeyed God's command and were banished from Heaven. Such is the inherent nature of man!

The people of Kazvin no longer saw butchered bodies hanging from the city gates; they no longer saw executioners mutilating and hanging their fellow-citizens, gouging out their eyes, cutting off their ears and noses, and this seemed strange and incomprehensible to them. At first, the people said:

"The new Shah must be a kind and timid man."

Then they began to wonder whether he really was so very kind and merciful, or whether he simply lacked a firm hand and was a weakling. In the end, they found he had endless other shortcomings as well. In a word, their peaceful life under a wise and humane ruler soon appeared terribly monotonous and dull to them.

The former officials noted this change in popular opinion and each waited for his chance to strike back, to foment discontent and disorder.

Shortly thereafter a mutiny broke out in Kazvin, led by the former head groom. He had met by chance with another former official and had said: "What are the people of Kazvin saying about the new Shah?"

"They hate him and think he's a good-for-nothing eccentric."

"As Allah is my witness, the simple people are wiser than we are. Do you realise how stupid we were to have voluntarily put an ignorant saddle-maker on the throne? We brought all this trouble on ourselves. The Shah has cast us aside, and only because we were devoted to the throne and served our country honestly and selflessly. He has degraded us so that every last dog in the province is held in greater respect than we. Mark my words, we have disgraced ourselves in the eyes of the whole world."

"But we never chose him to be our Shah! Such was the will of Shah Abbas! We had no other choice but to obey."

"I agree, Shah Abbas was our ruler, and his every word was our command. But now, when Shah Abbas is no longer our ruler, what's to prevent us from dethroning and killing this scoundrel, this cursed infidel who, they say, actually believes in the transference of the soul! After we get rid of him we can crown the most deserving member of the noble dynasty of Safawids. Everyone will obey such a Shah, for he will be of royal blood."

"You are speaking wisely, and I agree with everything you've said. But there are only two of us. What can we do? Don't you think we should go straight to the former commander of the artillery troops and talk it over with him? After all, he's also been dismissed."

The former commander was overjoyed to see them. He listened to their plans, agreed with them wholeheartedly and said he was ready to take part in an uprising against Shah Yusuf. However, he added that if they did not enlist the aid of the present head of the cavalry troops they would be doomed to failure. "He's a very dear friend of mine," the commander continued, "and I'll take it upon myself to gain his consent. I'll prove to him that under the infidel Shah Yusuf no one can be sure of his future, and that sooner or later he, too, will be dismissed, just as we were. I'll tell him he's duty-bound to help stop the evil before disaster strikes him, too. I'm sure he'll listen to me. Besides, yesterday the Shah reprimanded him publicly during a reception for having dared to enter a mosque for prayers when he was drunk. If he joins us, I'm sure the commander of the infantry will, too. They are cousins and brothers-in-law, so there should not be any trouble there. I suggest you both go to see the former chief of police of Kazvin. Bring him around to our side, and make him promise to use all his influence on the former police officials and street elders who were his subordinates until last week."

Each of the plotters went off to carry out his part of the scheme. Four days later they all gathered in secret and agreed that the time was ripe for an uprising. They decided to surround the palace at dawn on the coming Saturday, rush into the Shah's quarters, kill Shah Yusuf and proclaim a member of the Safawid dynasty the new Shah.

39

On the day designated for the uprising the armed insurgents, some mounted and some on foot, surrounded the palace before the gates were open. When Shah Yusuf learned of this he said the gates were not to be opened.

The uprising had caught the Shah unawares, for after he had his chief enemies, the head mullah, the commander of the army, the grand vizier, the treasurer, the chief astrologer and his teacher Movlana arrested, he felt he was safe. The blow had come unexpectedly.

Soon Shah Yusuf's supporters learned of the mutiny. They quickly armed themselves and headed in large numbers towards the palace, where they took their stand opposite the insurgents, who would yield to no persuasion, and so they decided to fight it out and opened fire.

The battle raged, for neither side would concede defeat, and every man was ready to sacrifice his life in order to defend his cause. After a short period of cross-firing, the two sides went into hand-to-hand combat. The bloody battle lasted for nearly four hours, with each side losing close to three thousand men.

Finally, the supporters of Shah Yusuf faltered. This happened when the ungrateful townsmen joined the insurgents. The Shah's supporters were defeated and fled.

The insurgents stormed the palace, knocked down the doors and rushed into the Shah's apartments, but could not find Shah Yusuf. He had vanished. Some said that he had taken part in the fighting, inspiring his supporters with his valour, and that he had fallen in battle. Others claimed that he had not been among the battling forces at all, but had disappeared as soon as the two sides had clashed. Be that as it may, he was never found among the dead, nor was he found among the living.

Having plundered the Shah's palace, the insurgents headed towards the bazaar, where they looted the shops and the caravan-serais. From there they headed first to the Armenian and then to the Jewish quarters of town, robbing and plundering, and committing villainous deeds.

As the sun set, everyone went back to his own home. The uprising was over. The pillaging ended.

The following morning the leaders of the uprising went to Arik Prison and set free the commander of the troops, the grand vizier, the treasurer, Movlana Jemal-ed-Din and the chief astrologer. They told them of the events of the previous day and asked them which of the men of the Safawid dynasty they considered worthy of being their new ruler.

At this Movlana said: "What day is today?"

The head groom said that it was the sixteenth day after the New Year. Movlana's heart brimmed over with joy. He announced that the terrible danger had passed, and that the promised blow had fallen upon Shah Yusuf the previous day. "You all know," he continued, "that there is no worthy prince of the Safawids who might be enthroned, for they are all either crippled or blind. Some were blinded by Shah Ismail II, while others were blinded by Shah Abbas. Since none of them can thus rule, it is obvious that Shah Abbas will again be enthroned."

At this the head groom remarked that they would all be only too happy to have such a just ruler as Shah Abbas return, for had they not all been so well off during his reign? However, to everyone's extreme sorrow, Shah Abbas had disappeared without a trace, having voluntarily abdicated, and his whereabouts were unknown.

Movlana smiled and replied that there had been a very good reason why Shah Abbas had acted as he had, but since that reason no longer existed and he knew where the Shah was, they were all to follow him and beg him to return to the throne.

At this, they all went to the house in which Shah Abbas had been hiding and solemnly escorted him back to the palace. Shah Abbas resumed his title as ruler of Iran, and life returned to normal again. It was as if Shah Yusuf had never existed.

I wonder at the foolishness of the stars. How could they have not perceived that the Iranians were deceiving them and that the saddle-maker Yusuf was an impostor, put on the throne by the wily Iranians? How artless the stars were! And how cunning it was of the smart Iranians to have outwitted them!

The stars punished poor, innocent Yusuf, having spared the true ruler of Iran, Shah Abbas, and for the next forty years they looked down indifferently at his despotism, cruelty and barbarity. One example of this fiendish cruelty was his treatment of his own sons, two of whom he had blinded and the third murdered in cold blood.

Perhaps, however, one should not blame the stars, for they had nothing against Shah Abbas personally. They simply had to do away with the man who occupied the throne of Iran on the fifteenth day after the New Year. Since the saddle-maker Yusuf happened to be the man on the throne that day, the wrath of the stars was vented on him.

Could the stars have foreseen that the Iranians might outwit them and place an impostor on the throne instead of the true ruler?

And how foolish the British were to have nearly started a war against such a dangerous people!

Djalil Mamedkulizade (1866-1932)

After almost 70 years readers can still hardly contain their laughter at the adventures of Novruzali, the protagonist of Djalil Mamedkulizade's story "The Letterbox". They laugh at this poor, downtrodden peasant who lives under such conditions that he has not the slightest notion of the most elementary developments of human civilisation: and they sympathise with him. The subtle, profound humour of this great writer has the power to evoke laughter mixed with tears.

Djalil Mamedkulizade's nom de plume is "Molla Nasreddin", the name of a popular sage well known in the East as a wise, resourceful exposer of oppressors.

In April of 1906, Djalil Mamedkulizade began publishing the satirical journal Molla Nasreddin *in Tiflis. This journal became the rallying point for a large circle of writers, both those who were concerned with enlightenment and revolutionary democrats. The journal was sharply critical of backwardness and fanaticism; it called on the people to fight for their freedom and played an important part in the development of realistic literature in Azerbaijan.*

Djalil Mamedkulizade left a rich legacy of novellas, stories, feuilletons and plays which enjoy great popularity in Azerbaijan.

The 100th anniversary of Mamedkulizade's birthday, which was marked by a gala celebration in the Soviet Union, took the form of a festival of Azerbaijanian culture.

The Letterbox

It was a cold November 12th, though no snow had yet fallen. The doctor examined the khan's ailing wife for the last time and said that she had improved and that they could set out on their journey in another week.

The khan, who had urgent business to attend to in Erivan, was in a great hurry. Besides, he was afraid that the cold weather would be bad for his wife, and thus the trip might have to be postponed. He sat down to write a short note to his friend Djafar-aga. It read:

"We are returning to Erivan next week. Since my wife is ill, I have a favour to ask of you. Would you please go over to my house and have the servants lay the rugs, make the stoves and air the rooms. Reply by telegraph. I have attended to the matter you asked me to.

Sincerely, Veli-khan"

He slipped the folded sheet into an envelope, put a stamp on it, addressed it and was about to summon his servant who would take it to the post office when he recalled that the man had been sent off on another errand.

Just then he heard someone at the gate. He looked out and saw a peasant named Novruzali from Itkapan Village who was a frequent visitor. Novruzali had never once come to the khan's house without bearing gifts of flour,

43

home-made noodles, honey or fresh butter. This time, as always, he came laden with offerings.

At the sight of the khan, Novruzali set his walking-stick against the wall and opened the second half of the gate. Then he led his mule into the yard and began unloading sacks and cheeping chickens from its back. He set the sacks by the wall, raised his eyes to look at the khan and bowed low in greeting.

"Why do you go to all this trouble, Novruzali?"

"It's no trouble at all, my lord! I'm your faithful servant till the grave," the peasant replied, brushing the dust from his garments.

The khan wondered whether he should not ask him to take the letter to the post office, since it was nearly one o'clock and the mail would soon go out. Aloud he said, "Do you know where the post office is?"

"How can an ignorant peasant like me know where the post office is, khan?"

"Ah, well, perhaps you know where the police-officer's bureau is then."

"Yes, I do. I went there last week to complain about our village elder. I swear by your head, khan, he's making our life unbearable. Besides, he's not a local man, and he hates us. Last week two of my calves disappeared and I went...."

"Wait a minute. You can tell me all about it later. Listen carefully now. There's a big house right across the street from the police officer's bureau and there's a box on the wall outside the door of that house.... It's called a letterbox. It has a long, narrow lid. I want you to take this letter there, lift the lid, drop the letter into the box and come right back."

Novruzali accepted the letter gingerly, holding it with both hands. He raised his eyes to the khan again, then went back to the wall and bent down to lay the letter on the ground.

"No! Don't put it on the ground! It'll get dirty! Hurry, mail it and come right back."

"Dear Khan, just let me hang a bag of oats on the mule's neck. He's come so many miles, and he's tired and hungry."

"No! Not now! You'll miss the mail. You can feed him when you get back."

"Then I'll just tether him, or he'll chew the bark off the trees."

"No, not now. Hurry! I want you to go as fast as you can!"

Novruzali put the envelope carefully inside his jacket. "The chickens are tied, Khan. Let me untie them and feed them. I've got the feed right here in my pocket." He put his hand into his pocket, but the khan said, "Not now! Later, after you've come back."

Novruzali picked up his staff and rushed off like a child. Suddenly, having remembered something, he stopped, turned at the gate and cried: "Oh, dearest Khan! The eggs are tied up in a kerchief. I'm afraid the mule will lie down on them."

"Stop talking and run! You'll be late!"

Novruzali was off.

"Wait! Don't give letter to anyone, and don't show it to anyone. Drop it in the letterbox and come right back. Understand?"

"I'm not a child," Novruzali replied as he went through the gate. "What do you think I am? The mayor won't get the letter from me!"

The khan went back into the house. "Well, light of my eyes, start preparing for the journey," he said tenderly to his wife. "I wrote to Erivan, and the house will be ready. Praised be Allah, you really are getting better. We can start out at last. And the doctor says a change of climate will do you good."

While he was talking to his wife, his manservant returned.

"There's a mule and some sacks and bundles in the yard, Khan," he said.

"Put the things away. Novruzali from Itkapan brought them."

The servant carried the eggs and the chickens to the kitchen and led the mule off to the stable. Then he untied a sack, took a pinch of flour and showed it to the khan. "It's top quality white flour, Khan."

The khan glanced at the flour, then told the man to bring in their dinner.

* * *

The khan had no further thought of Novruzali and the letter until after his dinner, which lasted for two hours. He then summoned his servant and was told that the man had not yet returned. This surprised him, but he then decided Novruzali had mailed the letter and had gone to the bazaar to buy something to eat. An hour later he had still not returned. Finally, the khan sent his man to the post office to find out what happened to Novruzali. The servant returned to say he was nowhere to be seen.

The khan went out to the terrace and lit a cigarette. He began walking up and down leisurely. "Something must have happened to have detained him," he said to himself.

At that very moment a policeman entered the yard. "The police officer asked you to come over to the station and vouch for your peasant or he'll be sent to jail."

The khan gazed at the man in astonishment. "Why," he finally uttered, "the man would never hurt a fly. Why was he arrested?"

"I don't know. Will you please come to the station? They'll tell you what happened."

The khan dressed quickly, said nothing to his wife so as not to upset her and set off for the police officer's bureau. As he passed the jail he looked in and saw poor Novruzali among the other prisoners. He was crouching in a corner, weeping like a child and wiping his tears with the flap of his long jacket.

When the khan learned the particulars of the case and had vouched for Novruzali, he was permitted to take the man home.

The first thing Novruzali did when they got back was feed his mule. Then he sat down by the wall and began weeping again.

The khan went into the house, lit a cigarette, came out onto the terrace and called to him. "All right, Novruzali, now tell me what happened. What a story! Someone might even write it up! And don't leave anything out. Tell me exactly what happened from the minute you left the yard till you were arrested."

Novruzali rose, came over, wiped his face with the flap of his jacket again and recounted the tale. "My dove! Forgive me, Khan, for the sake of your children! I'm not to blame for anything! I'm only a poor, ignorant peasant. How am I supposed to know about letters, or letterboxes, or post offices? Forgive me, I beg of you, or this will be the end of me. If I live I'll surely return your kindness. I have sinned, but what can I do now? It must be Allah's will. I'll be your faithful slave till my dying day." He came closer and bent down to kiss the khan's foot.

45

"Don't despair, Novruzali! I'm not holding anything against you. You haven't done anything to make me angry."

"Ah, Khan, you don't know the half of it! That infidel, the son of an infidel, took your letter, put it in his pocket and walked off with it."

"What infidel?"

"That Russian, the son of an infidel."

"Where did he take it?"

"Into the big house. The one with the letterbox outside on the wall. He went straight into the house."

The khan was silent for a moment. "But didn't you drop the letter into the box?"

"Of course I did! But the moment I did this infidel came along. He managed to open the box, stole the letter and was off."

"Weren't there any other letters in the box?"

"Of course there were! There were a lot of letters. He stole them all."

The khan laughed. "Wait, Novruzali! Start at the beginning and tell me everything, just as it happened."

"Dear Khan, I took your letter and went straight to the police officer's bureau. I saw the big house you told me about and went over and raised the lid of the box on the wall. I was going to drop the letter into the box, but something stopped me. I looked at the letter and then at the box, and didn't know what to do. I was afraid you'd be angry, and I didn't know whether to drop it into the box or not. Besides, I couldn't remember what I was supposed to do after I put the letter in the box: come back here or stay there. On the one hand, if I was supposed to wait there, how long was I supposed to wait? After all, Khan, you know I had my hungry mule here in the yard and the chickens with their legs tied together, and the sacks of flour. See, the sacks are still here, Khan. Let me call the man to help me carry them into the house. It looks like rain, and the flour might get wet."

"Don't worry, Novruzali, they'll see to it. Go on with your story."

"Well, I decided I'd better not drop the letter into the box. I put the lid down again and walked off and then stopped. I wanted to come back here and ask you what to do, but to tell you the truth, I was afraid you'd say I was a stupid ass, an animal with no brains. So I sat down by the wall to rest a bit. Then I saw an Armenian boy of about twelve or thirteen, not bigger than this, go right up to the box, lift the lid and drop a letter in that looked just like yours. He put down the lid and walked off. I called after that shameless boy to ask him how he could have left his letter there and walked away, but he didn't pay any attention to my shouting. Maybe he didn't understand me. Anyway, he didn't even look back. As soon as he was gone a Russian woman rushed over, dropped a letter in and hurried off. I felt better then. That meant the letters were supposed to stay in the box. So I said a prayer to give me courage and walked boldly up to the box. I raised the lid and dropped the letter in. I was just about to come back here when the Russian showed up. I thought he wanted to drop a letter in the box, too, but then I saw that the thief was up to something, because he stuck his hand right into the box. I knew then that the dog wanted to steal the letters. Forgive me, Khan, for tiring you with all this talk. Tell the man to open the gate for me. It's getting late, and I'm afraid I won't be home before dark."

"Don't be silly! Go on with your story."

"May my children be orphaned for your sake, Khan! May I never live another day without your blessing! Well ... there was the thief, pulling all the letters out of the box right there in broad daylight. Then he closed the box and was about to slip away when I ran over to him, grabbed his hand and said, 'Where do you think you're taking them? Hm? People didn't bring these letters here for you to sneak off with them. Put them back this minute if you don't want to get into a lot of trouble! Novruzali isn't dead yet, and he won't let you steal a letter his lord gave him. Think of what you're doing! Why are you taking something that doesn't belong to you? Don't your Russian laws say that stealing is a sin?' Please let me go, Khan! It's getting late, and it's getting dark!"

"Don't worry, you'll be back in time. Go on. What happened then?"

"Ah.... Where was I? Oh, yes! Hey! Watch out! The mule'll break the vines!" Novruzali wanted to run over to the beast, but the khan restrained him. "Ah, where was I? Well, I argued, and pleaded, and said that my lord would kill me, and asked him to at least return my lord's letter, but the Russian wouldn't give in. I could tell he wanted to run. Then the blood rushed to my head. I grabbed the infidel and threw him to the ground so hard that blood trickled out of his mouth. Then some men from the police officer's bureau came running out and they all jumped on me at once. Then they dragged me off to jail. May I die at your feet! I would surely have been sent to Siberia if you hadn't come to defend me. There were some other men in the jail there. They said I'd beaten up a Russian official. But what else could I have done? You can see I'm not guilty, am I?"

But the khan just laughed and laughed.

Night had fallen. Novruzali tossed the empty sacks onto his tired mule's back and, not having had a bite to eat all day, he set out wearily for home, prodding the animal on with his cornel stick.

Two days later the khan received a telegram from Erivan which read: "Received your letter. House in readiness." The khan and his wife left shortly after.

A month later Novruzali was summoned to court and sentenced to three months for having assaulted a civil servant who was carrying out his official duties.

Novruzali pleaded innocent.

Another month passed and the news of what had happened reached his master in Erivan. Now, for the first time, the khan stopped to think of a thing or two.

Abduragim bek Akhverdov (1870-1933)

Akhverdov continued the outstanding realistic tradition of M. F. Akhundov in dramaturgy and in prose.

His plays reflect Azerbaijanian society at the end of the nineteenth century: the struggle of isolated proponents of enlightenment against feudal, patriarchal mores.

Akhverdov's play In the Shade of Trees *is the first in the tradition of Azerbaijanian dramaturgy to deal with the theme of revolution and civil war.*

The writer was also productive in the sphere of prose. He was one of the most active contributors to the revolutionary-democratic journal Molla Nasreddin, *composing in the style and spirit of this literary school: with love for the simple labourer and a desire to help him overcome oppression and ignorance.*

The writer's stories and feuilletons expose ignorance, fanaticism, philistinism and egoism. "The Bomb" is a biting satire on the tsar's gendarmes and bureaucrats, rushing about in horror before the impending revolution.

The Bomb

Police Constable Kerbalay-Zal had served in the force for over 25 years.

"The cap doesn't go with your beard, and neither does the sword," his wife used to tell him. "Give up the police force. Open a grocery stall and trade away at your own sweet pace...."

"Wife," he would reply, "you don't understand the fascination of power. If they made you a policeman, you wouldn't leave it in a thousand years. And besides I've been serving in the force for more than 25 years In a year or two I'll get a pension. Then we can take it easy."

"Well, you know best," his wife would concur.

* * *

One day Kerbalay-Zal came home very upset.

He had been called up by the district police inspector.

"Kerbalay-Zal," he had told him drily, "I'm not satisfied with you. You're an old and experienced member of the force. The young policemen who have only just arrived here from Russia keep finding bombs or rifles and cartridges. Their police station gets a good name and they receive rewards themselves. But you haven't even come with as much as a broken axe. Either you must be taking bribes or you've got too old to do your job properly. If this goes on, we'll have to dispense with your services."

These words went through Kerbalay-Zal like an arrow.

At home his wife asked him why he was upset, but he said it was just a headache.

His wife put a bowl of abgusht in front of him. Kerbalay-Zal ate a little, but then pushed the bowl away and decided to go to bed. But try as he might, he could not get to sleep. Finally he got up, drank a glass of tea, and went out on his beat again.

Standing on the corner of Krovavaya and Neschastnaya streets Kerbalay-Zal began to ponder over the inspector's words.

It was well past midnight. Suddenly Kerbalay-Zal caught sight of a man approaching the house of the blacksmith Feyzulla, leading a horse by the reins. On the horse's back lay two sacks, which contained some kind of round objects. The blacksmith and the man with the horse carefully took down the sacks and carried them into the house. Then they led the horse away and shut the gates.

As he watched all this Kerbalay-Zal thought to himself:

"At last my star has risen.... Round objects in sack in the middle of the night.... Something funny there!..."

And without further ado he blew his whistle. The nearest policeman on patrol, Constable Potap, came running up to him.

"Potap, there's a bomb here...."

"Where?"

"They've just carried it into Feyzulla's house...."

Potap immediately passed this news on to Constable Ivan, Ivan told the senior police inspector, he told the district police inspector, he told the superintendent, who passed the word on to the colonel of the gendarmes, and within half an hour Feyzulla's house was surrounded by cossacks, gendarmes and police.

They knocked at the gates.

"Who's there?" asked Feyzulla in a sleepy voice.

"Open up!"

When he opened the gates Feyzulla went speechless with fear.

All he could say was:

"What's happened?"

"No talking.... It's a search."

They woke up Feyzulla's wife and children, turned everything in the room upside down, but didn't find anything. Then, on entering the room next door, they caught sight of two paunchy sacks.

"Mr. Superintendent, sir, there's the bomb!" Kerbalay-Zal gave joyous shriek.

Everyone froze to the spot. Nobody dared to go up close to it: "It'll explode and blow us all to pieces."

Poor Feyzulla was standing to one side with his hands tied.

Seeing the futility of the search, he managed to come to himself and cried out suddenly:

"Gentlemen, don't be afraid! Untie my hands and I'll empty the sacks myself."

His request was granted. Going up to the sacks, he calmly extricated the watermelons that were their real contents and rolled them towards the feet of the superior police officers.

On the following day Constable Kerbalay-Zal was discharged from the police force.

Nariman Narimanov (1871-1925)

An outstanding revolutionary who was active in affairs of state and in the Communist party, which he joined in 1905, Narimanov served as president of the Council of People's Commissars of the Azerbaijanian SSR and was also a member of the Central Executive Committee of the Soviet government. He successfully combined revolutionary activities and active participation in civic and political work with a career as a prosaist, playwright and ardent publicist.

Narimanov's works show the life of patriarchal Azerbaijan toward the close of the 19th century: the power of ready money and the mores of a mercantile environment. His stories, novellas and plays have a powerful accusatory spirit; the vivid colourful characters are based on an encyclopaedic knowledge of the era.

"The Adventures of One Village", the story selected for this anthology, is directed against religious fanaticism, backwardness and ignorance. With scorn and anger the writer exposes the social forces which instill superstition in the people and teach them to revere ancient, outmoded customs and to submit to coercion.

Continuing the traditions of M. F. Akhundov, Narimanov wrote simply, in a language that the people could understand. His style and attitudes are close to those of the nineteenth-century Azerbaijanian realists.

The Adventures of One Village

In the past I spent some time at a village in the Caucasus. It was a large, wealthy village. Anyone visiting this village for the first time could not fail to notice the difference between its two *makhallas**. One *makhalla* was situated on a mountain; its streets were narrow and dusty, and pisé hovels were crowded close together. The streets of the other *makhalla* were broad and clean; its buildings were properly constructed. The names of these *makhallas* were respectively Namelsem and Inmire.

So they had been called since our grandfathers' day.

The story goes that Namelsem and Inmire were prominent citizens. Each had attempted to organise public services for his *makhalla*. The name of each had remained to designate the respective districts.

The residents were as different as the *makhallas*. Each district had its own way of life. The residents of Namelsem had always been independent; they led a loose life and spent their time in a round of constant amusements and festivals.

If someone were to closely study the people of this region and their way of life, he would no doubt observe that they were able to live so tastefully and with so much pleasure by virtue of their heritage.

* *Makhalla*—a region, block, part of a village.— *Ed.*

The residents of Inmire, on the other hand, were hard workers. They sowed and reaped at the proper times, went often to the city, where they traded and gathered information, and made constant progress.

The inhabitants of Namelsem also went to the city, but they brought back only what they smelled and saw in the tea and coffee shops.

At that time there were not many schools in the towns. The residents of Inmire got the idea of opening their own school. But other villagers were somewhat opposed to this.

To resolve such questions, the headman would summon representatives from both *makhallas*. Representatives of Inmire would always come when no one from Namelsem appeared. Therefore the question of building a school was kept suspended. In a word, the residents of Inmire were zealous in fulfilling their social responsibilities and together accomplished much. They were careful to elect officials such as judges and a headman who would be worthy of the posts, people who would be productive, who would not be parasites or take bribes or betray the interests of the inhabitants. The residents of Namelsem did not interfere in public affairs. When they needed someone to speak for their interests they turned to Ami. Ami's real name was long and so they called him Ami for short. In any case there could be no question of calling Ami by his real name because it was considered disrespectful in the *makhalla* Namelsem to call adults by their names. Respectable people were called *Kerbelai,** meshadi, hadji****, master, and *Ami**—the latter name was only given to a person who was invested with great authority. In fact, Ami was the most authoritative person in that *makhalla*. Ami was so well-known that he was called by this name not only in the neighbouring villages, but in town. In short, he was called Ami.

Ami was seventy or eighty years old. But it must be noted that no one in the *makhalla* knew exactly how old he was. For as far back as anyone in the village could recall Ami had been as swift and daring as a falcon. He was tall, well-built, comely and had a black beard. He had riches to spare. He was the richest man not only in Namelsem, not only in the entire village, but in the entire region.

The inhabitants of Namelsem *makhalla* loved and respected Ami. This too had a reason. Poor *beks* were always borrowing money from him. Usually they could not repay the loan in time. Then Ami took over their land. Ami also lent money to others on interest. He was truly a good man. He helped the poor. He lent them money. But if a debt was not repaid on time, he remembered to show his power over the debtor. He punished him, just as father punishes son to teach him not to go back on a promise.... For this reason or for some other reason the people loved Ami.

And he deserved respect because in times of need he spoke in the name of the inhabitants of Namelsem *makhalla* without their knowledge: he tended to their affairs without troubling them. And the inhabitants of Namelsem were in need of such services. To deal with the headman, with the local chief of police was not simple and could even be dangerous. In addition when the chief of police or the police inspector came to the village they would be housed by Ami. This gave Ami's name even greater weight. Ami understood this; he knew his people and

---

* *Ami*—Uncle.—*Ed.*

** *Kerbelai*—a shrine of Moslem Shiites.—*Ed.*

*** *Meshadi, hadji*—pilgrims who have journeyed to a Moslem sacred shrine.—*Ed.*

was convinced that to be intimately acquainted with such eminent personages meant a lot to the residents of Namelsem. Even the residents of Inmire seemed to be rather afraid of Ami and pretended to love and respect him. In their hearts they laughed and rejoiced that Ami's authority grew with each passing day in the eyes of the inhabitants of Namelsem *makhalla.*

There was a reason for their rejoicing. The inhabitants of Inmire *makhalla* were perspicacious; they understood a lot. They reasoned that only an educated man could properly conduct the affairs of his people, a man who was well versed in the ways of the world. Ami had never been beyond the world of his village and understood nothing outside of it. In truth the residents of Inmire *makhalla* were farsighted.

To increase Ami's authority in Namelsem they purposely praised him and said to the Namelsemians: "How lucky you are to have a protector like Ami." And the residents of Namelsem *makhalla* told each other:

"That Ami is a bright man. Even our enemies respect him."

With this in mind they trusted Ami even more and totally entrusted their affairs and privileges to his guardianship. Things went so far that when the inhabitants of Namelsem had to decide something they did not bother to assemble and discuss it; there was no need. A hundred heads could not compare with the one head of Ami. Whatever he said was obeyed. So people remained calmly in their places. The residents of Inmire observed this and secretly grinned.

In truth these *makhallas* had been enemies since time immemorial. This made the position of headman a difficult one. Generally a headman did not last for more than two or three years. If the headman was from Inmire he supported his constituents. If he was from Namelsem, he supported the inhabitants of that *makhalla.* In short, due to bad luck or to some other reason the villagers could not find a neutral headman. Nevertheless, the headman supporting Inmire lasted longer because they were generally aware that Ami represented public opinion in Namelsem and did their best to oblige Ami. Naturally Ami was in no need of money. More than anything he wanted to be awarded a medal or a cross. And truly Ami wanted to experience all the pleasures of this world. Why not? Once a man has money, and all men dream of having money, he can buy anything, even authority.

Don't look so surprised! Money's power can make a man great; he can associate with great men. Nothing else is needed. Ami would give one man a lamb, another man a cow, a third man a wineskin with cheese.... And much, much more....

There came a time when the villagers were driven to despair by an outbreak of murders, petty thefts, and robberies. At their request, the authorities appointed a neutral headman. And truly it seemed that the new headman was a good person.

His name was Dashdamir*. And in fact he was as strong as iron. He was an educated man with good intentions. He set things in order straightaway. The thefts and robberies ceased....

Time passed and the headman noticed that the residents of Namelsem did not participate in village affairs. They did not come to the meetings even when called. Only Ami would from time to time appear to speak in the name of the people. For instance, they wanted to open a school in the village. All the prominent residents

---

* *Dashdamir*—Dash means stone, Damir—iron.— *Ed.*

of Inmire came, spoke, and made a clamour. But no one from Namelsem came to the meetings. Only Ami would come when he took it into his head....

In this way one day after another passed.... Finally Dashdamir the headman said to his wife: "I confess that the Namelsemians astound me. They are like sheep. And the Inmirians are like wolves. One must fear them. True, none of them are of noble descent. They are all poor men. But they know their rights. You have only to infringe on them and the whole district will attack you like a nest of hornets."

"You still don't know the residents of Inmire," answered the headman's wife. "If you want to make a name for yourself and advance to a higher position, take their side. They are vociferous. They make a fuss about the smallest matter. My father was from that *makhalla* and he told me a lot about the people."

The headman decided that his wife had a point. From that day on he looked differently upon the residents of Namelsem. When someone from that district came with a complaint, he would consult with Ami. Ami would consider the problem. If he liked the man he would recommend helping him, if not — he would send him away. On the other hand, if something happened in Inmire, the headman himself would go quickly to the site, attentively examine the matter and take measures.

In short, Headman Dashdamir conducted his affairs as he saw fit and managed to outlast all his predecessors. The chief of police respected him more and more.

Things went so far that the governor once visited the village and announced before all the elders: "For your services as headman I will award you a higher position." Ami too was presented at this meeting. The people told the governor that the headman was indeed a good person.

From that day on Ami began to approach the headman more and more. And why not? Ami saw that he was respected by the governor. Ami needed this.

There was a spring nearby. By ancient custom each *makhalla* was allowed to divert the water to its side three times a week. Once Inmire *makhalla* diverted the water to its side for four days. The Namelsemians told Ami about this. Ami agreed to speak with the headman. And in fact they met and Ami told him what had happened. The headman replied: "Inmire needed extra water this week and asked me for permission to divert the spring to its side for one extra day. Please don't meddle in the affairs of the headman."

Ami returned home. He was quite upset and frightened by the headman's remark. Ami had never heard such sharp words.

Ami decided that the headman must feel powerful indeed to speak with a man like himself in such a manner. He told the residents of his *makhalla:* "I told the headman about this incident. He regretted the occurrence and promised that it would never happen again."

This soothed the Namelsemians.

This incident was a test of both men. Ami relied on his money and good name, thinking: "Of course the headman cannot refuse me."

The headman was testing Ami's power by speaking to him sharply. He thought: "If Ami is truly behind his people something will happen. He will tell his people the truth, and the people will come to me and tell me their troubles in order to defend their rights...."

The headman was truly a wise man. Two days later the residents of Inmire again diverted the water to their side on an extra day. The Namelsemians again turned to Ami. Ami again promised to speak to the headman. But this time he was so frightened that he did not say one word to the headman. Instead he told the residents of his district: "I scolded the headman roundly, he begged me to forgive him and promised that it will not happen again."

The people believed Ami and calmed down.

The next time this happened, some of the younger Namelsemians took up spades and went to the spring. They found some youths from Inmire *makhalla* by the spring. The boys from Namelsem wanted to divert the water to their side, but the boys from Inmire prevented this. Harsh words were exchanged and eventually they fell on each other with spades.... People from both districts flocked to aid them. The headman came too. He arrested some youths from Namelsem, but said nothing to the people from Inmire. The inhabitants of Namelsem went to Ami and told him what had happened.

Ami made a clamour and began to threaten all concerned, saying finally: "What a shame that I'm ill today. You go back and calm down. You'll see what I'll do to that headman."

The trusting residents of Namelsem dispersed. On the following day Ami sent the headman a lamb and a wineskin of cheese. Then he came to see him.

When he saw Ami, the headman said: "I was very disturbed by yesterday's incident. Today I reported to the chief of police and to the governor. One or two of your people are going to have to be evicted from this village."

Ami smiled and answered: "Yes there are some black sheep in our *makhalla*. Some of those crazy young people ought to be evicted."

The residents of Namelsem *makhalla* waited patiently. Nothing happened.

The headman thought: "The people of that *makhalla* are like cattle. They will suffer any mistreatment patiently."

And the residents of Inmire *makhalla* laid siege to the headman's home on the following morning and began to agitate for the eviction of three persons from Namelsem. Three men were evicted.

After this incident relations between the two *makhallas* grew even worse. The citizens of one tried to do as much harm to the citizens of the other as possible.

When the Namelsemian women went down to the spring, young boys from Inmire *makhalla* laid hands on them. They even caught some young girls and kissed them. The panic-stricken women ran back to the village. Each told her acquaintances what had happened. The villagers did not know what to do. There was nothing but to tell Ami and consult with him. They came to Ami and told him what had happened.

To show how dear the *makhalla's* honour was to him, Ami threw his sheepskin hat to the floor and pounded the table with his fist. "Don't worry. I'll deal with that headman. Who does he think he is? I won't bother talk with him again. Any day now I'll be going in to town. I'll go straight to the governor and tell him everything."

In a few days the headman called on Ami. Ami ordered that the table be set. But the headman told: "Mr. Ami, I did not come here to dine with you. I have something to tell you. I've been hearing rumours that your *makhalla* is preparing to attack Inmire *makhalla*. I know that the Namelsemians will not disobey you.... The head official knows that too.... You know that if something happens you will be answerable...."

Ami was afraid. "Mr. Headman," he said, "I assure you that I am speaking for all my people. We would never consider such a thing. Our people would never commit such an unworthy act."

As the headman prepared to leave, Ami gave him a hundred rubles to distribute to widows and orphans.

After the headman had gone, Ami quickly summoned a man from the *makhalla* and told him: "The headman just came to see me. He's heard that our district intends to attack Inmire. I told him we could not forget the shameful incident that occurred by the spring. I told him I would inform the governor of this. The headman asked me to restrain our people because the guilty will be punished. We have to be patient. Everything will be sorted out and there will be peace. I answered that I could not agree with him. Things could not be left as they were."

Ami uttered these words in an angry tone, then thought for a moment. "In any case, if you are thinking of doing something like that, hold on. I'll go to the governor and set things straight so that the headman will be removed."

One of the men who had assembled at Ami's bidding answered: "Ami, you are our father. Whatever you say we will obey. But we won't let them lay hands on our women."

"Don't worry," said Ami. "I understand... You just stop those boys."

And the next day Ami actually went into town. He completed his business and returned toward evening. He not only failed to see the governor but was so frightened that he did not dare to pass the street where the governor was.

Rumours flew around the village that Ami had returned. The agitated villagers flocked to his home. "Well? What did he say?" they plied him with questions.

"Listen," answered Ami. "You know that for your sake I am ready to give up all my wealth. Money can do what nothing else can. What do you think happened? I spent what was necessary and smoothed things over. Now I'll deal with the headman. Go back to your homes and wait peacefully. You'll see how things will turn out."

The poor villagers had no alternative but to wait. Eventually several Namelsemians were arrested....

After this the inhabitants of Inmire became so bold that the Namelsemians were afraid to go out on the street at night.

With each day the *makhalla*'s plight increased. The headman saw what the district of Namelsem was capable of and feared nothing. He helped the Inmirians as much as he could, paying particular attention to their complaints and taking measures to alleviate them. And why not? The headman was an intelligent, wordly-wise fellow. He knew that there were bright, educated Inmirians living in the town. He knew that when something happened, the news would immediately circulate in the town; they would send one of their men to set things right.

The headman knew that if he allied himself with the Inmirians, his official affairs would go well. As for his relations with the *makhalla* of Namelsem, the headman took the law into his own hands and did whatever he felt like. Nevertheless, the chief of police and the governor in town respected him more with each passing day.

And there came a time when they needed a new police inspector in the town. They appointed Headman Dashdamir to this position. The news reached the village. The Inmirians were grieved. The Namelsemians rejoiced, clapping their hands with glee. On the eve of his departure, Ami gathered the residents of

Namelsem about him and said: "You know what that villain did to you. We'll show that headman that we don't approve of him. I suggest that we don't see him off or congratulate him when he leaves. It would be better if I alone went and told him a thing or two before he goes. Let him feel our displeasure...."

Everyone agreed to this.

In the morning, the residents of Inmire gathered at the outskirts of the village to see the headman off. From Namelsem only Ami appeared. One by one the representatives of Inmire paid their respects to the headman; some made speeches, a few even wept.

Then Ami came forward: "Dear, beloved Headman," he said. "In the name of the residents of Namelsem *makhalla* I congratulate you with all my heart. We will be sorry to part with you. You have been like a father to us. May God not consider that He has given us a surfeit of blessings." And he even pretended to be overcome by tears.

The headman didn't even notice that no one from Namelsem had come to see him off. He had never seen them. Ami had always spoken for them and he was there.

So the headman took leave of the village. He left, but he was still puzzled: "Extraordinary people these Namelsemians. Either they're very good or very foolish. I've done so much to help their enemies; I always humiliated them before their enemies. And yet they still sent their most respected representative, Ami, to congratulate me."

And truly the headman had not discovered where the people's loyalty lay; what god they worshipped; how clever they were and how honorable.

Suleiman Sani Akhundov
(1875-1939)

A writer and educator, Akhundov is one of the founding fathers of Azerbaijanian dramaturgy. His plays The Falcon's Nest *and* Love and Vengeance *were standard repertory pieces in Azerbaijanian theatres.*
S. S. Akhundov's stories are laconic and rich in social insights. They are quite popular because they reflect the daily life of the Azerbaijanian people with a vivid realism. A particular favourite among both youthful and adult readers is the story "Blacky" where Akhundov depicts the life and tragic death of a talented, selfless young gypsy girl who sacrifices her life to save a friend. The deliberate humanism of the story inspired a film of the same name which enjoyed a long successful run in Azerbaijanian cinemas.
"The Dinner Party" was written by Akhundov in 1905. It is typical of the style and frame of mind of a realistic writer and educator.

The Dinner Party

They had had a good meal with many fine drinks. Then coffee was served. As they sat sipping their coffee, someone said:

"Who do you think are the pillars of society?"

"The pillars of society?"

"The nobility, naturally," said their host. "No nation could exist without us, the beks. We are the pillars of society."

The merchant replied: "There could be no money if there was no trade. And no nation can survive without money. Which means we merchants are the pillars of society."

The scholar said: "A nation exists by its knowledge, and no system can exist without it. It will crumble and perish. We are the pillars of society."

The mullah said: "We are. We who serve Allah and keep the masses in check. If not for us, there would be no moral code. There would be uprisings. Blood would flow, and governments would fall. We are the pillars of society."

The officer said: "I agree with all you have said, but who comes forth to defend the nation when enemies attack? We do. We soldiers are the pillars of society."

The guests moved to the veranda to smoke. Some smoked cigars, others preferred hookahs. The discussion was resumed. In the yard an old peasant was loading sacks of grain onto the shoulders of some workers who then carried the sacks to the storehouse.

Their host said: "Let's put it to the old peasant. Whatever he says, goes."

They agreed, called the man away from his work and told him what the argument was about.

The peasant said: "If you're looking for the truth, sirs, I'll tell you that we peasants and those workingmen who are carrying the sacks, I mean all of us who work by the sweat of our brows are the pillars of society. No nation could exist if we peasants did not sow and harvest, and if they did not work."

At this he turned and went back to his job.

61

Mamed Said Ordubady (1872-1950)

One of the first novelists of Azerbaijan, Ordubady was also an active contributor to the journal Molla Nasreddin.

He combined a literary career with active civic and political work, participating in the struggle to liberate Iran of 1907-1912, an underground fight against the tsarist autocracy. As a result, he was arrested and exiled from Azerbaijan. Following the Great October Socialist Revolution, he fought in the ranks of the Red Army.

His four volume epic novel Misty Tabriz, *an excerpt of which is included in this anthology, depicts the revolutionary movement in Iranian Azerbaijan of 1907-1917. His other novels* Underground Baku *and* The Fighting City *show the life of the working people of Baku on the eve of decisive battles against the autocracy.*

Ordubady's books reflect both a historic era and the life of his people. He is a master at creating absorbing plots and vivid characters.

In Djulfa*

From the novel
Misty Tabriz

Our confederates in Tabriz were worried about two comrades in Djulfa. We had no way to deliver them from the clutches of the tsarist gendarmerie. It would not be easy to go to Djulfa to aid them. For that one had to have permission from the Russian consulate or corresponding military organisations of the tsarist army. Since there was no other way, I decided to turn to the consul.

The permit issued to us read as follows:

Abulhasan, a jewel merchant, and his companion Aga-Asad are bound for Djulfa on business. Abulhasan-bek and Aga-Asad are under wardship of the tsar's consul and the consulate therefore requests the military departments to give them their full cooperation should this prove necessary.

Once I was granted permission to travel to Djulfa I wasted no time and without telling anyone began to get ready for the journey. No one could be trusted. Spies swarmed about everywhere, chasing those who had just arrived in Tabriz or who were about to leave the city. They tried everything to find out the purpose of each passenger's journey, where and why he was travelling. Although we had been permitted to leave the city, we were nevertheless obliged to be careful because not only the consulate but the military authorities made a strict

* The events take place in 1914.— *Ed.*

check on anyone who had been granted such permission. Nina warned me: "It would be better if you didn't interfere in this. You know how dangerous it is. You're slipping a noose around your own neck."

"If they catch me it won't be so terrible," I answered. "I will have helped two comrades whose work is vital to the revolution. In this game we can't lose."

Nina fell silent. In such situations she tried not to upset me and herself maintained a calm façade.

* * *

The vehicle in which I was supposed to drive to Djulfa left early, at 6 a. m. I said goodbye to Nina and rode to the caravan-serai in a phaeton. The car stood awaiting its passengers.

Everyone was there. Only I and an unknown Russian girl whom the consul had entrusted to me were late. When I arrived, the passengers began to fret; they did not want to wait for the girl.

"Let's get going," they pestered the driver. "How many people have to wait because of one Russian. That's the last straw!"

The driver ignored their comments. He wiped the car, pretending that he was unaware of the passengers' agitation. I stood to one side and watched it all thinking that I had never once travelled this road without a female companion. True, this Russian girl whom the consul had requested me to protect had no resemblance to Nina nor to Miss Hanna. Perhaps she was a spy who had been charged to follow my actions. For this reason my travelling companion whose acquaintance I was obliged to make did not particularly interest me.

"What sort of devilry is this? Why aren't we leaving?" the passengers continued to grumble in dissatisfaction.

"Just because of a *matyshka** we have to be detained!"

"To tell the truth we aren't considered to be human."

"Obviously she's the driver's sweetheart. Look how he waits for her, not a protest, not a sign of anger."

"Let her come. We'll see what she looks like."

"What do you think she looks like? Like a hundred other such persons who are shuttling back and forth along these roads."

The vehicle's owner did not catch everything that was said but guessed what a good deal of it might be about.

"If the gentlemen knew what sort of girl she is they would not be angered at her lateness," he said turning to me. "If you buy something from these gentlemen they won't give up a bent *shai***; just look how they're crying out to go as though a hundred and fifty gold *toman* were scattered on the street."

"Ignore them," I interrupted him. "The girl who's keeping us waiting is no ordinary passenger. The consul personally asked me to take care of her. It doesn't matter. We can wait."

Finally the girl appeared. A Russian soldier carried her suitcase. The passengers who had earlier expressed their dissatisfaction now hurried to seat her beside themselves. The girl was young and unusually lovely.

The driver didn't want to seat the girl with the merchants and showing her a

---

* *Matyshka* is a common folk term for a Russian woman in Azerbaijan.— *Ed.*
** *Shai*—a coin of little value.— *Ed.*

64

place up in front turned to me: "I think you'll be more comfortable here. Please sit down beside the young lady."

I accepted his kind offer and sat. I was not dressed in the Iranian fashion and the merchants, deciding that I was not an Azerbaijanian, made indecent jokes at our expense.

The vehicle began to move. We had hardly driven off when the soldiers quartered opposite the caravan-serai began to check our permits. By the time we passed Adji-kerpi and reached the highway administration, they had checked our documents twice. During the second check I was able to look over the girl's shoulder. Her permit had been granted by the tsar's consulate in Tabriz. Her name was Kseniya Pavlovna Berezovskaya.

We sat beside each other in silence. Only three of the merchants did not let up. They kept up a stream of obscenities. Taking me for a Russian they had no qualms about gossiping about the girl, accompanying their words with cynical laughter.

Evidently hoping to curry favour with us, the merchants mentioned Nikolai II, praising him and calling him a just tsar and the father of the faithful. The passengers, just as everyone else in Tabriz, were taking no chances; each suspected that his neighbour was a tsarist secret agent. Words were weighed particularly when the conversation turned to politics or economics.

At the highway administration our documents were checked once again. Putting her permit back in her purse, the girl grinned: "We're obliged to show our permits so often that we might as well pin them on our chest. Look your fill, we ought to say, just stop plaguing us."

"It has to be that way," I answered. "We are quite close to enemy territory. Our military institutions have to be alert and careful. That's a cardinal rule in war-time."

Not one more word passed between us until we reached the settlement of Sofian. I observed the girl imperceptibly. She was bored and would not have been averse to some conversation. A long road stretched before us and there was nothing to occupy our time. We had to pick a harmless subject for our conversation, a subject that would jeopardize neither oneself nor one's interlocutor. The girl shifted restlessly in place. She obviously wanted to know what sort of person I was. It was the simple curiosity of a fellow traveller and quite to be expected given the prospect of a long, tedious journey.

"What time do you have?" she asked as if by chance.

"Five to eight," I answered. Our conversation broke off at this.

We were silent for another hour. Finally the girl found a topic. "Have you left Tabriz for good?" she asked.

"No. If I can finish up my business I hope to return in three days. It's difficult to know precisely."

"Are you a merchant?"

"A merchant? Not exactly. I trade enough to live without outside help."

"What do you trade in?"

"Precious stones. But this is impossible now because we have no way to communicate with Europe. We get the best stones from France, Italy and Holland. The war interferes with our trade relations with these countries. Right now I'm on my way to Djulfa to collect a small debt. Since the money can't be sent by post I'm obliged to pick it up myself."

The girl thought for a while and said: "I wouldn't mind trading in precious stones. If one could learn to distinguish among stones, one could also learn to distinguish among people. That is also an art. Not everyone can master it, particularly when young."

It seemed to me that the girl had some secret and I decided to continue the conversation about precious stones.

"Oh, Miss," I said sadly. "One can easily see the tiniest diamond under a microscope, but science will hardly suffice to comprehend the secrets of the human heart. There's no comparing man with stones. As we men study each other, we grow old. Both the simplest of mortals and the wisest of philosophers are as helpless as children when it comes to studying that most complex of nature's creations — man.

"For my own part rather than study others, I try to study myself. And it seems to me that apart from a few deviations to one side or the other there is a lot in common between me and any other man. In my opinion people are distinguished by their character, although different characters have much in common too, just like other phenomena in nature. Our consciousness and imagination cannot grasp the multitude of forms in the world. At first glance it seems that nature is not harmonious but chaotic. But science has proved that all natural phenomena have something in common, that all are in a sort of correspondence.

"The same is true of men, dear girl. There is also a common bond between men. This is why I decided to understand myself before all else. I am interested in human interrelations. I want to determine my own outlook, to understand my abilities and calling."

The girl listened attentively. She seemed to be pleased with the conversation. From time to time she even touched my arm and exclaimed: "Please go on! I like to listen to you."

And I was pleased that I had succeeded in making her take interest in an abstract philosophical discussion of nature; I had managed to avoid discussing political problems or recent events, subjects which I did not care to talk about. We chattered on during the journey from Sofian to Maraid.

When Maraid had been left far behind us, the Russian girl said: "You know I almost don't want our journey to end. I feel like riding on and on...."

"Why?" I asked. "Don't tell me you are enjoying the trip?"

"Well I wouldn't say that the route is very interesting. We've been jolted and covered with dust and the area between Tabriz and Djulfa is not very picturesque. There's nothing to soothe one's eyes. But I've enjoyed the trip because I enjoy listening to you. I feel as though I would never grow tired of conversing with you no matter how long the journey."

"I can't believe you'd be interested in what I have to say."

"Believe me I'm not one to sing false praises. I don't like to exaggerate other people's virtues and I have no reason to be hypocritical."

"How could I think such things about Miss?"

"I want to believe you. It's quite possible that another girl would not be interested in such themes. Each organism digests different kinds of fare in different ways, as they say. We each have our own interests. We read newspapers, magazines, novels and stories and pick out those elements that are to our taste. At times, works that have no artistic value also find admirers. As for me I am fascinated by the questions that you discussed. I feel that I understand you

66

very well. I have similar ideas but I've never been able to systematise and present them as you have. Unfortunately I am a poor judge of men, quite as helpless as those philosophers whom you mentioned."

"One of my greatest shortcomings is that I often do not know whom I can talk with and what I can talk about. One should always know the person with whom one speaks. It seems to me, and it is purely coincidental, that you were interested in what I had to say."

"I can't agree."

"Why not?"

"From what you say one might conclude that a teacher ought to study his pupil's inclinations, to consider his wishes and then structure his lesson accordingly, that he should adapt the lesson to the pupil. If a man studies the taste of his interlocutor before he speaks then he will involuntarily begin to imitate him and may end up with no views of his own. Isn't this the case?"

The girl had me cornered. I sensed that she was different from other girls I had known and decided that my lofty pronouncements about nature might have seemed like empty chatter to her. Hoping to correct my mistake, I wracked my brains for a topic of conversation but found nothing better than to ask her: "Do you read literary criticism?"

"Why? I do from time to time. One can hardly avoid it."

"If so then you've probably observed that one demand often made of a writer is that he should create for the masses. When a man speaks he should likewise consider the interests, tastes, and intellectual level of his interlocutor."

"But isn't it true that some writers are not read by the masses but still manage to search for truth and write inspired works?" objected the girl. "A writer should be concerned with one thing: he must choose his themes from the lives of the people, for he is part of this. Having selected his theme and passed it through the prism of his outlook, the writer clothes it in an artistic, colourful form. You too took the ideas which we discussed and as a talented narrator made them expressive and interesting. So you have found the method of instilling your thoughts in my consciousness. I don't want to annoy you, but here is a simple example: each cook can take the same piece of meat and prepare it in his own way. The result depends on his art and skill. Perhaps the comparison is somewhat crude but the same is true of ideas. Whether an idea is taken by a writer from life or from another person, once it is expressed in a work it belongs only to him...."

This Russian girl interested me more and more, although I knew neither her origins nor her profession. After conversing several hours with her, I concluded that a woman's beauty is not confined to her external attributes. A beautiful woman should know and love poetry, for poetry and women complement one another.

With this in mind, I asked her: "What sort of literature is closest to your heart?"

She raised her head and looked seriously at me: "Our conversation leads me to conclude that we are both morally justified in calling ourselves twentieth century men. But we're making a terrible mistake. We should have gotten acquainted before beginning our conversation. Rather than continuing to talk about literature, I suggest that we fill in that blank."

I extended my hand: "Abulhasan-bek."

"Kseniya Pavlovna," she answered, pressing my hand. "The gentleman's name indicates that he is not Russian but Iranian."

"No I am not Russian," I answered, being obliged to admit the truth.

"We can discuss that later. Now tell me where you intend to stay in Djulfa."

"It's difficult to say beforehand. In any case I can always find a room at a hotel."

"And if we were to choose the same hotel? Perhaps we could return together."

"You're going back to Tabriz?"

"I would have preferred not to return, but I must."

I resolved not to question the girl about her return to Tabriz. From her conversation I deduced that she had experienced some sort of misfortune. I decided not to refuse her proposition.

"There can be no question," said I. "If that suits you I am happy to comply."

With that our conversation ceased. The vehicle rounded Daradiz and speeded toward the north. A cold wind announced that we were close to Djulfa. It was impossible to converse. Strong gusts of wind carried away our words.

From afar, the roofs of the buildings seemed no larger than matchboxes thrown in the sand. Pointing to the north I said: "We've arrived! Do you see that ribbon glittering in the sand? That's the River Araks. You can consider us already in Djulfa."

*　*　*

Night fell. The cold wind of Djulfa raged. It tore loose from Mt. Kemtal to the southeast and Mt. Alidji to the north, whirling, flinging up sand and sprinkling it on the roofs of the buildings. I waited for dusk to go and find out about Aga-Mamed Gadjiev and Alekper. Shaking the dust from my clothes, I changed and a few hours later went down to the restaurant.

Dusk shrouded Djulfa. In the restaurant of the Hotel France life took its course. Passengers, both those who had just arrived from Iran and those who were leaving for Iran, were gathered there.

I sent the waiter to invite the Russian girl to share my table. She agreed. We dined until ten o'clock.

"Aren't you planning to rest?" she asked as we rose to leave.

"No, but if you wish to rest I won't disturb you."

"No, I wanted to meet the train from Tiflis. It arrives at eleven o'clock."

"I too have friends whom I must see. Let's meet here at midnight."

Having agreed, we parted. She sat in the phaeton and drove off to the station. Grigor-aga and I went to the square where the Commercial Bank is located. The soldiers' tents scattered on the banks of the Araks resembled pyramids on the banks of the Nile. I was reminded of Egypt. Even the cupola of the church opposite the Commercial Bank looked like the sphinx.

The wind howled like a hungry jackal but could not drown out the voices of the tsar's soldiers singing "God Save the Tsar!"

The thundering of the cannon passing across the Djulfa bridge was horrifying. It seemed as though the earth was shaking.

"Djulfa is different from the city you saw in 1909," said Grigor-aga. "It's no longer the rear, but a city on the battle-front."

And in fact military detachments moved along the streets of Djulfa, transporting cannon and field kitchens. Even in the Hotel France there were many officers.

Continuing our conversation, Grigor-aga and I went behind the Hotel Europe and, trying not to be conspicuous, made our way along small, empty streets to the home of Mamed-Hussein Gadjiev. A little farther on, a thickset, heavy man came out of the Hotel Niko and headed toward us.

"Go back to the hotel," he said when he came up to us. "We have something to talk about."

It was the junior gendarme officer, Khromtsov. We took different routes back to the hotel. As he went into Grigor-aga's room, Khromtsov stared at me and evidently recognised me. "I knew you in 1909," he said and graciously shook my hand. Taking a cigarette from his case, Khromtsov lit up and turned to Grigor-aga: "I wouldn't tell you the latest news for ten rubles."

"Don't be greedy," said Grigor-aga.

"I have something to add," I interfered in the conversation and slipped him a twenty-five ruble note.

Khromtsov's eyes lit up when he saw the money. He was astonished at such a large remuneration and turning the note over in his hands, stared at it attentively. "It isn't forged?"

"How can you think such things? I could never be so base as to give a forged banknote to Mr. Khromtsov. That would be disrespectful."

The junior gendarme officer slipped the money in his pocket.

"All right, what do you have to tell us?" said Grigor-aga impatiently.

"Give me ten rubles and then we'll talk about it," said Khromtsov calmly, sitting down.

Grigor-aga found a ten-ruble note and gave it to him.

Khromtsov took an order from his pocket and began to read. It was a warrant for the arrest of Aga-Mamed Gadjiev and Alekper Husseinov, believed to be hiding in the Hotel Safarov.

Putting the order back into his pocket, Khromtsov said: "Do what you have to tonight and in the morning I'll report to Colonel Shtraube of the gendarmerie that these men are not in Djulfa. Got me? See you later." Khromtsov left.

Grigor-aga and I exchanged glances.

"Send for Arsen," I said.

I was agitated and began to fret. Our comrades were in danger. "It's good that I was on time," I thought. "If I had waited one day it would have been disastrous." Thus reasoning, I paced quickly about the room. My nerves were strained to the limit.

Arsen arrived. We embraced each other. Without prefacing my words, I told him how things stood. Arsen stood up and announced: "I'll call the carter Avetis-aga immediately."

He hurried from the room.

An hour passed. At midnight Avetis-aga appeared. We discussed the details of getting Alekper and Aga-Mamed Gadjiev to Iran and he left.

I spent more than an hour waiting tensely. Finally Avetis-aga returned and announced that Aga-Mamed, wrapped up in fur and Alekper posing as the carter had crossed the bridge of Djulfa and entered Iranian territory. We calmed down. Now Aga-Mamed in the phaeton of an Iranian postal official would drive on to Alemdar. Alekper, using my own passport was headed for Tabriz.

When we had finished our business, a messenger brought a letter from the Russian girl. She wrote: "The people whom I was expecting did not arrive. As soon as you are free, send for me. Kseniya."

Abdullah Shaik
(1881-1952)

Abdullah Shaik is still remembered as a small, fragile old man with kind, wise eyes. An indefatigable worker, he enjoyed a productive career as a prosaist, poet, playwright, enlightener and educator.

He was first published in 1907. His stories paint a vivid picture of life in the pre-revolutionary town and countryside. With a masterly realism, as is evident in "An Undelivered Letter"—the story presented in this anthology, he depicts the difficult lot of workers in the Baku oil fields before the revolution. The writer's memoirs are a valuable gift to the younger generation.

An Undelivered Letter

It was a frosty winter's day. The sharpness of the cold burned your face. As though clad in mourning, the sky was swathed in a heavy veil, while the mountains and valleys were covered with a white shroud. Crows hopped warily about the snowdrifts on the street. Warmly-dressed, well-shod people emerged from their cozy, well-heated homes and rode off in horse-drawn carriages or proceeded on foot. The icy day and bitter frost did nothing, save please them.

Do all the sorrows and calamities of this world really fall only to the indigent part of humanity?

71

1

Kurban was sitting at the edge of the Shaitan Bazaar beside his fellow-villager, Mullah Ferzali, the street scribe who wrote letters and appeals for the illiterate. Kurban was frozen. With one hand he held the open collar of his threadbare shirt together, and with the other he tried to pull his tattered shoe off his foot, for it had frozen to his skin.

"Write a letter for me, Mullah. You know I always bring you a profit. I only left our village a year ago, but this is the fifth letter you'll be writing for me."

Mullah Ferzali rubbed his stiff fingers, pulled out a scrap of paper and laid it on his lap. "What do you want me to write?" He stifled a yawn.

Kurban moved closer and began to whisper, as if he were sharing a great secret: "First of all, greet the mother of my children. Tell her to take good care of them and to cherish them. Then write that, praise be to Allah, I am well. Tell her I'm sending them fifteen rubles with Gulam-Rza and will send some more money in time for the holiday. I want the children to have everything they need. Tell her I'll be home late this spring."

The mullah dipped his pen into the inkwell. He was about to start the letter, but the ink had become so thick it was impossible to write. Mullah Ferzali spat carefully into the inkwell, stirred its contents with his penpoint and got down to the work at hand.

Kurban drew his worn robe tighter around his body, covering the bristly hair on his chest and, bending double from the bitter cold, said unhappily: "My new master is an evil person. The well we're digging is more than 180 feet deep. We begged him to add something to our pay, because it's so hard going that far down, and the gas fumes are killing us. But that evil one, the son of an evil one, won't give in. He said if we don't go on digging as agreed, he won't pay us at all. It's hard to earn money here, Mullah. A man can envy your trade: you write five or ten letters a day, say a few prayers for others and, praise be to Allah, you have enough to eat. May Allah provide for you always! What else could a man wish for?"

Mullah Ferzali laid down his pen, pinched some sand from a hollow in the wall and sprinkled it over the paper.

"Ah, my friend, a fight always looks interesting from the sidelines. My job isn't to be envied, no matter what you say. Summer and winter I sit at the crossroads, waiting for clients. Sometimes my head begins to swim. There are days when I have no work at all, so I sit here, rubbing my empty stomach." The mullah shivered, drew his cloak more tightly around his shoulders and read the letter aloud.

Kurban listened intently. He gaped, as if he were about to swallow the words that issued from the mullah's mouth. He seemed pleased with the results, and at the close he said, his eyes lighting up: "Mullah, add my respects to Gulam-Hussein and ask him to look after the children until I get back. Tell him to write me a letter and tell me what happened to our red cow and whether he sold the blind nag. And write that I'll bring Anakhanum and Memish each a printed red kerchief when I come home."

After Mullah Ferzali had finished writing he folded the paper carefully, slipped it into an envelope and said: "Whom should I address it to?"

Kurban scratched his head in some confusion. "Just say that it should be given to the mother of Kurban's children."

Mullah Ferzali addressed it and handed it to his client. Kurban accepted it with trembling hands, examined it closely and was about to put it inside his robe when it slipped out of his stiff fingers. He bent down quickly, snatched it up, brushed the frozen bits of earth from it and laid it against his chest gently.

Then he took a ten-kopek piece from his pouch and put it into the mullah's hand. "Here. This is for you. I'll be back before the holiday to order another letter. You'll be getting a bit of business from me, just wait." He walked off, pressing one hand firmly against the envelope.

Kurban was in a hurry to reach Gulam-Rza's house and give him the letter, and then add a few words of his own. He was thinking that Gulam-Rza was a lucky man. He had saved up a bit and was now going back to their native village to visit his children. How beautiful everything would be there in another month!

The forests, mountains and hills would be covered with an emerald carpet. The flowers would be in bloom. The trees would be clothed in green and the swallows, those first heralds of spring, would have returned from warmer lands. Then the starlings and cranes would return to their old nests. Work would be in full swing in the fields and gardens. The fishermen would set out on the rivers and lakes. Ah, bitter poverty, what have you done to Kurban? You tossed him into an alien place, tearing him away from his wife and children.

A lump rose in his throat. Then his heart froze, his knees buckled and he fell senseless on to the powdery snow. When he came to a few moments later he raised his head, feeling wretched and terribly weak. Grand carriages, lively crowds and the happy faces of self-satisfied, warmly-dressed people flashed by. He glanced at all those well-fed people with hatred and bitterness. A great sigh escaped his bloodless lips.

Mustering his strength, he rose slowly, then quickly put his hand into his robe to make sure the letter was still there. Pressing it still more firmly under his arm, he started out for his friend's quarters again.

The door was locked. This was an unexpected disappointment. Kurban turned sadly away. As he wandered dazedly through the crowds of workingmen, he suddenly spotted Safar, another fellow-villager. Kurban hailed him and learned that Gulam-Rza had gone off to the city. "As soon as he gets back tell him that I have to see him before he leaves for his home. I want to give him a letter and some money for the family, and say a few words to him myself."

2

"You scoundrels! Loafers! When the well was shallow I was the head and you were the tail, and wherever I turned you crawled along after me. But now, when it's deep, you want to become the head. Every day you present me with a new ultimatum. Every day you come up with new demands. You say the well's too deep and it smells of death down there, and other nonsense. Imagine! You've lost all sense of decency. What you need is a good flogging!" their master, Hadji-Kuli screamed.

Safar and Tariverdi tipped over the tub of sand they had raised from the bottom of the well and then sent it down again.

"We still are the tail, Aga," Tariverdi said. "You know how dangerous it is working down there on the bottom now. Look at its maw. Just like a dragon lying in wait. A good conscience is a good thing, you know."

"Look over there," Safar added, pointing to the oil derricks in the distance. "Every inch of the ground there, no matter where you sink a pick, you'll hit a worker's bones. You can hear their moaning everywhere. And those who live in these fine, tall houses...."

"Go on and die if you want to," Hadji-Kuli shouted and stamped his feet. "You think money comes easily? You risk your lives, but we risk our fortunes."

"Safar! Hey, Safar! Kurban's yanking the rope down there."

The two workers ran back to the well. As they lay down on the ground to look over the edge a terrible roar of exploding gas threw them back.

"Allah be merciful," they whispered fearfully. "Now Kurban's dead, too."

Hadji-Kuli seemed not to have heard them. He walked over to the well and bent over cautiously. His eyes lit up and his lips parted in a happy smile. "There's an opening for the oil now! It'll come up in a fountain!"

"What about Kurban's body, Hadji? You mean it's going to remain down there?" Tariverdi said with seeming indifference.

His words had a sobering effect on their master, whose eyes now grew wide. Then he took two twenty-five ruble bills from his purse and muttered: "Here.... This'll be for whoever brings up the body."

Tariverdi looked over the side of the well and saw the bubbling oil rising to the surface. "Poor Kurban. You dug your own grave."

"Here," Hadji said. "Take the money and divide it between you, but not a word to anybody, hear?"

"What about his clothes, Aga?"

Hadji placed his hand gently on Safar's shoulder and said: "Bury them someplace here."

When they picked up Kurban's clothes an envelope fell to the ground.

"Poor Kurban. His letter was never delivered."

Yusif Vezir (Chemenzeminly) (1887-1938)

Vezir, who writes mainly short stories and novels, began his literary career in 1910 as one of the pleiad of writers united by their work on the revolutionary-democratic journal Molla Nasreddin.

He first won public acclaim with his novella A Pass for Paradise *(1913), which mercilessly exposed fanaticism and superstition.*

From 1916 to 1925, Jusif Vezir lived as an émigré in Turkey and France. When he returned to his native land and witnessed his people's achievements in the process of socialist construction, the writer was inspired to compose new stories and novellas.

In the late twenties and early thirties, Vezir authored a series of historical novels: Virgin Spring, Second Nature, *and* Students. *The latter shows how Russian students revolted against the tsarist authocracy.*

Many of Vezir's stories, including "Aksakal" *(which means "greybearded", "elder" or "sovereign"), show the heavy lot of simple, poor people and their longing for goodness and light.*

A Good Omen

Old Gulsum awakened with a smile that morning. She sat up in bed and smiled. The sun peeped in the window. She looked at it and said: "May I serve Allah always, and may Allah be with me always, as to this day! And may my dream come true, with Allah's help! I'll go to Alipashi-bek today and ask for the hand of his daughter."

Old Gulsum mused over this for a while and then broke into a smile again. "My son Faradj is rich and handsome. So what if he's of the middle-class? May I serve Faradj and his noble bride always."

Gulsum had been thinking about her son's eventual marriage for quite some time, but had not known whom to choose for a bride for him. She did not want a commoner for a daughter-in-law, and did not have the courage to approach the bek,* for beks never let their daughters marry commoners. They always managed to find sons-in-law as noble as themselves. Gulsum's background was not befitting them, for her husband had been a broker and her son was a merchant, which meant they spent their days at the bazaar, never returning home until evening. Besides, they had neither the manners nor the appearance of aristocrats.

Still, Gulsum had decided to approach Alipashi-bek. Perhaps she would not have taken such a step if not for

_____
* *Bek*—Moslem of noble birth.— *Ed.*

her dream. However, the dream had been favourable, and it would have been a sin to disregard it.

She had dreamt a horse had been standing by a hayloft, sniffing at some sacks of barley. Then the horse had reared and kicked over a barrel of water.

A horse meant hope. A barrel meant purity. And water meant clarity. However, the horse had reared up and kicked over the barrel. What could that mean?

Gulsum was puzzled. She scratched under her arms. Then she picked her nose. Suddenly she laughed aloud. Kicking meant dancing and merriment. A wedding. It was as simple as that.

Alipasha-bek and his wife were sitting by the window, smoking.

A serving girl informed them of Gulsum's arrival. Her mistress, whose voice was as deep as a man's, told her to bring the woman in.

Gulsum entered.

"What brings you?" the bek's wife asked softly.

"I wanted to see how nobles live. We want to become nobles, too." Gulsum said and laughed. The woman smiled. A trace of a smile smoothed the wrinkles on Alipasha-bek's face. They were silent for a few moments. Gulsum took in the room and confided: "My son Faradj had the walls painted just like yours. We could never have done it ourselves. The job cost us a couple of thousand rubles!"

Neither the bek nor his wife paid any attention to the remark.

They all sat in silence again. Finally, the old woman spoke up. "You know we are rich and never want for anything. Faradj is a good and modest young man. He'll be like a son to you. As Allah is my witness, he is worthy of your family! He is handsome and tall. Let him marry one of your daughters," Gulsum said and laughed with pleasure.

The bek's wife frowned. She looked at her husband. He looked at his wife, then glanced angrily at the stupid old woman. Ah, how he would have liked to hit her over the head with the hookah. Never before had a bek's daughter been married to a commoner!

However, he controlled himself and said, speaking with restraint: "I cannot give you my answer yet, Sister. We'll have to see what our aksakal * says." There was both irony and wrath in his voice, but the old woman sensed neither. On the contrary, she was overjoyed.

"The dream was a good omen," she said to herself as she went down the stairs. "The girl's as good as ours. What can the aksakal say? He'll surely agree."

Thus lost in thought she did not realise that she had descended into the inner yard. A huge hound dashed out from under the staircase and leaped at her. Gulsum screamed. The dog tore her clothing to shreds. No one came running at the poor woman's cries. She finally managed to break away from the dog and hide in a cold tendir,** pulling the iron sheet that served as a door over her. The dog had bitten her hands badly.

At last Alipasha-bek appeared on the balcony and shouted to his servants: "Tie up the dog!"

* *Aksakal*—elder.— *Ed.*
** *Tendir*—a clay oven.— *Ed.*

The dog was chained, and the mangled old woman was pulled out of the oven. The bek turned towards her with a smile and shrugged, saying: "See, Sister, aksakal says no."

Old Gulsum barely managed to reach her home. Three days later she died. So that was what the horse's rearing up and kicking had meant.

Seid Hussein
(1887-1938)

An outstanding prose-writer. He was born to a family of sailors. Before the revolution he worked as a proof-reader and editor at the printing-house "The Caspian". He was first published in 1908, beginning his career as a critic.

After the revolution he spent most of his time working in the field of education. His first stories were published in 1927 and they were quickly acclaimed by the public.

His simplicity and clarity were greatly admired. Seid Hussein seems to converse with his readers; with a rare sincerity he tells them about his own experiences and observations. "A Story About a Street" is written in precisely this way.

The major themes in the stories of this writer, who has made a significant contribution to Azerbaijanian prose, are the struggle between the old and the new as reflected in daily life; the liberation of women and the human quest for spiritual perfection.

A Story About a Street

Everything I am writing about happened, and happened not so long ago.

The street, whose story I have decided to tell, is in Baku. Thirty years ago this city was no less the political and cultural centre of Azerbaijan than today. The street in question is well known to the people of Baku. It will suffice to say that four mosques are situated along it. Two of them, the Hadji-Pirverdi and the Hadji-Abulgasan, enclose it on the east and west sides.

The East and West, moslem concepts of life and the western way of thinking, Islamic and European culture, all were absorbed into the street. Side by side with the magnificent multi-storied residences of the wealthy huddled delapidated shanties, whose inhabitants never caught a glimpse of the sun. Old moslem schools stood next to modern ones. Merchants girt in brightly coloured scarves, smartly dressed oil magnates in collar and tie, spiritual leaders in huge white turbans and tradesmen in top hats, poor folk, breaking their backs to earn a piece of bread, and the bloated rich all lived side by side, knew each other well and to an outsider might have appeared as one large family.

The life and soul, the backbone of the street was a certain Hadji-Aslan. There was not a single person, man, woman or child, who had not at one time or another heard the loud abuse of this distinguished citizen, the most popular man in our street.

To all the inhabitants of the street Hadji-Aslan was a "white beard" or person of authority, indeed, a fatherfigure. In the city council, of which he was a member, Hadji-Aslan was considered the true representative of the people.

This esteemed man was not only respected by the wealthy merchants and important oil operators, by the European-educated lawyers and spiritual leaders who knew the secrets of the "Kerbela", but his word was also law in the dukhanes (taverns) and opium dens, frequented by people with very shady pasts. No doubt this was precisely why Hadji-Aslan was well informed of any crime that took place in our street, and he knew about many of them even before they actually occurred.

Thus Hadji-Aslan was a very big man; a respected businessman, the leader of the *makhalla*, an "aksakal" and the true representative of the people, generally recognised and universally admired.

It was early spring. The street was alive with merrymaking and nearly every house had guests: the faithful were paying calls on one another to celebrate the New Year. Then suddenly, when the festivities were in full swing, Hadji-Aslan ordered all the gates and doors to be locked and bolted as quickly as possible — he was going to train his young hounds to hunt hare.

Hadji-Aslan hoisted his large, bulky body onto his horse, showed his hounds the hare which had been trapped in a field, rode ahead a little and set the animal loose. The dogs rushed after it, and Hadji-Aslan galloped after the dogs, urging them on with loud hollers.

Utter bedlam broke loose. The frightened people hid in corners. Children began to cry. The wretched hare raced along the street, looking for some hole to dive into. It was lucky. In the door of one of the old houses it spotted a small opening which had been made for a drain. The hare rushed through the gap and disappeared in a trice. The hounds tore after it in a frenzy. It so happened that the owner of the ill-fated house had locked the door, but in his haste had forgotten to block up the mouth of the drain.

Hadji-Aslan cursed not only the poor man, but also his wife, daughter and even his baby son lying in a cradle.

The man, scared out of his wits, begged forgiveness. His wife and children

82

sobbed and huddled close to one another. But Hadji became more and more infuriated.

"If you like," he shouted suddenly, "I'll take your wife out onto the street! Then you'll see what I do with her!"

Hadji-Aslan was capable of carrying out his threat. If someone dared to contradict him or simply did not wish to bow down to the omnipotent lord of the *makhalla*, Hadji-Aslan would stop at nothing.

The *makhalla* knew many stories of young girls and boys disappearing "without a trace" and returning home a few days later with puffy, tear-stained eyes.

"Your order was only about doors," blabbered the unfortunate master of the house through lips white with terror. "Do you think we would really dare to disobey...."

Whether because Hadji-Aslan had begun to cool off, or because the words "do you think we would really dare to disobey" had pleased him, he suddenly calmed down.

"Oh, alright then," he said peacefully. "So be it, I'll forgive you this time."

"May Allah lengthen your days!" cried the man joyfully, miraculously delivered from abuse. "May Allah not deprive us of your favours!"

And from that time onwards people in the *makhalla* praised Hadji-Aslan's magnanimity even more warmly.

However there was hardly anything remarkable about the occurrence and it was forgotten within a few days; people were used to happenings of that sort. But what happened with Mursalkulu was really out of the ordinary and remained in the inhabitants' memories for a long time.

Everyone loved Mursalkulu. He was a courageous man, yet modest and devout, and had never in his life been involved in any unseemly affair. He worked on one of Hadji-Aslan's steamers and with his meagre income supported his sister and her two orphaned sons.

This Mursalkulu was the only inhabitant in the *makhalla* who dared to speak out against Hadji-Aslan and his men when they embarked on some dirty business. Once or twice he had even been involved in fist fights with Hadji men and had put on a fine show.

Applauding Mursalkulu's courage and intrepidity, Hadji-Aslan decided that it would not be a bad idea to break in this bold fellow and make him one of his boys. However Mursalkulu flatly declined the offer: he preferred to earn his money honestly.

Hadji ordered the impudent fellow to be dismissed. However Mursalkulu quickly found himself other work.

For the first time in his life Hadji-Aslan was not able to do as he pleased. This put him in a very difficult position, all the more so because Mursalkulu's popularity and influence in the *makhalla* had increased. It turned out that there were others, too, who were capable on occasion of speaking out against him. To tolerate this was unthinkable.

Hadji-Aslan decided that to get rid of Mursalkulu would serve as a good lesson for the others. It was no trouble at all for Hadji-Aslan to carry out his intention — just a sign from him was enough.

One day during Ramadan, when the people were coming out of the mosque, four of Hadji-Aslan's armed thugs fell upon Mursalkulu. A heated fight developed in front of the mosque. The brave man had decided to set a high price on his life. Several bystanders were wounded in the fierce fight.

The outcome of Hadji-Aslan's "measure" was that four lifeless bodies lay by the door of the mosque. Mursalkulu, two of Hadji-Aslan's thugs and one completely innocent person, who by chance happened to be nearby, were killed.

However, even this was not a really unusual incident — the *makhalla* had seen worse. People only remembered the events which happened directly after Mursalkulu's murder.

On the following morning coffins stood in front of four houses: those of Mursalkulu and the man he had killed in the fight stood almost side by side with a gap of only a few feet between them.

Not a single person dared to mourn Mursalkulu or lament his spent youth.

Only the deceased man's nephew, a lad of about sixteen, stood in the doorway sobbing bitterly.

This was an obvious act of defiance. Hadji-Aslan had to avenge the victims. The coffin containing Mursalkulu's corpse had not even reached the cemetery when Hadji-Aslan's men dragged the sixteen-year-old nephew onto the street and tore him to pieces before everyone's eyes.

Perhaps you are thinking that the child's murder is the extraordinary incident we wanted to tell you about? Not at all! The street remembers a great number of occasions on which the blood of innocent children was shed. Children had been slaughtered before and this would not be the last time. It was what happened afterwards that is important.

Mursalkulu's sister was weeping. What could be more natural than a woman sobbing over the loss of her only brother, young, brave and strong! But what does a woman do if, while bitterly lamenting her brother, she suddenly learns that her son has been murdered, and running out into the street, sees his blood-stained body stretched out on the ground? The woman did not cry. She had no tears left. She only tore her clothes and hair and made terrifying animal-like noises. Only one name was discernible in her inhuman cries — Hadji-Aslan....

This woman was a mother. They had murdered her child. She no longer feared anything or anyone: commands meant nothing to her any more. And perhaps without even understanding what she was shouting, she continued to shriek one and the same word:

"Hadji-Aslan!! Hadji-Aslan!!!"

Not a single person went up to the woman, insane from grief; no one dared comfort her, though many sobbed, watching her from a distance. When Hadji-Aslan saw this, he immediately realised that his men had gone too far: this woman could disgrace his name. She had to be calmed at once.

"Calm down, sister!" Hadji-Aslan said in a soothing voice, approaching her. "Stand up and go home!"

The wretched woman heard nothing. She did not even realise who he was.

"Cursed be Hadji-Aslan!" she cried. "May the wrath of Allah be upon him!"

That was too much. The raving woman had to be silenced immediately.

"Stop this disgraceful behaviour at once!" shouted Hadji-Aslan angrily. "Aren't you ashamed of yourself? Stand up, I tell you!"

The woman continued to commit "outrages". She did not obey Hadji-Aslan's order.

"Alright then!" he said calmly. "Now I'm going to make you calm down!" And turning to his men, he ordered them to find the woman's younger son immediately and kill him too.

Only when the armed men were on their way to her house did the wretched woman realise what was going on.

And it was what happened next that made this incident so memorable.

The woman actually stopped shrieking and hurling abuse at Hadji-Aslan. She fell at his feet and began begging for mercy. Then she tried to get up and rush to protect her boy. As her legs would not carry her, the woman began crawling on all fours after the men searching for her child. She no longer cried, shrieked or begged for mercy, but began laughing loudly and unrestrainedly.

...Perhaps you have decided that all this has been made up, and that nothing of the sort really happened? It did, and not so long ago. Such incidents were very characteristic of our recent past.

2

This street has a long history, and in it are many blood pages! For Hadji-Aslan was not the only one of his kind; there were many like him, some weaker, some stronger. And each was honoured and respected by the local people.

The year 1905 arrived. Waves of revolution reached the Caucasus and swept over Azerbaijan.

The habitual, regular pace of life on the street was put off balance: disorder broke out.

The local authorities proved incapable of dealing with the situation. The city elders met in the council and formed a society called "Peace and Order" to "ensure public safety, put an end to violence and avenge innocent blood".

If you delve into the archives of the Baku city council or leaf through the newspapers of the time, you will certainly come across the familiar name of Hadji-Aslan, a member of the Baku council and one of the most respected citizens in the city.

At that time Hadji-Aslan was especially popular; he had to speak in public on quite a number of occasions. I remember one of them to this day.

Reaction intensified. A society called "The Union of the Russian People" was founded which fought in Baku against the actions of the city's multinational proletariat. Quite an important detachment of this commendable organisation was formed on the street with whose story we are concerned.

The detachment moved along the street. At its head pranced Hadji-Aslan with a line of Cossacks bringing up the rear. Flutes and drums rent the air and Hadji-Aslan's men, with their sheepskin hats pulled over their foreheads, danced spiritedly. Thus Hadji-Aslan's detachment entered the courtyard of the Great Cathedral. Here Hadji-Aslan was greeted by the city governor and other important officials.

Hadji-Aslan climbed onto the rostrum which had been erected in the church courtyard. People started making hushing noises.

"Citizens!" pronounced Hadji-Aslan in an imposing voice when silence had fallen. "Cursing the tsar is as bad as dishonouring his wife."

People began to applaud wildly.

"Citizens!" continued Hadji-Aslan. "Tell everybody that cursing the tsar is as bad as dishonouring his wife!"

The crowd of followers became noisy. Everyone began to repeat Hadji-Aslan's words loudly and joyfully, they expressed their joyful and exalted mood so well.

Then Hadji-Aslan died. The entire street went into mourning for the deceased, and spoke of nothing but his countless virtues and merits. The street had lost its lord, its protector. Thus, Hadji-Aslan had sowed the street densely with seeds, and each of them, carefully cultivated, had germinated. The shoots sprang up rapidly and spread out, but the time was not ripe, and so, no matter how high the shoots grew nor how far they extended, they could not come to fruition.

After the February revolution the First Congress of Caucasian Moslems was held in the Ismailia Palace, now the Palace of Culture. Many of Hadji-Aslan's protégés took part as professed representatives of the people. The Congress was to decide the fate of the Azerbaijan Turks. An uproar was caused by a woman appearing without her veil. The Congress was split. Some demanded that the woman be removed, others were of the opinion that she should be allowed to participate. All these differences of opinion prevented Hadji-Aslan's spiritual heirs from gaining the advantage and seizing control.

The October Revolution soon followed. Dark forces prevented it from penetrating into our street. Hadji-Aslan's disciples changed their colour as fast as chameleon. From time to time they began to raise their heads and take the offensive—"faith, the Koran and the Shariath". The dark, evil shadows of the past hovered above our street. But the ground was already giving way under the feet of Hadji-Aslan's descendants.

Two more years passed and the waves of October, sweeping across the Caspian, flooded the old streets, washing away all the scum in its path. Like a storm uprooting age-old trees, the purifying revolution ripped the weeds sown by Hadji-Aslan out of the native soil and scattered them to the four winds.

At last the street was clean.

**Gadjibaba
Nazarli
(1895-1939)**

*An outstanding prosaist. For many years he headed the Writers' Union of
Azerbaijan.*
*Nazarli composes absorbing and stirring narratives about events and
people at the time of the revolutionary underground and the Civil War.
"Kagraman's Story" is part of this cycle.*
*At times Nazarli presents his heroes in a romantic light and at times
depicts them in the stern, restrained manner of the realists.*

Kagraman's Story

The spacious room, divided by a thin partition, still bore the pitiful traces of the Civil War. Among the maps, posters and obsolete slogans on the walls glared bare bricks from which the plaster had crumbled and bullet holes, gaping like deep wounds. A fire crackled cosily in the hearth. An old samovar, polished to shine, puffed away on a table covered with newspapers. Golden sunbeams danced on its dented surface.

Four people sat at the table.

One of them, Kagraman, a middle-aged man with thick curly hair and a large, but delicately featured face, took

89

his cup from his lips, put it down on the table and began to search his pockets for a cigarette.

"Oh, Salman!" he sighed. "I can't help remembering the terrible tragedy that happened in that difficult year.... In your room."

It was not the first time that Salman had heard these words from Kagraman, but he simply could not imagine which tragedy his friend had in mind for the entire house was pock-marked with cracks and bullet holes, the stubborn witnesses of past battles.

Salman thought for a moment and asked:

"Which tragedy are you talking about? Not about the days of the revolt?"

"That's right."

"What happened in this house then?"

For a long while Kagraman watched the fire playing fancifully in the hearth, sat silent for a few minutes and, as if recalling the events which had happened long ago screwed up his large, wide-set eyes.

"As you well know the revolt in this town flared up in 1920. If I'm not mistaken, you were in town then, weren't you, Salman?"

"Oh no, I wasn't!" objected Salman. "The night before, I went to the station with the revolutionary committee and travelled by train to the headquarters of the thirty-second division."

"That's right, I remember!" confirmed Kagraman. "You left me here with four comrades. And when the enemy troops entered the town, you instructed us to guard this house. I remember it as if it were yesterday. The commander of the division said on sending us here: 'Don't let anyone enter or leave the house! Protect it to the bitter end!'

"Do you know why? This house on the outskirts towers above the other houses and you have a perfect view of the whole town from here. We were to retain this advantageous position at all costs, especially to protect the bridge from the insurgents. Headquarters promised to send us help in one or two-hours time.

"From here we could shell the bridge and the square.

"With us was a Komsomol member — a slender, frail, dark-haired girl with grey eyes. Her name was Siranush. Oh, Siranush! Never in my life have I met such a beautiful, brave young girl!

"I'm sorry, I've digressed a little from the story.... Let me see.... So, our task was to guard this house. We soon realised that there was little hope of being rescued as an hour later our troops had totally abandoned the town, and no one knew when they would return. But an order is an order. It was my duty to carry it out, I had to stay here ... until the last bullet.

"I found out that the house belonged to a very rich and influential man in the town. During the revolutionary uprising he fled with his elder son, leaving his wife, their ten-year-old younger son and a maid.

"Two days passed in comparative calmness. During this time not one of the house's inhabitants betrayed his hostility. However alarmed they were, they behaved correctly and even haughtily. It was as if they had no doubt in their minds that the counter-revolutionaries would certainly come out of this battle victorious and we would be punished according to our deserts.

"On the third day fierce fighting broke out in the town with the initiative being won alternately by our troops and then by the insurgents. Even our small fortress was affected: when the insurgents gained the upper hand the guarded house was stormed with a hail of bullets. When our troops managed to push forward there was a temporary respite and we were only hit by stray bullets."

The narrator grew silent, lost in his own thoughts. The fierce winter wind howled in the flue, and hurled handfuls of stinging snow and ice at the windows. Kagraman took a drag at his cigarette, blew a cloud of bluish smoke up at the ceiling and continued.

"It was nearly noon. Silence fell and lasted for about half an hour. Only in those days could you call this deceptive lull 'silence'. In fact, the shooting continued and only the cannon volleys ceased completely.

"It was not difficult to guess that both sides were preparing to attack. This proved to be so, as half an hour later mighty volleys of artillery blazed from all sides. The town seemed to tremble from the deafening rolls of thunder. Two comrades and I positioned ourselves by a window in one of the rooms on the second floor from where we could shoot at anyone who tried to cross the bridge. Suddenly the door opened and the maid came into the room. Unlike her normal self, she was upset and depressed. I immediately noted this change in her mood.

"'What's happened? What have you come here for?' I asked her. 'Go downstairs, or you'll get killed!'

"But she waved her hand in despair.

"'The mistress wishes to speak to you.'

"'What kind of conversation can we have at a time like this?' I replied with restraint, though in fact this request infuriated me. 'Can't you see what's going on outside? It's the end of the world! I can't leave this room.'

"'She's not far away,' the old women explained. 'She's here in the next room. The mistress wants to have a word with you about something important.'

"'About something important?' I repeated bewildered.

"'Yes,' she confirmed, 'it's very important....'

"'Alright, let's see what is bothering your mistress.'

"I informed my comrades, told them to remain on the alert, and then followed the old woman.

"It was the first time I had seen the wife of the house's owner at close quarters. Tall, dignified, beautiful, and blooming with health she stood by the wall with her pretty head thrown back. She was not a day older than thirty. Two tightly braided black plaits hung over her breast, and on her shoulders lay a white scarf which had slipped off her hair. I can see her ringed fingers running up and down its fringe as if it were today.

"When I appeared she walked up to an armchair in the corner and sat down gracefully.

" 'May I have a word with you, sir?'

" 'Look, I'm ... busy at the moment, but if it won't take long, please do.'

"Braiding and unbraiding the ends of her plaits, she stood up, approached very close to me and looked me steadily in the eyes.

" 'How courteous you are!' she said with a coquettish and gentle smile. 'Aren't you surprised to see a woman standing before you? And, what is more, a young woman.... It's strange, isn't it?'

"I didn't bat an eyelash, but continued to stand with one hand on my hip and the other holding the handle of my dagger. We were alone. I didn't like that very much. So, I thought, let's see what game you are up to, my beauty...."

...Kagraman paused and, sipping his cold tea, stared again at the fire in which blue tongues of flame licked the scorched logs. His friends sat in silence, waiting for him to continue, and if it had not been for the crackling of the logs in the hearth and the puffing of the boiling samovar, their hearts would have been heard beating.

"...I didn't move," continued Kagraman. " 'Please speak up,' I said. 'What do you want of me?'

" 'Lord, how terrifying you are!' she exclaimed, shrugging her shoulders, and clearly pretending to be frightened.

" 'In that case, I'm going, I can't wait!'

"I made a decisive step for the door. Suddenly I felt her soft, hot fingers touching my left hand. Outside, the booming of artillery and rattle of machine guns ripped apart the sky. The ever intensifying firing meant that the situation was becoming more and more grave with every moment. I drew my hand away.

" 'Time doesn't stand still! Say what you've got to say quickly.'

"She grasped my hand even more firmly and said in a pleading voice:

" 'Will you let me?'

" 'What?'

" 'Go out into the yard, go to my relatives.'

" 'Impossible. I've been ordered not to let anyone out of here,' I replied firmly and pulled the door towards me.

"As soon as I'd grasped the door handle she threw her bare, ivory-coloured, sweet-smelling arms around my neck from behind. I thought she wanted to grab my gun. 'Kill her!' flashed through my mind. But I immediately came to my senses. However, no matter how hard I struggled, I could not free myself from her powerful embrace.

"'Sweetheart! Let me. I'll come back and then I'll be yours!'

"It was a crude trick. Too crude. Her cunning and her words of flattery only aroused my anger. I did all I could to free myself from the encirclement of her arms. I didn't notice the door open and Siranush standing in front of me. She seemed to drop from the sky. Her angry stare wandered over the woman embracing me and then fixed on me, penetrating right through.

"'Comrade Kagraman!' she exclaimed, clearly trying to hide her embarrassment. 'I think the fighting is of more importance. Wouldn't it be better if you returned to your post?'

"I felt as if I'd been scalded with boiling water. I myself didn't feel I was in the wrong, leaving my post or in any other matter. No, I wasn't wrong at all.... But I felt so humiliated, so insulted before this Komsomol girl, that even now, remembering the incident makes me sweat.

"The woman looked Siranush up and down with eyes blazing with hatred, and then went into the other room. I tried to explain, to dispell Siranush's suspicions.

"'Believe me, Sima, she stuck to me like a leech. She was trying to get me to let her out of the house. This is the first time I've seen her. She's a very unscrupulous woman. Don't you believe anything else....'

"'This isn't the place for confessions. Anyway, I'm not interested,' said Siranush, indifferent to my explanations. 'Let's return to our post. It wouldn't hurt to remember that we're carrying out a special mission.'

"We left the room and went to the machine gun.

"An enemy detachment approached the house and opened up a barrage of fire. Bullets whistled through the window and you couldn't stand at full height in the room. I fell on the floor, protected myself behind a sack, drew Siranush to me and began firing the machine gun. A minute later about two hundred retreating enemy soldiers were running in all directions across the square. Then, leaving Siranush, I returned to my post.

"Then a comrade and I shot at the bridge with our rifles. A couple of minutes later from the next room came a terrible shriek that turned into long, drawn-out groans. My heart skipped a beat: Siranush! I rushed for the door and threw it open with a jerk."

...Outside, the snow storm howled like a wounded beast. Kagraman closed his eyes and pressed his temples with the palms of his hands.

"Siranush stood leaning awkwardly on the high back of the old armchair. She was as white as snow, her face, with its full, childlike lips, distorted by pain. Thick blood trickled between the fingers she held over the wound on her breast, ran down her old, patched-up cotton dress and dripped onto the floor. I seized her

93

in my arms and carefully laid her on the floor. She did not speak. Only a hollow moan escaped her breast from time to time.

"She was dying; her voice was becoming weaker and weaker.

"'Return to the machine gun! We must hold the square. We must.... Our troops seem to be advancing. We'll win for sure.... I ... I ... won't be here.'

"She could no longer speak, and only looked at me with trusting smile, moving her moist lips all the while.

"I watched the life slowly leaving her small, feeble body.

"'We shall win, Siranush! Believe me, I won't leave the machine gun while I'm still alive. To the bitter end....'

"I could say no more. I carressed her cold, blood-covered fingers. Her grey eyes suddenly became ever so bright.

"'I believe! I know...' she said with difficulty.

"A minute later her body grew heavy and her head drooped. I looked at her pale face for a long time. A smile had set on her lips. 'I believe....' Those were the last words I heard. She believed in that lofty cause, and for its sake she did not spare her youth, but took up arms. This is how Komsomol members died, and thus died Siranush...."

...Kagraman bent over the fireplace to hide his moist eyes and turned over the charred logs. The fire flared up and illuminated his sadly pursed lips and the scar on his chin, made by a stray bullet.

"That isn't all..." Kagraman began again. "Listen to what happened next.... The exchange of fire continued. Suddenly I heard a tapping sound, repeated several times, coming from the third room. It alerted me. There was a ladder there which led to the roof. And from it you could easily cross over to the attic of the next house and let yourself down into the street. Therefore, as a precaution, I had hung a lock on the trap-door to the roof. Opening the door noiselessly, I looked into the empty room. My attention was caught by a man dressed in black who had climbed up the ladder and was trying to break the lock. He didn't notice me. And it was no wonder. There was such a din going on all around that he could not hear my steps. I waited for a minute. The stranger broke the lock with a small crow-bar and raised the trap-door. I cocked my gun and shouted:

"'Stop, who are you?'

"Taking no notice of me, he started to climb out onto the roof.

"'Stop or I'll shoot!' I shouted again.

"He'd already managed to lift himself through the trap-door, and only his legs were left dangling. I shot once, twice. The bastard tumbled down the steps and fell heavily on to the floor. I went up to him, rolled him over and froze with astonishment. Who do you think it was?"

Kagraman's listeners' eyes widened. The samovar had long since stopped puffing, the wind had abated in the street, the fire had gone out and only the coals smouldered, flickering with dying lights. Kagraman smiled sadly.

"In front of me lay the mistress of the house, the woman with whom I had talked. Pressing her lips tightly together, she tried to overcome the pain. Silently, without a single moan. The bullet had struck her in the back and passed straight through.

"'Where were you going? Did you want to escape?' I asked.

"She was as stubbornly silent as before. Only her eyes blazed with hatred. I tried to dress her wound. She pushed me away, laughing hoarsely. A minute later her breathing ceased. From under her fur hat, two coal-black plaits slid out like shining snakes and lay at my feet.

"Even when dead, her smile was evil, vindictive and cruel."

...Kagraman finished his story. Somewhere across the street the first cocks began to crow. His friends sat motionless, each one afraid to break the silence, to frighten away what Kagraman saw as he gazed at the fire.

"It's time to be off."

Kagraman got up and went over to the samovar, limping slightly on his left leg.

"Thank you for the tea," he said, shaking his host's hand.

A cloud of cigarette smoke diffused near the ceiling.

**Beyukaga
Talybly
(1897-1939)**

A prosaist, journalist, and distinguished civic activist. An active participant in the Civil War, he edited the newspapers Kommunist *and* Novaya Mysl *and published publicistic, enlightening works.*

The writer depicts a wide range of distinctively Azerbaijanian characters. Erkek Tukezban (from the story of that name) is a striking example of Talybly's skill at characterisation. In Azerbaijanian, the word "Erkek" means "man". Tukezban is a female name. The combination of the two illustrates the tireless energy and courage of an emancipated woman who becomes the master of her own destiny....

Erkek Tukezban

Christopher Columbus discovered America. Newton discovered the law of universal gravitation. Turgenev discovered the Russian peasant.

If some pioneer had transferred his attention to the women of Azerbaijan, he would have found in one of the dark corners of this unknown world a woman by the name of Erkek Tukezban.

Erkek Tukezban was renowned throughout the entire district. She even had some credentials from the district Soviet council which were stamped on a red paper.

Not for nothing was she known as Erkek and not for nothing did she carry this red paper. But more about that later.

She looked about 35 years old — a swarthy woman of average height, not fat but not thin, an intelligent Azerbaijanian woman, a woman of the countryside in the full sense of the word, a woman like hundreds and thousands of others in Azerbaijan. Her movements were brisk. Her hair was black. She had large fang-like teeth, and she spoke in a loud voice. Her manners were rough and it was obvious from her hands and face that she was no lover of soap and water. But on taking a closer look at her and observing her movements and behaviour, it was impossible not to feel a certain liking for her. On her sunburned cheek, under her right eye, was a congenitally placed birth-mark which gave her face a distinctive expression. "Peppery" we would have called her in our area but for some reason her fellow-villagers had dubbed her "Erkek", which literally means "man-like" or "masculine".

If she had lived in a town, I would not have paid any special attention to this fact or troubled the reader with my story, for in the towns of Azerbaijan nick-names of all sorts are commonplace enough. It is quite usual for people to be called things like "Mother Sakina", "Foxy Fatima" or "Kheyransa the Pain".

But why, oh why had they named poor Tukezban "man-like"? The reader will find out in due course, but in the meantime, out of respect for our heroine of "unknown sex", I shall simply call her plain Tukezban.

So there you have her — an Azerbaijanian peasant woman of medium height and middle age, swarthy, not thin but not fat either.

Right from her childhood Tukezban had suffered from a certain "malady" which she has not shaken off to this day. And whereas other people are treated with various medicines and drugs, Tukezban had merely been treated with intensified doses of beating. She was cuffed and slapped by her father and brothers almost from the day she was born. However, this medicine had not had the necessary effect. Her malady, by the way, consisted in her gregarious nature. Even as a little girl, whenever she saw a small gathering of people, she immediately made a bee-line for it. She only had to hear a noise and she would be off like a shot in the direction from which it came, tying up her yashmak as she went. She did not know the meaning of modesty and was incapable of blushing. No gathering could ever be held without her: she was an invariable attendant at funeral and marriage feasts; she was always to be seen in the bathhouse and the mosque.... All her kin resented her behaviour. Goodness knows what people didn't say about her in the village.

Eventually her father's patience ran out and he managed to rid himself of his restless daughter.

In the village lived a farm labourer who was generally known as Asad the Fool. After Tukezban's father had had a short talk with him, he took her as his wife.

Many thought that Tukezban would now settle down a little. But no; her marriage made her feel even more at liberty and she began to appear in public even more often than before. Asad, being a very timid lad, was simply unable to cope with her; when he tried to rebuke her, she turned on him with her fists.

The village elders often abused Tukezban's father and husband for allowing her to be so self-willed and the old matrons did not accept her in their company. Some women liked Tukezban or respected her, but others were rather afraid of her; and there were some who even hated her. "Why have anything to do with her?" they said, "She has no sense of shame."

But Tukezban did not pay any attention to them and ignored the gossip and abuse.

Then, unexpectedly, a big event came to pass in Tukezban's life: Asad fell ill and died. All the cares of making a livelihood fell onto the shoulders of his widow; whenever it was necessary to go to the bazaar or answer a summons to some government office, Tukezban would jump on a horse and ride away without pausing to think about it twice. Ploughing, sowing and reaping became a normal part of her life. She also knew the meaning of poverty.

Thus the death of her husband was no great loss to Tukezban. The whole village marvelled at her capabilities in husbandry. However, the legends about her continued to circulate.

By that time Soviet power had become firmly established in Azerbaijan.

Tukezban did not understand politics; she had no idea why the Mussavatist regime had been overthrown and replaced by a worker-peasant government, but she heard from agitators who came to the village that she was now her own master, that she was free and independent, with the same rights as men.

One night, when she was returning home from her vegetable lot, Tukezban killed a big wolf with a rifle. This event raised her authority a little. In every house they talked of Tukezban's bravery, dexterity, ability and her other good and — for good measure — bad qualities. The group of villagers who had accused her of shamelessness and depravity gradually dwindled.

One day the news came through that the village would have to send a woman to Baku as a delegate. Nobody really knew what for or why. Everyone came up with a different theory.

The local mullah also gave an explanation of his own:

"So this is what we've come to," he said. "They've even started taking our women away from us!"

Finally it was learned from a man who had come in from the district centre that a women's congress was being convened in Baku and that the village could send one delegate.

The villagers began to haggle as to who to send. But they couldn't come up with anyone suitable. Who would agree to do without his wife, mother or sister?

Eventually, after a lengthy wrangling at open gatherings and secret caucuses the residents of the village unanimously agreed on Tukezban. Her candidacy was supported by men and women alike.

"After all, who knows what'll happen to her in Baku," the men reasoned. "If something does, then it's no great loss: she's a homeless woman and she shames us as well."

The women, of course, had no intention of nominating any other candidate. Tukezban's fate was decided: at an official meeting she was unanimously elected a delegate to the First Women's Congress, in Baku. She had formally mounted the first rung on the ladder of her career in public affairs.

Nobody realised that this would not be the end of the story, that this first step would be followed by others. Who could have imagined that, having mounted the first rung, Tukezban would take it into her head to clamber higher and higher? Who could have thought that Tukezban would make such a nuisance of herself? Who could have forseen that Tukezban would become the champion of the oppressed and the scourge of the oppressors? Who, finally, could have supposed that Tukezban would come to be known as "Erkek".

If any of the righteous heirs of Mohammed (holy be His name!) had been in the village during the elections and, inspired from above, given the residents a hint of what Tukezban had in store for them, the name of that confounded woman would never have been mentioned.

But there was no going back now. Tukezban became well known both in the local centre and within the Baku women's organisation. And having been drawn into public affairs, she did not sit idle. The upshot was that two years later, when new elections to the village council were held, Tukezban's name appeared on the list of candidates for the post of council chairman.

On election day the people gathered before the village council headquarters. The instructor who had come from the district centre made a speech and insisted on the active participation of women in the elections.

He then put the following question to the meeting:

"Shall we call the women together separately or with the men?"

Now anyone knowing our village would easily have guessed that, apart from Tukezban, the meeting was attended only by men.

On hearing the instructor's question, Tukezban jumped up from her seat:

"Together, comrades," she cried, "together with the men."

However, the time had still not come when women's proposals could be let through and the gathering voted unanimously for separate meetings. But as a result of the elections Tukezban ended up as chairman of the village council.

The whole village grew uneasy.

"What, aren't we men enough?" the menfolk asked each other. "Don't we wear the pants round here? And now some trollop is going to order us around...."

"What's going to happen? Now can a woman hold power?"

"Hey, what are you getting upset about? Tukezban isn't a woman at all. She's a man.... Just think: how many years was she married and she didn't have any children. Asad himself used to complain she was no wife to him.... Rather the other way round...."

And with these thoughts on their lips the indignant peasants dispersed and went home.

Right up until evening they relished the phrase "Tukezban's a man — Erkek", which was passed from mouth to mouth. The whole village was enthralled by the news.

And so, in the course of a single day, the heroine of our story, a swarthy woman of medium height and middle age, became a man. The question of the village's honour was resolved to the satisfaction of all.

Tukezban viewed her election to the post of council chairman as something quite natural and took over the business from her predecessor with due dignity. She carefully folded up the red paper that represented the credentials she had received from the instructor and put it in her pocket.

That evening, when the working day was over and the peasants were sitting (men and women separately) with their feet tucked under them on the street near the mosque, chatting and gossiping, a boy suddenly called out:

"Here comes Erkek Tukezban!"

And indeed it was Tukezban — walking along the street with a briefcase under her arm, a riding whip in her hand and a pipe between her teeth. She walked silently past the staring villagers.

"Just look at her. What arrogance!" one of the men hissed through his teeth. "As if her forbears had been rulers from time immemorial."

Nor could the women remain silent: each of them had something of their own to say — some good, some bad. Among the women was a certain townswoman who had fled from the Bolsheviks and was living in the village.

"Good God!" said one of the local women, turning to the townswoman and pointing to Tukezban's whip and briefcase. "Why, it's a real man."

The townswoman observed this scene with great amazement.

100

"Absolutely, my dear! The times are changing and customs have changed too. Women have become men, and men have become goodness knows what!"

Night fell. The village was plunged into its usual silence, only broken from time to time by the barking of dogs. Tukezban's election to high office had not disturbed its tranquillity and the people slept sweetly, not suspecting what awaited them in the morning.

When the sun arose, they all went about their work as usual. The secretary of the village council, Mamedali, a man of a somewhat light-hearted disposition, arrived at the council headquarters and calmly sat down in his usual place in the left-hand corner of the office.

But before he had even had time to get his breath back, in rushed Tukezban, strongly incensed about something. Her brows were knitted. Taking the chairman's place, she fixed her eyes on the paper hanging on the wall as if she wanted to devour its incomprehensible hieroglyphics with her eyes.

"How long do I have the right to put someone under arrest for?" she asked, having scrutinised the paper to her own satisfaction.

"For five days," replied the secretary.

"Five days?"

"Yes."

"That's a pity. A great pity. Show me where it's actually written."

The secretary got up and, walking over to the paper stuck to the wall, pointed with his finger to the appropriate clause in the appropriate resolution by the Azerbaijanian Government.

Tukezban also rose to her feet.

"It's a pity, a great pity," she muttered, "it should be more."

She went over to the wall and, placing her index finger on the paper — beside the secretary's finger — drew a line under the relevant clause with her nail.

"What other penalties can I impose?"

"A fine of up to 15 rubles and five days forced labour."

"Hmmm. That's not much either," said Tukezban, completely disheartened. "And where's it written?"

"Here." Once again the secretary pointed to the appropriate clause of the resolution and once again Tukezban marked it with her thumbnail.

Frowning she returned to her place.

Then, after a short silence, she turned to the secretary and declared. "I order that Mullah Rajab, his son Mullah Djafarkudi, his brother Safarkuli and his brother-in-law Seid-Gusein be locked up for five days. Write it down."

"Yes, ma'am," said the astounded secretary.

"I furthermore order that Gulam Guseinbek, Gusein Kulibek, Safaralibek, Sergeant-Major Khalil, Sergeant Akhmed and patrolman Suleiman be put under arrest — each for five days. Write it down...."

"Yes, ma'am."

"Furthermore, I order that Kerbalai Museib, Meshadi Samed, Gaji Mekhti and Mir Suleiman be fined 15 rubles each and forced to work five days cleaning out the main irrigation ditch. Write it down...."

"Right you are...."

Tukezban's wrath had cooled a little. Her face brightened up. She opened her briefcase and, taking out the red paper which she had received yesterday from the instructor, began closely scrutinising the incomprehensible marks on it. A smile

101

appeared on her face. Having had a good look at the paper, she folded it carefully, put it back in her briefcase and asked:

"Have you written all that down?"

"Yes."

"See that the order is carried out immediately. I'll show those parasites!"

"It shall be done."

Within an hour the converted stable which now served as a gaol was so full that there was nowhere to sit.

The children, wives and relatives of those who had been arrested had assembled in front of the council building and were waiting for Tukezban to appear. At first the villagers, who had slept peacefully all night and calmly started their day, did not believe what had happened. How could anyone arrest Mullah Rajab? How could anyone raise a hand against Gulam Guseinbek? How could anyone put Gusein Kulibek in gaol?

Their amazement knew no bounds!

Tukezban rode up to the council building on horseback with a whip in her hand. The people gathered there gasped when they saw her. Some of them were speechless with fear.

The crowd parted to make way for Tukezban. She nimbly jumped down from her horse and walked into the council building. The petitioners poured in after her. Their pleas followed thick and fast:

"For God's sake, take pity on us, don't ruin us, have mercy ... release our menfolk!"

"Out of the question," snapped Tukezban. "I won't let them out."

Seeing how adamant she was, the petitioners realised the fruitlessness of their attempts.

Five days went by. The arrested men were duly let out and, after fulfilling their terms of forced labour, returned to their business. But within two days of their release Mullah Rajab and a whole group of village parasites were arrested again.... And yet another group of kulaks were sent to clean out the ditches....

A week went by. Then a month. And a year.... Tukezban continued in her job. The local ditches were cleaned continually: Mullah Rajab spent two days of the week with his family and the remaining five in custody. After a couple of days at home he was often to be seen trudging wearily back in the direction of the council building, tripping over the tails of his long gown.

"What's up?" the villagers would ask him. "Where are you going?"

"To the usual place."

"Why, has there been another order for your arrest?"

"No, but why wait? I know my job."

Christopher Columbus discovered America. Newton discovered the law of universal gravitation. Ivan Turgenev discovered the Russian peasant.

If someone had taken an interest in the women of Azerbaijan and let us know the results of his investigations, then today Tukezban would not stand alone in the public arena on election days. She would be surrounded by women like herself. But there is no literature to give us an all-round picture of the Azerbaijanian woman. How many are there among them who are capable of serving as council chairmen or occupying even more responsible posts! Unfortunately, we have no idea whatsoever what talents lie hidden under the black yashmak.

But Erkek knew; even though she had not even attended literacy courses, she understood such questions perfectly well.

One day it was announced in the village that elections would be held to the co-operative board. It was Friday and the members of the co-operative had assembled in good time.

The meeting was duly declared open. Sitting beside the chairman and puffing away on her pipe, Tukezban followed the course of the debates. A list of candidates was drawn up and a token woman included in it. Each candidacy was put to the vote separately. Tukezban voted along with the others. As soon as the name Gokhar was read out, she raised both hands, then looked round and saw that she was the only person voting.

"Why don't you raise your hands?" she cried. "As soon as you hear a woman's name, you hide your hands in your pockets."

No one responded to Tukezban's reproach.

The meeting finished. Chatting in groups, the people dispersed and went home. Conversation, of course, centred on the co-operative. The instructor who had come from the district centre went out onto the street talking to Tukezban.

"Well, how do you feel yourself, anyway?" he asked her after they had discussed the composition of the new board.

"Huh, what do you think? Meetings in the morning, meetings in the evening and at night skirmishes with bandits. Those rascals have been giving me no peace for a whole month. I'm in the saddle all the time with my rifle slung over my shoulder. My back aches like hell. And the salary is not enough to feed a horse on...."

"But what about your land and crops? You're not likely to go broke are you?"

"I would have done. There's no helping it. Luckily the Armenian refugees turned up at the right moment. I took one of them on as a helper ... a young man. He had no one else in the whole wide world." Tukezban thought for a minute, "He does his best, the poor fellow.... Works from dawn to dusk.... I took a liking to him and now he's my husband."

"And how are you coping with the kulaks?"

"What can I say.... The bastards will kill me one of these days. Not that I'm afraid for myself.... I'll be sorry for my husband. If only you knew how hard he works!"

Soviet prose

Djafar Djabarly   *A work provoking only thought and not emotion is no work of art.*

...No matter how many admirable qualities a writer attributes to his character, if he has not shown him as a living person with all the passions of life, he will not inspire the love of readers and spectators; a writer should create living, full-blooded people with noble intentions and burning passions. In our books we must show a new man, one who is pure, strong, bold and worthy of our great epoch.

1934
Speech delivered at the First All-Union Congress of Soviet Writers.

Mekhti Hussein *My country is called the land of eternal fires. This poetic name has both a literal and a symbolic significance. In the underground treasure vaults of the Apsheron peninsula is that eternal source of fire, oil.*

But the name "The Land of Eternal Fires" can be more broadly interpreted. No matter what hellish flames might scourge the Azerbaijanian earth, no matter what trial the people might endure, like the legendary Fire-bird they will remain strong and eternally vital.

1960
The Land of Eternal Fires

Abdullah Shaik *Those who have endured the terrible oppression of the tsarist regime have a particularly profound awareness of the vital strength of the sunny spring brought by Soviet power.... The black clouds have dispersed; the darkness enveloping the people has vanished; the sun of Soviet power has risen, illuminating our land from all sides. The country has blossomed forth and the tears have been washed from the face of the earth.*

"With all my Heart." 1946.

Mamed Said Ordubady

...The Empire has fallen for ever. The enmity of the tribes
is no more,
And towards a happy future a great broad road we have
laid
We harness nature, we oppose the fate
We are never disheartened in labour, study and struggle,
We have dug a canal into Future through Time.
We have fought like heroes and mocked the despondent...

From "The Khan's Palace"

Seid Hussein

The waves of October, sweeping across the Caspian, flooded the old streets, washing away all the scum in its path. Like a storm uprooting age-old trees, the purifying revolution ripped the weeds sown by Hadji-Aslan out of the native soil and scattered them to the four winds.
At last the street was clean.

"A Story About a Street",
1927, Winter Nights

**Djafar Djabarly
(1899-1934)**

A brilliant playwright. A poet, prosaist, film scenarist, and translator. To the treasure-house of Azerbaijanian literature he brought the romantic spirit of a new epoch and a vision of the living truth, depicting these with an acutely social realism. His plays, among them Sevil, Almas *and* In the Year 1905, *were written in the years when socialism was being built; they form a vivid artistic chronicle of the people's struggle and victories.*

The zenith of Djabarly's poetry is the narrative poem "The Maiden's Tower". It is based on an Azerbaijanian legend.

Djabarly's prose is only a small portion of his creative legacy. But it is distinctive and pithy.

"Firuza" acquaints the reader with a liberated, spiritually mature Azerbaijanian woman.

Firuza

She was a young girl with a refined oval face, the dark, deeply-set eyes of a southerner, and black eyebrows which looked as if they had been painted on with a brush. I must confess she interested me very much. She seemed to be living through sort of emotional crisis. However, my position as a senior lecturer at the medical school made it impossible for me to question a student like her as to why she was so constantly pensive and drawn.

She was already in the last year of her course. Yet in all the four years she had been studying I had not managed to find out where she was from and who her parents were.

Imagine my surprise, then, when one day she stopped me in the corridor on her own accord. Her face alternately blushed and went pale, her lips trembled nervously. Stammering slightly she said: "Please excuse me, doctor, but there is something I wanted to ask you. I attend all the practical sessions and I went out to the country on the anti-malaria campaigns.... I wanted to ask you if it would be possible...."

She fell silent and blushed.

I smiled involuntarily.

"Go on, Firuza, don't be shy."

Overcoming her embarrassment, she continued:

"Doctor, I would like to work under you and attend your surgery hours. I have enough time for it."

117

And on the following day, at the appointed hour, she turned up with a white smock under her arm.

After my surgery was over, Firuza set about putting the place in order. She had just started on the blood tests when the door bell rang. I opened the door. Before me stood a tall man in a long military greatcoat, looking rather troubled by something. I recognised him with great difficulty. He was an oil-rig worker whom I had treated for malaria several years ago and who had once written a piece in a newspaper to the effect that I had refused to treat a patient after surgery hours.

He greeted me and, smiling with embarrassment, said:

"Do you remember me, doctor?... We nearly went to court once over a piece in a newspaper...."

And, smiling again, he continued:

"I've come to you for help."

"Are you ill?"

"I don't think so," replied my visitor. "It's just that I've lost my way, doctor."

"What do you mean you've lost your way?"

"I can't find our house."

I looked at him closely, assuming that he was in need of medical aid. But I decided not to offer to examine him as he had not asked me himself. His face wore an anxious look, his glance strayed absent-mindedly around the room.

"It's strange, doctor ... but I can't find our house," he repeated.

I began to wonder whether he had suffered some brain damage and asked:

"Have you actually forgotten where your house is located?"

"No," he replied quickly. "Let me give you the full story. My name is Mamed. I'm 25 years old, and almost all my life I've lived in Baku,— in the hilly part of the city. I used to know all its highways and by-ways, I remember very well that we had a little house in Chemberekend, in that blind maze of crooked streets and ruins. At the back of our house the roof almost levelled with the pavement of a crooked lane which was always heaped with piles of dung ... and a few steps away there was a cemetery."

He spoke in an agitated manner and this agitation grew the further he delved into his recollections.

"I was a child. I well remember how the water-carrier brought us water in four pitchers on a run-down ass. One day, when my mother, who was still young then, proffered him a token so he wouldn't lose count, the water-carrier kept hold of her hand. Mother indicated me with her eyes.

"I remember that behind the cemetery there was a bare patch and a reservoir which the rain water drained into. The people took drinking water from it. My father used to scratch around there with a wooden plough trying to grow a few sackfuls of barley. He worked for the owner of some oil wells but sowed barley as well because his wages were miserly."

...From the laboratory the voice of Firuza reached our ears. She was singing a Turkish song that ran something like this:

> *"My love was the hero of the wells,*
> *He sucked the black blood from their depths,*
> *He cleft the earth's crust with a drill,*
> *Forced it to yield up its riches,*
> *And drew the black gold from its bowels...."*

"Who's that singing?" Mamed asked suddenly, looking up at me, his eyes alight with curiosity.

"My daughter," I replied, in order not to distract him from his narrative.

"A pleasant voice," he commented. Taking out some cigarettes and sighing deeply, he uttered as if to himself:

"She often used to sing like that too."

His face assumed an expression of sadness, he became pensive. I observed him without speaking.

"Yes, doctor, I remember everything. I remember how, one day when I was a child, father took me with him to work. He tied a rope round him, the other end being wound round the drum of a hand-winch, and went down into the oil well. For a long time the drum revolved, letting out the rope. Then everyone began bustling about. They pulled up a bucket with some blue clay in it and let it down again. Then they pulled my father up. He was terribly pale. 'What's the matter?' asked the boss, knitting his thick brows.

"'It's impossible, boss. The gas chokes you and there's something humming below. Maybe a gusher will strike, I could be killed....' Angrily gesticulating, the boss cried: 'A whole year you worked without complaining and now when it's become a little tougher, you throw in the towel. Who will go down into the well for you now that the difficult part of the job lies ahead?'

"And he ran up to father and struck him hard across the cheek.

"I started crying, but father whispered almost with a groan, 'Boss, ... it's dangerous down there. I have children to support....'

"And he looked in my direction. Our eyes met. He seemed to be ashamed to look at me, ashamed that he had been struck in my presence. After all, in my eyes he was stronger and more powerful than anyone in the world.... He turned his eyes away.... I was not weeping any more, I was burning with hatred for the boss. But the boss, not sensing this, came up to me, stroked my hair with the same hand he had only just struck father with, then took some money from his pocket and handed it to me — 30 rubles it turned out to be....

"'Go down, Meshadi Ali. Don't be afraid. If God wills it and the oil flows, I'll buy you a fur hat, a skirt for your wife and some shoes and a shirt for him.' The boss indicated me.

"Father was wavering.... The boss continued his efforts to persuade him and handed him 20 rubles. Father came up to me with a faltering step, took the money out of my hands, put it in the small pocket of my old tattered overcoat. Then he wiped my tears, untied the knot in his handkerchief, gave me a piece of bread

119

to eat, kissed me on the eyes, said a prayer, and went down again into the well. He was down there for a long time. I couldn't eat anything, although I was hungry...."

Once again Firuza's song could be heard from the laboratory: Mamed leapt up from where he was sitting.

"Who's that singing? Ah, yes, you said it was your daughter."

Sighing deeply, he sat down again.

> *"My love was the hero of the wells,*
> *He sucked their black blood from their depths,*
> *He cleft the earth's crust with a drill,*
> *Forced it to yield up its riches....*

sang Firusa.

I drew nearer to Mamed and, trying to make sure that he did not notice my suspicions about his medical condition, asked:

"Well, what happened to your father after that? Is he still alive?"

"No ... he...."

And taking a breath, Mamed continued:

"When they dragged him out, he was unconscious. I ran up to him. Father was just lying there, his face blue, his eyes wide open and motionless.

"'He's dead,' said the boss slowly. Suddenly there was a rumbling sound in the well and a mighty fountain of oil spurted out, tossing the winch up into the air.

"'Hurrah!' cried the boss with glee, instantly forgetting about the dead man. The workers dragged me away.

"On the orders of the boss they slaughtered a sheep on the spot — on the strength of their jubilation. I kept trying to get to my father, who was lying under a geyser of oil. Every time the workers held me back.

"At last the boss got round to doing something about father. They took him by the legs, dragged him away, laid him on an old cart, covered him with some rags and wheeled him home via the outskirts of the town.

"Don't worry, doctor, I'm completely well," said Mamed, suddenly interrupting his story when I grasped his hand and tried to take his pulse without him noticing it. "I'm in full possession of my faculties. I remember everything. I even remember a Russian woman who used to go past our house with flowers — on her way to the cemetery. I once ran up to her and asked her for a flower.

"She looked at me with surprise and gave me two flowers. I ran to the cemetery and put them on my father's grave. Then I lay down beside it, hid my face in the ground and wept and wept, soaking the fresh hummock with the burning tears of a child. It was a cold autumn evening. I ended up frozen through and shivering all over.... I was ill for almost three months after that."

Mamed fell silent.

"Maybe I'm keeping you, doctor?" he said.

"No, on the contrary, your sad story interests me very much," I hastened to reply.

"...When I couldn't find our house, I happened to read your name on the door and called on you as an old acquaintance, who once treated me. I wanted to find out a few things."

"But how did a completely healthy and strong man like you suddenly lose your way and forget where your house is?"

120

"I haven't forgotten. I swear it was in this district and yet I couldn't find it. And the neighbours' houses aren't there either. The whole district has vanished."

"When did you leave Baku?"

"Six years ago. When I arrived back here yesterday it was evening and I headed for our house straight from the station. But it wasn't there. Our dusty, dirty crooked lane had gone. Instead I saw a broad avenue,— well paved, bustling, full of traffic, and running through the whole city. Behind our house, where the heaps of dung used to lie, a five-storeyed building has gone up. Even the people have changed somehow. Instead of shapeless figures wrapped up in the black yashmak there are gay young people on the streets and I didn't see a single woman or girl wearing the veil."

"So your house has been demolished?"

"Only our house? But what about the neighbours' houses? Old Chemberekend with lop-sided shanties has disappeared almost entirely. In my perplexity I climbed a hill I recognised. I remembered the road well. But the old cemetery had gone too. I couldn't even find my father's grave. Where the cemetery used to be there is now a beautiful park with broad avenues. And my father's grave is now part of a flower bed.... I tried to find the narrow little path that led to our house but I couldn't. Instead I found a broad asphalted road with thousands of cars and trucks and buses speeding along it in an endless stream.... I got the impression that a violent earthquake had swallowed up all of gloomy old Chemberekend and a new town had grown up with beautiful houses, wide streets and a lovely green park. In the end I went back to the station...."

"But surely you don't disapprove of what's happened, do you?" I asked.

"No, I don't disapprove. But where's my family, where's my mother — she's an old illiterate woman — where's my sister and my wife?"

"You had a wife here?"

Mamed went pale and, sighing deeply, replied:

"After my father's death we lived on the pittance my mother earned by taking in washing. We half starved — in winter we shivered in our pitiful rags. After the Revolution I met the same worker who had dragged me away from under the black fountain of oil on the day my father was killed,— it was he who had brought his body home.... Usta Samed his name was. Learning that I was looking for work, he said, 'I'm working as a drilling foreman for the Azerbaijanian Oil Corporation. If you like I'll take you on; we need men just at the moment.' I followed his advice and joined the professional training classes at the same time.

"Soon afterward Usta Samed moved onto our street, and I began to visit him often. He had a beautiful daughter. She worked in the Ali Bairamov Cultural Centre. And studied there too. We became friends and fell in love with each other. Usta Samed turned out to be a very good man. Despite the fact that he was a foreman and I was only an assistant, he agreed to our marriage. I raked some money together, enough to buy two satin dresses, then I added to these my mother's only gold ring and we got married. A few months later I was sent off to continue my education. I studied in Moscow and Leningrad, then enlisted in the Special Far-Eastern Army. At first my wife and I wrote to each other but

121

suddenly she stopped answering my letters. Maybe it was because of my change of address, but maybe....

"Not long ago a mate of mine wrote to me that he had seen her. She was living with some doctor. I know that hardship probably forced her to. She really did love me. But it's difficult for a woman being all by herself."

I rang for tea.

"There's nobody here, doctor. It's Masha's day off," I heard Firuza's voice from the next room.

Again Mamed jumped up from his seat, but did not say anything.

"But if you can't find your house, you can still find your father-in-law," I said in order to renew the conversation.

"I've looked for him. I was on the oil fields today. I went round the bores inquiring.... But things aren't the same as they were before or even what they were like back in 1928. You hardly ever see people smeared with oil now. They're all cleanly dressed. The old dusty roads have disappeared and the ox carts and draught horses.... Everywhere there is gleaming asphalt and automobiles. And almost all the fields have tramlines or small railways running through them."

"So you didn't find Usta Samed?" I asked impatiently; I was familiar enough with the state of things on the oil fields without his comments.

"No. I didn't find him," replied Mamed, "I was told he had become an inventor and had been sent to America to learn about the American oil industry. This, of course, I was thrilled to hear. I remembered him as a worker who had toiled under the lash, who was ready, for a morsel of bread, to go down into a grave dug by his own hands, into a dark pit of poisonous gas, to meet certain death.... And now this same worker can unleash his energies, and become an inventor."

"And did you find your wife?" I asked.

"No. Nobody knows anything about her, or about my sister."

"Are you still a student?"

"I'm a machine engineer."

There was a knock at the door.

"Come in," I called.

Mamed was holding his cigarette case in his hands, getting ready to have a smoke. The door opened and Firuza entered in her snow-white smock.

"I've put away the instruments and I'm off now," she said. "Today Aslan is performing at the Conservatoire. He got me the tickets. Zuleikha and Aunt Bala are probably waiting for me already."

Mamed was looking closely at Firuza, who was standing with her back to him. He rose and made an impulsive step forward, but dropped his cigarette. When he bent down to pick it up without taking his eyes off Firuza, the rest of the cigarettes spilled out of the case. On hearing the names Zuleikha and Bala, he quickly stood up again. I was following his movements attentively. Catching my glance, Firuza also turned round and looked at Mamed.

Then he caught sight of her face. He seemed to gasp. And Firuza, who was usually reserved and self-possessed, appeared agitated.

"Firuza!" he said in a soft voice trembling with emotion. He seemed to be ready to throw his arms around her.... And the most surprising thing was that Firuza showed no signs of wanting to stop him. Her dark eyes were beaming. But Mamed suddenly froze, the blood drained from his face and his eyes lost their gleam. He became pensive and, hardly managing to get the words out, asked in a voice that was hardly audible:

122

"Do you live here?"

"I live at my own place," answered Firuza.

"Where are mother and Zuleikha?" asked Mamed, looking her straight in the face.

"We all live together. We've been given an apartment in Shaumyan Park. Let's go and you'll see for yourself," replied Firuza.

"You'll take me to your place?"

"Of course. In fact, I'm surprised that you came here and not straight to our apartment."

"I looked for you but couldn't find you. By the way, who is this Aslan you were talking to the doctor about?"

"Let's go, and you'll find out," replied Firuza with a smile.

"I can take you in the car," I offered and left the room.

When I returned Mamed's face had completely changed; his eyes were alight again. He was laughing and Firuza was wiping her eyes.

"Well, the car's ready. Let's be off," I said.

"All right, doctor," answered Mamed, in a voice that had already completely regained its usual strength, and briskly stepped out ahead of me.

"Is it your own car?" he asked, when I sat behind the wheel and switched the engine on.

"It was a reward for speedy and successful eradication of plague when it spread through into a border zone...."

And the small car rolled off along the mirror-like surface of the asphalt road. From time to time I turned round and looked at Mamed. One glance was enough to realise how surprised he was to see the bustling streets bathed in electric lighting, the new multi-storeyed buildings, the gay crowds of young girls.

As we were driving past the new Press House he gave a gasp.

"Good God! When did they manage to do it?"

I stopped the car and asked Firuza to take the wheel. She attended classes at a driving school and had a certificate and licence and often drove the car by herself. When she sat behind the wheel, Mamed was even more staggered. A minute later he again exclaimed:

"Good God! What are they doing?"

"Who are 'they'?" I asked.

"Our people. Only the day before yesterday, the day I arrived, when I was walking along the Kubinka, I saw a ramshackle house being pulled down. And today there's already a lovely square here covered with asphalt. There's nothing remarkable about the fact that in two days they've pulled down a rickety house, evened out the ground and asphalted it over. What is surprising is that the trees that have just been planted there are already blossoming and thick with fresh spring leaves. Only yesterday I was walking along the old esplanade where camels

123

used to shriek and the long-bearded brokers and dervishes used to bustle about, juggling with their toothless snakes and singing of the feats of the old imam and the coming of a new one. But what I did see yesterday? The whole ramshackle hodge-podge, so typically oriental, had disappeared, and in its place lay a shady garden with streams of cars, trams and buses whizzing round it. And beside it,—instead of the old dilapidated one-storeyed Khanum-Caravan-serai in where they used to smoke opium before the Revolution—a massive seven-storeyed building had gone up."

We were travelling along the smooth highway leading to the township of Shaumyan. Firuza drove with assurance.

Mamed was observing her closely.

"Take this very Firuza now driving the car," he continued. "What would she have been even six or seven years ago? A downtrodden ignorant woman. And yet here she is today about to qualify as a doctor. It's a real revolution, a revolution in life, customs, in the minds of the people...."

The car stopped by a six-storeyed building. Firuza took the key and we went up to the second floor.

On entering the apartment, Firuza turned the switch. A blinding light flooded the room and the dazzling parquct floor reflected our figures. She then went up to the high window and opened it. A branch covered with fresh leaves peeped into the room.

"Hello!" Firuza joyfully greeted it.

Mamed stood enraptured in the middle of the room, viewing the broad white ceiling, and the walls and furnishings.

"This is my room, this is my bed, and that's Asker's," Firuza was telling him.

Mamed's face lost its cheerful expression.

"Who's this Asker?" he asked with a hushed voice.

"My husband, the one who's going to be a doctor; they wrote to you about him," answered Firuza calmly. And without giving Mamed a chance to come to himself, continued, "And here's Zuleikha's room, this is Aunt Bala's, this is the dining room, there's bathroom, kitchen, store-room, here's the balcony. Go and have a look round."

They had already returned to the room in which I was sitting when suddenly the door opened and three figures rushed noisily in: a youth aged about 20 and a young girl holding a well-dressed little boy by the hand.

"Firuza, this swindler wants to do me," said the girl with a ringing laugh. But seeing me she ran up, hugged me around the neck and gave me a juicy kiss on the cheek.

"You be the judge please," she said. "Your son Aslan is a swindler; he wants to do me."

124

Aslan, pretending to be angry, interrupted her:

"Zuleikha, I forbid you to kiss other men...."

"It's none of your business. I'll behave as I like," the girl retorted.

But Aslan, already smiling, added:

"And to kiss in the presence of strangers!"

"What strangers?" the girl looked round and only now caught sight of Mamed. She became embarrassed and closely scrutinised the guest.

"Brother, my dear brother," she cried out at last, weeping and laughing at the same time.

"Isn't that great to have a wife who kisses all men except you and in your presence as well!" Aslan exclaimed, "I'm divorcing you. Come on, we're going to the court-room right away."

"It's none of your business. I'll kiss when and whom I like. Let's go and get divorced if you want."

"What's this about a divorce, Zuleikha? So you decided to get married behind my back?" said Mamed smiling.

Laughing merrily, the girl replied:

"Well, that's none of your business, brother. What sort of despotic behaviour is this? I'll marry when and whom I like.... Those times have gone when red-bearded match-makers arranged marriages for poor maidens, when they gave them in marriage to rich old men against their will."

"Just think, only yesterday you were still a snotty little schoolgirl!"

But Zuleikha would give no quarter to anyone.

"That was yesterday, but now I'm a teacher: I teach arithmetics, geometry, algebra and trigonometry. I even have a testimonial for good work. Here! I'll show you if you like!"

"You should have just said 'I teach mathematics'," Aslan interrupted her.

"I'll say what I like."

Firuza came into the room carrying an electric kettle.

"Don't you dare kiss my husband. He's not common property!" she said seeing Mamed and Zuleikha embracing.

"It's none of your business, I'll...."

But Zuleikha did not have time to finish her customary phrase before Aslan exclaimed:

"But my Zuleikha's common property, is she?"

The women laughed loudly.

Mamed's face became serious. Embarrassed, he asked quietly:

"What husband, Firuza? You said you had another, someone called Asker, who was going to be a doctor...."

And again the women burst out laughing.

125

Then suddenly Zuleikha grabbed the little boy she had brought in with her, lifted him up and exclaimed:

"Here's her husband, the Asker who says he's going to be a doctor. He's exactly six years old...."

And she almost threw the child into the arms of his father.

Mamed pressed him tightly to his chest.

"Here's my husband. Do you recognise him?" said Firuza with a smile taking Mamed by the ear. "And now go and wash your face."

Mamed laughed guiltily and only embraced the child even more tightly.

But before they had time to leave the room a stocky woman with rolled up sleeves burst in. Barely having crossed the threshold, she called out in a thunderous voice:

"Firuza!... Give me a sheet of paper and help me to write a piece for the wall newspaper. That loafing bureaucrat is keeping some planks and iron parts in the yard under the house; he's ruining them! I demanded that he take them away, but he answered: 'You don't have the right to shout at me. I'm head of the materials section and I'm responsible for the materials....'"

"Well, of course, mother, you don't have the right to interfere in another person's business, to say nothing of shouting at him," said Zuleikha.

"What do you mean I don't have the right? I'm a member of the local committee. Maybe he doesn't realise what he's doing or maybe he's deliberately spoiling materials," the old woman angrily objected, taking hold of Asker who had run up to her and lifting him up in her arms.

"Aunt Bala, I'm getting married," exclaimed Firuza, running into the room. "Here's my husband. Get acquainted."

And almost by force she dragged the old woman in after her.

"Well, so what, my child," said the latter, emerging from the bathroom. "Maybe my Mamed will find himself someone else too."

"And I've found myself someone else," said Zuleikha, running up to me and embracing me.

"Isn't that great! Everyone kissing except us. Aren't we human or something!" exclaimed Aslan, pretending to be angry.

"It's none of your business! Firuza, give me the grammaphone."

The record started turning. Zuleikha jumped up, ran over to Aslan and the couple began whirling in a dance.

"I don't know what sort of reunion mother and son had," she was telling Aslan, "I only know that when they came into the room Mamed was washed clean and mother's face was all covered in soap."

I was sitting facing a mirror, which reflected part of another room. I could see Firuza sprinkling her husband with eau de cologne; then they gazed at each other, Firuza embraced him and their lips met in a kiss.

"Well, so what," I thought. "Socialism and kissing are hardly incompatible."

To be honest, I envied their happiness, their youth, their sparkling eyes, and regretted that I wasn't 25 any more....

Then Zuleikha sat down at the piano. Firuza and Aslan started dancing, while little Asker forcibly dragged his grandmother to her feet to partner him.

Mamed sat down next to me and said quietly:

"I now understand everything, doctor: what old Baku was and what it has now become; what this family was and what it has now become. How could a newcomer not be perplexed? And you thought I was ill and casually tried to take my pulse. Revolution, doctor, — it's affected everything — life, economics, the way the people live, the way they think. It can even change the age-old laws of nature. That's why a square planted with trees turns into a sea of blossom in a couple of days and a cemetery comes to life as a park for cultural recreation."

Mamed was right, of course, but all the same I advised him to find another place for that mirror.

Suleiman Ragimov (b. 1900)

A master of epic prose, distinguished novelist and civic activist. Named People's Writer of Azerbaijan.

His childhood years were spent in want and poverty.

At the very inception of Soviet power Ragimov began to play an active part in civic affairs. He graduated from the Azerbaijanian University.

Ragimov began writing in 1930. His novels Shamo *and* Sachly, *novellas* Ainaly *and* Mekhman *and cycles of short stories reflect the struggle of the Azerbaijanian people for freedom and happiness, their past and present way of life, and their historical achievements in the process of building socialism.*

Many of Ragimov's stories, novellas and novels deal with ethical questions. "The Key to Life" introduces us to a modern country boy whose arrival in the city involves him in a series of interesting, instructive adventures.

The Key to Life

1   It was another burning-hot summer day. Flames seemed to come from the sky. Doors and windows in every building had been thrown wide open. And I too had opened the windows and door of my office, one room of a vast tall building on Naberezhnaya Street. I looked through the window at the sea, so close you could almost touch it. Its glassy stillness was frightening.

My light silk shirt clung disgustingly to my body.

Although it was becoming more and more difficult to breathe, I continued to work, examining the papers that lay before me, trying to reflect on what I had read, making notes in the margins, and ceaselessly wiping away the sweat that streamed down my face, neck and chest with the end of a towel slung over the back of a chair.

Suddenly I heard an indistinct rustling. "Don't tell me that's a breeze?" I rejoiced. But it had only seemed to be so. I leaned back over my papers, when the distant sound was repeated. This time, craning my neck, I looked around me. But what was this? Someone's small fist was attempting to knock at the soft leather padding on the open door.

Who could be knocking on an open door? "Come in!" I called in a deliberately loud voice, hardly able to contain my laughter.

On the threshold, shifting from one foot to the other, stood a short boy. Beneath his blue worn suitcoat could

129

be seen a sateen shirt which had not been tucked in. His thick, pitch-black hair twined in disorderly curls. I looked closely at the boy and immediately realised that he was hardly acquainted with city life. I asked him politely where he was from. He evidently thought that I would not recognise the name of his village and so named the centre of the region.

"From what family?"

"I'm Garanfil's son."

"Which Garanfil?" I was fairly well acquainted with the inhabitants of the regional centre, hell, I spent my childhood there, went to school there, and then taught school, and if I couldn't recall who this Garanfil was, then it was worth questioning the boy about his other relatives, friends, and acquintances. For in the end it would be determined whose kin he was.

I tried to recall who this Garanfil could be. "You say Garanfil," I turned to him. "Who is this Garanfil?"

The little fellow angrily shot back: "Your sister Garanfil." Then immediately abashed by his own sharp tone, blinked his eyes and sniffed earnestly.

Rising noisily, I threw my arms around him. I embraced and kissed him and rumpled the pitch-black curls, slapping him on the shoulders and on the back.

Then we sat down and suddenly fell silent. My God, more than anyone in the world I loved my sister Garanfil. How could I forget Gara* — we called her Gara because she had pitch-black curls. Once we dressed her in my long shirt, because she looked like a boy, and just then the red-bearded dervishes came up to us and, muttering a prayer for each with a vacant expression, turned to my father (gazing affably at Garanfil): "May Allah protect and have mercy upon your curly-headed son!"

Affectionately tousling Gara's hair, the dervishes departed. Our laughter followed them as we mimicked and repeated the words of their prayer for Gara, and even father, who had a great respect for dervishes, could not keep from laughing.

Father loved Garanfil the most of all the children. He also called her Gara until she was quite grown-up and had married.

How could I have failed to recognise the son who so resembled Garanfil?

I felt guilty and harshly rebuked myself. I swore that at the first opportunity I would go back to our village, see my relatives, visit Gara and ask her to wash my grey head, her alone — my favourite sister who had at one time been more tender to me than a mother. I controlled myself with difficulty, and, I must confess, was glad that the two of us — uncle and nephew — refrained from tears. After all in such a respectable establishment it would have seemed somewhat odd.

"Well, what's new, how's life treating you?" I asked as naturally as I could and began to question him about Garanfil, before all else of course about Garanfil, and then about all the rest of our relatives and countrymen, friends and strangers, until we had gone through all the inhabitants of our village.

"How many brothers do you have?"

"There's six of us," said my nephew looking up at me.

"And I only know one," I thought, once again getting angry at myself. But recalling how my nephew had carefully knocked on the soft padding of the open

---

* *Gara*—black.— *Ed.*

door, I had to smile, and suddenly I felt good, as though a burden had been lifted from my heart.

"Now you tell me what made you knock on an open door? You could have walked right in." I reached for my towel and wiped the sweat that streamed down my face.

"It's better to have permission in the biginning," he said, lowering his head. "Without permission, it isn't right."

"And where was my secretary who should have been sitting by the open door at this time?"

"She didn't allow me to come in."

"Where did she go?"

"She went to get a drink of water, and ordered me not to let anyone in."

"Why didn't you wait for her?"

"I was afraid she wouldn't relent even after she had gotten her drink...."

My nephew, who had not been frightened off by the big city, who had found his way around this vast building and quickly contacted his uncle, began to interest me, especially when he uttered this last keen-witted observation.

"Why did you come to Baku?"

"I want to go to school, Uncle."

"What grade did you finish?"

"I went to school seven years in our village."

"Why didn't you go to the neighbouring village and enroll in the ten-year programme?"

"To tell the truth there are a lot of kids in our family and father's getting old. I want to study without being a burden to the family."

"Hm.... Where do you want to study?"

"At a technical school."

"What kind?"

"I want to work in the oil fields."

I must confess that I could not understand why a country boy who had grown up in a small village would want to enter not an agricultural institute but a school for those who wanted to work in the oil industry. I leaned toward him screwing up my eyes as though taking aim:

"Can you pass the examinations?"

"If I had the sort of uncle who...."

"Uncle. Another uncle? You just found your own uncle. What do you mean?"

"I mean the kind of uncle who would be useful, you understand?" said my nephew calmly.

I was amazed by this unexpected glibness and resourcefulness coming from the shy nephew who had so anxiously wiped away his tears.

"All right, suppose that your uncle arranged for you to enter a technical school. Then what? Who would study for you and pass the examinations?"

"From then on it has nothing to do with my uncle."

"Hm ... excellent. But would you be able to study at a technical school? Do you think you could learn to handle the technology, the complex machinery?"

"That's exactly what I want to do," answered my nephew with dignity. "I decided to enroll in a technical school for oil workers and to enter the technological department. I won't study anywhere else. Even if they invite me without any examinations. During the few days that I've been in Baku, I've looked into the curriculum. I'll make it."

"When did you arrive?"

"One week ago today."

"And you waited until today to come by!... Couldn't you have come to see your uncle right from the station?"

"I found myself a place in the dormitory."

"Were you afraid your uncle wouldn't take you in?"

"No," said my nephew, wiping the sweat from his tanned arms with a crumpled handkerchief. "Not because of that. I knew that your children were in the country."

"It's good that you knew about that."

"Yes, but I knew that they went away in the other direction, not our direction."

"Why not? How did you know? Perhaps they did go to your part of the country."

"No. Then my uncle would know his remaining five nephews."

"But the nephews don't know their uncle."

"If they didn't know him, how could they seek him out in such a large city, in such a big building?"

"Perhaps because of examinations..." I said, having resolved to pin down my nephew. "Perhaps during examinations an uncle would come in handy."

"Not at all! I'm not worried about the examinations. I rely only on myself so far as they're concerned."

"But you said that if you had that kind of uncle...."

"Well, it wouldn't hurt if they knew ... that I too ... that someone is backing me. That's so they won't put someone else in my place, someone who has that kind of uncle, but who hasn't got it up here." He tapped his forehead expressively with one index finger.

I must confess that my nephew was pleasing me more each minute. He was not afraid to contradict me and even to argue with me. I thought to myself: "It's natural that he should be smart, being the son of Gara who we love precisely because of her resourcefulness and intelligence." It seemed to me suddenly that I was speaking to Gara, that once again we were mimicking the red-bearded dervishes, laughing and frolicking together.

Our conversation grew more and more animated. I reassured my nephew. It was only just to help him ... I would help him as much as I could so that those other uncles would not worm their nephews into a position that by rights should go to my nephew.

The boy's swarthy face blushed slightly. I paced about the room, glancing surreptitiously at my nephew who sat decorously on the edge of his chair. What hopes he had pinned on his uncle.... I went over to him and rumpled his curls, kissing the forehead darkened by the sun.

2

Several days passed. It became even hotter. Already I was having difficulty breathing. Fortunately I had to go to the provinces on business. That evening, at twilight, I drove off. By morning I was on the slope of snow-capped mountains. I

132

spent a week in this area without, I must confess, thinking about my nephew who was taking his examinations in Baku's unbearable heat.... But it was time to return. I rejoiced upon learning that the north wind was blowing in Baku and that not only had the city cooled down, but it was cold enough for people to wear suits, even light coats. But by the time I reached Baku, the north wind had ceased to blow.

"Strange, very strange," muttered Baku's citizens who had importunately been deprived of the saving coolness and, as always, found themselves at the mercies of an oppressive heat. It is well known that Baku's climate depends on the north wind; when it blows, it's winter, when it is calm — summer. But no matter how you figure things, it won't make them any easier.... After work I would sometimes get into my car and drive off, no — speed to the sea, to Buzovny. But more often than not, overburdened with business, I simply rushed home and hopped into a cold shower....

Up to my ears in work, I completely forgot about both my newly discovered nephew and my own children. There was no time for such thoughts.

In this way a month passed. But one day, my secretary entered my office and announced: "Your nephew wants to see you."

Suddenly I felt terribly awkward. How could I have forgotten about my nephew. I rose and walked to meet him: "Well, what's new? How's life treating you?" I said and, although I extended my hands to him, I guiltily lowered my eyes.

"Everything is fine, Uncle," he said.

I reproached myself silently; how could I have left the boy to the whims of fate, taken off to manage my own affairs and then not even inquired about him upon returning? Now, possibly, it was too late....

"Well, how are things with you?"

"Things are all muddled up, Uncle."

"Why?"

"Because all the uncles who own cars have perched on the roof of the technical school."

"What are you talking about?"

"They're climbing in through the attic and writing their nephews' names into the enrollment lists."

"And you?"

"My name isn't on the list."

I began to bustle around like a hunter who has driven his prey from its lair, or rather like the victim itself as the hunter catches sight of it. What will I tell my nephew now? What will I tell my sister? Although, who knows, maybe the news won't worry her at all. Maybe she will be glad that her little squab has returned? But in any case to act like I acted, as her brother and his uncle.... Your nephew asked for help and you didn't offer him a hand, didn't do everything that was in your power so that he could become an oil worker if that was what he wanted.

"Yes.... Hm.... Maybe you ruined things for yourself.... Probably failed an examination."

I raised my head and met the gaze of my nephew. We stood face to face.

"No," he declared firmly. "Not one examination."

"Then what happened? Why weren't you on the lists?"

133

"As if it wasn't quite clear. Those who have uncles are on the lists, those who don't are stricken off."

"That's impossible." I called my secretary and ordered her to find the phone number of the technical school's director.

I called in the presence of my nephew. Stealing a glance at him, I noticed that the boy had grown gloomy. He was swarthy anyway and his face grew even darker. "Why.is this?" I thought. "Did he actually fail or is it because his uncle seems indifferent?"

I phoned the director of the technical school once, twice, three times.

"The uncles are tying up the line!" muttered my nephew, staring at the ceiling, in a tone which did not suit a boy from the country.

Finally the line was free. The director of the technical school picked up the receiver. I gave my name, inquired about his directorial health, about the health of his children (although I wasn't sure if he had children), and he complained that he was up to his ears in work and had no rest what with constant phone calls. This of course was a hint, and a pretty transparent one, but I was implacable.

"I wanted to speak about my nephew." I clearly articulated his name, patronymic, and last name of my little squab and asked the director to look at the lists more carefully.

"Right away, right away. I'll leaf through them and check them over.... What is your nephew's problem?"

"I would like to know what subject he failed. What should he do now? Perhaps he should prepare to take the examinations again next year?" I glanced at my nephew and he looked at me. I saw anger in his eyes, not so much at me as at my sister, his mother.

"There's your important brother," they seemed to say. "There's our precious uncle whose name we always swore by."

I held the receiver to my ear and waited. At last the director, as though having freed himself of great burden, said: "Your nephew is listed. He was rated excellent on everything and admitted to the technological department."

"But why isn't his name on the lists posted on the board?"

"Because we haven't posted the names of school-leavers accepted by the technological department."

"Please repeat his last name."

He repeated it.

"Then Aslan-zade is on the list?"

"Yes, yes. Aslan-zade. He came through his trials like a true *aslan**. But there's something wrong with his vision. Evidently he was dazzled when he looked at the names of departments on the lists."

Having no desire to prolong the conversation, I thanked the director for the good news, hung up the receiver, and, turning to my nephew, congratulated him on being accepted into the technical school for oil workers.

"After you called," said my nephew thoughtfully. "Thanks to uncle's phone call," he added neither cheerfully nor sadly.

"No, you have only yourself and your knowledge to thank for it, my boy."

"Not at all," he shook his head. "Without uncle's phone call they would have refused me. I have no doubt."

---

* *Aslan*—lion.— *Ed.*

For a long time he assured me that only because of my phone call was he, my nephew, accepted at the technical school. I could not convince him of the contrary and ceased to insist upon it. In the end, the most important thing was the result.

3

My nephew attended his classes regularly, studied diligently, and was given a scholarship which allowed him, as he expressed it, to live without any obligations. From time to time he stopped by to visit me and we engaged in short, but lively conversations. We became close friends.

When I was in a bad mood, he had only to come by and my face would involuntarily clear. Suddenly I would feel like talking about something gay, like joking.

"Well, how are you, engineer?" I would ask.

With an embarrassed smile the boy would answer: "There's a long way to go until I'm an engineer, Uncle."

"Why so? You'll graduate from the technical school, your uncle will help you enroll in an institute, in the technological department. Before you can say 'knife' you'll be an engineer."

"No. That's enough of that!" my nephew would protest. He still could not rid himself of the idea that he had been accepted at the technical school through the grace of his uncle. He was convinced of this and felt himself doubly obliged to make his way on his own.

"You can't get along without your uncle," I joked, winking at the other members of my household. "It'll be hard to endure competition."

"If uncle's call hadn't flashed over their heads like lightning at the very height of the heat wave — remember how hot it was? — you would have never made it through the tests, right?"

"I am well aware of it!" said my nephew.

No matter how heavy the burden of gratitude and the fears of seeming not grateful enough, he evidently did not wish to free himself of it.

"Maybe I will get on without my uncle," he said, smiling affably to soften the blow.

"Without your uncle you may find yourself in a difficult position," I smiled too. "Without your uncle the Baku heat will burn you to a cinder — poof! What do you say to that?"

"Now 80° centigrade couldn't affect me!" declared my nephew categorically. "When I finish the technical school I'll go to work in a factory."

"And then? What about a higher education?"

"Then we'll see how things turn out...."

"Perhaps my nephew wishes to get married," I said looking at the boy suspiciously. His pitch-black hair gleamed, his suit was painstakingly pressed.... Somehow I was certain that my nephew would not be slow to get married. Well, as they say, God help him, he'll master his trade, get a suitable job, and settle down to married life, I reasoned.

At last my nephew finished the technical school and went to work at one of the oil refineries. He was absorbed in his work. It was obvious that it fascinated him.

135

Now all of our conversations revolved around problems of refining oil; one after another these crowded my nephew's head, although he was only a technician. He had many new worries, duties, and plans.

But I began to notice that things were not going smoothly for him. He would come with a sullen face, frowning, and answer my questions in monosyllables, evasively.

One day he came by directly after work, openly agitated and disturbed. I pretended that I had noticed nothing unusual.

"Well, how are things, engineer?"

"Those noose is tightening, Uncle."

"What noose?"

"I had a run-in with the director."

"With the director? How did that happen?"

"We had a strong difference of opinion."

"Aha. About what?"

My nephew frowned, muttered something and fell silent. Evidently he was embarrassed by his own confession. He certainly found someone to pick a quarrel with, I thought to myself. If only it had been some shift engineer or at the worst a shop superintendent. But the director of that enormous factory.... What was it that they couldn't agree on?

My nephew left, but I continued to think about him and could not stop worrying. Maybe he had begun to behave badly or was connected with trouble-makers? How could it happen that out of a thousand workers at that factory, he alone — that little squab, my nephew who occupied such a lowly position — caught the director's attention and became a thorn in his flesh. Why, the boy had only worked there for two or three months!...

The more seriously I considered all this, the more my anxiety increased. The next day I found the phone number of the director of the factory where my nephew worked and called him. I was told that the director had gone to the shops. Two hours later I phoned again and was told: "The director will not be in today. It is useless to keep calling."

"And when can I find him in?"

"Tomorrow. At ten o'clock sharp."

I slept restlessly and woke early the next morning. I waited and waited until the clock struck ten.

Finally I pick up the receiver and dial the number. I give my name, apologise for taking the director from his work and straight away turn the conversation to my nephew.

"Do you know Aslan-zade? Several months ago he finished technical school and came to work for you...."

"Know him? I know him well," interrupted the director. "I know him best of all."

"What do you mean?"

"An inveterate debater."

"Does he behave poorly? Or has he fallen under a bad influence?"

"Not at all."

"What then?"

"He fancies himself an inventor. But he's biting off more than he can chew. As they say, he's trying to put both feet in one shoe. Then he comes and claims that things are lagging behind, that I don't encourage initiative, that I don't make way for what is new and progressive!"

"Tell me about this, please!" I said noncommittally, restraining my laughter with difficulty.

The director at length and not without bitterness assured me that neither heaven nor earth could set a limit to my nephew's pretensions, that not a day went past without him getting into an argument with someone, and when they didn't want to listen to him he would announce: "I will stop at nothing!... I'll take this to the highest authorities!..."

"Excuse me, but do his inventions show the slightest spark of thought?"

"You see ... hm ... to predict something like that is difficult, difficult...." He breathed out noisily. "I would appreciate it if you would give your nephew a good scolding the next time he comes by and convince him to leave us in peace. When the boy actually invents something ... worthwhile, useful, then we'll talk about it and accept it ... and install it...."

To tell the truth I calmed down after this conversation. Even if the inventions of my nephew, the little squab, were not quite functional yet, nevertheless, it wasn't a bad start, not bad at all....

On his day off, he stopped by. I asked him how he felt and then give him a proper reprimand: "It's no good, brother. You've gone too far. You abuse people and quarrel. And who is it you pick on? The director of the whole enormous factory."

My nephew hung his head and listened to me. But as soon as I mentioned the director he exploded like a powder keg. "If they told me I had only an hour to live, I would still argue with him and never be appeased."

"And why, my dear boy? Why don't you feel obliged to respect your elders and superiors?" I asked angrily. "Have you young folks forgotten the difference between seniors and juniors?"

"A senior worker ought to know his place too," said my nephew, changing countenance. "He ought to be able to respect his subordinates."

"Don't be so stubborn and arrogant!" I altered my tone somewhat.

"Just try it. People like our director sense your weak spot, grab you by the scruff of the neck and put you in your place."

"Look here, it wasn't all that long ago that your mother hatched you!"

"What do you want me to do — crawl back into my shell?"

"Let's have a little more civility, my boy."

"I can't be more civil, Uncle."

"Oho! And why not, my child?"

"That director is like a stone wall, Uncle!" he said. His face darkened so it looked like a sooty strip of felt. "He has old-fashioned views. Believe me, I'm not alone. All the young workers at the factory are unhappy with him."

"And I suppose you are a leader?"

"Yes."

I tried to collect myself and to think how best I could explain things to him — admonish him, persuade him? But I realised that at that moment my words could not affect him. I pricked up my ears: although the boy had chosen the right path, he might still go astray, he was already in an unenviable position....

"Yes," I said. "That's how it is. Just let a man feel he's independent and he

137

thinks he can do anything, doesn't listen to his superiors. Whoever heard of such a thing? How dare you speak to me like this?"...

In a word, leaving him alone, I went into the other room, took a book from the shelf, and hurriedly leafed through it. Then I collected my papers, put them into folders, went out on the balcony, glanced at the sea, went back inside.... And although this actually took only a few minutes, God knows how much time seemed to have elapsed, but when I returned he had left. He got up and left. My children threw themselves on me, demanding to know why I was so harsh with my nephew. There's nothing to be surprised about, they said. Of course the boy left. And he was absolutely right, and so on and so forth.... But I thought that I was right, not he! He'd fallen into evil ways too quickly.... What evil ways, you ask?... Arrogance.... Yes, arrogance!... It couldn't be overlooked.

...Weeks slipped past and then months. There was a storm and then the whitecaps disappeared, emotions subsided. Once again we were together, I and my nephew, the little squab. We greeted each other. He sat and hung his head strangely, either with guilt or distress. Still he regrets it and who knows, I thought, perhaps he wants to ask my forgiveness. But all that had passed and there was no sense in reliving it. It was better to speak about the present. I was about to tell him this when our eyes met and I saw something in his that made me keep silent. I looked at my nephew's hand: it was already inserted in his trouser pocket. It emerged with a small bundle which it quietly unwrapped. What do you think I saw? A massive gold engagement ring. Small beads of sweat appeared on his skin as he handed it to me....

"Uncle, do you know anything about gold?" he asked, blushing with embarrassment.

I tossed the ring gently in my palm.

"May Allah send his blessings!" I said. I could not reproach him. Hadn't I, thirty years earlier, acquired just such a ring without saying a word to anyone? "Well, congratulations, my boy."

"Is it gold, Uncle?"

"To tell the truth I don't know much about such things," I laughed. "I bought your aunt a ring, but that's the only time in my life when I was in need of gold."

"I just want to know if it's gold or not."

"Who did you buy it from?"

"The person who sold it."

"In a store?"

"No," my nephew told me what had happened to him.

He was sitting on a bench reading a book, quite alone. Then a well-dressed man sat down beside him, "a gentleman" as my nephew put it.

The man coughs respectably, sneezes, lights up a cigarette, glancing sideways at my nephew, and finally turns to him. He politely poses various questions, perfectly harmless questions which one could answer or not as one pleased — nobody would take offense at such questions. But one of those harmless questions interests him more than the others; is the young man married or a bachelor? Oh, a bachelor, but no doubt he is already preparing to get married. It's high time! And he has just the thing for a man who is about to marry.

He takes out the engagement ring.

"It will be difficult for me to part with this, but if you want it, I will give it up."

"Why are you selling it?" asked my nephew.

"I'm a poor man, my dear fellow. I have expenses and I need money."

"In that case why don't you take the ring to the market?"

"I confess I'm afraid of being cheated." The gentleman looks at my nephew firmly and serenely. "I'm afraid of swindlers, my friend. I'm afraid that my ring will slip through my fingers and then I will have nowhere to turn."

Undoubtedly the glitter of that golden engagement ring blinded my nephew, as a man is blinded on a sunny day. Behind the glitter he saw ... a newly-fallen virgin snow and a bright sunny day. Behind its glitter he saw.... But let's forget the details.... Let us instead watch what the gentleman is doing. He gazes tenderly on my nephew. He watches how the boy holds the ring in his hand for a long, long time. And he says: "Friend, I can see that you like the ring. Take it. Consider it a gift."

"How can I take a gift from you?" protested my nephew. "What will people say?"

"No one will say anything. The ring is mine and I give it to you.... There's an old saying: 'Do a good deed, throw a fish into the sea; if the fish doesn't learn about it, Allah will.' There's no need to be acquainted or to be good friends. A good deed is never forgotten. He who has done a good deed is always rewarded."

"No, forgive me, but I can't accept your gift."

"In that case, why don't you buy it?"

"Where could I find so much money?"

"You can buy it for less."

"I confess that I don't have very much money in my pocket."

"How much?"

My nephew carefully rummages in his pockets and empties them. There are about three hundred rubles.

"Is that all?"

"All I have besides this is my watch, I swear it."

"And now much is your simple, metal watch worth?"

"I bought it for three hundred rubles."

"I'll take the loss. It's enough to know that the ring won't go to some scoundrel."

Silently, my nephew takes off his watch and with some embarrassment holds it out to the ring's owner.

Taking my nephew's small hand in his, the fellow shakes it firmly and disappears, instantly and without warning. Suddenly the boy feels the prickings of spleen; he is possessed by a vague anxiety, and he decides to turn to his uncle, not suspecting that his uncle has no idea of noble metals.

To tell the truth I bought a small golden article only once in my life, as I said earlier, and it never occurred to me to examine it or bite it.

Tossing the weighty ring in my palm, I said: "If this is real gold you've got it for a song." I looked at him significantly.

"And if not?" My nephew turned pale. "If it's not gold?"

"Then you've been cheated. They've cleaned you out. Really do you think one can buy such things from strangers?"

"I thought if there's a chance to buy it cheaply, why not?"

"And if you paid too much for it?" I began to scold my nephew. "My friend, this isn't your first year in the city, you've finished a technical school, you claim to be an inventor, you've made the director of a large factory miserable, and yet you buy an engagement ring from a total stranger. You invent things yourself, but you haven't the slightest idea about inventions." I turned the so-called engagement ring in my hand.

Just then my daughter returned from school and upon being told what the problem was clasped her hands in dismay. She also turned the ill-starred ring over and over in her hands, this way and that.

"You know what," I said to my nephew and daughter. "Go to the nearest jeweller's and they'll tell you the truth, the whole truth. Gold or not gold. Three thousand rubles or three kopecks."

My nephew who had been struck dumb, as they say, by my words, left in embarrassed silence. My daughter followed him.

Suddenly I seethed with rage. If I had my hands on that "gentleman" I don't know what I'd do to him — but it wouldn't be pleasant!

"Well, hello! So quickly? What's the verdict?"

My nephew silently threw the ring onto the table. "Worth all of ten rubles," he said, wiping the sweat from his forehead. "Ten rubles, no more, no less."

My daughter stood to one side, biting her finger.

"Are there others in the store like it?"

"As many as you like. A whole cartload."

No, say what you like, my nephew and I were very upset.... It wasn't only the monetary loss. My nephew's first endeavour had come up against a stone wall.

"We failed in that undertaking." I said.

My nephew hung his head. To tell the truth I didn't know what upset him more — the fact that his first endeavour had come a cropper or the fact that the person he had taken for a "gentleman" turned out to be a swindler, a base, brazen liar.

Suddenly, tossing his head, clenching his teeth, and screwing up his eyes as though he had been burnt, he wrenched open the door and dashed out as though shot from a gun. My nephew, that impatient little squab who had no self-control and had so feared my reproaches and complaints, had rushed off somewhere. Where had he gone? Well, I knew where. He had run into the garden to sit down once again in the place where he had had the pleasure of making the acquaintance of the "complete gentleman". He would sit there for a while, then get up, wander around that bewitched area, look around him. No one. Yes, now there was no one. The "complete gentleman" had disappeared. But he was somewhere. Somewhere he walks the earth, walks, but from time to time sits down on a bench next to young people who are ready to get married, just as he sat down next to my nephew, and he offers them a ring, absolutely free.... He walks the earth, that strange character, but he has no right to. This was the conclusion of my nephew, the little squab. And it was the right conclusion.

4

My nephew left, and when my agitation at this episode with the engagement ring had somewhat subsided, I shook with suppressed laughter: "To be sure, the boy was engaged." There's no hurry. He's the youngest in the family. Why should he outstrip his elder brothers? I wanted to share this thought with my nephew there and then, but we met some two weeks later. I won't hide the fact that I was very happy for him.

"Well, at last! Why haven't you come by? Where have you been? Has your "gentleman" turned up? That gentleman certainly tricked Aslan-zade but good!" I ribbed my nephew, "and not at night time, but in broad daylight, and not in some dense forest, but in the city gardens, in the most crowded place. No, I must confess he did it cleverly, like a master!" I mocked the boy, laughing and slapping him first on one shoulder, then on the other.

"Yes," my nephew affirmed bitterly. "You're right, Uncle. I'm ashamed to own it to anyone."

"Well, what do you think," I glanced cursorily at him. "Perhaps we'll buy another engagement ring."

"No, Uncle. That's finished. All in the past."

"But why? How can that be?"

"I have to study. I need a lot more education."

"That's true. You must study a lot, learn a lot. But why have you put off enrolling in an institute? A technical education on a secondary school level isn't very much. You should become an engineer. Otherwise, little brother, you'll never invent anything of value."

"I know, Uncle. I know. But that's a difficult business. The most difficult thing for me is to pass the examinations. Then, you know, I'm working so hard already, if you add the burden of studying to that...."

"That is precisely why you have to study," I insisted. "You've got oceans of energy. You could move mountains. What should you do with it ... wander around the city and waste precious time? Think about it, boy."

"I'll think about it, Uncle."

"Not to mention that the engagement ring was a counterfeit. You shouldn't be hurrying anywhere right now."

"Yes.... But I must find that swindler. Myself. Find him and turn him in to the proper authorities."

"That's all fine and dandy, but it's difficult. And is it worthwhile?"

"I'll search him out, Uncle." Lightning flashed in my nephew's black eyes.

"It'll be hard. It's hard to find one creature among a million others in a big city! Hard."

"I'll find him."

"Just watch out. Don't get into a fight under any circumstances," I told my nephew, being quite convinced that he would indeed find the man. "Don't forget the law and the courts. No arbitrary sentences! I know you get excited, but none of that! To hell with him! Catch him and drag him right off to the police station. Get out of harm's way."

"I admit it will be hard for me to control myself, Uncle. I'll give it to him once or twice first, what say?"

"Alright, alright. Maybe once or twice.... But don't forget what I told you. By the way how tall is he?"

"How tall? Oh, about three times as tall as I am and about twice as broad — a real elephant."

"Watch out. Apart from everything else he might crush the life out of you. Better not to tangle with him."

"No, if I, say, once or twice ... only twice, Uncle ... I won't rest until.... I can't promise anything in that respect.

141

Time passed.... I can't say exactly how much time passed since our last conversation, but I was already preparing to seek out my nephew, the little squab. "Where could he have disappeared this time?" I thought on one fine, autumn day, as I strolled along the seashore. Suddenly someone is calling me. I turned around and it's him.

"*Salam*, Uncle."

"*Salam, salam*, Nephew.... Have you completely forgotten the old man?... Well, what's new, how are things? Tell me!"

"Honestly earned goods don't disappear!" said he, proudly showing me the watch on his wrist. "Look. Even the band is the same."

And he told me what had happened.

...Each day my nephew had scarched for the man. He walked and he looked, walked and looked, on the ground and in the sky, in trains and in stores, on streets and squares. He was indefatigable, as though he held a magical iron staff in his hands; his legs never wearied, as though he were shod in magical iron boots. My nephew searched for the "complete gentleman" here, there and everywhere. Finally, a few days ago, my nephew entered a large store and caught sight of him drifting among a thick stream of people and as he went showing something to a young, well-dressed woman who drifted alongside him. My nephew saw how that "something" gleamed dazzlingly in his cupped hand and how the woman, opening her purse, took out a packet of hundred-ruble notes.... At that moment my nephew Aslan was transformed into a young lion with sharp claws. He flew at the man.... This put an end to the adventures of the "complete gentleman". My nephew kept his word; he gave it to him two times, no more and no less, just as he had promised, nimbly snatched back his own watch, and immediately turned his prisoner over to the police.

"But the money...." I asked him. "Where are your three hundred rubles?"

"That's the matter for the court to decide on," pronounced my nephew like a true lawyer.

"Why didn't you take the money like you took the watch?"

"I'll get my money through the courts."

"Well," I thought, "my nephew is making progress. My lessons were not in vain. What respect for the letter of the law...."

But I saw that he was ready to slash at the very shadow of that rogue.

"Strictly between us," he whispered ominously in my ear, "I'd like to burn all those rotters and parasites at the stake...."

"Well, well, but you just...."

"Yes of course. I, ah...."

"You shouldn't excessively give way to your emotions. Not to excess...."

And I taught my nephew the next lesson: one must control oneself even when this seems almost impossible. In no case should one start ... (I never said what should't be started, just shook my fist at him and he understood precisely what I had in mind.)

Peacefully conversing in this way, we strolled along the boulevard, then, picking out a bench, sat down and both began to ponder. I was thinking about the work that I had just begun to write. In one place I hadn't succeeded in describing the sea the way I wanted. A few strokes were lacking. Looking at the sea, I wondered what these were, and I must admit that I forgot about my nephew seated beside me.

He coughed.

"Ah, that's you! Forgive me! This writing business is intolerable sometimes. Suddenly imagination spreads its sails and carries you off along unfamiliar waves to unknown places."

"I understand," said my nephew.

"How could you understand that? Or have you fallen ill with the same complaint as your uncle?"

My nephew coughed again. "No," he said. "Not at all."

"Perhaps after your attempt to buy an engagement ring failed, you turned to poetry?"

"No, I haven't become interested in poetry, Uncle."

"What then?"

My nephew pulled a rolled-up newspaper from his pocket and handed it to me. He unrolled it. It was a factory newspaper. On the front page I saw my nephew's picture, and beneath the picture was an article. I slipped on my glasses and slowly began to read it. The article said that my nephew's invention for the time being had been implemented at one factory and resulted in a yearly savings of hundreds of thousands of rubles, but when it was instituted at other factories, such savings might amount to millions of rubles....

So that's how it was! My nephew had not abandoned his quests and the difficult path of the inventor. Even the director of that enormous factory had not managed to discourage him.

In addition, the article stated that Aslan-zade was studying by correspondence at an industrial institute without discontinuing work.

"Is this all true, or did a friend write the article?"

No sooner had I posed this puzzling question to my nephew, when something gleamed in his hands. I started gently. But no, this time the object was not made of a precious metal: it was an ordinary iron key on a gleaming brass chain, the key to the personal apartment of my nephew, the little squab.

Only six years ago he had timidly knocked on my open office door.... Only six years ago....

He had not simply folded his arms and waited for an apartment. In his free time he had worked to construct an apartment building for workers at the oil refinery. He helped as best as he could and learned yet another trade — that of a brick-layer.

I took the key from him and turning it over in my hands, began to think. "Key!" A good word! It always lends itself to symbolic generalisations.

But we won't give our key any such significance. Let us merely congratulate my nephew on his new apartment with all our heart. He has a flat of his own with bath and balcony. And I'll let you in on a little secret. Right now uncle wouldn't be adverse if his nephew considered buying an engagement ring.

And how would Gara look at all this, Gara, at whom the red-bearded dervishes smiled after gaily praying for her?

What do you think about this, my sister Garanfil, mother of the nephew who sits alongside me and thinks! What is he thinking of? For the time being we won't ask him. When we all get together, he'll tell us himself.

Agreed, Nephew?

143

Ali Veliev
(b. 1901)

Formerly a farm labourer, Ali Veliev has a superb knowledge of the country, of folk traditions and the life and mores of peasants. The pre- and post-revolutionary countryside, its people and their struggle for a better lot, is the underlying theme of his stories and novels; these include Kagraman, The Road to Guradjuli, *and the two-volume* Budag. My Contemporary. *The story "He Didn't Come" carries on this tradition.*

He Didn't Come

It's a pity I don't know how to write. If I was more literate, I would unburden my heart on paper, I would write about my life. No doubt there are other people who have felt the same grief as I have. My life is a long story, and my heart is like a closed book. I'd like to write everything down, that people might know what I have endured over these years. "Drop by drop water can wear a stone away" the saying goes. But I did not give in, I held out....

I'm now over sixty. The collective farm chairman has done me proud: he has appointed me watchman over the vegetable garden. The fruit and vegetables grown in our village are renowned throughout the entire district. Anyone who samples our honey-dew melons will long remember their wonderful taste and aroma. To say nothing of our water melons; they're so big that you can't get your arms around them ... and when you cut them open, they're as red as blood and sweet as honey. As to the roasted peas they used to sell in Shusha, these were also grown in our parts. And anyone who has not tried our beans has only himself to blame....

I keep watch over the vegetable garden. It's a long way from the rice field, in the upper part of the village. A huge plane tree grows near its edge.

My grandfather once asked his father how old that tree was. The old man replied that no one in their family

145

knew it. When you stand beside this tree and look at the vegetable garden, you get the impression that it's a flock of lambs lying there in hiding. In a word, there's no denying it ... we reap a rich harvest here. May God grant our farmers good health.... But that's just by the way....

The summer can be very hot in our parts. And if it wasn't for this spreading plane tree, I'd have a hard time under the baking sun at my age. When it gets really hot, and the crickets do their chirping, and the snakes become vicious as ever, I lie down in the tree's shade and have a good puff on my chibouk. Then all my tiredness goes away, and I forget about everything in the world.... I forget it all but not for a minute can I forget Murtuza. I can't get him out of my head. I just keep seeing him there before my eyes.

I've seen a great deal in my day, what haven't I suffered during my life but it all went by and was forgotten. Only Murtuza's behaviour I can't forget....

Summer was already nearing its end. But for some reason the heat did not abate. Even after noon it did not get any cooler. One day, when I was gathering some melons and piling them up in a heap, my wife suddenly called me in a loud voice. Now, my Gulgadam would not have called me for nothing. She knows I can't stand women who don't leave their husbands in peace for a minute and keep running after them. And then, Gulgadam knew I was working, guarding community property. So she wouldn't have bothered me over some trifling matter. Something must have happened....

The river lay between us; I couldn't work out what my wife was saying and she couldn't hear my voice. She stood there for a while, shouting something out. Then I called out at the top of my voice, really straining myself, but all in vain. Gulgadam went away, and I returned to the garden. Still puzzled by what had happened, I began counting the melons again. Then the son of my sister-in-law ran up, joyously unfolded the news that Murtuza had arrived from Baku in his car and demanded a treat for this information. Murtuza, he said, was now in the district centre but he would be returning to the village in the evening and staying at our place. I gave the boy a few honey-dew melons and strictly instructed him to tell my wife to tie the sheep up before I came home and lock up a couple of turkeys and a few chickens in the barn.... After the boy had gone, I marked the melons and headed back to the village myself. My heart was beating with excitement, my mouth dry from thirst, and the walking was hard work, but I hurried as fast as I could. By the river I got my breath back a little. When I was crossing the bridge, I heard a familiar voice. Was it Murtuza calling me? I looked round, and listened carefully. There was no one about, and the river did not make all that much noise in that spot. I crossed the bridge and, as I was going past the mill, I heard that voice again.... It was Murtuza's voice after all. But where was it coming from? If it was Murtuza calling me, why didn't he show himself? I leaned against a rock a little further up from the mill and began to look carefully around. I didn't see anyone. I called at the mill but heard nothing but the rhythmic knocking of the mill-stones. There was certainly no sign of Murtuza in there. Vexed by the mystery, I continued on my way. The road from the river to the village ran uphill and was covered in stones and ruts. I turned onto a small path and took the shortest way home. And here again I heard Murtuza's voice. I stopped dead. Putting my hand up to my ear, I shouted: "What is it you are saying? Speak louder.... What do you keep hiding for, like the moon behind the clouds, or are you a bashful bride?"

146

But there was not a sound in reply—only silence all around....

Although the dry wind was still blowing, breathing had become easier. A fresh stream of cool air refreshed the body.

My thoughts gave me no peace. I felt like clutching my head in my hands and running away. But where to? Right to the village, of course. Gulgadam was waiting for me. In the evening Murtuza would be calling on us, the house would be full of people.... Engrossed in my thoughts, I reached the top of Gazayagla Hill without noticing it. This hill blocks off the village of Yemlikli and here lies our cemetery. I stood for a while by a grave with a tall tombstone. Here lay the remains of my brother, Murtuza's father.

This grave was very dear to me because Museib was my only brother. Ah, the pity of it! May you grieve as I have....

I remembered the past, when the first collective farms in and around Yemlikli were being set up, or rather when we were setting them up. Museib was in the forefront of this movement. He urged the people to join the collective farm. But, as the saying goes, there's a jackal in every wood. And so it was in Yemlikli. There were a number of wicked people living in this village—the kind who forced poor peasants to work for them for a mere pittance. They tested the strength of their fists on the poor wretches and flaunted their power around the village; for them other people were not even human beings. Of course, the collective farm was not in their interest, and therefore they went out of their way to frustrate our plans. One of them was that boastful swindler Islam. Three or four times in a row he warned me: you tell your brother to leave us in peace and do a bit less tongue-wagging; it'll be better for him if he just keeps quiet....

Was there no one else for him to have a go at? I gave him a real telling-off and sent him away. It turned out he had threatened Museib five or six times. Museib paid no heed to his words. This made Islam furious and he shouted: "If anyone harnesses my bullocks I'll cut his fingers off. If anyone dares to sow a field ploughed by my plough, I'll cut his hands off. If anyone gives my cows to the paupers, I'll tear his tongue out. If anyone shares my sheep out among the rabble, his mother will weep bitter tears afterwards." That was how he threatened us and every now and then he would send someone to tell Museib: "You'd better just sit quiet. I wouldn't like to be in the shoes of anyone who touches me." But Museib did not deviate from his path, did not give in. And then Islam lay in wait for him one night and shot him in the back.... Since that day I have felt as if my wings had been clipped, as if my back had been bent. My heart was wrung with pain.... Everything went dark all around.... Good brothers are not so easy to find, and especially ones like Museib. How painful it is to recall those days....

At that time Murtuza was still in his mother's arms. He was a sickly child and often ill. There wasn't a single doctor we didn't show him to or a single person we didn't consult with. They all maintained the same thing: "The child is weak, look after him." Look after him! But how? He was not even six months old, when his mother abandoned him and remarried. Poor Gulgadam was forced to take the child and nurse him herself. After the death of our only son Gulgadam's milk had dried up but it appeared again when she began feeding Murtuza.

The little boy quickly began to recover. In three or four months he had blossomed to such an extent that it was a pleasure to look at him. We both doted on him. No sooner had I put him down that Gulgadam would make him comfortable on her back. Up until the age of seven Murtuza slept together with

Gulgadam and would not part with her by night or day. On the day he went to school I killed a sheep. Gulgadam and I grew so accustomed to the boy that we couldn't be without him for a minute. This was chiefly because Murtuza was the only son of my only brother. But, besides, we had no children of our own.... And it seemed to me that heaven itself had sent this boy to us. We pandered to all his whims. He never had to ask us for anything twice. But, to tell the truth, Murtuza was a lad after everyone's heart. God had endowed him with a good head on his shoulders. When he graduated from secondary school with top marks, Gulgadam and I had a bit of an argument. My wife said: "Let's send him to Kirovabad: after all it's close to home. You'll be able to visit him pretty often." But I couldn't go against Murtuza's will, I didn't want to offend him. In 1947 we saw him off to Rostov. The house seemed empty after his departure, as if all the life in it had flickered out. My wife and I could not eat or drink. In a whole day we could not even manage a single loaf between the two of us. Not a month went by without us sending Murtuza money and parcels. Gulgadam made up her mind to let him have 500 rubles a month. "The child's so far away from home," she would say, "after all, he'll have friends. People will look at him, what will they say? We must strive for all we are worth to make sure that Murtuza doesn't feel himself an orphan."

May God grant you good luck, but Gulgadam took more care of Murtuza than if she were his own mother. Indeed, even a mother who had borne him in her womb, could not have done more to please him. There was nothing that Gulgadam wouldn't do for the boy. She would send him everything—from her own home cooking down to woollen socks and mittens. My wife and I regarded him as our own son. To tell the truth, after Gulgadam had done so much for Murtuza, I began to respect her a great deal more than before. She was an exceptionally kind-hearted person....

Another five years went by. Ten months of the year we sent him money and presents and during the two summer months we did nothing but regale him with tasty tit-bits at home. We were like birds feeding their young from morn to evening. I don't know about Gulgadam, but I couldn't sit still from joy when Murtuza came home. If I'd had wings, I would have taken off. It had been my hope that Murtuza would qualify as an agronomist and return home, and all my weariness would be gone. Gulgadam too would finally rest from her labours.

People who knew us regarded us as happy, and spoke about us with envy: "they didn't mix him or bake him but found him ready-made," they used to say. These words were unfair—for a start, we didn't find him ready-made. And in the second place our bun didn't bake very well: it remained moist inside while the crust was burnt. When Murtuza was in his last year of studies, we made an agreement with him: that as soon as he received his diploma on graduation from the institute, he would go straight to Baku and get himself assigned to work in our village. We also had dreams of marrying Murtuza and having a wedding that would last three days and three nights. Gulgadam and I had made up our minds to give our son and daughter-in-law all the nicest and finest things in our house.... But our dreams were not destined to come true....

When Murtuza graduated from the institute, we heard nothing from him for a whole three months. My wife and I became anxious and fretful. But what could we do? We sighed and moaned and walked around all gloomy. Sometimes we consoled each other. Then suddenly we heard that Murtuza had got married in

148

Baku and was already working at the Ministry. This news left us thunder-struck.... We walked past people on the street with our heads down, ashamed to look them in the eyes.

Of course, Murtuza did the right thing in getting married. But it wasn't nice that he had taken this step without our consent. He had humiliated and offended us, trampled on our hopes. Our only son, whom we loved, cherished and prayed for, had arranged his life in his own way, without remembering about his parents.... Maybe it was because he was young and didn't understand — "young and green", as they say.

But why had the girl's parents, who had given their daughter in marriage, not thought of this. After all, we have our own laws and customs. Young people should respect their elders. What about Murtuza's duty before his father and mother? Why had I been denied the chance to dance to my heart's content at my son's wedding? And surely it wasn't fair that a woman who had given more than 20 years of her life to her son and worried about his happiness day and night, was not even able to sample the nuptial pilau.

For ten days we walked around finding no peace of mind. Then we calmed down a little and began to admonish each other. Finally we decided that, regardless of what had happened, it was up to us to make the first step for we were older people. In the autumn we would get ready and go off to see our daughter-in-law....

...This is what I was thinking about as I hurried on my way. I was so engrossed in thought that I didn't notice that I was already home.

My thoughts were interrupted by Gulgadam's voice. My wife was calling me, hurrying me on.... And indeed there was plenty to be done at home.

I quickly slaugtered the sheep. The meat was too fatty and I even wondered whether I would find suitable pieces for shashlyks to roast over the fire.

Cutting up the carcass made me sweat profusely. Indeed, I thought, I'm really getting old. I used to do this job without even raising a drop of sweat on my forehead....

I cut some firewood for the cauldron, and killed a couple of turkeys, two roosters and half a dozen chickens. I took this sin upon myself, too....

The fire raged under the cauldron. While Gulgadam and her sister Kubra were scalding the birds and the rice for the pilau was soaking, I wiped the spits with an old piece of felt. Then I went out onto the balcony. And while I stood there, looking down and waiting for our dear guest to show up, Gulgadam and Kurba finished what they were doing and started assembling all the cooking for the table....

In the country, of course, it's not easy to receive guests from town. You don't know what to do to please them. They might notice some shortcoming and immediately start making fun of it: how can country bumpkins be expected to know how to serve food.... They'll drop it in the ashes and bolt it down just the same. Well, Gulgadam and Kubra really tried hard, they didn't want to disgrace themselves....

It was so pleasant up on the balcony that I didn't want to go down again. Then I noticed that the sun had already set. First the village became enveloped in a huge shadow, then the darkness seeped into everything around as if covering it with black dye. Neither the flame in the hearth nor the fire in the yard could repel it. But nobody came. Then I sent Kubra's eldest son to the district centre, instructing him to tell Murtuza that his father and mother had been waiting and waiting....

When the boy had left I set to roasting the meat. I strung the edible inwards of the sheep on four spits. The ribs and fatty tail I decided to serve separately. Murtuza loved shashlyk made from soft meat and six spits were specially prepared for him. Gulgadam kept taking an occasional look at the pilau, to make sure it didn't get cold because of the bent cauldron lid....

Kubra's son returned quickly — the district centre was just down the road — and informed us that Murtuza was at a meeting and the meeting would not finish till late. This news upset us but there was nothing we could do but have patience and wait. However, it got hopelessly late and there was still no sign of Murtuza. We couldn't stand it any longer and I set off after him myself.

As I walked I expected any minute to hear the sound of my son's car.... I would be lit up by the glare of its headlights and the car would stop. Murtuza would jump out of it and throw his arms around my neck, kissing me and weeping. And, calming him down, I would sit in the seat beside him, as befitting for a father and son, and we would drive home together....

Such were my thoughts when I reached the district centre. The sweat was running down me in torrents: I set off straight for the Party district committee. There was nobody there. The man on duty — may God grant him health — explained that the meeting had finished. I inquired about Murtuza, and learned that he had left in his car for Baku. The man on duty added that he had apparently received a telegramme saying that tomorrow was the birthday of some relative on his wife's side. That was why he had been in such a hurry....

I couldn't believe my ears. I would never have thought that Murtuza could act so unworthily, so unreasonably. But ... facts were facts. He had left as inconspicuously as he had arrived. I had to return home with nothing to show for my pains.

The moon rose. The dusk dispersed and it became light as day — so light that one could see the tyre marks of Murtuza's car....

I felt so tired and heart-broken that I could barely drag myself along.

When I reached Ay-Iokhush hill I stopped. The night was quiet. Involuntarily, I breathed a heavy sigh. It expressed everything — my shattered dreams, and hope, and resentment, and pain.... Only an echo responded, and it did not carry the sound beyond the river as it usually did, but died away somewhere nearby.

Yet all the same I felt some relief; I didn't feel the pain any more. But my legs wouldn't carry me....

When Gulgadam and Kubra learned what had happened, it was as if boiling water had been poured over them. They sank down onto a chair with their arms folded and their heads drooping.

Murtuza didn't come. The pilau remained untouched. The fire in the yard burnt itself out and became covered with ashes. The spits with the cold shashlyks on them lay beside it. Swarms of midges flocked to the light and circled round the table. The unwanted melons floated in pails of water, pressing close to one another, as if afraid that they would be cut up all for nothing....

I say nothing of my own labours, or the fact that all Gulgadam's efforts turned out to be vain.... I was more dejected because of something else. What would they say, those people who had no special liking for Murtuza and us? They would most likely blame us: "You can say what you like but after all you're only his

150

uncle...." But others might put it more bluntly: "Of course, if he were your own son he would have come straight home! But Murtuza — what was there for him to remember here?"

But these words did not distress me all that much. It would be a shame, though, if Murtuza was not acting of his own accord.... Maybe his bride had laid it down as a condition before marrying him that he should have nothing to do with us. I don't like old people, she might have said, especially if they're from the village. They're all ignorant and unscrupulous: give them an inch and they'll demand a yard.

But they're wrong to think so.... And I think they're wrong to call me an old man in the village.... Very well, Murtuza didn't come, that's his business, let his bride turn her nose up at us, but all the same I'm going to travel to Baku for five or ten days and find them. And I'll tell them that I've come all this way just to say two things to them: firstly, that when a tortoise leaves its shell, it doesn't like to go back to it; and secondly, that the more fruit there is on a tree, the lower it bends....

No, I probably won't go anywhere. Evidently, the Murtuza I knew is gone forever. Otherwise he would certainly have called on us. But he didn't come.... He humiliated us, shamed us in the eyes of others....

Ah, if only I could write it all down for myself! No doubt there are others who have been through what I have. They could read and learn about my sorrow.

Seifulla Shamilov (b. 1902)

Shamilov is the author of many stories dealing with past and present Azerbaijan, with the pre-revolutionary Azerbaijanian countryside and the socialist reconstruction of Azerbaijanian society. In some of his stories, Shamilov takes a stand against religious fanaticism and fights for a new life and the modernisation of family relationships.

Shamilov's writing is characterised by a striving for authenticity. His artistic generalisations are based on concrete realities.

His story "Lachin" recreates one of the most exciting episodes in the history of pre-revolutionary Azerbaijan.

Lachin

The horses were exhausted from climbing the many hills of the road that wound along the edge of the forest. We turned off, tethered them on a meadow at the foot of yet another hill and went down to the foaming, churning, turbulent river.

It was the middle of June. A golden wheat field billowed on the other bank. In the distance rows of steep hills gave on to the majestic, snow-capped peaks of the Minor Caucasus.

The breeze from Mt. Munguz, which was shrouded in mist, relieved the stifling heat and caressed our faces. All of nature was at rest, as calm as the clear face of a pregnant woman. Yet, all was expectancy. The earth was preparing to give up its bounty, for the harvesting would begin in a day or two.

The villagers of the valley had already taken their sheep to the summer mountain pastures, and we were to follow in order to keep count of the flocks. My young companion and I were accompanied by an elderly guide from the vicinity.

He settled back, took out his pipe, filled it with home-grown tobacco and said, "If Allah is with us, we'll soon reach the pastures. Look around and see how beautiful everything is here." He got out his flint, struck it against a rock, laid the smoldering wick on the tobacco and dragged on the pipe.

153

"I'd really like to climb some of these mountains," I said.

My companion was lying on his stomach on the grass. He picked up his gun and sighted something. I followed the direction of the barrel and noticed a grey structure on the steep hill beyond the river. It resembled a cupola. Then I, too, took aim. I felt someone barely touch my arm. It was the old guide, cautioning me not to be hasty.

"There can't be anyone there, can there?" I had not seen a soul. He smiled and replied.

"If the earth could speak, my son, would it tell you whether there was anyone there or not?"

"What do you mean?"

He tamped down the tobacco with his thumb, raised his head, looked off at the strange structure and sighed. "Well, I'm no historian. Through the centuries my people have let their bards sing of our joys and sorrows. Then white-haired old men like me pass the songs and legends down for future generations. This has always been our way, and that is why my people will never forget their heroes. I'm sorry for those who are nameless and whose names go into the grave with them."

I tried to guess what he was driving at, lay down my gun and turned to face him. I felt he wanted to tell me about something of importance and was thinking of a way to begin. But why did he seem upset? Perhaps he had witnessed some terrible drama, an often occurrence in these parts in the past? At any rate, I wanted to hear what he had to say. "Why'd you think I was aiming at the cupola?"

"There's no other target over there."

"What's so wrong about aiming at it?"

"Maybe nothing. But you shouldn't."

My companion had long since laid down his gun. He was listening to our conversation.

"You see, son, you young people should take good care of that structure. It's a monument to the past." He was silent for a moment and then continued, pointing to the top of the hill: "There was once a large settlement over there. Girls used to come down the winding paths to the spring for water at daybreak. It's difficult to imagine it now. One day that cupola will crumble and then no one will ever know that there were people here once."

"Is it a tomb?" I asked, interrupting his train of thought.

He was in no hurry to reply, but knocked the ashes from his pipe, stuck his hand into his pocket, pulled out his pouch and began filling it again. Finally, he spoke: "It's a very long story, son."

"We're in no hurry."

He exhaled the acrid white smoke and embarked on his tale. "See that mound?" He pointed to the edge of the field across the river. "There used to be houses and outbuildings starting from there and all along the bank right up the cupola. Nothing was ever planted over here. This is where the cattle was put to pasture. See that crooked old plane tree? There were shops there, though not many." He fell silent again. "I was twelve or thirteen at the time. The village was called Yaradulu. The elder's name was Bairam-uzbashi. He was a red-faced, beardless, stocky man with a terrible temper and a hatred for all the poor people of the village. They always tried to keep out of his way. He was in the habit of strolling through the village, carrying a long whip. The women avoided his gaze, the men

154

tried not to appear on the village square, not even on Sundays. The children would scare each other by shouting: 'Bairam-uzbashi's coming!'

"He used to ride to town on Thursdays, and when he and his escort of Cossacks returned it was as if brigands were galloping down the road. Bairam-uzbashi never let a shepherd, a peasant or a woman pass without having his fun. If he noticed a good karakul hat he would wink at the Cossacks, and one of them would spur his horse and snatch it off the man's head. There was no stopping Bairam-uzbashi. He was the lord and master there.

"On Fridays he would go down to the spring and sit there for hours, staring at the girls and young women carrying their pitchers on their shoulders as they came for water. He would often annoy them. If he took a special liking to a girl, he'd tell his men to kidnap her. Or he would ask a pretty girl for a drink of water and then grab her the moment she came close enough. If a girl or a young woman resisted, he'd make sure that she and her family paid dearly for the snub. He'd accuse her brother, husband or father of stealing and then had them run out of the village or thrown in jail. Since he had official power over them, no one dared to go against him. The district police officer, Tatishvili, was of a mind with him. Everyone hated and feared the elder, and there was not a single decent soul who respected him. He could only count on the support of his flunkeys, the Cossacks, and on the tsarist officials, those embezzlers of public property and bribe-takers."

"I can see he was pretty much like a god," I remarked.

"Nothing halfway about it. He had absolute rule there. He was God. The peasants had no place to go to complain, and even if they did, who would listen to them? Some may have even tried to, but he was never reprimanded once by his superiors."

I wondered at the infinite patience of the villagers. "Go on with the story."

"Bairam-uzbashi had company every single day. He and his cutthroat band would have regular orgies, drinking themselves stupid. He kept getting fatter and fatter until he began to look like a hog. Whenever a peasant came to him with a request or a complaint, the man would vow by the mane or the hoof of the elder's horse, or even his cow, to convince the elder of the truth of what he was saying. They were simple-minded folk, and even vowed by the moustache or the hat of the elder. Even the mullahs, those so-called descendants of Mohammed, never once went against him, because they were afraid to arouse his anger. No matter what the elder said, they'd always nod and say: 'That's right.'

"I couldn't say that Bairam-uzbashi was a religious man and feared the wrath of Allah. He drank vodka, was an adulterer and played games of chance. He never fasted or prayed. But once in a while he'd wander into the mosque during prayers. He never sat cross-legged on the floor as the peasants did, but always had a chair brought out especially for him. I could go on and on, telling you about him."

We were silent, pondering over the old man's words. I decided that he had been carried away, as is sometimes the case with elderly people, and had forgotten about the strange cupola on the hill. As I was about to remind him of it, he resumed his story:

"One day I saw everyone running towards the village square. The women who were standing on the roofs of their adobe houses were looking at the square and beating their heads and knees in anguish. I followed the crowd." The old man dragged on his pipe. We could see he was hesitant to recall some terrible event of

155

the past. "What we saw there was inhuman. I never imagined such a thing could have happened.

"Several days before the blacksmith Lachin had shot at a Cossack who had been annoying his betrothed. Lachin knew what lay in store for him and disappeared from the village. Now Bairam-uzbashi was taking it out on Lachin's mother. The unfortunate woman was dragged to the square and tied to a tree. Then they shaved her head, put a black cloth over her face and began whipping her, no matter that she was a woman of over sixty. Bairam-uzbashi had found himself a vantage point on a rise and kept shouting to the Cossacks to whip her as hard as they could. The lashes fell upon the woman's bruised body as Bairam-uzbashi roared like some crazed beast:

"'Hey! Where are you? You who shot at my Cossack! Why don't you come to the rescue? Let's see how brave you are!' Then he turned to the moaning woman and said: 'You're being whipped on account of your son. I'm waiting for him to come and protect you. Well? Where is the dog? You think there's no law left? That anyone can do as he likes? You think you can get away with anything? I'll show you what law and order are!'

"Everyone was too terrified to move. No one came forth to defend her. The people feared for their lives and the lives of their kin. There would be no mercy for anyone who stood up for her. That cursed fear paralysed them. Then a brave man appeared. I shall never forget that scene. His courage gave me new faith in my fellow-men."

The old man scratched around in the bowl of his pipe again. My companion lay on his back, looking up at the sky. I thought he was miles away and had no idea of what we were talking about. Suddenly, he raised his head and said:

"Well? Go on. What happened?"

The old man lit his pipe for a third time. "He was just like any other man, but I've never known anyone as bold. Bairam-uzbashi had barely finished speaking when a man dressed in rags and with a dirty bandana tied around his head stepped forward. He was carrying a sickle. The jagged steel of the blade glinted when he raised his arm quickly. Bairam-uzbashi fell like a rotten tree. There was a great commotion on the square. People jostled each other in their haste to escape from the scene of the crime, so as not be numbered among the witnesses, who certainly could not look forward to having an easy time. A small group of startled Cossacks and several villagers who were bolder than the rest clustered around the headless body of Bairam-uzbashi. 'What a blade! It cut off his head at a stroke!' one of them said. The terrible elder of but a moment ago was now a headless corpse."

My companion prompted: "Who was the reaper?"

"A very brave man. His big heart had absorbed the hatred and wrath of the entire village, of every man, woman and child. He was from our district." There was no mistaking the pride in his voice. "His name was Lachin, which means Falcon. He was the old woman's son. His body lies under the grey cupola on the hilltop. It is a sacred spot, not to be used for target practice."

"We didn't know," my companion said ruefully.

I seemed to have come awake after having had a terrible nightmare filled with the horrors of the past when the rich ruled the people as they wished.

Evening had crept up on us. The sun had set beyond the mountains and the moon, a glittering sliver, now rose in the sky.

156

"So Lachin was arrested," I said.

"No, he disappeared as quickly as he'd appeared. He was gone without a trace. A long time after, one of Bairam-uzbashi's former soldiers came upon him sleeping at the edge of a forest. He struck Lachin with his axe and killed him. No one remembers the murderer's name, but Lachin will never be forgotten. There is no village there any more, but whenever the people pass by his grave they think of the brave young hero. Yes, he was a freedom-loving Falcon at a time when black ravens ruled the land," the old man concluded.

In the stillness that followed we could hear our horses tearing up little clumps of fresh grass and frog croaking on the river bank.

I was still under the spell of the old man's story and felt I could actually see young Lachin coming down the mountain, a simple peasant who had risen up against evil and tyranny to defend human rights.

The old man was also looking at Mt. Munguz. His beard seemed very white in the gloom, and his eyes sparkled. I gazed at him with tenderness, for here was a true preserver of the history of my people.

Yusif Shirvan
(b. 1910)

Shirvan's favourite theme is the romanticism and heroism in the life of modern-day youth. He describes the studies, labour and noble impulses of his friends, the young men and women of Azerbaijan at work on the fields of collective farms, on the celebrated Neftyanye Kamni, in the city by the blue waves of the Caspian, and on major construction projects. "First Night" is one of Shirvan's finest stories about a youthful contemporary, a "hero of our times".

Dedicated to two of the discoverers of Nef-
tyanye Kamni: Fuad Samedov, laureate of the
Lenin Prize, and Kurban Abbasov, Hero of
Socialist Labour.

First Night

Scores of people crowded the small pier: red-cheeked young women, delicate girls, grey-haired mothers, youths, and mature men. "Have a good trip!" they called out. From time to time one heard: "As soon as you get there, let us know!" "Don't worry about us!" "Until we meet again!"

Aidyn alone scanned the borders of the crowd, hoping to see Nailia.

Until last evening he too had a person dear to him, one who inspired dreams and filled his heart with gladness. Suddenly a storm broke out.

All day they had been together. But that evening when Aidyn told Nailia that the next morning he would leave for Neftyanye Kamni, she frowned.

"Before I took that for a joke. Then suddenly I saw that the joke wasn't funny. What now? Everything is clear to me. You're deliberately going there. Evidently you wish to part with me."

"I'm not going to Neftyanye Kamni to play games, or to amuse myself. I've told you that time and again. I'm going there to work. I must go."

159

"To work!... And I suppose you can't find work on dry land? You can't work in Lok-Batana, in the Bay, even on Peschany Island? If I didn't know you so well I wouldn't speak this way now. You're always seeking out adventures. You're a romantic. Well I hope you realise that it's too late to be Kurban or Kaverochkin. They were the first to explore the area, but now everything has been explored. For a long time now, we've been extracting oil. Remember how many years ago they drilled the first well. There is no more romanticism. It ended with them. Now there's no difference whether you work there or here in the Bay."

Upon hearing this Aidyn burst out laughing. Nailia stood, her nerves on edge.

"You laugh! But I'm serious about this. I don't want that kind of life. Half the time we would be separated. I won't be imprisoned in that kind of life."

"Nailia, you must be joking."

"Absolutely not. This is my final decision. For a month I've told you the same thing. I'm repeating it for the last time. I don't want to spend all my time looking out the window, fearing for you. Each time when the wind rose, I would think: I wonder how they're doing today, what is happening. There would be eternal fear and terrible nightmares. No, I don't want my life to waste away from the waiting and fear. We were close friends, but all that is finished. Forget me! I won't make you choose me or your work. That would be ridiculous. Aidyn, I feel that your duty, your career, your work is dearer and more important to you than I am. That is your business. I don't have the right to forbid you to think that way."

A lump rose in Aidyn's throat. He could only answer: "Nailia, what are you saying?" But the girl continued without listening to him:

"They say that the heart is glass. Your decision has shattered my glass heart into a thousand splinters. They can't be glued together again. You can't glue them together. Everything is finished. You can go now."

Upon saying this, Nailia left swiftly.

* * *

Aidyn slept badly that night. For hours his mind wandered. He did not think about parting with his beloved girl-friend. He did not even believe that he had been spurned once and for all. He hoped Nailia would relent and regret her decision. For hours he listened for the ringing of the telephone. He waited for Nailia to call.

None of his hopes materialised. Just before morning he drifted off to sleep. Then at seven thirty he phoned Nailia's home. He was informed that she was still sleeping.

Half an hour later, already holding his suitcase and ready to leave, he called again. This time a gentle female voice answered: "She's gone to work!"

The laboratory where Nailia worked was close to their home. She never left the house before eight o'clock. "Maybe she went to the landing to see me off," Aidyn thought. He quickly took leave of his mother and left the house. But Nailia was not waiting on the pier.

At nine o'clock the steamer left port. During the preceding hour he had scanned the entire landing. Each person to arrive seemed at first to be Nailia, then came close enough for him to realise that he had been mistaken.

Now the ship, rounding the harbour and emitting a stream of water like a small fountain from its stern, proceeded on course. Aidyn's head spun. He closed his eyes and held on to the rail. At last feeling that the ship rolled along the waves rhythmically, he opened his eyes.

He was not alone on the deck. It was crowded. One red-cheeked youth played a pleasant *mugam* * on a small accordion. Several people gathered around to listen. Three or four young chaps stood some distance away, and, looking toward Peschany Island, quarrelled among themselves about something. The derricks scattered along Ilyich Bay moved swiftly away from them and gradually began to sway to and fro. Mount Bailov and Mount Bibi-Eibat slowly sank beneath the horizon.

The sea which had been smooth as a mirror in the Gulf of Baku looked different here. It was no longer calm. But the large steamer paid no heed and moved along the path spread for it by the morning sun, keeping a course to the east.

Aidyn remained standing on the deck. Just as a burn grows more painful with time, the bitterness of parting increases as time passes. Still the steamer continued, carrying him forward.

When the steamer had passed the Apsheron Peninsula and entered the open sea, it began to rock more and more. The sea grew rougher. Grey storm clouds chased each other hard across the sky. All this only added to Aidyn's misery.

The ship at last reached Neftyanye Kamni. They docked at the harbour long past noontime.

This was not Aidyn's first visit. As a student he came here several times for practical training. The last time he had stayed over a month. Each time he arrived with his fellow-students and with teachers assigned to conduct the training sessions. Now he was alone, no longer a student coming for practice, but a specialist, a geologist. Here he would seek out new treasures together with the experienced geologists who had discovered these secrets of the depths, this mineral wealth.

On shipboard no one had paid any attention to him, but ashore the man on duty smiled as he checked Aidyn's papers and said: "Welcome to Neftyanye Kamni!" After this he told him the address where Aidyn should report. Aidyn wasn't so much pleased by this behaviour as soothed. The sadness that had oppressed him since morning weighed a little less heavily on his mind. At the quarters of the head geologist he was received even more cordially. As soon as the young secretary heard his name, she showed him to a seat and asked about his "sea voyage". Aidyn didn't feel like admitting that the heavy seas had tormented him for the last two hours. So he answered simply:

"Not a bad trip."

The girl scrutinised the sea through the large open window. "You were lucky," she said. "Today the sea is relatively calm."

"Today the sea is relatively calm...." The words seemed strange to Aidyn. He looked through the window and it seemed to him that the girl must be joking. Beyond the window waves reared up high into the air and came crashing forward with a roar. The large building shook as though there was an earthquake, and a deafening rumble filled the air without cease.

Aidyn asked when he could see the head geologist.

"Right now he's taking the place of the director of the oil-works and is out at

* *Mugam* — a folk song. — *Ed.*

sea. It's quite likely that you won't be able to see him today. But he'll be here tomorrow morning at eight."

With these words the girl picked up the phone, informed someone that a new geologist had arrived, and asked where he might spend the night. Evidently she wasn't pleased with the response.

"No, no.... Only in the place where our geologists and engineers are living. The place you're speaking of is crowded and uncomfortable. I can't send him there. Then wait a minute and I'll consult with the deputy director."

She made another call, requesting that the new geologist be housed in dormitory No. 3. The answer appeared to be positive. She smiled and then began to argue that the newcomer should be given a single room.

"I have to argue with them every time. They simply cannot understand that there's no place for bureaucracy at Neftyanye Kamni. I've got you a place in a good dorm and what's more — a good room. The windows face south. True, it's a double room, but your roommate sailed to the mainland yesterday. For ten days you'll be living by yourself. Do you know the building?"

Aidyn confined his answer to a shrug of his shoulders.

"In that case I'll show you myself."

"Don't bother. Just give me the directions and I'll find my way."

The girl paid no attenion to these words. "Come on," she said, as she rose from her seat.

* * *

As they walked, the girl, assuming that Aidyn was here for the first time, recounted the history of Neftyanye Kamni and described how it was to live there.

To a newcomer this seems like a terrible place. His heart sinks, but then after a little while he gets used to it. Those people who return to the city really get homesick for this place.

"You seem awfully pensive. Perhaps you're sorry that you came here...."

"No, no.... Just the opposite.... The seas were a little rough. That's the reason."

The girl looked at the sea and said with amazement: "You think these are 'rough' seas? You've never seen the Caspian when it's rough! True, today's weather forecast predicted a light gale. But nothing serious will come of it. Last year we had a gale like that. Now what *I* call a storm," the girl extended her hand toward the open sea. "Look there. About half a kilometre from us they were drilling. During the gale, before our very eyes, the drilling platform sunk to the bottom of the sea. The workers were rescued with great difficulty. On that day the waves overflowed the dike. However no one was frightened. Work continued everywhere. On that day our chief again replaced the director of the oil-works. He was at sea for eight hours and working together with everyone. He visited all the oil-works and there were a few faced with tremendous danger. Once the launch that he used for getting around the stations overturned. The head geologist swam to the platform. In fact he carried one of the drillers who couldn't swim back to shore with him. That's what *I* call a storm. That's what happens when the Caspian is 'agitated'. But this? Our boys don't pay any mind to these waves. They don't consider them 'waves'."

Aidyn liked the way she told her story — calmly, with enthusiasm but without agitation.

The girl led him to a building constructed on one of the new steel islands. There were many such buildings here. The spacious room on the second floor pleased Aidyn. The girl left. In a little while the girl on duty had made up his bed and announced: "There you go."

The moment he was left to himself, bitter feelings began to pain him again. For a long time after the secretary had left him, her image hovered before his eyes. Her description of the gale, of the terrifying seas as though these were an ordinary occurrence forced him to think. Involuntarily Aidyn compared her to Nailia.

Nailia was a physician. She had completed her education. The secretary seemed younger. Perhaps she had not even finished high school. She worked at Neftyanye Kamni, far from Baku, surrounded by violent waves and terrifying gales. How coolly she reacted to the difficult life!

Twilight had come. Aidyn nevertheless did not turn on the light. He remained standing at the window, deep in thought. He didn't like the bloody colour of the thick clouds gathering to the south-west. It meant that tonight, or at the latest tomorrow, the weather would get much worse.

He had not yet got down to work. He did not know where he would be working: in what sector, on what drilling platform. He had heard a lot about the head geologist. As a student in the institute he had heard about the great part played by this man in prospecting in the area of Neftyanye Kamni. In the newspapers the head geologist was described as a bold man. Aidyn had seen his name among those of other Azerbaijanian oil workers on the list of men awarded the Lenin Prize in the preceding year. He had imagined the head geologist as a man of medium height, robust, with a powerful build. But that same year, when he arrived at Neftyanye Kamni for practical training, he discovered that the head geologist was tall, and extraordinarily thin, with an oblong face, that he had a habit of inclining his head to one side, that he spoke to everyone calmly with a smiling face. Aidyn realised that his imagination had erred. Later he witnessed the strong will and boldness of the head geologist who had, at first glance, impressed him as a weak, feeble person.

Aidyn had come to look upon the head geologist — his work, his actions, his authority in the collective — with great respect. Later he resolved to emulate the head geologist, to work the way he did. He set himself a goal: to be like the head geologist in every way. This explained why, upon graduation from the institute, he announced that he wanted to work only at Neftyanye Kamni, thereby provoking Nailia's anger.

It was already eight o'clock when he realised that he was very hungry and went to the cafeteria.

After dining, he went out on the square. Several administrative buildings, stores, and a clubhouse stood on this square, the largest at Neftyanye Kamni. All around the square, bushes and flowers were growing in enormous planters giving the square the appearance of a public garden. Gaily coloured benches adorned the square. A loud-speaker hanging on one pole broadcast light music. Nearby ten or twelve youths and two girls who had heard the music congregated.

Aidyn knew no one here. So when he wanted to cross the square, he kept close to the buildings and, catching sight of a brightly illuminated cinema, headed in that direction.

The auditorium was not crowded. That day they were showing a tastelessly done film. The wheels of a speeding train rolled endlessly across the rails amidst darkness and a constant procession of telegraph poles. A lot of time was devoted to showing how two passengers, seated in the lurching carriage, drank vodka and conversed. One was disturbed and lost in thought. He told how he was going to work the virgin lands. His wife had opposed the idea, not being eager to leave Moscow. So he had divorced her. As he spoke, he frequently filled his glass with vodka and drained it.

Aidyn suddenly realised that there was something in common between this man and himself. But he, Aidyn, would never seek consolation in a glass of vodka. And he would never forget Nailia.

Aidyn became angry with this man and with the director who had made such a weak film. He did not wait to see the end, and left the cinema. Already it was eleven o'clock. The square was empty. The wind, which had managed to grow stronger, battered the flowers in the large planters, tearing off their petals. All seemed to be trying to hurl the flowers in their boxes into the sea. Telephone lines and electric wires howled like hungry wolves; the waves gnawed at the steel piles beneath the square. Aidyn saw nothing better to do than return to his room. When he had passed the cafeteria and came into the open he felt the full strength of the wind. He clutched at the brim of his hat with one hand so that the wind would not carry it away. To keep his footing, he grabbed onto the railings along the road. Suddenly he heard the honking of a car. He pressed against the rails. Two buses crammed with passengers rode along the dike giving off sounds that seemed like a hollow knocking along the planking of the piles. They were headed for the drilling stations which from a distance flickered in the raging sea as though they were blinking. Shortly thereafter a car loaded down with pipes passed Aidyn. At the entrance to the dormitory he encountered a group of about fifteen persons. All were wearing the helmets of oil workers. All were in their working coveralls. All wore heavy boots. Aidyn greeted them — all were still strangers to him — and continued down the corridor. Then he noticed that a bus had pulled up to the dormitory and that these people boarded it.

He entered his room. From the room next door came the sounds of a radio turned to a programme of songs by Byul-Byul-ogly specially prepared for the anniversary of Fizuli's birth. Leaning against the window he began to listen to that unforgettable voice.

Below, the merciless sea beat against the pilings; the blows of the waves grew increasingly stronger. Through the din came the majestic voice of Byul-Byul, filling the heart and caressing the ear.

Against his will he suddenly remembered Nailia and her parting words which like an axe had severed the threads of his hopes and love. His heart sank within him. He tried to drive such thoughts from his mind. But Nailia's angry eyes, welling with tears, her trembling lips and nervous face would not fade away; her image rose before him as though living. Her biting words rang in his ears. He almost cried out. During this time several cars were approaching the building from the opposite side. Two cars stopped in front of the dormitory. Some twenty men emerged from them: they were smeared with oil and clay. Evidently they had just come off duty. They headed for the wide front doors. Shortly afterward their steps resounded along the corridor and doors creaked throughout the building.

Time passed, a few minutes in all, and the noise decreased. Aidyn lay in bed.

In the middle of the night he was awakened by a great din. Doors slammed and hurried footsteps filled the hall. Heavy boots resounded against the plank floors.

Aidyn sat up in bed. It seemed the wind and waves had grown still more violent. He remembered that at such times, in case of an accident, people run to help, regardless of their calling or position. So he quickly dressed and followed two workers who were slipping into their mackintoshes as they went. A truck stood by the doors of the building. Everyone who exited boarded this truck. The truck in front of it was already filled with passengers. Someone's voice could be heard from inside it:

"Hurry up!" came the command.

A passer-by, looking at Aidyn, said: "Don't get under foot. If you're going, get in the truck."

His voice roused Aidyn, who leaped into the truck. The truck took off. Its passengers seemed to maintain a deliberate silence. As though guarding a secret, they did not speak of what had taken place. When they passed utility poles, Aidyn caught a quick glimpse of their faces. He noted that they were frowning and guessed that something serious and extraordinary had occurred.

The truck turned off the central platform onto a narrow road leading to another platform. It continued for several minutes then stopped at a small square. The passengers poured from the truck onto the platform. Aidyn got out with them. They were met by a few men. One whose face was hardly visible in the dim light, said, with evident exhaustion: "Get into the cutter as quickly as you can. The electricity has been cut off from six drilling stations. They can't even pull the bits from the holes."

The cutter, tied to the pole from which a lantern hung, rocked mightily. People hopped in. And Aidyn hopped in. He was aware that at such times even a little help was a source of strength. A tall man was the last to spring into the cutter. He made his way to the bow and stood scanning the horizon ahead. The cutter spurted from the dike and speeded through the pitch-black waves.

For the first few minutes Aidyn was distraught. He wondered, could he do something, help in some way at the site of the accident?

The farther the cutter sailed from the pier, the more the waves hurled it up in the air and then down again. Each time the cutter rose and fell, Aidyn closed his eyes in fear and then sighed deeply. Despite the strong resistance of the waves, the cutter speeded forward. Before them, amidst these waves, emerged a drilling platform. At times it vanished, and then appeared and seemed to approach their boat. Its lanterns came closer and shone more clearly. At last they reached the drilling platform. The motor's rumbling died down as the cutter decreased its speed. The man who had remained standing at the cutter's bow called out:

"Ahoy! Mardan! Can you hear me?"

Amid the thundering of wind and waves came an answer:

"Ahoy! We hear you! Be careful! Keep the cutter farther out or you'll hit the piling...."

"What's happening?"

"We pulled the bit from the hole. We're getting ready to change it, but I'm afraid that we're not going to get any electricity."

"What do you hear from platform 315?"

"Nothing since the current was cut off. Their transmitter isn't working."

"Do you need anything?"

165

"Nothing right now. But if you can, tomorrow morning send us water and cigarettes."

"Will do. Don't worry. Tell the boys hello. Tell them to hold tight and not be frightened by the gale."

"Don't worry about us...."

"Roger. We're heading for 315."

"Good luck. And be careful!"

The cutter tore loose of its moorings and took off. Soon some black sea monster took shape before them.

"Must be the drilling platform," said someone.

"Right. That's 315. Hold tight to the rudder ... we'll put in here. There might have been an accident right on this spot."

"Did they transmit a message?"

"Since early morning their transmitter hasn't been working. But the neighbouring drilling platforms have been complaining that their current's not flowing. Probably there was an accident at this platform."

A powerful wave drenched the men in the cutter. Aidyn could taste the bitter water on his lips. The cutter rose in the air and then fell. Close before them appeared the outline of the drilling platform. A thin, tall man, holding those around him by the shoulders, stood erect:

"Akhmed! Akhmed! Can you hear us?"

"Yes, yes. We hear you," came an anxious voice from the drilling platform.

"Are you all alive and well over there?"

"Yes, yes ... alive and well."

"How are things with you? What's the situation?"

"What? I can't hear you."

"I said, how are things, what's the situation? How come the current isn't flowing? Did the transformer burn out? What's going on?"

"No, no ... nothing burned out. We're not getting any electricity from 275. There's a light at that platform. Probably the cable broke."

"Why isn't your transmitter working?"

"It stopped working early this morning. The tubes must have burnt out."

"How are the bits?"

"The bit is deep in the ground. We were drilling when the electricity was cut off. Probably the filling hasn't hardened around the hole yet."

"Do you have water and bread?"

"Can't hear you!"

The cutter nearly capsized. The helmsman changed directions. The tall man repeated his question.

"Thanks! Don't worry. We don't need anything. Just give us electricity before the filling hardens or else the pipes will be stuck down there."

The tall, thin man was already turning to the pilot:

"Take the cutter farther out and anchor it, Nadyr. Can you hear me? We'll have to dive in and swim over to the platform. There we can get the cable and bring it back. We can turn around slowly then and see where the break is. I know it isn't easy to dive into the water in a storm like this. But we have no choice. Can you do it?"

"I'll do it. But the cable's so heavy, I'm afraid it will weigh me down and prevent me from swimming. In any case, if I can't do it, I'll let you know."

Aidyn aroused himself.

"If you'll allow me, I'll go into the water and look for the cable with him. Just tell me where it lies in relation to the drilling platform."

A swift enormous wave delayed the answer.

"Damn water gets right down your throat. Comrade, I can't see your face and I don't recognise your voice. Please identify yourself."

Aidyn gave his name and the reason of his arrival at Neftyanye Kamni.

"Aidyn ... Aidyn.... Sounds familiar. Are you a good swimmer?"

"I'm a superb swimmer. You don't have to worry about me."

From the left came a voice: "I'll dive into the water. This comrade is a novice. He has no experience in such situations."

"Don't worry about me. I can stay in the water as long as necessary."

The tall man joined the discussion.

"If there are two men in the water it can't hurt. You can help each other. We'll be waiting close by. You won't lose touch with us."

Without waiting for orders, Aidyn took off his street clothes.

"I'm ready."

"I'm ready too, Comrade Aidyn. Listen to me. Stick close to me," said Nadyr and jumped into the water. Aidyn waited until the cutter rose on the waves and jumped in after him.

"Can you hear me?"

"I hear you."

"Swim behind me so that we don't lose sight of each other."

Aidyn could see nothing. He only heard Nadyr's voice. And from time to time he felt his hands touching him.

Nadyr swam up to one of the piles and grasped it tightly.

"I've reached the drilling platform. Be careful. Don't let the waves throw you against the piles. Hold onto me. That's it. Now let's find that cable."

Evidently the men on the drilling platform heard their voices. A hoarse voice responded: "Go to this side. The cable begins here."

Although Aidyn held firmly to the pile with one hand, the waves tossed him up and down. From Nadyr's voice he gauged the direction and, holding onto the piles, began to swim behind him. Suddenly he heard Nadyr's loud cry:

"Be careful! Watch that the waves don't knock you against the piles!"

Aidyn shifted carefully, trying to keep his back to the waves. In a little while Nadyr's voice was right alongside him.

"I found the end of the cable. Give me your hand. Here. Hold on. Don't be afraid. It won't come loose. Got it?"

Aidyn held onto the cable at the place where it was attached to the pile. Before he could answer, a wave swept over his head, filling his mouth with bitter water. He began to cough.

"Boys! What's happened? Why aren't you speaking?"

"We've found the end of the cable and we're swimming over to you."

Aidyn couldn't see the cutter. But he heard Nadyr's voice clearly.

"Follow me. Hold on tight to that cable. If..." Nadyr's voice faded out. A large wave lifted Aidyn into the sky. Suddenly he felt that a burden had been lifted from him. He realised that the cable had slipped from his hands.

"Nadyr, where are you?"

"Here I am. I let go of the cable. But you hold on tight."

167

Aidyn, not answering him, dove into the water. He spread his arms wide and began to circle around beneath the surface. He had no idea how long he stayed under water. His arms were already weakening when he felt the cable with his fingers. But he couldn't grasp it right away. He had to circle around one more time beneath the surface. This time he grasped the cable firmly and surfaced.

"Comrade Nadyr! Where are you?"

Nadyr's voice was already distant. But another voice close by rang out: "Here we are! Swim over here." Aidyn heard the command clearly.

Having convinced himself that Nadyr was alive and well, Aidyn swam to the cutter. The waves swept him to one side. He could see nothing, but he heard voices from the cutter and tried to swim towards them.

In the east, the horizon slowly lost its dark colouring. This helped Aidyn make out the dim silhouette of the cutter. Holding onto the cable with one hand, he swam to the cutter. After prolonged torments at last he caught hold of the cutter.

Strong hands took the cable from him and lifted Aidyn onto the cutter. The weakened Aidyn fell as though he had been shot.

"Thank you. Comrade Aidyn. Nadyr, Nadyr! Where are you?"

From the other side of the cutter came Nadyr's voice. They pulled him into the boat.

"Ah, so you're here too? Even though the cable tore loose from my hands I didn't worry. I figured that you were holding tight."

Aidyn's voice trembled. Through his chattering teeth he managed to speak: "I let go of the cable too."

"How did you find it?"

"It wasn't easy. I had to dive down several times into the water."

"The cable's broken off here," said another voice.

Then came the voice of the tall, thin man. "Stop the cutter here and drop anchor," he commanded. "Now we'll have to search for the other end of the cable."

"Let's go over to 275," suggested someone. "There we can take up the cable, go in this direction, and find the other end."

"A good suggestion. But it's going to be hard to keep the cable on the surface while we sail over there, find the other end and come back here again. It will be simpler to dive for the other end. Murad, lengthen the end of the cable a few metres ... five or six should do it. Kerim, get ready. Aidyn and Nadyr are tired. Now you go into the water."

Nadyr protested. He stood up and leaped into the water. Aidyn, not waiting for orders, also rose and leaped after him. Soon he held onto Nadyr's hand. Both began to search for the end of the cable.

Filling his lungs with air, Aidyn dived deep into the water. The water was still pitch-black. Nothing was visible. It was hard to get one's bearings. After Aidyn had dived and surfaced several times, he felt the cable. He grasped it with his right hand. With only his left hand free he began to swim with the current. When he lifted his head from the water, the first thing he saw was the horizon. But the cutter was a good distance away. With one hand he held firmly to the end of the cable, that was pulling him down, and swam towards the cutter. The clouds lay almost on the surface of the sea. But the sea, meandering like a snake, did not permit the clouds to lay right on its surface. There was some space between the sea and the clouds. The redness of the dawn like molten steel pouring from a blast-furnace, flowed out and filled the space between the black waves and the grey storm clouds. Now the drilling platforms scattered about the sea could be clearly discerned.

The men in the cutter, noticing that he was having a difficult time swimming to them, took up the anchor and sailed as close to him as the cable, whose end was in the cutter, would permit. Seeing that the cutter sailed towards him, Aidyn summoned all his strength, but the cable kept dragging him down.

Suddenly it seemed to him that a huge piece broke loose from the grey storm clouds and fell on his head. His head vanished in the clouds. The waves embraced him more tightly, and the strong hands of the sea began to pull him down, to the bottom. But the clouds didn't want to let him go. A struggle began between the waves and the clouds. The weight of this struggle lay on his shoulders.

* * *

When he opened his eyes he was in a rather large, bright room, lying in bed amid snow-white sheets. At his head sat two women and a man dressed in white gowns. The moment Aidyn's eyes opened, the man let go of his hand and breathed deeply: "The crisis has passed." Turning to one of the women, he continued: "Give him an infusion. Then leave him in peace. Let him rest. It he feels like eating give him some chicken bouillon. I'll come by later on."

Upon this, the stout man left the room. Aidyn glanced at the black-eyed woman who was gazing at him solicitously and asked at length: "Was I taken ill?"

"No. But you were floundering in water all night."

"Is this a hospital?"

"Yes."

"When did they bring me here?"

"Three hours ago.... For three hours we've been trying to bring you round. You've got a strong heart or we would have had a bad time of it."

"What time is it now?"

The black-eyed woman looked at a clock. "Eight-thirty. But we've talked enough for now. It's time for you to rest. You'll probably be staying here for several days."

"Nothing of the kind! I'm not ill. I haven't even been to the place where I'm going to work. I have to get down to work. I have no intention of staying here...."

A familiar voice was heard beside him.

"Last night at 2 a.m. you got down to work." It was the voice that had taken command and given orders to everyone through the night in dusk. Aidyn turned to face it. There stood the head geologist. One of the conquerors of Neftyanye Kamni. Exhaustion was evident on his face.

The head geologist took Aidyn's hand in his big bony hand and squeezed it gently. "We owe you much thanks. You helped us enormously last night. It almost seemed as though you were sent precisely to help us."

Aidyn was not able to answer him.

The black-eyed woman whispered: "He's very tired. He must be left alone."

* * *

When Aidyn opened his eyes for the second time the sun had already illuminated the room through the window on the opposite side. This time beside the black-eyed woman stood the secretary. Her large, almond-shaped eyes gazed tenderly on Aidyn.

"Hello, Comrade Aidyn. Good afternoon.... I came to congratulate you. We received a telegramme from the ministry conveying official gratitude to you and Nadyr." The secretary paused and, altering her voice, added: "There were two calls from home. They asked for you. I don't know who Nailia is, but she's very worried. I was obliged to tell her that you were out at sea. Nailia asked if you would call her when you returned...."

Nailia.... Nailia. She had turned from him because he had come here, to Neftyanye Kamni. She had told him that he, Aidyn, must forget about her. And then suddenly, she had called him, not once, but twice.... Aidyn shot a glance full of gratitude to the secretary who looked very much like Nailia. He smiled. The girl smiled back and handed him a bunch of narcissuses which she had hidden behind her back. Aidyn took the bouquet and, to his own surprise, asked: "Is your name Nargis?"

"No. My name is Firangis. They brought me the narcissuses today from the mainland, from Mardakyany."

Mardakyany.... He had met Nailia in that summer settlement, at the holiday home. That was in February. Many narcissuses grew in the garden of the holiday home. Every day he presented Nailia with one flower. On the day he was to leave, Nailia gave him a bunch of narcissuses. A bouquet just like this one....

From that time on, Nailia always sent him a large bunch of narcissuses on his birthday.

170

Music resounded from the radio. A man sang with a pleasant, gentle voice: "My love is in the sea...."

He smiled again and his heart began to beat anxiously. The room seemed magnificent to him, the nurse and the secretary—tender and dear. It seemed to him that morning had come only at this time. The gloomy weather that began yesterday morning was beginning to lift.

Abulhasan
Alekperzade
(b. 1906)

Alekperzade was first published when still a student. The theme of his earlier stories is the formation of new psychological attitudes and a new morality; he also comes out for the liberation of Azerbaijanian women from restrictive, customary social roles.

In 1930 Abulhasan wrote Ascent, *a novel dealing with collectivisation. A World Collapsing, writen in 1933, is an epic canvas of the Azerbaijanian people's fight to establish Soviet power.*

During World War II Abulhasan participated in the heroic defense of Sevastopol. His wartime experiences are reflected in his novel Bastions of Friendship *which chronicles the struggle to liberate Sevastopol from the first battle to the triumphant deliverance of this city-hero. Abulhasan gives a vivid description of the role of an Azerbaijanian unit in battle. "Sing, Nightingale, Sing!" likewise deals with the Second World War. Here Abulhasan recounts the exploits of reconnaissance agents.*

Sing, Nightingale, Sing!

"Battery, fire!"

Long-range artillery fired a volley. Flames burst from the long gun barrels. Storehouses shook and the forest trembled. No sooner had the sky absorbed the roar of the guns when the order rang out anew:

"Fire!"

And the guns thundered again.

The signal rang out: "Aircraft approaching!"

Deftly, but without hurrying, the gunners moved their artillery 100 metres to the side.

Five enemy planes dropped twenty bombs. The earth seemed ready to split from the explosions. All around trees were uprooted.

But this time they were still unable to inflict perceptible losses. The enemy planes circled over the battery's encampment and then flew away.

The battery occupied its previous position. Once again the voice of the battery commander Akhmedov was heard: "Fire!"

So things had continued for ten days.

Everyone, from the commander to the private, rejoiced at the battery's successful operations. But artillery commander Sergeant Asker was particularly ecstatic. During the evening calm, he amazed everyone with his strange request. He would turn towards the forest and call: "Sing, my nightingale, sing!"

173

What was even more surprising, the timid, cautious song of a nightingale responded from the forest. If the nightingale was late in answering his request, Asker himself would begin to sing:

> My dear one, I pluck flowers
> And make rose water out of them;
> But if my nightingale dies,
> I will revenge him....

So each time, Asker would ask the nightingale to sing, and the bird, as though it understood this, would answer his request.

There was nothing miraculous here. True, the sergeant did not know the language of the birds, he had no idea where the nightingale made its nest. But he had studied the habits of this bird and, what is more, he knew that the nightingale should console people and help them forget their suffering.

The war continued and Death walked the earth. But Spring brought joy to the land, strewing its blossoms all about and spreading green carpets across the plains. The evenings turned a gentle orange, and to keep all this beauty company, Spring planted a nightingale at the tip of a tall poplar tree and ordered it to sing.

The sergeant felt spring with all his being. When his heart overflowed with feeling, he sang:

> I'm in love, I wait for spring,
> Like a letter from my beloved.
> The nightingale sings merrily
> Awaiting spring.

After this, the nightingale began to warble. Its song was like the babble of clear water on a hot day.

The entire detachment listened to the nightingale.

"How wonderful that our nightingale isn't frightened by the thunder of the guns and doesn't fly away."

Asker beat his chest and boasted: "I keep it here. If it weren't for me, the nightingale would have flown away long ago."

Several days later, early in the morning while the sergeant was preparing the artillery for battle, an owl hooted; the sound came from the same place where the nightingale's song was usually heard and it sent shivers up the sergeant's spine. Asker was no coward; he feared nothing and he had looked Death in the eye many a time, but now fear clutched at his heart.

The owl's cry didn't drown out the nightingale's song. Asker listened. He wanted to find out the location of the owl. Its wail rang out, now far away, now somewhere in the immediate vicinity.

Asker hated this bird; for him, it was a symbol of fascism and he was ready, if permitted, to bombard the cliff and turn everything upside down to force that cursed owl to be still once and for all....

Meanwhile the nightingale trilled diligently. He was not concerned with his terrible enemy or with anything in the world. Asker listened to the warbling of the nightingale and the wailing of the owl, fearing that in the end the nightingale would run out of breath. At times, he felt that he was afraid for himself rather than for the nightingale. He tried to convince himself that the owl was only an ordinary bird, that its terrifying voice was given it by nature, and that to take it for

174

an evil omen was giving in to superstition and ignorance. But his efforts to comfort himself were in vain. No matter how he reasoned he could not stop the pounding of his heart. He had a premonition that the owl would bring misfortune both to the nightingale and to himself, Asker, and his battery.

Akhmedov, the battery commander, found out about Asker's naive misgivings.

"Don't worry," he said. "We'll find that owl, destroy his nest, and then our battery's nightingale will sing again."

Enemy planes raided the battery several times that day. One soldier was seriously wounded during an attack.

Sergeant Asker hurriedly made his way over to Akhmedov.

"Comrade Commander," he said, "since that owl's made his nest here we've had bad luck."

Akhmedov also thought of the losses and failures. But his thoughts differed from the gloomy forebodings of Asker.

Early in the morning, the battery had hardly begun to shell behind enemy lines when a group of enemy bombers appeared above them. This time the bombs damaged a gun; several men were wounded and there were some casualties.

As soon as the explosions died down, the owl began to hoot. Although the battery commander was not a superstitious man, he too angrily exclaimed: "Damned bird!"

The rest of the day passed in melancholy silence. As though in mourning for the dead, the nightingale also was silent. But the owl rejoiced. Now its hooting echoed in the distance, now it seemed right beside the camp. The weather also raged at its screeching and turned gloomy; clouds covered the sky, the wind angrily shook the tree tops.

To the accompaniment of the wind, the battery commander said: "Get ready! We're abandoning this position after supper."

One of the detachment commanders who was friends with Akhmedov asked: "What, frightened of an owl?"

Sergeant Asker, depressed by the events of the day, asked an ostensibly casual question: "Are we leaving the nightingale?"

"It left before you," answered the commander.

"No, Comrade Commander. It didn't fly away. It was offended. That's why it doesn't sing."

Akhmedov restrained himself and did not rebuke Asker for his fancies. Asker went off by himself and sang:

> *I'm in love with a rose;*
> *The rose suffers when its petals fall off.*
> *Strange gardener, don't come into this garden —*
> *The nightingale will take offense, the rose will take*
> *offense.*

Everything was ready for their departure. Asker had already fastened his knapsack. Akhmedov, who had been keeping an eye on him all this time, said: "Come here."

Asker jumped up, smoothed his uniform and ran over.

"Yes, Comrade Commander!"

Akhmedov stared at the sergeant: "Where are you going?"

"Aren't we breaking camp, Comrade Commander?"

175

"You're going to stay."

The sergeant did not want the commander to repeat himself. "Very good, Comrade Commander!" he said, saluting.

"I'm leaving you here to catch that bird."

Asker smiled. At first it seemed to him that the commander was joking. Then he thought: "Why should he joke? We did speak about not abandoning the nightingale."

"Thank you, Comrade Commander," he said. "You know how precious this nightingale is...."

The commander interrupted him. "You're not going to catch the nightingale."

"Then let it be a quail.... It's hiding somewhere there, in the poppies or the wheat field and it sings without cease. I've travelled all through the Caucasus; I know fowlers and I've heard a lot of bird songs, but I've never heard such a pleasant call."

The sun had already set. Akhmedov could not see the sergeant's face, but he sensed his agitation.

"You're not going to catch any quails," he said gently. "Quails ... nightingales, what are they to us? Let them live in the wild and sing."

Asker was puzzled. Was the commander joking after all?

Akhmedov made things easy for him. "Don't waste your time guessing, Asker. You're going to catch that owl!"

"The owl?" Asker marvelled. "We're leaving, aren't we? Let it hoot to its heart's content. What would we do with an owl?"

"First, we'll catch it. Then we'll figure out what to do with it."

But he was obliged to explain a thing or two to the sergeant. Having given the necessary instructions and seen the sergeant off, Akhmedov summoned his deputy commander:

"Is the battery ready?" he asked. Upon hearing an answer to the affirmative he began to make the necessary preparations.

"Order the men to leave their guns as they are. Two or three carts should proceed down the stony road and make a lot of noise. Warn everyone not to make a sound after they leave. Post sentries and let everyone else sleep. The men who go with the carts should return along the other, sandy path. Have them wait a few hours. Make sure everything is quiet. Then we'll see what happens with our owl."

As soon as the rumbling of the carts died down, the owl screeched several times.

"Let it howl," thought Akhmedov. "It'll help the boys."

Neither the battery commander, the political instructor, nor the artillery commander slept that night. They sat and listened intently to the sounds of the night. Each wondered what hid behind that deceptive silence....

Suddenly there was a whistle from the cliff; a grenade exploded and someone yelled: "Hands up!"

Several shots rang out and then silence fell again. A pleasant lyrical voice cut through that silence:

> My dear one, the rose is lovely
> Until it's plucked!
> The nightingale will shed tears a hundred times
> Before it wins the rose in the garden.

176

"Asker is coming with his prey," whispered the political instructor.

And sure enough before ten minutes had passed, Asker appeared. He saluted and gave his report: "Comrade Commander, your order has been executed. We've caught the owls. But one didn't hold out...."

They entered the trench. Asker began a hurried account of the operation.

"As soon as the carts thundered into the distance they came out from their cover. We proceeded with caution. I took the lead and the men followed. We could hear the rumbling of the carts and a sort of rustling close by. The owls began to listen too. About ten paces from us I heard laughter and then a terrible wail. I kept mum. Two men were talking, quickly, curtly, like barking dogs. One went back into their shelter and began to transmit something on a radio. The second cried out a few times, imitating anowl, and then followed his friend. I signalled to the men to come close; I wanted to take the birds alive. But they heard us. One leaped out and threw a grenade.... I shot him. We took the second one intact."

They brought in the prisoner, a hefty chap. Even in the feeble light of the wick-lamp his fair hair and freckled face with its large square chin and green, treacherous eyes could be clearly seen. He did not conceal his gaze and looked about him like a cornered wolf.

Akhmedov pointed to the radio: "With regard to this, everything is clear. But why would he screech like an owl?"

The political instructor translated the commander's question. The enemy, without lifting his gaze, remained silent.

"Why, that was what betrayed you," continued Akhmedov.

The German only repeated the word: "Nachtingall.... Nachtingall...."

"He doesn't want to speak so let me explain it," interrupted Asker. "They were screeching to spite the nightingale. That dead orangutan did the screeching...."

The prisoner was led off to unit headquarters. Akhmedov passed through the battery and remarked to the political instructor: "Now we'll see an interesting battle. The enemy is relying on his 'owls'. But who'll tell him what's happening in the battery now?"

Dawn was near. A fresh wind blew. Like a delicate, graceful beauty, the thin crescent moon merged its pale light with that of the dawn. Dimly twinkling stars hid and melted into the brightening sky. The world luxuriated as though it had never known blood and suffering; it was drunk with the aroma of flowers. The birds had begun to sing, but their discordant chorus was not joined by the nightingale.

The nightingale was silent.

"Battery!" came the sharp warning command. The men shuddered. "Fire!"

The gunners did not allow the enemy to finish his dreams. Shells rained on the enemy. Shelters and command posts were destroyed; the explosions rooted out long-standing fortifications and trenches.

When the firing ceased, Asker went to one side. Not only he, but the whole battery thirsted to hear the nightingale.

"Sing, my nightingale, sing!" cried Asker just as he always did.

The nightingale was silent.

Others also called to it in vain.

The nightingale had disappeared.

The soldiers looked questioningly at the battery commander. Akhmedov took a few steps forward, then gave a long drawn-out shout: "Sing, our nightingale, sing!"

The nightingale was silent.

Below, in the wheat field, a quail trilled gaily and thrushes sang in the bushes. But the nightingale was silent.

Everyone expected that it would begin to sing and that soon they would hear its warbling that so delighted the soul.

There was no telling how long they might have waited had not a soldier holding a piece of paper approached Akhmedov.

"Comrade Commander, I found this in the pocket of the dead Fritz. Read it. Maybe it's important."

Akhmedov held the letter out to the political instructor: "You know German. Read it!"

The political instructor read the letter to himself. Everyone present, including Asker, saw his face grow darker and darker as he skimmed the lines.

"An owl, a real owl!" he said. "Listen to what he wrote." He began to read aloud: "My friend, you know that I can't endure birds, flowers and things of that nature. That nightingale began to make me nervous at night. We were sent here on a mission but he trills above us, pays no attention to bombs or shells, just sings and sings. The Red Army men love that bird. I began to screech like an owl to spite it. You know how owls are feared in the East; people hate them. I thought that the nightingale wouldn't be able to bear it, that it would fly from the owl's cry. Far from it!... Finally I went out to hunt the nightingale down. I wore a Soviet uniform. The artillery rumbled in the distance and so it was easy to shoot the nightingale. It didn't die immediately. But in this country you can't pity even the birds. I smothered it with my foot. In a few hours we'll cross back to our side; I'll take the dead nightingale with me so that together with this letter, you'll receive a dead Crimean nightingale from me."

For some time, the political instructor held the letter in his hand; that executioner, that sadist had not even taken pity on a harmless bird. No one knew what to say.

Akhmedov looked at Asker, whose face had clouded.

"Don't grieve, Sergeant. There's more than one nightingale here.... Why, there are hundreds of nightingales...."

As if to confirm this, a marvellous warbling was heard.

The men of the battery happily exchanged glances and cried out with joy: "Sing, my nightingale, sing!"

The nightingale sang.

With a voice filled with anxiety and pain, it sang a song of freedom, calling them to take vengeance on their enemies in the name of life, in the name of spring.

Mekhti Gussein
(1909-1965)

Prosaist, playwright and critic. People's Writer of Azerbaijan and State Prize Winner.

Mekhti Gussein entered the field of literature as a journalist. Before writing his first story, he worked actively on many newspapers and magazines. As a correspondent, Mekhti Gussein was constantly in the thick of things and had close contact with people from many walks of life. His first story, "The Sheep-shearing" was published in the magazine Zhenshchina Vostoka (Woman of the East) in 1927. This was followed by other short stories about the Azerbaijanian countryside and its people's struggle against patriarchal, feudal attitudes in order to build a new life. Mekhti Gussein was quickly acclaimed as an outstanding Azerbaijanian novelist. His novels High Water, Combat, Apsheron, The Black Rocks, *and* Morning *are vivid pages in the history of Azerbaijan's renaissance. These are powerful, realistic narratives about oil workers in old and new Baku. The story included in this anthology. "The Rivals", also deals with this theme.*

Gussein is a strictly realist writer. His writings are almost always based on factual material drawn from life.

Rivals

1

"What did you say?!" I couldn't believe my ears. "And you wouldn't even bat an eyelash?"

"Not an eyelash. Word of honour, if it were in my power I would tear foreman Eibat's heart out with these very hands."

I couldn't doubt the sincerity of those words. But it was strange that foreman Pirveli wasn't even excited; he wasn't overcome by any momentary fit of anger. He stood, as stern and serious as usual, in front of my desk. I had heard of and read about it in books, and now I became convinced myself: the restrained, inner anger of a man is frightening. I was sure that if a stranger who didn't know our renowned oil industry worker, foreman Pirveli, had been in my office then, he, upon meeting Pirveli's hard stare, even terrifying in its austere calm, would have thought: yes, this grey-haired giant would really tear out the heart of his rival (yesterday's friend!), drill foreman Eibat, without thinking twice.

I had reason to be amazed. I had known old Pirveli for many years. The originality inherent in him alone, the tact, affability of character, and love of life of this Herculean-cut man fascinated me.

A thought flashed through my mind: Maybe I had idealised him?

I didn't want to believe that. But then what had induced him so suddenly to change his attitude towards Eibat, an old friend and no less a celebrated drill foreman than he himself?

Foreman Pirveli turned and slowly, with heavy steps of his huge, truly pillar-like legs, moved towards the door.

"Explain? As if you don't know yourself?!" His inflamed, drooping eyelids narrowed and a sneer formed on his lips. I saw how his fleshy cheeks became deeply flushed and his forehead, covered in sharp wrinkles, broke out in blotches. "To a real man, a sense of pride in his own work is more dear than his own stomach. Until now I thought that Eibat was made of the same stuff. If he is acclaimed then I have a share in his glory as well. It seems I was mistaken. Now I can see that I am not appreciated. Eibat should be indignant about this injustice. And since he says nothing, it means his conscience is not clean."

"I understand what you are talking about. Eibat was awarded the title of Hero...."

I shouldn't have opened my mouth. With that remark I as much as poured the fat into the fire.

"And you?!" he raised his voice. "Aren't you our manager? Why have you kept quiet?"

"But you know that I don't give out medals and titles of honour...."

Foreman Pirveli approached the edge of my desk with an ominous sluggishness, and, taking his right hand from the pocket of his quilted jacket, inclined in my direction.

I'll admit my heart skipped a beat. I thought: now he'll bring his huge fist down on my head like a sledge-hammer, and if I don't breathe my last in that very instant then my head will certainly be knocked to one side.

Pirveli must have guessed that I flinched. He grinned glumly and, it seemed to me, sadly, and taking a brown wooden tobacco-box out of his pants' pocket, began to roll a thickly-packed cigarette. He licked the edge of the strip of newspaper, got it to stick with difficulty, and lit it with a simple lighter made from a rifle cartridge case during World War II. I knew well that he was never without this lighter.

A thick, yellow-bluish cloud of smoke floated over my desk, swirling and changing form and hue.

"I know that many of you like to talk about truth and justice," he continued just as heatedly. "But then why, in requiting some according to their deserts, do you forget about others? I am not working for glory nor for all kinds of trinkets. But I have taught more than 100 pupils, and each one now has a profession under his belt. And they will say: 'Well, what's the use of working as eagerly as Pirveli — do they appreciate him?' How has Eibat surpassed me? For example, he has drilled 50 wells, and I sixty. He has worked 40 years in the industry, and I forty two. He has 5 wells in the sea, and I eight. Maybe Eibat has more children? No, I have kept pace with him in this, too. I have three daughters and a son, and Eibat — a daughter and three sons. So what! Today's girls are as good as boys in every respect."

"Of course, *usta**, indisputably!" I agreed, hoping to bring him back to his

---

* *Usta* — a polite form of addressing a professional. — *Ed.*

former disposition. "You have become grey serving the people. You don't have to explain anything. I know it myself."

"You know, but it seems there are those who don't."

"You are not right, *usta.*"

I shouldn't have objected. He dragged violently on his cigarette a few times and flung it, still lit, into the ash-tray on the desk.

"Not right?! That means I am lying? In the papers — Eibat; in the magazines — Eibat; on the radio — Eibat; in the movies — Eibat. Soon they will probably move the television studio into his home. A couple of days ago my wife asked me: 'Ah, Pirveli, why are you so unlucky? How did it happen that they gave Eibat the award you should have received, and they made him, not you, a Hero of Labour?' I flared up and said a lot of rash things.... Afterwards I was sorry. I hurt the poor thing for nothing. What had the old woman done wrong?"

"Ah, *usta...*"

"Don't interrupt!" he almost shouted.

"Foreman Pirveli!..."

"Yes, I am a foreman! But I see that it is not enough just to be a drill foreman!..."

He turned and quickly, with a vitality unusual for a man of his age, left my office. He didn't even say goodbye.

2

I had planned a trip to foreman Pirveli's drilling platform in the sea for the next day.

In the morning, in the management offices, I recalled our talk of the previous day, hesitated, and thought: Pirveli is offended and angry. It would probably be better to meet with him in a few days, after he has cooled off. I considered foreman Pirveli to be of noble nature, to which a false pride is alien when it does something out of anger and is truly sorry the next day.

However around ten o'clock in the morning I received a telephone call from his drilling platform. Gyurbat, a driller on the day-shift, was at the radio set. He announced that the brigade had lost patience waiting for the filling materi- al — hematite — which they had been promised delivery yesterday morning yet, and that all work on the site had been suspended.

While talking I heard a second voice near the receiver and understood: foreman Pirveli stood beside the driller and prompted him. He was indignant with the red-tape.... What are you saying, foreman?... Aha, he is warning: better not infuriate him or else he'll take the receiver himself....

I assured Gyurbat that I would check everything immediately and find out who was to blame for holding up the hematite. I contacted the drilling bureau on the inside phone and learned that the fill for foreman Pirveli's well had left the storehouse on schedule.

Then I myself went over to our wharf, which was surrounded with motor-boats, freight barges, and launches.

The sea was calm and smelled of oil, that particular smell to which you never become accustomed yet which doesn't oppress the sense of smell. It is pleasing to me. The grey sky seemed to hang over the very water. Sea-gulls shrieked hysterically. "The weather is turning foul!" I thought.

Workers were loading all sorts of equipment for the drilling platform, including hematite, into the hold and onto the deck of the old barge.

"Hallo, boys. I've come to give you a hand!" I said jokingly. "Can't you manage by yourselves? You promised our giant, Pirveli, to deliver the hematite. Why did you let him down? Aren't you afraid that the old man will blow on your tub in anger and then we'll have to fish you up from the bottom of the sea?"

Some of them laughed, but the majority went on as if they didn't hear me. I saw that the workers were really rushing. The loading tempo pleasantly stunned me. Most energetically of all worked the captain of the barge, Volodya Timoshchuk, a light-haired young lad. He finished tying a rope around a crate of spare parts for the drill mount and came up to me.

"We expect a Northerly, comrade manager. We are in a hurry. Foreman Pirveli's hematite has been on the dock for three days now. The day before yesterday we couldn't put to sea, the motor conked out, the gaskets were punctured. We fixed it. Yesterday I saw old Pirveli. He so scalded me with his stare that I still shudder."

"I'm sailing with you."

I was amazed myself at the suddenness of my decision.

3

Climbing from the barge onto the main derrick of Pirveli's brigade I saw that the situation here didn't look a bit like the one Gyurbat had described to me over the radio. The drilling was in full swing.

I understood. Foxy Pirveli had taken an original preventative measure in demanding the fill in good time.

Gyurbat, catching the mooring lines of our barge, saw me, became embarrassed, and lowered his eyes. He waited for me to chew him out for lying. But I myself had worked for a long time as a drill foreman and silently approved of such methods. I had used them more than once myself, as in the majority of cases the tempo of drilling suffers because of delay of equipment and fill.

"Where is Pirveli?" I thought. "Why doesn't he show himself?"

In spite of myself, a strong desire arose inside me to see him and learn whether he had become himself again after yesterday's talk.

"Where is your foreman?" I asked Gyurbat.

"He went to smoke...."

"He probably saw me on the deck of the barge from afar and decided to hide," I realised. "Yes, it looks like the old man hasn't cooled off yet."

I walked along the main derrick, greeting the workers.

All of them were amicably disposed towards me. I knew from my 12 year's experience in the oil industry that there are few hypocrites or smooth-talkers among oil workers. Some of them knew me for a long time. We had worked on the drills together. After the institute I was a drill foreman for two years. Work brings people closer together. I became attached to them and they to me. I will admit that to win the respect and friendship of these common workers is not so easy. But when you win it, it is pleasing and, yes, even beneficial.

I asked Gyurbat how deep the bit had gone.

Yes, foreman Pirveli was, as they say, strong not only in words but in action as well. On that day they had drilled more than 200 metres above the norm. All the equipment was running smoothly. Each member of the brigade was at his post.

It is gratifying to visit such a collective. You think: Ah, well done, lads! This is what our working class is like! And an acute feeling of pride in those people, impossible to express in words, swells up in your heart. And in the evening, at home, your wife and children feel that "papa's in a good mood!", and are also glad.

I recalled how Pirveli left me yesterday, all worked-up and upset: not good!...

"Did your foreman go ashore for the night?"

I asked Gyurbat this question, but the mechanic Yakhya answered: "No, he didn't."

"Why not?"

"We don't know. All evening the old man was gloomy. He returned from the management offices, called us all together, pulled a paper out of his pocket, read a report about the coming holiday, and then announced: 'Before the holiday arrives we are going to double our quota. Clear? Who wants to say something?' No one said anything. Figures speak for us...."

Yakhya looked away and sighed deeply, as if regretting something. "I don't understand what's happening with our old man. Yesterday, all evening, he walked around like a storm cloud, muttering under his breath: 'What for, what for, I shouldn't have said it....' Said what? To whom? I couldn't help myself, and asked. He glanced at me so strangely, shook his head, growled: 'Oh, nothing, I blundered!...'"

The roar of a motor-boat interrupted our conversation. We looked towards the sound and saw foreman Eibat climbing up the steel ladder onto the main derrick.

My heart skipped a beat. "An ill wind has brought him here! There he is — the rival!..."

Leaving the workers I hurried to meet Eibat.

"Where are you headed, *usta*?"

"To my well, 109. On the way I decided to pay Pirveli a courteous visit and at the same time get things off my chest."

"What, is there a reason?"

Eibat passed alongside me and hailed the workers.

"Where is your wise foreman?" he asked, and turned to me. "Please, Comrade Manager, sit in on our little chat, you can be a witness. I have a few warm words for Pirveli. But where is he, that teacher?"

You would think that Pirveli appeared out of thin air like a magician.

"Greetings, here I am. And how long has it been since you conferred the title of teacher on me?"

The workers laughed loudly. It was evident that the exchange of caustic remarks by these famous veterans amused them. It seemed to me that the laugh meant they considered their foreman the victor.

Eibat took Pirveli by the elbow with a strong hand and led him towards the cabin. He took a few steps and turned around:

"Let's go, comrade witness."

What good could be expected from their conversation? "I have to go," I decided. "If they quarrel I'll keep them apart."

185

The workers, not displaying any curiosity in the conversation of the two men, dispersed for their posts.

A swooping gust of wind almost carried my cap into the sea, on which steep-banked white-capped waves already danced.

4

The plank walls of the cabin were almost completely pasted over with coloured pictures from magazines, postcards, and also clippings from newspapers from which you could construct a detailed chronicle of Pirveli's famous brigade. It was hot here from the electric heater which stood on the floor in the right-hand corner.

On a low table, covered with a sheet of light-blue pasteboard, an electric kettle puffed and rattled, boiling over. A thick jet of steam burst from its spout and made a damp spot on the wall.

Foreman Pirveli turned off the kettle, removed the top, and, keeping his face to one side so as not to burn himself, pulled a package of tea from the oil-cloth bag which lay on the floor and poured a sizeable dose right into the kettle and covered it with the top.

"Please sit down wherever you like," he offered and lowered himself onto a wooden bench.

Foreman Eibat and I sat down opposite him.

"Answer me please, dear friend," spoke up Eibat first. "Why have you suddenly begun to fight with my shadow?"

Foreman Pirveli, with an indifferent look on his face, as if no one had spoken to him, bent over without standing up, got a freshly-ironed towel out of the bag, folded it in four, and covered the kettle with it.

"He doesn't want to begin the conversation without offering his guests tea," I thought. "A diplomat!"

However Eibat was in no mood to wait.

"Be so kind as to tell me," he asked offendedly, "what I am to blame for? Oh, leave your kettle alone, for God's sake!"

"I won't force you to drink." Pirveli, not raising his eyes to his interlocutor, took the tobacco-box familiar to me out of his pocket and began to roll a cigarette. "And as to your reproach that I am fighting with your shadow, you are mistaken. What do I need your shadow for when you yourself are right here in front of me?"

"Then explain what happened."

"Don't be in such a rush, I'll tell you right away." Pirveli spoke slowly on purpose, with pauses, and it seemed that by this he wanted to drive his guest to distraction. He lit his cigarette with his lighter, took a few puffs, and continued just as gravely: "I don't know who told you what, but it will be better if you hear it from me personally."

Was this a dig at me? But my conscience was clear. I hadn't had any opportunity to tell foreman Eibat of our talk yesterday.

"Your wife had a talk with me," answered Eibat. "She phoned us yesterday and said: 'Where is justice, Eibat? You are continuously extolled over the radio. Why don't they praise my Pirveli as eagerly as that? You,' she said, 'will become enemies in the end.' If there weren't any such discussions in your home she wouldn't have spoken with me in this way. I can't remember a time when you weren't the first to congratulate me when I was awarded a medal or something

186

else. What has changed? The postman has been besieging my home for over a week. Only you remain silent. Why?"

"You ask why I keep silent?" asked Pirveli, avidly puffing on his cigarette. The menacing appearance of his rival obviously didn't phase him. "There is something I don't like, that's why."

"You're jealous, eh? I see. Hostility has won out."

"Hostility has nothing to do with it. I'll lay everything on the line right away and you'll see. Do you remember, at the very height of the war, your well in the sea spouted a powerful fountain of oil? A week later you received the Order of the Red Banner. Right or not?"

"Well, true."

"And didn't my well thunder over all Azerbaijan then? What did I receive? Nothing. Right or not?"

Eibat lowered his eyes, couldn't find the words to answer, and moved his hand from the table to his knee.

"You keep quiet?"

"But in return you got a large bonus, a heap of money."

"Not money did I expect. I can't stand sons of bitches who work only for profit, saving for a rainy day." Pirveli rested his elbows on the table and bent a finger on his left hand. "That's number one. Listen further. In the last few months you drilled four wells with a total depth of nine thousand metres. And I drilled four wells, depth—twelve thousand metres. On one of them we managed without hematite. Right or not?"

"Right," growled Eibat.

"I didn't hear. Louder!"

"Right, dear friend, right. Am I denying it?"

"But they made you a Hero for that, and passed me over again. Right or not?" The old man bent a second finger. "Look, that's two. Or am I incorrect?"

Eibat obviously had his back forced against the wall. I felt that in his heart he acknowledged the fairness of Pirveli's words.

"But you know I don't give out titles!"

"You don't give them out. True. But tell me, where, when, and to whom did you protest: 'You're not being fair!'? Maybe, there was a time?... Did you protest? No! Then answer, can I consider you a real man?"

"A-a-ah, Pirveli. It turns out that you are a vain soul!" Eibat contemptuously pursed his thin lips and shook his head.

I noticed that Pirveli's hands trembled and I understood that Eibat's words had deeply hurt him.

No. Foreman Eibat didn't have the right to accuse Pirveli of vanity. That was an insult.

"You are wrong, *usta*," I intervened, placing a hand on Eibat's shoulder. "More than wrong. Yesterday Pirveli said it well: 'To a real man, a sense of pride in his own work is more dear than his own stomach.'"

Pirveli placed his extinguished butt in the ash-tray and raised his eyes to me. They were filled with sorrow.

"It isn't even a matter of professional honour, son. I told you I have many oil-worker comrades who are younger than me. I have pupils! That's why I have become vain in my old age! I guess I have become foolish!" He filled a pear-shaped glass with tea. "All right. The talk is over. Let him go...."

During the weary pause I noticed the fury of the waves lashing against the foundation of the well. The wind battered the door of the cabin.

"Really, became foolish," sighed Pirveli and, stooping again, took a tin box with sugar out of the bag and placed it on the table. "Have some tea. Warm yourselves. The weather is freezing. It is stormy again."

"By the way, I didn't come to argue with you," said Eibat despondently. "I wanted to challenge you to a competition, draw up an agreement."

Pirveli brought the glass to his lips and slowly took a sip.

"We are not going to draw up any agreement."

"Why is that, *usta*?" I blurted out.

"Because I am far ahead. I, that means my brigade. So far there is no one equal to us in our oil field. Though...." Pirveli smiled craftily. "We are also competing."

"Here's another riddle. Who can figure it out?" muttered Eibat.

"For some, a riddle; for others, no."

I will say frankly that Pirveli's words seemed puzzling to me, too.

Noticing my perplexed look he suddenly said softly, addressing Eibat:

"Go, get you brigade together, and tell your lads that Pirveli isn't going to compete with anybody." He brought the glass to his lips once again and glanced towards me. "Are you interested why, Comrade Manager? Because we are competing against tomorrow!" It seemed that Pirveli had forgotten the unpleasant discussion and he smiled simply and amicably, jokingly clapping Eibat on the back. "Well, famous hero, have you figured out the riddle?"

Foreman Eibat got up from the bench.

"You are bitter, Pirveli. I can see what is in your heart." He moved closer to the door.

"Ah, Eibat. I wouldn't have been so honest with anyone else." His voice was hollow and depressed. "I told you everything that was on my mind, you and our manager there. Let's let it go at that. Sit down, have some tea. A storm is building up. Where can you go in your little boat? Accidents easily happen."

"The first time, or what?... Well, all the best!" And he left.

Pirveli sat with downcast eyes, reluctantly sipping his tea.

The cabin quivered from the blows of the Northerly.

"We shouldn't have let Eibat go," grumbled Pirveli. "We should have talked him out of it. This sea is a wild animal, I should know...."

5

On leaving the cabin we were enveloped by a piercing wind that drove and drove ridges of foamy waves over the sea.

Eibat's motor-boat hadn't gone very far yet. Following it with his eyes, Pirveli let out the ear-flaps of his hat and did up all the buttons on his quilted jacket.

"He shouldn't have, he shouldn't have gone.... We are much closer to shore — less than a kilometre — and in a storm even we try not to stay here. I can imagine what it's like where they are — hell! If Eibat is smart he will get his lads and return to the shore."

"Who knows what it will be like in half an hour," I interjected. "This is the Caspian. The wind can die suddenly and you will be the first one to regret that you bolted for shore."

Pirveli sullenly shook his head as if he had a premonition and went over to the derrick, continuing to follow the dark dancing spot on the waves with his eyes.

And the Northerly gathered strength as if it had gone wild.

Half an hour later work on the well was stopped. Mountains of water fell on our main derrick with a roar, threatening to wash away and crush everything in its path.

"How are they, in the open sea, on 109?!" I wondered anxiously, looking at the motor-boats which passed by our well. They seemed so helpless. First they flew along the crest of a gigantic wave and then fell into the abyss of the sea, disappearing from view.

But still the boats went on, fighting metre for metre in the raging watery element. The brigades working in the sea were returning to land.

As a rule, in a storm with wind force over 5 drilling is stopped and the workers set out for shore. After the accidents that occurred last year the central board issued a special order about this.

I returned to the cabin and sent a radio message to 109: "Everybody on shore immediately!"

But even after that I felt uneasy.

When I left the cabin to join foreman Pirveli, who was at the derrick, a gust of wind nearly swept me into the sea. It is a wonder I was able to save myself at the last moment by grasping the steel rail of the derrick with both hands.

"Djalal, son," Pirveli turned to me, agitated. "Give the order to send the launch for them! Don't ignore my advice!"

189

It wasn't difficult to grasp his train of thought. The old man knew that in such a storm a small motor-boat wouldn't be able to dock at well 109 and even if the workers, risking their lives, managed to get into the boat, it was hardly likely that they could reach shore safely.

"You're right, foreman," I answered. "Hurry and get ready. Let's go to the settlement. We have to take urgent measures."

6

We were only 200 metres from the shore when the launch left the wharf and passed by us. It seems the workers in the drilling bureau judged as we did and sent our best life-saving launch to assist the brigade working far out to sea.

I turned to foreman Pirveli. His face was now not so sullen.

"Now it's not so bad." It seemed to me that he was smiling. "This launch can cope with a hurricane."

However our joy was premature. The storm ran high. No one could remember a storm of equal strength on the Caspian for the past 25 years. By four in the afternoon the wind velocity had reached 13. A few derricks in the sea were swept away by the frenzy of the storm, including the exploratory well 109.

A radio message from on board the launch brought terrible news: "Foreman Eibat died from a skull fracture; two of his brigade are near death."

The news stunned the workers' settlement and soon after — Baku. When the launch with the rescued and wounded oil workers on board, and also with the body of foreman Eibat, turned against the wind and slowly approached the dock, I was standing in the crowd on the shore. Our entire settlement had come, from the little ones to the grown-ups. I recognised the faces of the district executives.

A hazy dusk crept in over the raging Caspian. The fierce Northerly beating the caps of the waves, showered a cold, watery spray over the crowd.

The people were emotional to the breaking point, though many didn't want to believe that Eibat was dead.

Hospital attendants in white smocks boarded the launch with stretchers. First they carried off the wounded; lastly — the deceased.

Suddenly I heard:

"Hey, out of the way, let me through!..."

Working his shoulders like a battering-ram, a man in a worker's quilted jacket made his way to the last stretcher. He was broad-shouldered and tall, a giant, at least two heads above the tallest in the crowd.

Who in the settlement didn't know our Pirveli? It was he.

He stood, like a mountain, in front of the attendant who walked in front of the stretcher carrying Eibat's body, and said:

"Wait a moment."

The thin attendant, with high cheek-bones, respectfully and, it seemed to me, a little apologetically looked into the giant old man's face and then so softly that I hardly heard, requested.

"Pirveli, let us through."

He didn't.

The attendants had to put the stretcher on the ground.

The crowd quieted and waited to hear what he would say.

He silently bent down on one knee in front of the stretcher, embraced the dead body, and sobbed so hard a chill ran up my spine.

The crowd answered with the wail of many voices.

Such is the custom: The people mourn with their heroes.

Mirza Ibragimov
(b. 1911)

Shortly before the revolution, a poor peasant journeyed from Iranian Azerbaijan to Baku in search of work. He made that difficult journey together with his son Mirza; the boy's mother remained on the other side of the River Araxes.

Many years passed. Mirza Ibragimov became a distinguished writer, a prominent scholar and public figure in Soviet Azerbaijan. He is a laureate of the State Prize, an active member of the Academy of Sciences of the Azerbaijanian SSR, and People's Writer of Azerbaijan. For many years he has headed the Writers' Union of Azerbaijan.

Ibragimov began writing as a youthful worker in the oil fields.

His stories, novels (such as Daybreak, A Confluence of Wates *and* Pervane), *and plays depict a wealth of characters. The writer is acutely concerned with the struggle of peoples for peace and happiness on earth. Ibragimov is particularly attentive to ethical questions and to problems of everydaylife and family relationships (as is evident in his story "The Heart of Medina"). We have selected his historical tale of the revolution "Peri-hala and Lenin" for this anthology.*

Peri-hala
and Lenin

1

It was a day of unpleasant weather, with sombre grey clouds drawn down over the horizon like the knitted brows of a lonely old woman long used to waking hungry and going to sleep hungry. The leaden sky hung low over the village of Almamyk as though trying to press its cottages down into the ground. The incessant wind from the mountains was cold, and the mud never dried for weeks even when the rains had been brief.

But impassable roads did not prevent news from town reaching the village with incredible speed.

That was why a cluster of men had been gathered since morning by the haystack behind the barns.

"It looks bad for our masters, they'll be legging it out of Baku soon — if not today, then tomorrow," said the farm-hand Veli, a grey-eyed young fellow, short but sturdily built.

Hadji Gulu, richly bearded, in a tall hat and good cloth *chukha*, cast an uneasy look at the brown, weathered face of the bold-tongued labourer.

"The hungry chicken dreams of grain," he said with a reproving headshake. "There you sit, waiting for them to invite you to a dish of halva. But in Russia, they say, people are wandering about the steppe eating grass like cattle. The Bolsheviks have gone crazy with hunger. How can they ever get here, starving and barefoot as they are?

General Denikin's got the bit in his teeth, he's hammering them everywhere!"

The stableman Nazar, a flaming red-head — hair, moustache and even eyelashes were copper colour — laughed defiantly.

"Keep that yarn for them as'll believe it, Hadji! The Bolsheviks threw Tsar Nicholas off the throne, you think they can't deal with some General Denikin?! Take a sniff and you'll smell the thunderstorm coming. You'll see, if you live long enough; they'll be rising in Georgia and Armenia any minute. Why then should our Azerbaijan stand aside?"

His fingers shaking with anger, Hadji quickly rattled the carved beads of his rosary along their cord. He wanted to stamp down this stableman grown so impudently assertive, so lacking in respect for an elder.

"Well, well, so here's a stableman who can't even master a wretched nag telling me what's going on at the end of the world! I am old enough to be your father! And I swear by this beard, before the Bolsheviks have time to rub their eyes, they'll be finished off by hunger and the British. That's what everyone says, not me alone."

The stableman, taken aback by this attack, flushed like a girl. The farm-hand Veli came to his rescue.

"May Allah have your beard in his keeping, Hadji! Naturally, your foot is wiser than our witless heads.... But in the name of the Almighty forgive me, a foolish one, when I nevertheless remark that if you believe all the gossips your ears will soon be packed like the road to the miller's in a year of good harvest! Now, isn't that true, Hadji?"

Veli said all this thoughtfully, without a smile, but his hearers laughed; they understood, and the mockery seared Hadji Gulu's heart.

"You just wait," he hissed, "wait for the Bolsheviks to fill your belly with rich pilau! They've got Russia well fed-up, now it's the turn of Azerbaijan!"

"Lose no sleep, Hadji," said the farm-hand in the same tone, "the Bolsheviks'll never come here, of course.... We're just wagging our tongues to pass the time in bad weather. But they say Lenin himself in Moscow has given strict orders to help our Baku with everything possible. Money. And grain. And clothes. What d'you think of that, Hadji? Like it?"

Hadji Gulu was purple with fury; he wanted to punch the labourer's head and shout, "Out of my sight, you scum!" But in these times it would be unwise, so Hadji with an effort swallowed his rage. Only his fingers swiftly rattling the beads betrayed it.

Nazar silently stirred the mud with a worn shoe, its nose turned up like a cock's comb.

The watchman Djafar-ami who up to now had been sweeping the floor back in the adobe barn, now came to the doors, put down his broom and straightened up.

"May Allah grant long life to Lenin," he said reverently. "They say Lenin is the first friend of all poor folks in the world."

Hadji Gulu cast a look of disgust at Djafar-ami; everything about the old man — his grey hair, his straggling beard, his thin bent figure — literally everything irritated the wealthy man. Hadji turned away as though to swallow the gall rising in his throat.

"Listen, Veli," he suddenly asked the labourer. "You know everything, tell me — what faith is Lenin?"

Veli evidently guessed Hadji's guile; he made no reply, just scratched his head with a simple-minded look. But Djafar-ami called out from the barn.

"Moslem! No doubt about it, Lenin's a good Moslem!"

Hadji Gulu glared at the old man.

"This is nothing for your addled wits, getting underfoot like a dirty mat! Sweep the barn and give praise to Allah for his goodness!" Under his breath he added, "I've been told Lenin worships idols!"

The stableman Nazar stroked his red moustache.

"Nonsense! Idol worshippers live in Iran, not Russia!"

"Maybe he came from there," Hadji insisted.

"Think an idolator would dare throw down the Padishah from the throne? Use your brains, Hadji. It just couldn't happen. Lenin's a Christian. That's a sure thing."

Djafar-ami wasn't to be put down.

"I know it for certain—he's a Moslem! A True Believer and a fighter for justice!"

A heated argument began and no one can say how it would have ended but Veli settled it.

"Lenin isn't of any faith. He wants to bring the Kingdom of Heaven down here onto earth, to help all who have nothing! He wants to free people from their bonds."

"If that's how it is, it's good," said Djafar-ami.

A carriage descending a hill some distance from the village put an end to the argument.

"Look, men, that's the bek's phaeton," said Hadji Gulu, peering through narrowed eyes. "What's made him take to the road in weather like this?"

"Can't be!" This was the stableman. "What the devil does he want to break his wheels for on these roads?" But still Nazar was alarmed.

Old Djafar-ami picked up his broom again, just in case, but remarked as he went. "A two-horse phaeton, but who's in it I can't see."

At last the foam-spattered horses hauled the phaeton to the village and the people, running up, saw stout Shakhbaz-bek lying back in it, in a Cherkess coat and grey astrakhan hat. The bek had never been noted for good nature, but today—whether he was tired or whether some trouble had hit him—he glared at the people as savagely as a wolf.

The exhausted horses were steaming; mud was thick not only on their legs, but even on their flanks with the dangling bells and tassels. The laquered phaeton was a sorry sight, and mud had spattered the fine cloth of the bek's coat and the driver's weary face.

As soon as the horses, panting harshly, had pulled the phaeton to the middle of the village square, it was surrounded by a close ring of peasants—men, women and children. Silently, unwinkingly they stared at the bek and their looks were lowering, like the autumn clouds that pressed down over the village. Then suddenly Veli walked through the crowd with the air of one who had decided that you can't die twice, and death will come once anyhow.

"Well now, looks like there's reason in the talk that the masters' days are ended," he laughed loudly. "The bek's looking like a funeral, as if all his ships had sunk in a stormy sea!"

The bek descended heavily from the dipping phaeton and the crowd retreated.

"What's that you're yapping, cur?" he snarled.

Veli was no shivering coward.

"I'm praying for your honour! For the sun to come out and dry up the road so you can go your ways to town, and quick!"

The boys sniggered but their mothers shushed them. The bek glared at the crowd, black as thunder, then turned back to the bold labourer.

"Really? And what other blessing did you ask of Allah?"

"I prayed the creator to give our bek many long years and excellent health that we sinners might live forever in the shadow of his glory! And if you permit it, most gracious bek, I can say more."

"Hold your tongue!" Hadji shouted peremptorily. "The bek's tired after the road, he needs rest. You can come afterwards with your stupid talk!" He reached out to the collar of Veli's shirt to give the impudent fellow a good shaking.

But Veli quietly put his hand aside.

"All people know I am not the one for empty talk. But if there is real need, I'll speak out to the governor himself!"

"Bek, all men know this impudent farm-hand's got neither sense nor shame!" Hadji wailed, with a fawning smile for the bek. "I beg you, benefactor, pay no attention." He shook a surreptitious fist at Veli. But Veli was not to be quelled.

"Allow me, bek, to ask one question, a very important one."

"Take him away," Hadji Gulu was nearly dancing. "The bek is tired, worn out! Hey, men, make way, make way for the high-born bek! And kick that farm-hand out!"

Angry voices came from the crowd.

"The farm-hand's created by the Almighty, as much as you, bushy-beard!"

"Isn't a farm-hand a man, too?"

"Let him speak, don't stop his mouth!"

Hadji Gulu had apparently gone too far, a risky thing in those days. The wily bek saw it was time for him to interfere. He raised his hand for quiet and without looking at Veli said, "Ask your question."

"Long life to the honoured bek," Veli began, when the square was quiet. "What I want to ask is — will Kyazim's home be torn down at last? Will the bek build in its place a big house with windows and balconies?"

The bek's thick black whiskers moved ominously; with a jerk he raised the leather whip, but Veli did not shrink back, he stood his ground with a mocking smile. And the bek lowered the whip to clean the mud from his smart top boots.

"The ruins of Kyazim's hut, and the whole of the village, be it accursed of God, I shall sell to this gentleman, your guest and mine," said the bek with malicious pleasure, and gestured with his whip at the phaeton.

There was a general gasp. Only now the people saw a pale gentleman wearing a top-hat and frock coat and wrapped in a plaid, huddling in a corner. He looked with a crooked smile at the startled peasants.

2

The clouds of spring washed the orchards, fields and meadows with gleaming torrents and floated away to the south. A thick grey mist lay over the village, over the bare skeletal apple trees in the orchards. The peasants, who with the coming of spring toiled from dawn to darkness, could hardly tell the time when day ended and evening began.

But Peri-hala saw everything, she felt and noticed everything. She had no orchard, no cow, no home of her own. For many years now, winter and spring, after hard day labour for wealthy neighbours, after work in other people's yards, on other people's land, she went to the edge of the village, sat down on the ground hugging her knees, her head on her arms, and let her thoughts have their way.

One look at her worn, patched skirt of black sateen, her crushed blouse torn at the elbows, her cracked dark feet — she went barefoot summer and winter alike — would have told an observer that Peri-hala was deeply sunk in poverty.

It was true. Need had been her cradle, poverty her faithful companion, and misfortune her fate, her constant friend in life.

Yet if one looked more closely, one could see that Peri-hala's movements had a natural grace, her tall form had not lost its beauty, her eyes held the lucidity of thought, and her braids beneath her black kerchief, grey too early, were a worthy crown; she was not so pitiful or helpless as might seem at first sight, she would always be able to uphold her dignity.

Once Peri-hala had known happiness, she had had her own home, loving parents had caressed her and a fine youth with a high, ardent spirit and eyes of courage and devotion had pressed her to his heart; her children had played round her feet ready with the obedience of village children to do whatever she, their mother, told them.

When she herself was a child her father had told her that beyond seven rivers, amidst seven mountains, there lived a hypocritical, wily, sweet-speaking old sorceress confined within seven magic circles. She was called with a strange name — Time. Day and night she twirled her spindle, spinning the thread of men's destinies, and then threw the balls of thread into the valley. Wild winds carried them in all directions and tore the threads, and the fragments got caught on the thorns of wild roses, and on mountain cliffs, or fell into streams and floated away with the current. And sometimes the mad sorceress herself tangled the threads of men's fates, and crushed the balls and struck them one against the other and tore them, casting the fragments upon the wind.... That was why there was confusion and grief in the world, why such bitter tears were shed by the poor and the unfortunate. And if one suffered constant misfortune while another basked in the sunshine, if you were racked with sickness while your enemy fattened and grew rich, if one neighbour lost his home while another who was lucky and wicked rode on the crest of the wave, all this came from that vengeful sorceress, for all the threads of men's destiny were in her crooked fingers. You could strive and struggle to get on, to have a place in the sun, while she tangled the threads and doomed you and your family to eternal poverty. All people must submit to her malice, and they call her "Time". And there had never yet been anyone brave enough to challenge her openly, to go single-handed to fight her and — even at the cost of his own life — to save humanity from eternal suffering.

Today, from the moment she left the village, Peri-hala had gazed at the cottage and garden, so absorbed that she did not see the red calf stray from the herd and make its way into a green strip of wheat. She could see from where she sat that the rain had washed away part of the back wall, long unplastered. Yes, let a

197

wall go two years without plastering and whitewashing and it will soon begin to crumble. And there was a crack in the reed thatch, wind and rain would enter and widen it. And the orchard! It hurt her to look at it. Nobody had tended the trees for a long time now, nobody had clipped the dry branches or dug around the roots, and the trees had aged before their time like Peri-hala herself. The abandoned apple trees seemed to lament: "Where are you, our masters? Come back!" Peri-hala heard their plaint and her heart broke with sympathy. Her eyes which had just been shining with hope dulled, as though the mists of sorrow rising from the heart had drawn a veil over them. And tears rolled slowly down her cheeks, lined and dark with sun and wind.

"Hi, Peri-hala, wake up, get up!" called a ringing voice. "That red calf will soon have eaten the bek's wheat field clean!"

That was Veli. The unrepressible jester, who would not stop making jokes even when he went hungry for several days on end, who'd think nothing of mocking even at the vile sorceress who tangled people's destinies.

"What's wrong, Peri-hala?" he shouted. "Look up and smile!"

Coming closer, however, Veli saw the tears in her faded eyes and her gaze fixed on the adobe cottage standing in the orchard, and understood everything.

"These cursed times," he said, embarrassed, and making her sit down again he ran himself to the bek's field brandishing his staff and shouting at the calf.

The spreading apple tree which stood taller than the others, casting a cool shade in summer onto the house door and sheltering it in winter from the biting winds, seemed to look affectionately at Peri-hala.

The whole history of the small orchard had started with that tree. Kyazim, Peri-hala's husband, had planted it the first day after their wedding, carefully arranging the roots in the hole. Then Peri-hala watered it abundantly from the nearby ditch until it grew tall and strong. And when its branches began to spread, on moonlit nights and sunny days Peri-hala and her husband would sit beneath it, and she told him her joys and troubles, and together they knew the light of love and the dusk of life's trials. Here she sang lullabies to her children, and the tree echoed her voice with the music of its leaves.

This two-windowed cottage, the orchard with the flowering trees, this nest built and feathered by the constant toil of her family for many years, was swept away by the storm in an instant. Peri-hala might forget her own name, the name of her first-born son, but never would she forget that terrible evening.

Kyazim had returned from the field where he had been watering the winter crops, their son Nazim with his shepherd friends had driven the flock down from the high pastures and slept at home. Their daughter Telli, a little girl of ten and sickly from birth, was feeling well that evening, even well enough to be naughty. And Peri-hala, seeing it all, happy in her family, ran from house to garden and her agile hands seemed to get the work done like lightning. It was a clear warm evening so they had supper under the apple tree; Peri-hala put on the small copper samovar and was collecting the dishes to wash up when Shakhbaz-bek and two bodyguards suddenly appeared.

Kyazim and Nazim jumped up from the carpet where they had been sitting and with a low bow begged the honoured guest to partake of something. Peri-hala quickly drew a veil across her face as the custom was and went somewhat aside, but not too far, waiting for her husband to say what he wanted.

The bek, however, did not sit down, he beckoned Kyazim to him and said

198

something in a low voice. Peri-hala saw her husband start and back away from the bek and heard his trembling voice.

"I shall be forever the servant of you and your children, gracious bek, but I implore you to give up this unjust intention."

"What difference does it make?" cried Shakhbaz-bek, angrily. "I'm giving you the same land for a hut, and I'll help you grow as good an orchard.... But I've taken a fancy to this place, I'm going to build a new house. With balconies. With a high roof!"

"I'll die before I agree, bek!" said Kyazim boldly, seeing that pleas were unavailing.

"Oh, you'll agree all right," Shakhbaz-bek gestured contemptuously and his servants giggled subserviently. "The land's still mine, there's still money owing on it.... So hold your tongue! Talk about not agreeing—on my land!"

"We've paid the debt a long time ago," cried Nazim, who had kept silence up to now. "It's not true, what you say!"

"What! You Bolshevik puppy!" the bek howled, purple in the face. "Wagging your impudent tongue! You think I'm deaf? Eh, no, I hear everything. I know everything! I know all about your talk with the shepherds!"

Nazim turned pale but did not drop his eyes; he boldly returned Shakhbaz-bek's hate-filled glare.

"I know, too, honoured bek, that your servants have sharp ears," he said with obvious mockery.

Kyazim stopped his son; he knew that a string could be stretched only so far, after that it would snap.

"Be quiet, my son, the bek is our master, our protector. He is older than I am, not to mention you. So don't be so bold, be quiet."

"I'm afraid your paternal teaching has come too late," the bek said threateningly and left the courtyard without turning back and without a word of farewell.

A few days later Nazim was arrested. Then came dark times. Kyazim was summoned by the police and the interrogating attorney again and again. Supercilious officials came to the house demanding the deed of purchase. Some papers were found but others had been lost—in those days most business in rural parts was based on trust, without papers. So very soon a mounted man took Kyazim too away to the town, and Peri-hala and little Telli were thrown out of their home by the bek's men. This was followed by the sad news that Kyazim had died in prison—heart failure, it was said; the probability was that he had been beaten to death. Little Telli's weak life flickered and went out like a candle flame in a wind. Peri-hala was alone under the autumn skies and none dared help her or take her under their roof, they all feared the wrath of the bek. All but the farm-hand Veli. He gave Peri-hala shelter in the shed where he himself lived.

Then the poor woman started going out to work as a day labourer, watching the herds of others, or cleaning manure out of a shed, or digging in neighbours' orchards....

When Veli had driven the calf off the bek's field he returned to Peri-hala, sat down on the grass beside her, and took a piece of barley bread and a couple of eggs out of his patched wallet. His hands were large and rough, and Veli himself, although short, was sturdy and thick-set. His large hand broke the bread and gave Peri-hala a piece of it, and a hard-boiled egg.

199

"Don't refuse it, take it, you need strength. Evil never went unavenged in this world, that I truly believe, Peri-hala! And punishment there will be for the villains who have treated you so wickedly."

Veli cared for her like a son, he urged her to eat.

"You know, Peri-hala, the lid is clamped tightly down on the cauldron, but the steam is already rising. Happiness will smile on us! And the masters will be pushed off to a hotter place!"

"Which masters?" Peri-hala turned her thoughtful eyes from the adobe hut and orchard to look with surprise at the young fellow.

"Masters like Shakhbaz-bek, and the Sultanovs, and other wolves in sheep's skins — that's the kind I mean."

"I don't know, my son, I don't know," she sighed wearily. "I think only the Almighty can understand what's happening these times. Of course, the devil's temple of gold and guile must fall.... When ants feel the coming of death, they grow wings. And our masters the beks have grown wings and dagger horns. But I look at the destinies of men and wonder; fate raises a True Believer to the heights, and then casts him down into the bottomless pit. How can you control this treacherous fate? How can you know what will come tomorrow, how can you look into your future? To me it seems that none can stand against Shakhbaz-bek."

"Eh, Peri-hala, you have seen many stout posts that have been chopped up for firewood!" the farm-hand said. "Lenin — you've heard of Lenin? — Lenin has turned all Russia upside down, and today there's a government of workers and peasants ruling in Petrograd. Soviet power!" he shouted the words, intoxicated by their sound. "Those fine beks shake in their shoes at the very name of Lenin. On the other side of the mountains our Daghestan brothers have already raised Lenin's banner. I know that for a fact! And if not today, then tomorrow the Baku oil men will do the same! I know you don't believe me, Peri-hala, but it is Lenin, Lenin who will give you back your son, your house, your orchard. Lenin himself!"

Not once, not twice — many times on winter evenings when the lowing of cows and the bleating of sheep broke the dark frosty silence of the village, Veli had told her about Lenin with all the eloquent power of his heart. It seemed that this farm-hand, this digger of manure who had never seen anything but the muddy tails of sheep, had nevertheless a keen vision that could see from this god-forsaken village what was happening in the world. Allah himself must have sent him to give hope and courage to Peri-hala in her days of misery, to be her staff and support. And the woman, grateful, prayed with all her heart for long life and all happiness for the youth.

"I do believe it! Why should I not believe?" said Peri-hala, but her voice was weak and uncertain. "God himself would be happy to hear such good news from your lips, my son! But I see it is those whose lamps are dark for lack of a coin to buy oil who love to talk about Lenin. Where can Lenin find the power to feed all the hungry, to comfort all the sorrowful? May the Almighty strengthen him and save him from the guile and malice of the vile sorceress that confuses human fates! When you speak of Lenin, a light shines in my heart!"

Peri-hala rose and went quickly to the wheat field where the red calf was again nosing in.

200

3

Shakhbaz-bek and the little merchant in frock coat and top-hat with the sharp, pale face did not come again to the village.

Their departure was followed by that of the farm-hand Veli and the shepherds — suddenly, at night. Where had they gone? To seek their fortune elsewhere? A day passed, another drew to its close with no news about the lads, as though the ground had swallowed them up.

Again the village was filled with contradictory rumours and talk. Some said they had gone to the oil wells in Baku. Djafar-ami warmly approved.

"What is there for poor men here in the village? Here each man holds out his hand and says, 'Give!' But never have I heard of any who say, 'Take!' The peasants have always been hungry, poor and wretched. So it was and so it will be to the end of the world. But if our lads become workers, and oil workers, too, they'll get somewhere, you'll see!"

Many were inclined to believe that Veli and his friends had been arrested and were now in jail. Hadji Gulu, a man of dignity, a man of cautious judgement, constantly repeated, "In broad daylight, before all good people, that ragged scum, that son of a stray dog, insulted the highly-placed bek!"

But Peri-hala, to the surprise of all, listened with an impassive face, although earlier she would certainly have spoken up in Veli's defence. And this did not mean the sympathies of her tormented heart had dried up, it was because she alone had bade god-speed to the farm-hand and shepherds when they left to fight grim battles.

At a late hour Veli firmly closed the door of the shed and lighted the clay lamp.

"The stars are fading, soon dawn will come, Peri-hala. The winds are knocking at our chutters. We must go, for now it is the turn of our Azerbaijan. The time has come — either we crush them, or they us. If I die, remember me with kindness. If I have injured or hurt you, forgive me. For you, Peri-hala, have been a mother to me!"

"I have two sons, Nazim and you," said Peri-hala and blessed Veli before his journey. "I wish you all that is good, my son."

"Not a word to anyone, Peri-hala!"

"The grave will speak sooner than I."

Veli blew out the lamp and darkness enfolded them. The door creaked.

Then Peri-hala ran after the lad, panting, and stopped him with a touch on his shoulder.

"What is it, mother?" said Veli.

A wave of happiness flowed over Peri-hala — it was so long since anyone had called her mother.

"My son! You are going to Lenin. I understand everything now. Tell Lenin that your mother called Peri lives in the distant Azerbaijanian village Almamyk, that she sends Lenin a greeting from her heart, that she prays he may be saved from the malice of the wicked sorceress who tangles the threads of human fate!"

Veli should have said: "But Peri-hala, how could I ever come to see Lenin?!" Only he had not the courage to disappoint her. And after all, anything might happen! What if the farm-hand Veli really did happen to meet Lenin?

"I promise I'll give Comrade Lenin your message!" he said in a trembling voice, and vanished into the night mist.

Days passed, many of them, but no news came of Veli and Nazim. This was a great grief to her. News there was, however, of all kinds, hardly a morning without it. The people were excited as they are before a great holiday, the peasants' faces were bright and their hearts beat fast. It was like that moment when the first refreshing gusts of wind reach the villages from the great storm raging in the mountains.

At last came the long-awaited day, crimson banners flamed on the hill, and horsemen came galloping along the road where Shakhbaz-bek's phaeton had once crawled. Nobody could yet distinguish their faces, but a wild shout went up:

"Bolsheviks! Partisans!"

Within a few minutes armed riders on foam-spattered horses poured into the square. They wore clothes of every description—shirts, *chukha* and wadded jackets, top boots and shoes of home-made leather. There were not enough rifles and pistols for all, some had their grandfathers' sabres and daggers at their belts. The group was led by the farm-hand Veli—gay and happy, and a stranger youth with hair long like a monk's and a neat beard. Behind them the stableman Nazar lurched awkwardly in his saddle.

Peri-hala stood modestly back in the crowd, but suddenly people parted to let her come forward, as though they knew instinctively what this day meant for her and willingly gave her first place.

Veli jumped lightly from his horse and embraced her.

"Your day has come at last, Peri-hala! I sent your greeting to Lenin by Comrade Narimanov* when he went to Moscow. You'll have to forgive me, I didn't get as far as Moscow myself this time.... Lenin was very pleased and he said, 'My thanks to Aunt Peri, I wish her all health and happiness.' And Lenin told my brother, your son, Nazim, to go home to his village."

Veli led up to Peri-hala the lad beside him—gaunt, long-haired but with a bold, direct look.

"Don't you recognise him?"

"My son!" she screamed as she held out her arms; her happiness was so great that her legs gave under her and she almost collapsed into Nazim's embrace.

4

When Peri-hala came to herself she found she was half-lying in her son's arms. A meeting had just ended, Veli who seemed to be everywhere at once had just called on the peasants in a flaming speech to unite under the banner of Soviet power and was now climbing to the roof of Shakhbaz-bek's house to hoist the red flag. For a staff he used a spade handle. He kissed the edge of the flag, fastened it to the handle, stood erect and shouted with all the force of his powerful lungs:

"Long live Lenin! Long live Soviet Azerbaijan!"

"Long live Lenin! Hurrah!" rolled over the square in stormy delight.

The wind caught the flag and it streamed out proudly, a joy and inspiration to all.

* *Nariman Narimanov* (1871-1925), Azerbaijanian revolutionary leader and writer.— *Tr.*

Peri-hala was recovering her serenity and understood it was no dream, her son was alive, and with her. She rose and walked with confident tread to her house. Nazim and Veli watched her in silence. Without a tear, although she might well have shed many, without a word she knelt and kissed the ground by the threshold. In the orchard the flowering apple tree awaited her, fair and festive as a bride, and Peri-hala went to give it her caress, she stroked its trunk and branches with a trembling, wrinkled hand.

Veli and Nazim seated themselves on the ground beneath the thickest branches of the apple tree, reluctant to break the quietness of the recovered home. After going round the garden and looking at the house, Peri-hala joined them and sat down on the grass. Her eyes reflected the feeling of quietness and peace.

"So dreams can come true," she said softly, as though musing aloud. "Although even in my sleep I never dreamed of such a blessed day."

Veli wanted to answer her softly, in the same tone, but underestimated his own voice and it rang like a trumpet.

"This is only the beginning, Peri-hala. We shall see still more wonderful days — my heart misses a beat when I think of it!"

5

From the day when the rising sun cast its golden shimmer over the red flag on Shakhbaz-bek's mansion, life was completely different in the village, although the Elder, Shakhbaz-bek's morose agent, still growled ominous predictions.

"The wheels of fate can sometimes roll back again. Wait, soon a new prophet will come, the holy Mekhti, and punish with a heavy hand the disruptors of ancient customs, the defilers of our patriarchal ways!"

Hadji Gulu kept out of sight for some time, hiding in his house; then, however, he took courage and emerged onto the street, the collar of his *chukha* unfastened, and jabbed his finger into Veli who was passing, a pistol in his belt.

"Just look at him, the way he struts! You'd never think it was the same farm-hand with ribs sticking out like some stray cur's, no, you'd think it's Ker-ogly himself!* Fire consume such an order of life!"

People clustered round.

The ex-labourer quietly patted Hadji Gulu's globular belly.

"Never mind we'll soon melt down all this fat! We'll see what your ribs look like!"

"That isn't your sunflower oil, it's mutton fat, it's not melted down so easily!" Hadji retorted confidently, trying to comfort himself with the idea that this was just one more of the impudent fellow's jokes, and not an earnest of big changes.

He went back home, ate rich bozbash** and lay down to sleep.

As soon as the village meeting elected Veli chairman of the Poor Peasants' Committee and he at once raised the question of dividing up the land and livestock of beks and wealthy men Hadji Gulu fastened his collar firmly and could neither eat nor sleep. He raged.

* *Ker-ogly*—hero of an Azerbaijanian epic.— *Ed.*
** *Bozbash*—soup made of mutton with peas and potatoes— *Tr.*

"It's the end of the world!" he growled to the Elder, and his friends, other wealthy landowners. "Have you heard—they've made that foolish, half-crazy Peri-hala a member of the village Soviet! A woman!—giving orders to us, men! What could be more hateful to God?"

One day a messenger came to summon Hadji to a village meeting; they were held almost every day now. And at this meeting Peri-hala spoke.

"It's awful to think how we peasants lived before," she said to the silent crowd. "As though they'd bound our mutilated hands and feet and thrown us into a dungeon. All our lives long we never saw the life-giving sun! But even that was not the worst. The worst was that we became blind, we took our sufferings for granted and nurtured no hope for liberation. The wise man who freed our hands and gave liberty to poor people said: 'Learn to read, tear away the veil which has covered your eyes!' So now I, Peri-hala, propose that we carry out Lenin's words at once, and open women's courses for the liquidation of illiteracy."

Try to object, thought Hadji Gulu, and Veli, or Nazar, or that jailbird Nazim'll have his hand at your throat; so he fought down his fury and asked meekly, "Would it be voluntary or by force?"

"What?"

"This teaching women to read."

Peri-hala did not know what to answer. It had never entered her head that there could be women who would reject Lenin's words.

Veli, standing alongside, answered for her.

"Voluntary, of course! But husbands or fathers who prevent women from coming will be dealt with, and with all the sternness of revolutionary law." He gave Hadji Gulu a very straight, grim look.

Hadji fastened the collar of his *chukha* more firmly and hurried home. For some days he went nowhere, collecting the rumours brought from the village by gossips. That insolent Veli, helped by men from the partisan column, had actually began measuring out the land for that arbitrary and unlawful redistribution, while Peri-hala, that wretched beggar, was going about the houses making lists of men, women and youths for literacy courses. Then Hadji Gulu heard the stableman Nazar had gone to the nearest town to get a teacher, textbooks, exercise books and pencils. Hadji shuddered nervously at news like this, but swallowed down his curses.

Peri-hala and Veli had no time to sit and chat these days—too much to do. Veli had matured, he looked stronger and somehow bigger; even elderly peasants no longer called him "the farm-hand Veli", but "Comrade Veli". Peri-hala had changed, too. Widows came to her with questions, young girls for advice. She was invited to conferences in town. When the bek's land was divided and apportioned, she was present, representing the village Soviet. She was busy from morning till night, but still found time to set her own home in order. She plastered the walls afresh, rethatched the roof and put a fence round the blossoming orchard. Previously adobe huts had never been whitewashed in the village but Peri-hala now whitewashed hers, and the result was so pleasant that passers-by stopped to look. The other women were quick to follow her example, so a new custom arose. But when the walls gleamed white, rubbish lying about the yards became an offence. Peri-hala swept hers up and burned it, and her neighbours did the same. The whole village looked pretty and cheerful, as though dressed in new clothes.

The spring weather became warmer, the sunshine generous, and one day Peri-hala's heart leaped as she saw tiny green apples, no larger than walnuts, on the branches of the biggest tree. It was like a gulp of fresh spring water to her parched soul. She felt as if her own youth had come back to her. The orchard had been waiting for its mistress, and in the autumn it would reward her for her care with an abundant harvest. Now there was no danger from night frosts or hot drying winds or the careless hand of passers-by. When the apples swell with honey-sweet juice, she thought, I'll gather a whole basketful and send them as a gift to Lenin. The wish was so strong, it caught her breath. Oh, if only I could see Comrade Lenin just once, and talk with him, she thought. The dream was too precious to speak about even to Veli or her son. They might laugh at her.

Days passed, weeks passed, filled with work, organisation, meetings and literacy study, but the dream never faded, it became a secret, burning desire. A person can become accustomed to anything, even the boldest dream, and Peri-hala began to think: is it really so impossible? Lenin is no khan, no bek or rich nobleman, with armed guards to keep the common people away. He is our teacher, the herald of our glorious hopes! At least, that's what Veli says....

Peri-hala had an utter faith in Veli.

If they told Lenin a peasant woman in Azerbaijan wanted to see him, to tell him all that had gathered in her heart, surely he himself would invite me to come, she assured herself.

But the vile sorceress was not sleeping, again she tried to tangle human fates.

One morning Peri-hala was wakened at dawn by wild shouts: "Fire! All out! Fi-i-ire!" She ran outside and gasped. The red flag no longer floated over the village Soviet, formerly the bek's house, instead grey clouds of smoke billowed out from under its metal roof.

Of course the peasants were soon on the spot and put out the fire, but nobody could or would say who had snapped off the flagstaff. Veli and Nazim discussed it for a long time. They called Nazar and Djafar-ami to join them. This was clearly the beginning of a fight, a fight to the death.

That evening Peri-hala found only five women at the literacy lesson; usually there were thirty or more. And those five, drawing their veils over their faces in embarrassment, told her:

"They say we are losing the True Faith when we learn to read. Bringing shame on ourselves!"

"Lenin's power will soon end."

"There'll be a new government, and they'll hang all who go to study. Don't be angry with us, Peri-hala, but we can't come any more."

Gossips ran about the yards whispering that Soviet power had fallen in Gyandja* and Nukha, and those who had given the bek's land to the poor had been hanged on the square.

Veli saddled a horse and gallopped away to town for help; neither he nor Peri-hala knew what to do, what to tell the waverers, how to fight the open enemies.

The chairman of the district revolutionary committee came, a tall, curly-headed young fellow with blazing black eyes. He was in military uniform, a gold star on his cap.

* Now Kirovabad.— Tr.

A meeting of the whole village was called. The peasants came slowly, with reluctance, either because they feared the secret agents of the bek, or because now they had got land they had lost interest in speeches.

The chairman explained the situation in the young Soviet republic — clearly and plainly; he spoke about the desperate efforts being made by the counter-revolution and ended on a note of confidence:

"The people, the workers and peasants stand firmly round the Communist Party, round Comrade Lenin! No power can break the strength of Lenin's just cause!"

They clapped him, they thanked him for an interesting report, but it was Veli's speech which was the real success.

"One day in the forest an oak sapling complained to his father, the big oak: 'Father, look how ruthlessly that axe treats us trees.' The oak tree rustled his mighty boughs. 'That, son, is because its handle comes from one of us — it's made of oak!'" Veli's eyes twinkled and there was general approving laughter. "We needn't fear Shakhbaz-bek, hiding out in some hole. The danger comes from his servants, his hired men who hide among us until their time comes."

It was like a signal. All eyes turned to Hadji Gulu and the Elder, who stood somewhat aside.

"It wasn't the bek himself, it was his servants who tore down the red flag, who soiled Lenin's banner with their dirty hands!" he continued, and his voice gained strength and confidence as he felt he was carrying the people with him. "But we'll find them, and make them answer before the law and the people! And you, comrades, if you ever see the hand of a traitor reaching out to the red banner grip that vile hand and hold it, and let the enemy cringe in fear before our wrath."

The Elder and Hadji exchanged livid looks and moved back, but did not leave the square.

Peri-hala was asked to speak. She did not wait to be urged, she knew one must not keep silent in such difficult times, that the right word was as effective as a rifle.

The old life was still vivid in her memory. Suffering is not quickly forgotten. And was she the only one who had known hardship? So Peri-hala felt this was the moment to remind the peasants about the black days when misfortune and sorrow lived in every peasant house. Then, carried away, without realising what she was doing, she told her listeners of her most cherished dream — to see Lenin, to please him with a gift of the sweet, juicy fruit from Almamyk.

"But I must tell you truthfully," she caught herself up. "Now I feel ashamed when I think of my dream. And why? Because Lenin would ask: 'Who threw down the red flag, who abused what is sacred? And how could you hang a padlock on the doors of the literacy school? Don't you know that learning is light, ignorance is darkness?' And I should have to tell him: 'Comrade Lenin, we villagers are asleep, we have not yet had enough of snoring under a dirty greasy quilt, a little more and we shall sleep ourselves blind!' No, better sink through the earth than stand before Lenin with such things to say!"

Peri-hala concluded with a wry smile, and there was a deep silence. The peasants, shamefaced, stared at the ground or at their boots.

This made Peri-hala feel better. People are not lost if they still retain a sense of shame.

The chairman of the Revolutionary Committee gave her a new flag.

"Raise it upon the village Soviet again, my son," she said to Veli. "This is Lenin's banner, eternal. I know that every honest man will guard this flag now like the apple of his eye!"

6

The days of summer heat passed, followed by the chill of autumn. In the gardens the leaves flamed, faded and withered. Under the apple trees they lay like copper coins. The ripe apples were small amber suns in Peri-hala's orchard. She had picked none as yet, only collected the windfalls.

Nazim and his friends the shepherds were soon to drive the flocks into the valley, and Peri-hala decided to gather the apple-harvest with her son, and invite Veli too to come, to select the very best of the crop as a gift for Comrade Lenin.

But the days of happiness are like spring flowers, each one fairer than the last — so say the old and wise.

The Revolutionary Committee chairman galloped up and stopped before Peri-hala's house.

"We've come for you, Peri-hala, prepare for a journey!"

"Come in and sit down, sit down, you're welcome," said Peri-hala, who had not properly taken in what he had said. "I'll have tea in a moment, sit down here, on the carpet."

"There's no time, Peri-hala, thanks! Did you hear what I told you? You must get ready for a journey, there's been a telephone call from Baku. A delegation's going to Moscow from Soviet Azerbaijan for the anniversary of the October Revolution. And you're to be one of the delegates."

Everything swam before her eyes, her legs felt weak, she had to cling to the door-post. But then a wave of wild joy swept through her as she realised her dream was to come true, she was going to Lenin in Moscow.

The chairman gave her no time to think.

"Get ready, hurry, the train leaves Baku in three hours, we've barely time to get to the station!"

Veli and Nazim had seen the horse at the gate and arrived in the nick of time. Startled, delighted, they helped Peri-hala collect her few things, picked the finest apples, large, golden fruit, and packed them carefully in a basket. Those would be for Vladimir Ilyich Lenin.

Nazar brought a grey horse, quiet but swift-footed, and Nazim and Veli helped her to mount.

"Good luck! Tell Lenin all about our village! There's been this and that, of course, but all the same, our village has put up a whole detachment of partisans to fight for Soviet power. That means something! And the poor have been given the bek's land, at last they're forgetting their poverty. Good luck, Peri-hala! Give Comrade Lenin our respects, our love. We shall always be faithful to him and his cause and his banner!"

Peri-hala sat before the big casement windows of her hotel room, admiring the majestic city.

Baku too was a large city, but even after Baku, Moscow enthralled her imagination. On the way people had told her about it, but still she had not imagined such size and scale, so many wonders and beauties as this great city held. It made her heart beat and caught at her breath. From the moment she set foot on the stones of Red Square and saw the walls of the Kremlin where Lenin lived and worked for the well-being of all people on earth, an inner power, a feeling of inspiration such as she had never known had welled up in Peri-hala.

The previous evening she had been with the delegation from Azerbaijan at the celebration meeting in the Bolshoi Theatre. The theatre had been packed with workers, peasants in bast shoes and home-spun coats, soldiers in greatcoats dark with campfire smoke, and party and administrative officials in leather jackets, all impatiently awaiting the arrival of their great leader. The theatre was cold, the red velvet curtains were faded, the gilt was dulled, the lights in the crystal chandeliers burned at half strength, but to Peri-hala, and to all there, everything glowed as though the sun were shining, because of the name on the lips and in the hearts of all — Lenin.

At last the great moment came. The curtain trembled and slowly rose. There was a breathless hush, then a storm of clapping, a roar of voices: "Hurrah! Long live Comrade Lenin!" People rose as Lenin crossed the stage with rapid steps, head slightly bent forward, and took his place on the platform.

Emotion dimmed Peri-hala's eyes, she could distinguish nothing, but after a moment she mastered herself, her sight cleared and the figure of Lenin imprinted itself forever in her heart.

Peri-hala would have felt no surprise if Lenin had been a giant, like the heroes in the old folk legends. Yet the more she looked at him, the more she felt that he could be only what he was — thick-set, quick in movement, with twinkling, penetrating eyes, with a smile sometimes firm and courageous, sometimes very kind, and that high bulging forehead. To the end of the meeting she never took her eyes off Lenin's face, behind whose brow lay so much wisdom and keen, penetrating vision.

Again a secret longing awoke as she remembered what Veli had told her and how the peasants had approved.

"You must talk with Comrade Lenin!"

She seemed to hear not only Veli's voice, but those of the villagers.

"You must talk with Comrade Lenin!"

How can I face people when I go home if I don't do as they said, she thought, and whispered imploringly to the leader of the delegation, an old Baku revolutionary sitting beside her:

"Try to get Comrade Lenin to receive us Azerbaijanians — just for a moment!"

If only it could be arranged, she would tell him all that was in her heart.

"Go in, please, Vladimir Ilyich is waiting for you," said the secretary, and all rose, making way for Peri-hala to go first.

She smoothed her pleated blue sateen skirt, smoothed the black kerchief on her head and with small steps and a pale face went into Lenin's office.

Lenin was looking through papers, marking them in pencil. He jumped up with youthful lightness, looked at her with smiling eyes, came out from behind the table, took her hand, seated her in an armchair and with a gesture invited the other delegates to be seated.

"I suppose we need an interpreter?" said Lenin with an inquiring look at his secretary who went out, returning in a moment with a swarthy youth in army uniform.

Peri-hala felt her heart sink — Lenin was looking expectantly at her, as though he wanted her to speak first, and the other delegates too had turned to her. And everything which had filled her mind on the journey and in the hotel vanished, leaving a void. But Lenin guessed her quandary.

"Comrade Narimanov has told me a great deal about the situation in Azerbaijan, and how hard the lives of women are," he said, his friendly eyes on Peri-hala's face. "It's to be expected! For long ages peasant women in Russia and in the East led approximately the same kind of lives. The lives of working women were essentially alike everywhere."

Peri-hala was already at her ease; Lenin talked so simply, he was like an old friend who knew all about her, all she had endured. There was such a kind simplicity in his look and manner that she felt she could talk to him as she would to Nazim or Veli.

"Thank you, Comrade Lenin," said Peri-hala, "thank you for all your thought for us poor people. You and Soviet power have opened the doors for us into a new, good life."

"Oh, but we haven't come to the really good life yet," Lenin said seriously, and there was worry in his narrowed eyes. "We have many difficulties — we are short of bread, short of textiles, winter's here and there isn't wood to heat even the hospitals and children's homes. Transport is disrupted, the trains barely crawl — you know about all that better than I do. And illiteracy, ignorance, superstition — those are dangerous enemies. No, we still have a long way to go to reach really good days." Lenin concluded with convincing frankness.

Peri-hala understood Lenin's concern, but did not altogether agree.

"The peasants of Azerbaijan have land, and they're freed from the yoke of the beks. This is a big thing! We are our own masters."

Her words pleased Lenin. He looked quickly from Peri-hala to the other delegates and asked with eager interest:

"So Azerbaijanian women understand that Soviet power has freed them from the age-old darkness? Yes? And the peasants really do see the Soviets as their own, people's power? Tell me, Comrade Peri-hala," Lenin glanced at the interpreter, who nodded — yes, this was the correct form of address, "tell me, do the village Communists, and non-party supporters of Soviet power, understand that the whole East is watching Azerbaijan? That it is extremely important for our entire policy? Your workers, your peasants, your Red Armymen are the first in the East to raise the banner of socialism!"

Peri-hala did not understand exactly what socialism was, but she remembered how Veli had raised the red flag over the village Soviet building, formerly Shakhbaz-bek's mansion, and how enemies had stretched out dirty hands against this sacred emblem, but the chairman of the Revolutionary Committee had brought another red flag, which would fly proudly forever.

"It is for you, comrades, to make Azerbaijan a model Soviet republic, so that the oppressed peoples of the East may look at your achievements and rejoice, seeing their own future!" Lenin continued forcibly, and his eyes held that challenging sparkle which always captured his listeners. "And in this great work, women take one of the first places. In our model republic, women must be raised to unprecedented height, they must have respect, influence and complete freedom. All the blessings of culture must be given to women! For the East, comrades, this will be of exceptional agitational importance."

Again Peri-hala did not understand all the words used, but she was aware of the essence of Lenin's speech. The delegates were deeply stirred, Lenin's words made them feel they were growing eagles' wings.

Lenin put detailed questions to them: how had the beks' land been divided, had the poor peasants horses, ploughs, harrows, didn't they want to cultivate in common the land they had received? Peri-hala found it extraordinarily easy to talk about it all; when she replied to Lenin she was talking about her own life; she was only surprised to find him interested in just the very things she had thought of as petty, everyday matters; to him they were important.

Asked about schools, Peri-hala said the village Soviet had decided to draw all the women into literacy courses, even those of forty. She spoke frankly of difficult days when not even the girls came to lessons, and some husbands still would not allow their wives to go.

"That is *adat* for you," said Lenin and the delegates all nodded. The power of ancient custom was still great. "Well, all that will pass," said Lenin. "How about textbooks in Azerbaijanian? And exercise books?"

Even this he thought of! Peri-hala at first was ashamed to complain about having one primer for five or six, Lenin had quite enough worries without that. But looking into his penetrating eyes she felt ashamed — you cannot conceal the truth from your father!

"They take turns reading, we're short of books, Comrade Lenin, very short. But there's something else we want to ask you."

"What's that?" Lenin asked alertly.

"There are three hundred villages in our district, and a good many people can read now, but there's no newspaper in Azerbaijanian," said Peri-hala with deliberation of an elderly peasant. "And there aren't any printing machines in the district. If you could send us one, then we could publish at least a monthly newspaper and write about village affairs and needs in it. It could be read aloud in the evenings for those who can't read themselves. It would help us, really it would."

Lenin jotted something down in his notebook and turned to the other delegates asking them questions about their affairs.

Unseen by Lenin the secretary signed to them — time to go, Lenin was tired and had a lot to do. They rose.

"Comrade Lenin," said Peri-hala in a trembling voice, "may Allah protect you from the wicked wiles of the sorceress Time dealing in human destinies, may he make your life so dear to all a long one!"

"The sorceress dealing in human destinies — and you call her Time?" Lenin's eyes twinkled. "H'm, that's interesting. A sorceress, eh?"

Encouraged, Peri-hala told Lenin the old legend.

"An interesting legend," said Lenin, after listening intently. "The people knew how to express the idea that in the old society a man's fate depended on the accidental combination of circumstances, and all fair dreams were destroyed. But from now on, Time is our ally, never again to tear or tangle human fate. We Communists shall make this sorceress work for people.... As for the counter-revolutionaries, h'm, we'll deal with them!" Lenin laughed gaily.

Peri-hala suddenly remembered the basket of apples still standing in the outer room; pushing the other delegates aside, she went to fetch it.

"This is the fruit of my orchard! That orchard you restored to me, Comrade Lenin!" she said, flushed with excitement, and held out the basket. "I dug the soil myself. When there was no water, I watered it with my sweat. Take them — a modest gift unworthy of you, but offered with all my heart." She picked the biggest apple, red as the cheek of a mountain girl in the winds of winter, and laid it in Lenin's hand.

He stroked it, he sniffed the fragrance that seemed to bring the warmth of the sun into the cold· office. And Peri-hala saw that his hand, although small, was strong.

"What a fragrance," Lenin sighed. "You know, there's a Moscow worker I knew well, very well. A staunch Communist — yes, Ivanov, a splendid man." Lenin turned to Peri-hala as though they were alone. "He was killed at the front a little while ago leaving a wife and four children. How pleased they'll be with your gift! Thank you on behalf of the Ivanovs — thank you!"

Now death itself will not be terrible, thought Peri-hala as she left Lenin's office, tears in her eyes.

But she had no wish to die.

Less than a month after the delegation's return, Veli galloped along the mountain trail from town and called to Peri-hala across her fence, "Peri-hala, they've brought a printing machine! And type! Everything! Baku printers have come, too. Lenin hasn't forgotten us, he did as he promised!"

"Lenin's words and actions are one, my son," said Peri-hala from her doorway. She raised her head and with quiet satisfaction looked at the crimson glow of the sunset.

Just think, she mused. Lenin — Lenin himself hasn't forgotten, he did what was asked by a peasant, yesterday's farm-hand. I must work, work hard, to show gratitude for such concern!

Two weeks later, the first issue of the district newspaper *Along Lenin's Path* came out.

Enver Mamedkhanly (b. 1913)

Enver Mamedkhanly's prose is remarkable for its subtle lyricism and elevated romanticism. Regardless of his subject, be it the elevating love of the great poet Nizami Ganjevi for the slave woman Afag, the harsh trials of Fatali-khan*, the life of Baku oil workers or the joys and sorrows of a girl from Iranian Azerbaijan — Enver Mamedkhanly never fails to win the reader's heart and his sympathies, to convey his agitation, liking or scorn.

The story "Ice Statue" is characteristic of Mamedkhanly's lyrical prose.

---

* Fatali-khan ruled the Kubin Khanate in Azerbaijan in the eighteenth and nineteenth centuries.— *Ed.*

Ice Statue

Winter of 1941. A frosty night. Everything in the vicinity, alive or dead, seemed frozen stiff. The air bit like a snake and the blood froze in one's veins.

On one such night a solitary shadow moved across a boundless snowy plain in the Ukraine.

A young mother was fleeing her village, hurrying ever onwards, towards the East fleeing her village which had been seized by the fascists, fleeing to salvage her self-respect and her child.

Ahead was the river, along which the front line stretched. She could hear the roar of the Soviet guns on the other side.

The young mother rushed on; no matter what she must reach her own people. She must carry her child across to the great, free land on the other side. Even if she had to die during this frosty night, a sacred cause lay before her — to save the symbol of her first love!

The mother trudged on and on tirelessly. But the snowy fields seemed boundless. She was exhausted, and the frost pierced her body like a blade. Suddenly it seemed to her that her child was freezing in her arms. She looked about her and her desperate eyes sought a nook, a place of refuge where she could bundle her child more warmly. Two black shadows rose ahead of her — two trees, growing closely side by side. She leaned against them for a second to regain her breath.

213

Her strength was already abandoning her. The frost licked her face with its burning, icy tongue. Terrible words pounded in the mother's breast: "The child is freezing. He will not live through this frost!"

But the mother fought off this dreadful thought.

No! No! She would not surrender the baby she had torn out off the clutches of the enemy to the icy embraces of the frost. Let the entire world turn to ice, let all life on it freeze, she would tear her maternal heart from her breast to warm her child with its heat....

She removed her woollen jacket and muffled up her child in it.... Minutes passed, but to her they seemed like months, even years, an eternity. The frost burnt her like red-hot iron....

And once again she felt that her darling child, and not she, was shivering and freezing.

She took her woollen shawl from her head and wrapped it around her child. Now the mother's exposed body was defenceless against the frost. She felt the proximity of death and knew that she was freezing. She had no more strength left.

She took off her blouse and covered up her child even more warmly. She was going to die anyway, but the child must live! A mother has to save her child! With her last ounce of strength she pressed the child to her bare breast with all her maternal love and whispered:

"I have nothing left to warm you with, my darling, except perhaps my heart. To the last beat its warmth is yours!"

The mother fell silent, but copper strings twanged in her ears.... They were tensing and bursting. The mother could no longer see nor hear.... She pressed closer and closer against the tree. The severe winter night decked her in a new array; the frost's icy fingers spun delicate crystal patterns on her....

Morning came, clear and frosty, like a sharp unsheathed sword glinting in the air.

Before the trees stood three men in white camouflage gear—scouts. They stood silently, motionless with their heads bared.

Before them was a scene they would not forget for the rest of their lives—the ice statue of a frozen woman.

For a long time they stood before that sacred altar without stirring.

Finally one of them approached the trees and the statue of ice. Inspired by a faint hope he peered into the bundle which the frozen woman clasped to her breast. With fingers trembling with emotion he unwrapped the cloth and ... saw a pair of child's eyes staring at him from within. The young soldier started and involuntarily drew back.

"He's alive, he isn't frozen," he said in a voice hollow from emotion.

The child smiled, squinting from the morning sun.

The soldiers who had passed through fire, water and deprivations, could not hold back their joyful tears. Raising their heads, they gazed once more at the majestic statue of the mother and whispered, as if in prayer, an oath of ruthless revenge.

They returned, carrying the child in their arms. But the ice statue, that personification of the grandeur and strength of maternal love and self-sacrifice, became a bronze memorial in their hearts, urging them ever on to grim vengeance.

Ilyas Efendiev
(b. 1914)

"Your idea of happiness is always the triumph of good feelings and impulses," says one of Ilyas Efendiev's heroines to her beloved. Her words also apply to the writer himself, for his works are a hymn to goodness and noble impulses.

Ilyas Efendiev's stories, novellas and plays are rich in emotion and lyricism. Many of his works, including the story "The Roofer and the Red Flower", deal with contemporary youth and its search for a place in the sun.

The Roofer and the Red Flower

The sun was rising as old Kara and his apprentice climbed up onto the roof of a house in the upper part of the town.

Both were tall and well-built, in rough oil-stained shirts. The old man had a worn brown cap pulled down over his eyes, but the young man's head was bare to sun and wind, his black hair parted on the side. In his right hand the old man held an ancient pipe, seasoned to a coal-blackness.

They walked along the roof from end to end. The young man asked, "Shall we make a start?" The old man nodded.

The young man climbed down the ladder and the old man took out his tobacco pouch and began unhurriedly filling his pipe, examining the place of their work through eyes narrowed against the sun.

The old kir* with which the roof was covered had softened and spread. Here and there were wrinkles and cracks.

Then the old man saw it—in one place where the kir had blistered and broken a flower had pushed through the crack. It was bright red, it blazed like a ruby under the rising sun. Young, green leaves surrounded the glowing petals like a guard of honour.

The old man lighted his pipe, his eyes on the flower. He had often seen things like that in his long life laying the kir,

* A sort of natural asphalt or bitumen, deposits of which were to be found in Azerbaijan.— Tr.

217

usually in the spring or autumn, and always, when he bent over such flowers, he had the feeling they wanted to tell him something. But what? The old man never thought deeply about it. He was content to look.

The sun broke away from the horizon and rose over the sea. The old man straightened joints that creaked a bit, pulled the peak of his cap lower over his eyes and looked to the east, his legs in their rough boots widely straddled. He looked as though he had been standing there from the beginning of time and would go on standing until its end.

The old man's face was darkened by the sun. Its lines were etched deep, like the furrows on autumn fields.

The lad's black head rose over the edge of the roof. He stood on the top rung of the ladder to hand up the bag of tools. Then they both took crowbars and started breaking the old kir off the roof and throwing it down into the yard.

When that part of the work was finished and they descended the old man unbuttoned his pocket and took out a ruble.

"Here!"

"I've got money."

"Go on, take it."

The lad ran off, the money in his hand. The old man watched him with approval. Then he sat down in the shadow of the wall and lighted his pipe.

He seemed to be watching the passing people and traffic. But in his seventy years the bustle of the town had ceased to interest him. He looked beyond it all, as though for something at the far end of the street. Just what he expected to see he himself didn't know. He just looked.

The lad came round the corner with a paper bag under his arm and a newspaper in his hand.

"Is that today's?" the old man asked.

"Yes. Nothing much in it. Like to see?"

Pipe in mouth, the old man leisurely unfolded the paper while the lad took a bunch of *vezeri* out of the bag, and dived into the house gate calling "I'll wash them" over his shoulder.

When he returned the old man had spread the paper and laid out bread, sausage, cheese and two bottles of beer. Then he took a knife with a horn handle dark with time and began to slice the sausage.

"D'you think we'll be through by seven?" the lad asked suddenly.

"With the work? I expect so." The old man looked at him. By seven. The boy was young. He remembered his apprentice days when he had asked the same question. Plenty of water had flowed under the bridges since then, yet sometimes it seemed like yesterday.

They finished eating, folded up the newspaper with the remains of the food and lighted a fire under a great smoky cauldron, brought the previous day.

For half a century the old man had known that cauldron, with its bubbling hell's brew of pitch. How many years had he, like that young fellow now, rolled up his sleeves to stir the kir, felt it softening, surrendering to the strength of his arms.

The first time he experienced it he had been a lad, just apprenticed to an old master who was likewise called Kara, the hereditary name of roof-layers. They had worked at a great height, covering the roof of the academy building, the finest in town. Only then it had a different name, Ismailiya.

Again the old man thought about the deceptively swift race of time. It was just fifty years ago, on a Friday, when he and his master started pouring the kir on the roof of that building. It was the last Friday of Novruz-bairam. They worked till sunrise. Then they brought fresh *chureks* from the neighbouring eating house, and a pot of good tea.

In the evening Usta* Kara had invited him home. Fires had been blazing by the gate and children screamed with excitement at the flames.

Gyulsum-badji, his old master's wife (God rest her soul, she was a good wife to Usta Kara!) brought pilau with *gourma*, then tea in pear-shaped glasses, and eastern sweetmeats.

He remembered it all, down to the smallest details. He could see them before him — Usta Kara and Gyulsum-badji.

Now the young fellow was mixing the kir, leaning his weight on the long handle of the spade. It puffed like thick dough. The muscles on the lad's sunburnt arms tensed and relaxed. Big drops of sweat stood out on his face.

The old man drew on his pipe and looked approvingly at the lad. A good, strong lot, kir-layers! At last he knocked out his pipe on a stone.

"That'll do now," he called. "Let it boil. And you sit down and cool off a bit."

The lad laid down the spade and took out a handkerchief. It was the first time the old man had seen him with such a well-ironed one. (He had only an old grandmother to look after him.) Carefully, as though afraid of creasing it, he wiped the sweat off his face.

"I'm going to get a drink," he said.

"Go along."

"Shall I bring you some?"

"No, thanks."

As the lad made for the gate, the old man called after him, "Don't drink too much. Not long since you had that sore throat!"

* * *

The sun was low, and plenty still to be done. The lad hurried, filling bucket after bucket, and the old man, standing on the roof, drew them up and poured the kir out in a thick, even layer.

At last the old man pulled his watch out of his pocket, found it was a quarter to seven, and leaned over the edge.

"Pack up now. We'll finish tomorrow." And added, as though to himself, "My back's aching a bit."

The lad's face lit up. He put down the bucket.

"Well, if you don't need me any more?"

"Go along, go!"

"Tomorrow, then."

He threw his jacket over his shoulders and hurried away. But the old man — he had no need to hurry, he had nowhere to go. He climbed down slowly, to avoid rocking the ladder, picked up the bucket and dipped it into the seething kir. Then he climbed up again to the roof and pulled up the bucket....

When the job was finished — he had promised to finish it that day and didn't intend to break his word — it was already dark. Slowly he went to the shore and sat down on a bench close to the water. An oleander grew beside it.

* *Master.— Ed.*

219

He loved those hours when work was done, loved that seat by the water, loved the sea.

There were plenty of strollers. Couples passed, walking very close together. But the old man didn't look at them. Lamps hung overhead, but he had no eyes for the promenade lights. He looked at the sea, at the quivering lines of light stretching out from the shore.

There were lights in the bay, the riding lights of vessels. Warning lights flashed in the distance. The sea gleamed, edged with a lacework of foam. It breathed with elemental life, its movement was restless, unrestrained, eternal. And the old man felt a renewed strength when he communed with the sea.

He smoked two pipes, then rose. His way took him past a house he had covered with kir not long ago. As he passed he could see through the lace curtains a brightly lighted room, a laid table, a man and two children sitting at it. They were having supper.Gay music came from the radio.

...The old man opened the door of his small room on the outskirts of the town and turned on the light. There was an unshaded lamp hanging from the ceiling, a table covered with worn oilcloth, chairs, and an iron bedstead in the corner covered by a threadbare quilt. Everything worn out, but neat.

The old man unhurriedly removed his jacket and hung it on a hanger by the door. He went into the tiny kitchen that led off the room and took a jar of sour milk from a shelf (a neighbour brought it every day and put it there for him). He ate it, then returned to the room and switched on the radio to listen to the news. After the news, the plaintive folk songs called *segyakh* were announced.

At one time he had liked nothing better than listening to *segyakh* sung by Khan Shushinsky. But now — now he turned the radio off. Since he had learned that his son Djavanshir would never come back from the front, he couldn't listen to *segyakh*. Because his nerves had become too sensitive. Because his heart was too filled with sorrow to endure any more....

So the old man switched off the radio and went to bed. But sleep would not come.

The one person who used to come to the old man every day, that apprentice lad, hadn't appeared for ten long days. Why? But how can you ask the young?

He rose and turned off the light. For a few moments he could see nothing, he was plunged into dense darkness, unrelieved, like eternity itself; he sank into it. But his thoughts continued, and with them came light and hope.

He thought of the lad's surprise tomorrow when he saw the work was finished. And how they would start on the neighbouring houses. And how the people living in them would thank him and invite him in.

People had always been well satisfied with his work, they respected him, he even had a waiting list. And the craftsman Kara was proud of it.

His last thought before sleep overtook him was of the lad mixing kir.

The next day they covered the neighbouring house. Again the old man worked on the roof, the young man on the ground. When they were nearing the end, the old man saw a girl standing nearby as he stooped to raise a bucket. She was in working overalls. A bright red ribbon held back her short hair. She had evidently just washed, the hair over her forehead was still wet. She stood watching the young fellow, her hands behind her back; and he scooped up bucketfuls of kir extra fast, so that each time he spilled a little on the ground.

220

Just a curious passer-by, the old man thought, people often stopped to watch them. But when the work was finished and he climbed down, the lad jerked his head in the girl's direction.

"I want to introduce you, master."

The girl came closer to the old man, looking up at him from under her brows. Then she smiled suddenly. Her teeth were very white and the ribbon in her black hair was red.

The old man pressed her hand gently, then got out his pipe.

"Do you work?" he asked as he cleaned it.

"She's building the new film studio," the lad answered for her. "She's just come from there."

The girl remained standing in front of the old man, looking silently into his face as though waiting for him to ask her something more. But he asked nothing.

"Well, if you don't need me any more—"

"Go along, go along," the old man said.

The lad hesitated a moment, then turned and they walked away.

"Rashid," the old man suddenly called him.

When the lad came back, the old man pushed a three-ruble note into his hand.

"Why, have you been paid already?"

"No, but—"

"Thank you!" The lad dashed off to overtake the girl.

After that the girl started coming every evening. As soon as Rashid saw her he would hurry, and the kir would splash out of the bucket onto the ground. Then as soon as the master allowed the lad would snatch up his jacket and they would go away together.

The old man asked no questions. They'd tell him themselves when it was time. But from that evening when the girl with the red ribbon appeared, he lived in a world of dreams. He imagined the young people's wedding, and how the first baby, if it was a boy, would be called Kara. Every day in the life of the future young family passed before his eyes. Time and again he counted over the money he would get when they had renewed the roofing on all the houses in the block, and in his mind went over all the things that would need to be bought for the wedding.

One fine Sunday something unexpected happened.

The old man had just returned from the bath-house and was making tea in his lonely room when there was a knock.

This time the lad was not alone. But the old man was happier to see him than ever before.

"Sit down, sit down, both of you." He began to fuss. "It's stuffy in here," and he opened the only window.

Both boy and girl were in their best. The lad wore a snow-white shirt and a blue tie. A tiny gold watch shone on the girl's wrist.

Suddenly the old man felt the lad wasn't his usual easy, carefree self, something was troubling him, and a certain apprehension mingled with his pleasure in the visit.

"It's lovely weather today," said the old man suddenly.

Rashid gave him a quick look. It was the first time he had ever heard an idle remark from his master, or seen a meaningless smile on his face.

221

The old man rose, went into the kitchen and brought back three glasses of tea on an old-fashioned tray with painted flowers.

"You shouldn't trouble, master," the young fellow said. "My girl would have brought it...."

"Trouble! Lord, what trouble is this?..." The old man looked away from them. "You sit here, just a moment—"

The lad caught his arm.

"But master, we've had dinner. Please don't bother. Or maybe you're hungry yourself?"

The old man shook his head.

"Then sit down, I've something to say."

The young fellow had never before seen the old man fussy or confused.

Silence. It lasted longer than the old man could endure.

"Drink your tea, or it'll be cold," he said.

It was the first time in many years Rashid had heard such sadness and affection in the old man's voice. It caught at his heart. He quickly picked up his glass and drank the tea in a couple of gulps. The old man held out his hand for the empty glass, but Rashid stopped him.

"Thanks, I don't want any more."

The old man looked at the lad.

"This morning two men came from the fortress," he said. "I told them we've a lot of work as it is, we could only do it after the fifteenth."

The young fellow glanced at the girl. Silence again. At last Rashid straightened with a jerk.

"Master, I shan't be coming tomorrow."

"What's that—?" The old man's voice was stifled.

"I shan't be coming to pour kir."

"Why not?"

"I'm going away to study."

"Where?" The old man pretended he didn't understand.

"To study at the transport technical school."

For a couple of minutes the old man said nothing.

"Won't you find it difficult?"

The lad understood what the old man had in mind.

"It'll be all right, we'll manage," he said.

"I'll be working, and he can study," the girl suddenly intervened in men's talk. "You see—"

She paused, picking her words.

"You see, times change, the time for kir-layers is past. They don't use kir for the roofs of the new houses."

That was true, the old man thought, they didn't use it, not for the new houses. Pitilessly, the girl continued.

"It's not like it is for you. Rashid's young. He has to think of the future."

Yes, of course, he has to think—

"Though honestly," the girl's voice seemed to come from somewhere far away, "I know you're like a father to him. For a long time Rashid wouldn't agree to leave you."

The old man raised his head and looked at the girl with new eyes. This girl whom he was used to seeing in close-fitting overalls, with a red ribbon in her pitch-black hair. She was so small, and so strong.

222

The girl picked up the lad's glass and her own (the old man had not drunk his tea) and went out into the kitchen. When she returned Rashid rose with a sigh of relief. The old man rose, too. They stood for a moment in silence. Then the habitual words slipped off Rashid's tongue.

"Well, if you don't need me —"

"Go along, go along."

"Goodbye, master."

"Goodbye to you, and all happiness."

They were at the door when the girl turned suddenly, ran impulsively to the old man and kissed him, standing on tiptoe.

Then they went. The door let in a bright shaft of sunshine. Then it closed, and the room was sombre with its usual dim light.

The old man stood by the door as though trying to remember something very important. Then he went to the window. But they had already vanished round the corner.

He slipped his hand under his jacket and took out his pipe. He was careful and unhurried, as usual. Then he put on his cap and went out.

With his quiet, steady walk he went to the public garden, familiar from childhood, where the kir-layers gathered on Sundays.

The sun turned the horizon golden and gilded the decorations on the Academy building.

As he walked, in his mind he went over the houses he was to cover with kir in the coming week. He thought about life, old yet eternally young, and its simple, wise laws.

**Gylman
Musaev
(b. 1914)**

Musaev's works appeal to both young and old alike. The writer engages his readers, regardless of age, in a sincere, serious dialogue on themes that concern them. His style is clear and simple. Realistic narrative is interspersed with frequent lyrical digressions.

Gylman Musaev has also authored many stories and a series of novels that deal with historical themes.

He was awarded the Mirza Fatali Akhundov Republican Prize.

"My Servinaz" is one of his finest works.

My Servinaz   Our village really is far from the sea. You can't even see the water if you stand on the roof. Actually, it's quite a distance from the cottages in Tugai where we spend the summer. But who cares! Summer and winter, we could sense the nearness of the sea on all our crooked little streets. On hot August nights, when everyone sleeps outdoors on the flat roofs, the distant rumbling lulls you to sleep.

There's an ancient fortress in our village which we are very proud of, because it's part of our history. The death of our ancestors and the birth of the village children are all reflected in its stone walls. When you climb to the top of the tower you see the sea lying at your feet. It seems that if you hold out your hand you can scoop up some water. From times long past our village has been bound to the sea. Late in spring, when the days become increasingly hotter, we take our flocks to the sea, to the shallows near the beach, where we bathe the sheep. They bleat loudly as we wash and comb their fleece till it is white. The water is still cold at that time of the year, and standing in it makes you feel that the sea is sticking invisible icy pins into your feet and legs. There are melon patches right behind the dark strip left by the high tide. You no sooner touch a watermelon with the tip of your knife than it splits open, and the melon juice is like cool honey.

225

There's good reason why the melon patches cluster on the strip of land along the coast. The water seeps up through the ground there, and that is just what the melons need. However, when the *khazri*, that vicious wind from the sea, begins to blow, it is pitiful to look at the place.

A year ago the wind blew day and night for a whole week early in spring. The surface of the sea, which is usually as flat as glass, cracked and swelled. Then it seemed to have gone mad, pouring into the gardens, crushing and tossing about the tiny cantaloups and watermelons, which were like fledgeling sparrows fallen from a nest. The sea was indomitable. When it begins to boil, it is like a wild beast, and when it exhausts itself, it's as mild as a ewe-lamb. After the *khazri* had spent itself, the sea appeared exhausted. We were sorry for it, quite forgetting that it had robbed us of our cantaloups and watermelons. Though the sun had not yet pecked through the sky, much as a chick through its shell, we went down to the beach to breathe in the coolness of the sea.

It really is wonderful to gaze at the azure blue of the water, with the sky reflected in the sea and the sea in the sky. We could not actually say where one ended and the other began and forgot all about the rest of the world as we stood there gazing at the water. After a day or two our tiny melon vines sprang back to life, though ooze still covered the rows. At last it, too, disappeared, for the sun's hot rays beat down upon the sand, bleaching it white. We would stretch out on the beach and give ourselves up to the sun.

The strong wind had built up little sand hills here and there along the edges of the melon patches. Some were bigger, some were smaller. The fine sand, which seemed to have been put through a sieve, was like silk in our hands. We would stay on at night, sleeping right on the sand, with our shirts as our only covering.

Our melon patch was next to the shepherd Gadir's patch. Perhaps his furrows were deeper, or perhaps there was some other reason for his success, but be that as it may, his cantaloups and watermelons were always larger than anyone else's. When his daughter Servinaz touched the tip of her knife to the ring of a watermelon it would split open with such a loud sound I could hear it from afar. Ah, that Servinaz was a real tomboy! She was hot-tempered, but always cooled off quickly and was very kind. She wore the same cotton dress all summer long. It seemed as though it had been dyed in henna, and it reached above her knees, so that her sunburned legs were always bare. Her large dark eyes burned and glowed so intensely that I usually tried not to look into them. She noticed this once and said:

"Why don't you look at me when you're talking to me?"

"I don't know."

"I didn't know you were that shy. Boys aren't like that."

Though she was my age, there wasn't anything I could say. I couldn't very well tell her that my heart pounded and thudded whenever I did look into her eyes. She would have probably called me a coward. Still, I felt as though I could have spent the rest of my life sitting with her on the sand hill that had suddenly appeared between our melon patches. When I sat next to her, the breath of the sea, seeped

226

as it was in fish and heady from the smell of sage that grew all around, could not snuff out the fragrance that was hers alone. There was so much I wanted to tell her! Yet, I could not utter a word. I was peeved at my mother, who, I felt, had brought me up to be so tongue-tied. I had read so much and knew so many poems by heart. But what was the use of it? I was always afraid I'd say the wrong thing.

One warm summer evening we were alone on our sand hill. The sea lapped at our feet. The moon had just risen, but we could not look at the water, for the moonlight blinded us. The tangy smell of sage filled the air. Servinaz sighed and said:

"Why do you read so much?"

"I want to be a poet."

"What will you write about?"

"About the sea and the gulls."

"And what else?"

"About you."

She glanced at me and laughed. "About me? What can you write about me, silly?"

"I'll say there was a girl who was as brown as a berry, and who was more mysterious than the sea. Her eyes..." here I bit my tongue.

"Well?" Her mischievous eyes darted at me.

"I'll write about the cantaloups and watermelons. I'll say that the tastiest melons of all grew in our melon patches. And I'll write about the smell of sage."

Servinaz lay back on the sand with one leg crossed over the other, as boys do. Her short dress rode higher up on her thighs, revealing her firm, bronze legs. They glowed in the moonlight. She crossed her arms behind her head and was silent. I turned towards her. Her eyes were shut. She sensed that I was looking at her, opened them and sighed.

"You're funny. What's there to write about watermelons that might be of interest to anyone?"

"Dont worry. People will read about them. Anyone who hasn't ever tasted them will."

"Don't write about watermelons. When you grow up I want you to write about the stars. Of how they drift into the sea. You know how beautiful that is, seeing the stars fall into the sea? First one star slips down and then another, and another. They say that double stars are lovers' stars. If they fall together it means their wish will come true. When I sleep on the balcony at home I can see the Milky Way. Sometimes I feel it's pulling me up into the sky and carrying me off across the sea to the stars. They're so beautiful! I wish we really could reach them."

She sighed and closed her eyes again. Something strange and mysterious inside me stirred from having such a girl lying beside me with her eyes closed. That evening I felt like shouting at the top of my voice, so that everyone would know how happy I was. I wanted to shout so the tired sea would hear me, and the sleepy moon, and the dozing evening. Instead, I barely uttered: "What do you want to be when you grow up, Servinaz?"

"Me?" A wonderful, kind and trusting smile lit up her face. "What can I be?" she said, but did not open her eyes. "I haven't read as many books as you, so I can't say that I'm going to be an important person when I grow up. I don't want to be anybody special. And I couldn't, anyway. I can only help people. You know, be of help in some way. I don't know how to do anything else."

She did not open her eyes as she spoke. Her small breasts rose and fell under her thin cotton dress. God, how beautiful she was! Her long lashes cast faint shadows on her cheeks, and her moist lips were as dark as cherries in the moonlight. I despised myself for not having ever kissed them yet.

She was silent for a while and then said, "Tell me a story. About mermaids. They say they're all great beauties. And that they're covered with scales, like fish. Did you know they have a palace at the bottom of the sea? When Grandma was alive she told me that mermaids come up when the moon rises. They weave filmy cloth from the moonbeams, but I don't know what it's called, and they make themselves lovely gowns of it. Then, as soon as their gowns are done, they go back down to their pearly palace at the bottom of the sea and dance there. Do you think it's true?"

"I don't know. I never even saw my grandmother."

"I loved my grandma very much. And I loved the stories she used to tell me. But Grandpa hardly ever talks. He's like you. Wouldn't it be nice if things were like they are in story-books? Then we could see the people in the fairy tales and talk to them. We would go off to fight the evil monsters with them. Then I could put salt on my finger, like Melik-Mamedov, and it would be a charm to keep awake all night."

We heard someone snoring. The sound would now become very loud, now die away.

"Who's that?"

"Grandpa." Servinaz smiled. "He always snores."

The sound was indeed coming from their melon patch. Her grandfather was sleeping on a roof supported by four poles. Servinaz rose and tossed back her long hair.

"Let's go for a swim. I'm glad he's sleeping. He'd never let me go." She did not wait for me to answer but grabbed my hand. We ran down to the water, jumping over clumps of sage. A rotten old rowboat lay on the beach. Ever since I could remember it had been lying there on its side with its bow buried in the sand. Servinaz was the first to reach it.

"Don't look! I'm going to get undressed."

228

I sat down on the damp sand, turned away and did not notice when she had undressed and entered the water. A few moments later she called to me: "Hey!"

I turned around. The water was up to her neck. Still, her firm breasts appeared momentarily. I looked at the clothing lying on the sand. She was nude. She was nude in the sea. She seemed to me like one of the mermaids she had just spoken of. Her hair floated about her shoulders. Who knows, perhaps she had unbraided it to cover her nakedness.

"Well? Aren't you coming in?" she called, and her voice sounded loud above the still sea.

"No. I don't like to bathe at night."

"Scaredy!"

I pretended I hadn't heard. Actually, I disliked the idea of bathing in the dark. It was a strange feeling that the moment I entered the sea, water snakes would curl themselves around my legs.

Servinaz swam about for five minutes or so. I could hear her hands cutting through the water. There didn't seem to be anyone else on the beach except us. Now and then a few dogs would start barking near the summer cottages. The heady aroma of sage tickled my nostrils. At night the cliffs, distorted and pocked by the wind and the waves, loomed up eerily from the sea. Each time Servinaz headed towards them I would call her back. Someone fired a gun. We were used to that. It meant someone who was alone in one of the cottages was signalling to the world that the cottage was not abandoned. At last Servinaz shouted:

"Hey, Scaredy, turn away! I'm coming out!"

I jumped down from my perch on the boat. My hand, either from force of habit or because I was unable to control the feelings that had come over me, began writing her name in the damp sand. First I drew some circles and then filled in the letters of her name. I could hear her come up onto the beach and begin to dress, but I did not stand up until she stood beside me. For some reason or other she spoke in a whisper:

"Come on!" Then she saw the letters in the sand. "Did you write that?"

"There's nobody else around, is there?"

We started out in silence. Then Servinaz said with a smile:

"I bet no other boy would've turned away."

I liked what she had said and wanted her to repeat it.

"What did you say?"

"Nothing. Come on. Hurry. If Grandpa wakes up and sees I'm gone, he'll go crazy." She took my hand again and pulled me along. "If it was up to him, he'd never even let me talk to you. He said he, meaning you, is a big boy now. And you, meaning us, shouldn't pal around any more. Grandpa's funny. I don't know why he's so worried when we're together." She looked at me saucily.

229

I didn't know what to say and so asked in turn: "Do you think he's right?"

"That's what I asked you."

"Well, I am asking you."

We always put up scarecrows when the melons began to ripen. I found a worn old hat and set it on a pole in the middle of the melon patch. Servinaz made a real scarecrow. It had a hat and a jacket. When I got closer I exclaimed, "Those are Sattar's!"

She nodded. "They were lying by the road, so I picked them up. See, the birds are so scared they're keeping away."

These were a very ordinary jacket and a hat so old the brim was glossy. Once again the terrible scene came back to me. That night the whole block had awakened from the scream:

"My mule's burning! My mule's burning!" It was the kerosene man, Sattar.

Flames soon engulfed the street. It seemed the very walls of the houses were burning. We all ran to the fire and saw two flaming torches spinning around. One was Sattar, the other was the mule. As we stood there, paralysed by fear, Servinaz rushed up to Sattar with a large blanket which she threw over him. She then began pulling it tighter and tighter around him. The people finally understood what she was doing and rushed over to help. Sattar was saved, but his poor mule burned to death. The mule used to carry the cans of kerosene from town which Sattar then sold in the village. The poor beast's coat was soaked with kerosene, and so it burned like a torch. We were all sorry for Sattar, too. His mule and his hat were landmarks in the village. Besides, he was the only one of the local men who wore a hat.

Now his scorched hat and burned jacket had become a part of a scarecrow.

Servinaz sighed and said: "If Grandpa'd let me, I'd buy Sattar another mule with the money we get for the melons. I'm so sorry for him!"

It occurred to me then that if Servinaz were a boy, she'd never have a penny to her name.

* * *

I had graduated from our village seven-year school and was leaving to continue my studies in the city. As I was setting out on my journey in a horse-drawn cart early that morning, I saw Servinaz. She was so downhearted she looked as if she might burst into tears. Servinaz came over to me and said in a choked voice:

"All boys are faithless. Don't be like the others. Don't forget us."

I did not return home until the following summer and immediately set out for the melon patches near the beach. The one next to ours that belonged to Servinaz's grandfather was barren. Then I saw her younger brother. He told me she was dead. Three months before a village woman had been washing some blankets and rugs in the sea. Her two little girls had gone in swimming and were caught by the undertow. Servinaz heard their cries and came running. Though she saved the children, she lost her own life.

All my dreams crumbled. I went down to the beach. The water was the same, the weatherbeaten cliffs that smelled of seaweed were the same, and the rowboat was still there with its bow buried in the sand. Everything was the same. But my Servinaz was no more.

There was so much I wanted to tell you, my Servinaz. I'm no longer the tongue-tied boy I used to be. Can you hear me? My dreams of the past and of the future have become waifs without you. I had been silent for so many years, storing up all that I wanted to tell you. Today I have finally found the courage to do so. Can you hear me? The air is once again filled with the heady fragrance of sage. The scarecrow you made became lop-sided and then toppled over. I raised it and set it straight again. Your grandfather doesn't snore any more. The poor old man is haggard from insomnia now. And I wrote a poem about you. I called it: "My Servinaz is more spirited than the sea."

Suleiman Veliev
(b. 1916)

Suleiman Veliev was born in the settlement of Romany on Apsheron near Baku. His grandfather and father worked in the oil industry and he too worked in the old oil fields of Baku.

During World War II, he fought on the front and was held prisoner in fascist concentration camps in Germany and Italy. He joined Italian and Yugoslavian partisans in the Resistance. He travelled to Egypt, Iran and Iraq.

He characteristically describes events that he himself has witnessed. As a result his scenes of pre-revolutionary Azerbaijan are vivid and precise; he has proved himself a master at depicting the worker's movement in the years before the October Revolution and the burdens of wartime tasks. We have selected his sketch of the city on the sea, the renowned Neftyanye Kamni, for inclusion here.

His latest novel Knots *deals with Veliev's favourite heroes, the labourers and oil workers developing new oil deposits in Shirvan.*

A Town at Sea

It is not so easy to get to Neftyanye Kamni. Only in clear, fine weather does the Caspian seem to issue permission to pass over its waters, and one can reach the fabulous township sprawling over the fitful waters.

A vessel called the M/S *Babazade* cruises between Baku and Neftyanye Kamni. It has been called after the man whose bold insight first penetrated beneath the sea bottom to reveal its horde of petroleum and who now, in a new guise, over and over makes the same difficult but by now rutine trip. The M/S *Babazade* carries oil workers from Baku to the derricks rising straight out of the sea, to a settlement of blooming gardens, canteens, a club, a medical centre, workers' hostels and even a book shop standing on concrete foundations amidst the sea. On off days it takes them back to the city, to their families and friends.

In one of the cabins we saw an exposition devoted to that outstanding Soviet geologist whose life work is associated with the "black gold", the principal wealth of Apsheron.

From the boat there opens up a view on the coastal town of Khanlar, so named after Khanlar Safaraliev, a revolutionary killed in 1907.

Once Aga Neimatulla, the famous specialist on oil, drilled several inclined wells there, but to his dismay

233

instead of oil found only hot water and mud. Experts, however, established that this was salubrious mud that provided relief against rheumatism and other ailments. A mud clinic was opened in the town, which is now famous all over the republic.

This mud was evidently a companion of oil. Incidentally, Naphthalan oil, extracted in the village of Naphthalan, itself possesses many curative properties. It is a miraculous medicament, like the fairy-tale water of life. People suffering from rheumatism converge on Naphthalan from all parts of the country and go home hale and hearty.

The boat churned on, little by little, the shore melted in the haze. And as if in response to our fervent anticipation the first derricks rose out of the water.

It all started when inclined drilling of wells reaching out far under the sea bottom was invented. Oil workers tried building concrete, earth-filled islands at sea. On the suggestion of Babazade several old, scrapped ship hulls were anchored far at sea. From them the first offshore wells were drilled, and they are functioning to this day. Neftyanye Kamni, however, reckons its birthday from the time the so-called trestle method was elaborated and light, tough structures could reach far out to sea, spanning the deeps from support to support. This is a hundred kilometres from Baku. Who would ever have undertaken to drill a well that long beneath the sea bed?

After a journey of a little over three hours we disembark at the unusual community, itself a miracle of modern engineering.

We approach the first derrick, which we had sighted from the boat. A marble plaque attached to it bears the inscription in tarnished gold letters: "The first well, drilled by operator Kaverochkin, which marked the beginning of offshore oil production. Yielded first oil November 7, 1949. "

The name of Kaverochkin is known all over Azerbaijan, for he headed the first party that gained a foothold on the Caspian Sea. Working day and night for three months, battered by hurricane winds, he and his companions drilled the first oil-yielding well, opening up the treasure-trove under the Caspian. In that fierce struggle with the elements, when the wind reached force 13 on the Beaufort scale, Kaverochkin, Sadykhov, Gasanov perished like heroes....

Yes, the Caspian may be grim indeed. Even now, when the Neftyanye Kamni has grown into a veritable township and everything is done to ensure the safety of one and all, the going is sometimes hard. The trestles have become wide streets, at the centre of the community is a mooring square, with an eating place, club and book shop brightly lit up at night. Trees grow and flowers bloom on earth brought from the mainland. Truly a fairy-tale garden on the high seas. For the celebrations of the 50th anniversary of Soviet power, a boulevard was opened, with game pavilions and benches to sit on in the shade of the trees.

On the day of our arrival the Caspian was majestically calm, sparkling gaily in the sunlight. It was hard to believe that here was the second stormiest body of water in the world after the Bay of Biscay. Perhaps it was because the heroic oil workers had harnessed and tamed it?

Now it was the attractive, bountiful Caspian that is rich not only in oil but also in some of the finest fish varieties, notably of the sturgeon family. Caspian sturgeon, in fact, accounts for a substantial share of the world's caviar production.

In general, it must be said that nature has generously provided our Apsheron Peninsula with riches. One need but name saffron, one gram of which is literally worth its weight in gold.

However, there is no need for digressions: a trip to Neftyanye Kamni is interesting in itself.

This forest of derricks is in reliable hands. The fields are in the charge of Kurban Abbasov, a pupil of Kaverochkin, past-master of offshore drilling, deputy to the Supreme Soviet of the USSR. After the death of his elder friend he took his place and drilled the second well into the sea.

At a distance from the derricks I noticed a cylindrical structure rising out of the sea. It looked like an oil tank, but seemed too small.

"That little tank holds no more no less than twenty thousand tons of oil," remarked a passing oil worker, evidently observing my inquisitive look.

"Impossible!"

"It's the height of a twelve-storey building," my chance companion laughed. "Simply most of it is below the surface, that is about forty metres."

He was silent for a while, then asked, "Did you see the pumping station?"

Without waiting for an answer he led me to the pumping station that pumps the extracted oil to the reservoirs and tankers. It all seemed so simple, but it would perhaps stagger the imagination even of such a bold master of fantasy as Jules Verne himself.

I have spoken of Neftyanye Kamni as of a town, but even so it was strange to come on a door with the notice "Town Soviet" over it, so out of place the very down-to-earth notion of a municipal authority seemed to be out at sea.

Here are some brief notes from my writing pad.

The population of the township is over six thousand. They represent almost thirty nationalities. Of course the word "population" must be understood in not quite its conventional sense: these people live both at sea and in Baku, where each has his flat or room.

Neftyanye Kamni has an Oil Technical School, where the workers can continue their education. The Palace of Culture runs an amateur arts circle. Performers from Baku often come to supplement the amateur concerts, and People's Artist of the USSR Rashid Beibutov, People's Artist of Azerbaijan Shovket Alekperova and many others are frequent guests there.

We guests of Neftyanye Kamni and the men returning home after work sit in the boulevard before boarding the boat which in a few minutes will take us back to Baku. The sea stretches out all around. Several black rocks looking like the wet backs of seals now hide beneath the swell, now appear again. It was these rocks that gave Neftyanye Kamni its name — Oil Rocks. Before, even the bravest fishermen feared approaching them in their flimsy boats. The rocks were slippery, oily — no one suspected then that it was oil that made them like that. It was impossible to climb them, but very easy to be shipwrecked on them even in a minor storm. Occasionally blue lights of burning gas flickered about the black rocks, and this "satanic" fire frightened people off.

Once again the *Babazade* hospitably invited us to its deck. At sea one more surprise awaited us: a floating drilling rig. Such rigs are searching for oil in the Soviet Union for the first time, and one hardly knows whether to call the men at the wheel oil workers or sailors.

Not long ago I read in the newspaper *Baku* that a whole floating installation is under construction. It is designed for drilling wells down to 6,000 metres under a tremendous layer of water. The installation will have a displacement of 9,000 tons, its platform will be 60 metres long by 45 wide and its overall height will be 7.5 metres. It will be the largest floating drilling rig in the world. The huge installation will house a veritable automated plant. The workers will have not only well-appointed cabins to live in but also a hall which can be used as a cinema, a club or recreation room.

The new floating rig will first be towed to the neighbourhood of Neftyanye Kamni, where it will commence test drilling at difficult sites. Then the string of trestles will perhaps go farther still out to sea, and with it the green boulevard of rustling trees and blooming flowers.

Baku has rightly earned the name of "Oil Academy". It is not accidental that Baku oilmen can be found in many parts of the country, where they help develop newly tapped oil riches. I myself met them in Eastern Siberia, where our southerners were undaunted by the unaccustomed frosts and frozen ground. Baku oil workers were once urgently summoned to neighbouring Turkmenistan to help put out a well fire.

Oil production in Azerbaijan is steadily mounting, and more than half of the output comes from the Caspian Sea, a treasure-trove from which the toilers of Neftyanye Kamni retrieve the black gold.

But don't think that the sea oil costs a lot.

Although the building and exploitation of all these structures call for substantial outlays, the offshore oil costs only about one-third that of oil extracted on the shore in Baku. First of all, because the riches concealed in the sea bed exceed anything we know on earth. The oil there does not have to be pumped out—usually it gushes in a mighty fountain.

Our boat approached Baku. The old Bibi-Eibat oil field on the shore hove into sight. It was there that more than one hundred years ago Azerbaijan's first oil derrick was erected. It was there after visiting this oil field that Maxim Gorky remarked so aptly and with such pain: "This city, standing at a treasure horde, is unequalled in the poverty of life and nature."

That was what our Baku once had been. Now our ship approached the fine sea front with trees rustling along it, and we were greeted by the festive glow of thousands of evening lights. Against the darkening sky rose new beautiful buildings erected in Soviet times when the national wealth has come to belong to the people and serve as a source of their well-being and happiness.

Imran Kasumov

(b. 1918)

A dramatist, prosaist and public figure, Kasumov is known far beyond the confines of Soviet Azerbaijan. The film On Distant Shores *adapted from the novel of the same name (which Kasumov wrote in collaboration with Gasan Seidbeili) has played in cinemas in many countries. His play* A Man Casts Anchor *was produced in Moscow's Maly Theatre.*

"A man should not only survive, he should prevail". This is one of the themes of Kasumov's story "The Summit Ahead" included in this anthology. It shows his characteristic laconicism, profound subtext, and rejection of rhetoric and superfluous ornament.

In recent years the writer completed a documentary narrative about the glorious daughter of Azerbaijan, Djeiran, who participated in the French Resistance; it is titled "French Gobelin".

A novella for reading and the cinema written on the basis of a true story heard from climbers of high mountains.

The Summit Ahead

A tall, slender girl in a worsted sports suit walks down the passage of a sleeping car.

She passes by the open doors of several compartments.

In one four lads, arms thrown over each other's shoulders, sing a comic college song on the eternal subject of the heartless, desiccated professor and the torments of their fellow-student for the benefit of their listeners, who sit crowded closely on the bunks....

In another a tow-headed lad in a thick sweater is showing tricks to two oh-ing and ah-ing girls: he rubs a coin into his forehead and retrieves it from the heel of his shoe; swallows the coin, demonstrating empty hands, then takes it out of his ear. He takes a doughnut from the table, then another, dispatches them into his mouth, and, to the girls' indignation, pats his belly sheepishly — they're gone for good this time....

In another two students sit in the soft light of the table lamp while a third finishes a sketch with swift, confident strokes of a pencil....

The girl passes on, and only on the dark coach platform finds the one she is looking for standing at the door half opened into the rushing night.

"And stubbornly he seeks to be alone," she comments in a sing-song voice, fingering a long string of beads on her chest. "I've been searching the whole car for you, Kyamil."

239

"I can't sing or show tricks or draw," Kyamil says with a wry grin, puffing at the stub of his cigarette.

He is a very tall, solidly built, black-haired lad, also dressed in a sports suit.

"But they can't climb mountains like you," the girl says.

"I suppose that's so," the lad agrees reluctantly.

"Then let's go," the girl urges him. "Let them sing and show tricks for themselves."

"No, Sevda," Kyamil says, shaking his head.

He flings the cigarette stub out of the open door.

"It'll be the same old thing. As soon as I appear in the compartment, Sasha will stop showing his tricks and offer to go over my paleontology with me, and our whole choral quartet, to brush up my historical materialism," he adds.

"To each his own," Sevda says, compressing her lips.

"Certainly," Kyamil agrees with her again. "I was looking forward to the holidays to tell them just that."

"And you will," Sevda says fervently, moving closer to him. "I can already see the main institute vestibule, the wall straight ahead, and your picture on it, Kyamil.... Everyone who passes remarks: There's our most famed alumnus...."

Her vehemence slightly embarrasses Kyamil.

"Meantime a long list of students' examinations arrears hangs there," he says thoughtfully. He touches Sevda's neck. "Will you give me these beads, Sevda?"

"What for?" she asks with surprise.

"There's a rock cairn on the top of Mount Garlydag. In a few days they will lie inside that cairn," he says in a solemn voice.

"How nice," Sevda exclaims, clapping her hands. "By all means!"

They stand side by side and see their reflection in the window glass.

...Their heads reflect in exactly the same way in the blue water of a small mountain lake. It is morning, and upside down in the lake are Sevda, Kyamil and, a little behind them, the sky with Garlydag in the company of two lower peaks rearing into it its snow-capped head.

"Of course, Garlydag isn't the tallest mountain in the Caucasus, but climbing it is rated in the 'top difficulty' class," Kyamil says thoughtfully.

His hand traces the outline of the peak on the water.

"Three 'sentinels' bar the way to the top, and you have to be a rock-climber and an ice-climber there," Kyamil goes on.

"You'll overcome those nasty sentinels," Sevda whispers with conviction.

"Several teams of climbers have been on Garlydag and erected the cairn there," Kyamil goes on without paying attention to her words. "But I...."

"What?"

"I'll place your beads in it after a traverse of the three adjacent peaks," Kyamil's hand describes a triple arc over the mountains.

Sevda hastily removes the beads from her neck.

Kyamil takes them, opens his mouth to say something, but is interrupted.

"Kyamil!" someone shouts from aloft.

Kyamil lifts his head.

They are sitting on a steep, grass-covered bank, a sheer cliff rising behind their backs with Garlydag and its neighbours in the background.

A rope ladder hangs down the cliff, several lads out on a training hike are standing at the top, while midway a girl is suspended caught in a rope rung.

"Kindergarten kids," Kyamil grumbles.

He jumps to his feet, runs up to the foot of the cliff and, clinging to rocky juttings, expertly climbs to the girl and loosens the ladder. The frightened girl cautiously continues her descent.

"You'd have done better to join a housekeeping circle and learn to make salads and soups," Kyamil throws after her.

Easily, without the help of the ladder, he climbs quickly down.

And finds himself next to an elderly balding man who has just appeared.

"Are you the party that's going to scale Garlydag?" the man inquires.

"Uhuh."

"I guessed at once," the man says, smiling, and extends his hand. "Kurbanov, base manager. Who's going with you?"

"One magician and one lyrical tenor," Kyamil says.

"Joking aside."

"I'm not joking," Kyamil assures him. "If you can't have what you want better want what you have."

They walk slowly towards the brightly painted clapboard bungalows of the base....

Sasha and Tofik, the shortest of the singers, appear, walking towards them.

"Meet Alexander Bochkov and Tofik Alizade, both with second-grade ratings," Kyamil introduces them to Kurbanov. "You can look them up in the voucher."

Kurbanov greets Sasha and Tofik. Together they approach the porch of one of the bungalows.

"One day for checking equipment, medical examination and rest," Kurbanov says. "The whole team ascends to the western saddle. You pitch a bivouac there, fix your return deadline, and three of you go on together with Faramaz." He nods in the direction of a summer pavilion.

Kyamil, Sasha and Tofik turn to look.

Faramaz is a very old man. Wearing a *chukha* with decorative cartridge rows on the breast, he sits on a tree stump in front of the pavilion, a heavy, knotty stick lying at his side, and silently fingers a rosary, looking at them from under bushy eyebrows.

"Some companion," Kyamil mutters.

"I bet he's seen Lermontov or fought with Shamil," Tofik exclaims with sincere admiration.

"Ekh, forgot my camera on the cot," Kyamil says, snapping his fingers in dismay. "He'd make a fine picture sitting on that stump."

"I wonder how a rucksack and crampons will look on that relic," Sasha muses, scratching the back of his head.

"He'll be in his *chukha* and with his stick," Kurbanov says. "That's how he always goes."

With a gesture Kurbanov indicates the climbers.

Faramaz nods his acquiescence.

Kurbanov draws a triple zigzag with his hand, meaning a triple traverse.

Faramaz nods agreement.

"So," Kyamil exclaims, "first a kindergarten to the bivouac, then venerable pensioners...."

...The bivouac: several tents, portable crates with supplies, an antenna over one of the tents.

The camp is on a moraine field in a small saddle high up in the mountains. Behind it gleams the sugar head of Garlydag with its two companion peaks. Kyamil, Sasha and Tofik are strung out, fully equipped, across the moraine. Faramaz, with nothing but his stick resting shepherd-fashion on one shoulder, is up in front. Lads and girls stand by the tents, seeing the climbers off.

"The last departure deadline is noon of the fifth day," Kurbanov says to Kyamil.

"It's six fifteen on my watch now," Kyamil says in a business-like voice, comparing his watch with that of the base chief.

"What'll we do without you?" one of the lads asks when Tofik comes abreast of him.

"Sing in trio at dawn and dusk, and I'll join you up there," Tofik says, laughing and pointing to the sky.

"Farewell, better half of mankind!" Sasha calls out. He removes the ice axe from his belt and manipulates it in front of the girls, but it slips to the ground.

"Misfire," Sasha says, bowing foolishly, and goes on.

Sevda overtakes Kyamil.

"You haven't forgot anything?" she asks hurriedly. "You're sure you haven't?"

"Of course not," Kyamil says endearingly, patting his breast pocket.

He looks over the send-off party.

"Well, here's the full complement: Goodbye, *do svidania, khudafis, salud, arrividerci!*" he calls out.

He quickens his steps and catches up with Faramaz.

"*Aufwiedersehen!*" one of the lads calls out.

"*Adieu!*" someone echoes him.

"*Do svidania,*" the parting cry rises faintly over the hills.

The girls mill about Sevda.

"You know," she says dreamily, looking after the file of climbers vanishing into the distance. "He'll come back a celebrity...."

"And what if he doesn't?" a freckled girl says.

"What d'ye mean?" Sevda asks fearfully.

...Kyamil wipes his forehead.

The four are standing on the highest point of the first height of the route, which is blotched here and there with white spots of snow.

"There are caves lower down," Faramaz says, pointing with his stick. "We can spend the night there."

"What do you mean 'spend the night'?" Kyamil asks angrily. "It's hardly past noon. By nightfall we'll have passed the second peak."

"It's worse camping there," Faramaz says impassively.

"On we go," Kyamil says, leading the way.

As impassively, Faramaz overtakes him and goes in front.

"Perhaps we should pitch camp?" Sasha suggests.

Kyamil halts.

"In the cave we can make ourselves comfortable: cook dinner, listen to the radio," Sasha pats the transistor dangling on his chest.

"Anyone second the motion?" Kyamil asks, turning to Tofik.

"Second the motion? Motion, motion," Tofik sings to a familiar operetta tune. "Camp for the night? Camp for the night!"

"All opinions have been voiced. The decision stands: we climb over the second peak," Kyamil sums up, following the guide. Sighing, the lads shamble after him.

The descent is easy, the rope is slack. A pair of feet in soft, felt-topped *chustas* pass by, followed by another pair in rock-climbing shoes, then another and another....

The guide's feet gingerly test a snow-covered ledge. The knobby stick digs into the ground, then a slow step forward....

Another descent. The crest of the second peak can be seen behind the climbers' backs, their going is much harder now.

The rope connecting the three passes over the shoulder and under the armpit of each man; guide holds the end.

Faramaz seems slow, but behind his slowness one senses the experienced highlander. He selects a convenient position, slackens the rope and looks expectantly up. Kyamil does not hold up the team: in two or three movements he is already next to Faramaz. Sasha, bringing up the rear, is in high spirits.

But Tofik is evidently unwell: he licks his cracked lips and every metre of the descent requires an effort of the will.

Unable to gain a firm foothold on the place vacated by Kyamil, he sways.

Regaining his balance, he accidentally pushes a stone.

The stone rolls down towards Kyamil. With an agile movement Kyamil kicks the stone aside. Gathering more and more rocks on its way the rumbling mass cascades into a dense bank of clouds.

Below the clouds hollow explosion-like thunder shakes the silence.

Sasha makes a sign to Kyamil that Tofik is poorly off.

"Have some lemon juice," Kyamil suggests. "We won't be long now."

"Don't mind me, boys," Tofik reassures them. "I'm all right."

But he takes the flask from Kyamil and makes several gulps.

In the tent Tofik drinks avidly from a mug.

Drops of water roll down the sleeping bag from which he has stuck his head out to drink.

Sasha makes him comfortable again, pulls up the zipper of the bag and covers him with blankets.

He walks over to Kyamil, who is sitting on a round stone, grimly opening a tin with a knife in the light of a pocket torch fastened to the tent pole.

Broth is boiling in a pot on a gas stove at his side, a little way off lie several thermos bottles.

A gust of wind buffets the small nylon tent.

"He's running a fever," Sasha says softly, sitting down next to Kyamil.

"I noticed it earlier," Kyamil says moodily. "I reached to pull him over and felt his hand was hot. Is he asleep?"

Sasha nods silently.

"We should have stopped in the caves," he says with a sigh.

"Sure, we'd have had central heating and carpet runners on the floor there," Kyamil says in a serious voice.

"Still...."

"Still we're one lap closer," Kyamil says, pointing the knife upward.

Sasha moves over to him.

"Do you think he'll make it?" he asks in a whisper, nodding at Tofik.

He is sure that Tofik is asleep, but he isn't and, licking parched lips, listens to the conversation.

"Won't make it?" Kyamil frowns. "Well...."

Abruptly he changes the subject. "Rouse that relic of the eighteen-thirties. Breakfast's ready."

Sasha directs the torch to another corner of the tent.

"He's not there," he says, surprised.

"Here I am," comes from outside, and Faramaz clambers in. "Cleaned the snow a bit. There's always lots of snow here," he informs them.

Deftly Sasha pours the broth into mugs.

"Have you been here often?" Kyamil inquires curiously.

Tofik continues to watch them through half-closed eyes.

"Not often," Faramaz says indifferently, sipping his broth. "Been with the elder Abalakov, been with two *Inglisi* and Japaridze, been with our scouts in the war," he ticks off the fingers on his gnarled hand. "Been with Fatma."

"Been with the elder Abalakov?" Kyamil says distrustfully, turning to Sasha. "I wonder what *he* needed him for?"

"You don't happen to have acted as guide to Tenzing, Tiger of the Snows?" Sasha says sarcastically.

"No," the old man shakes his head simply.

"Oh, I forgot," Sasha says gaily. "Tenzing's a guide himself, besides he lives in Nepal and climbs the Himalaya."

"Wait a moment," Kyamil says, pulling his sleeve. "I know both the Abalakovs, I've heard of Japaridze and read about the scouts' making their way from here to the German rear," he recalls. "But Fatma...."

"My old woman," Faramaz says impassively.

He falls silent and buries his nose into his mug.

"Sclerosis?" Sasha says inquiringly, touching his head with his finger.

"Probably," Kyamil shrugs.

"Faramaz," Kyamil addresses the old man. "What if we leave the sick one here and then pick him up on the way back?"

"No," Sasha says firmly.

"Yes," Kyamil says as firmly.

A heavy silence follows.

Sasha's and Kyamil's eyes meet, and both refuse to be outstared.

"Snow will bury him," says Sasha.

"We'll dig him out," says Kyamil.

"There's no such law," Sasha says vehemently.

"Yes, there is," Kyamil says without batting an eyelid. "Three don't wait for one."

Silence again.

Faramaz pushes back his plate and looks from Sasha to Kyamil and back.

"Time we were going," a casual voice says from the corner of the tent, and Tofik enters the circle of light, dragging his rucksack. "A breakfast chat is a pleasant thing, but why climb this high for it?" he remarks just as casually, and begins to collect blankets and thermoses.

"Tofik," says Sasha, taking a thermos from his hands, "I'll stay with you."

"Why?" Tofik asks quickly, and then answers himself, addressing them all.

"Because I almost fell on the traverse, got scared and out of fright decided to pretend I was ill?"

"But you *are* ill, you've got a cold," Sasha says indignantly. "You're coughing."

"Sure," Tofik says. "Pneumonia, pleurisy, consumption. Give me that thermos."

"Tofik!" Kyamil intervenes sternly.

"Sorry, Kyamil," Tofik says, packing up the gas stove. "I really got scared and decided I'd sleep it out in the bag while you make the climb...."

He stands up and adjusts the rucksack on his back.

"Sorry," he says again disarmingly. Throwing aside the door flap, he goes out.

...Stubbornly biting his lip and trying to walk with a rhythmic gait, Tofik climbs up the névé-covered slope.

In front are Kyamil, Sasha, Faramaz.

It is a gloomy early morning with gusts of wind.

Sasha draws abreast of Faramaz.

"The worst thing is when it's even like this," he says, puffing. "You hardly notice when you start gasping and shift from third into first gear."

"It *can* be worse," Faramaz remarks philosophically.

"And the wind, damn it," Sasha curses good-naturedly in an attempt to keep up the conversation. But Faramaz is silent, looking down at his feet.

Sasha falls back, waiting for Kyamil to approach.

"What are you thinking of?" he begins to pester Kyamil.

"Of the weight of beads," Kyamil replies enigmatically. "How much do you think a string of plain women's beads may weigh?"

"Imitation?" Sasha inquires in the careless voice of a connoisseur.

"Imitation?" Kyamil asks incomprehendingly. "Plain glass beads, a long string."

"One hundred grammes," Sasha says confidently. "Why?"

"Thanks for the information," Kyamil says, indicating that he has no intention of elaborating.

Sasha lags behind again waiting for Tofik to come up.

"Bearable?" he asks cheerfully.

"Go along," Tofik responds through clenched teeth. "Look after yourself, spinning like a top."

"Everyone in the blues," Sasha complains. "Could it be the broth?"

Faramaz disappears behind a crest, followed by Kyamil.

"After this turn—the summit!" Sasha announces triumphantly as he too disappears.

Without stopping, Tofik reaches for his flask, swallows some juice and makes a face.

He hastens to the crest, rounds it and halts, disappointed.

The summit of Garlydag is not there. Only the last "sentinel": an almost smooth, sheer wall beyond which one guesses the beginning of snow and ice fields leading up to the summit which is hidden behind a dense, billowing shroud of mist.

"No go," Faramaz says, pointing up with his stick.

"No go?" Kyamil queries worriedly, though he has understood the guide's meaning only too well.

"Garlydag is hiding," Faramaz says phlegmatically. "We'll have to turn back."

"What?" asks Sasha, taking it for a joke.

"Back?" Tofik involuntarily betrays his relief.

"Back?" Kyamil knits his eyebrows. "Go back when we're so close? One more turn and...."

"Seven or eight hundred metres," Sasha estimates.

"Retreat? Return to the camp? Have a heart, old man!" Kyamil's voice rises to a shout.

"You can't go," Faramaz persists. "The clouds are coming up."

"Hell with them! Let it spew fire and brimstone, let it collapse," Kyamil rages. "Forward!"

"I won't go," Faramaz shakes his head.

"No one's asking you," Kyamil snaps. "Sasha, Tofik, come along!"

He takes a grip on himself.

"Let him remain," he says in a low but imperative voice to his companions. "We'll go alone. In any case, what can that mummy of a man add to all we have? He's only a nuisance."

Leaning on his stick, Faramaz watches them impassively. The mountaineers recede in the distance.

They reach the "sentinel" and knot the climbing rope.

Selecting several folds, Kyamil begins to scale the wall. Sasha and Tofik follow.

Kyamil pulls himself up on his arms, gets a foothold on an outcropping, throws the rope over a ledge, draws himself up, then helps Sasha. Sasha begins to help Tofik while Kyamil shifts to the right, looking for a new outcropping to pass the rope over.

From a distance they look like outlandish insects zigzagging their way up a black-and-white wall.

Faramaz gives in.

When, after the next lap, Kyamil gains a small jutting ledge he is dumbfounded to see the old man there.

"Pitons," Faramaz demands.

Without another word Faramaz takes the pitons and makes his way up, using only his stick, which he presses into hardly noticeable fissures.

Sasha gains the ledge.

"It's a trick," he exclaims admiringly, watching Faramaz's soft *chustas* twinkle above him. "Like an automation."

Straining with all his weight at the rope, Tofik finally gains the ledge, completely exhausted.

"Forward!" orders Kyamil, following Faramaz.

Tofik waits till Sasha makes room for him, and when Sasha's feet are above his head squats down, pulls out the flask and takes another convulsive gulp.

Faramaz makes his way up a shallow trough in the cliff, his body almost perpendicular to its sides, his hands pushing into one edge of the hollow, his feet into the other.

From below Kyamil can see only the skirts of his *chukha*, girdled with a thin belt, and the rosary swinging at his wrist.

When he reaches the end of the hollow Faramaz hammers a piton into the rock.

Using it as a pulley and helping each other, the climbers negotiate another dozen metres.

The climb is very difficult and at times it seems impossible for people to move along such a wall at all.

Faramaz's hands grasp a small, hoar-frosted outcropping and he slowly pulls himself up.

Kyamil's hands appear and repeat the old man's movements.

Sasha's hands, then Tofik's....

The most difficult part comes.

The "sentinel" is cleaved in two. They must pass over to the other slope, and the climbers span the crevasse with a telescopic ladder.

Balancing with his stick, Faramaz walks steadily across.

Easily, without stopping, Kyamil crosses.

Slower, but also agilely, Sasha gains the other side.

Tofik also walks well, but when there is two rungs left the ladder begins to slip down.

One moment Tofik is dangling on the rope, the next he is with his comrades.

In spite of the cold beads of sweat appear on Kyamil's forehead.

"What are you thinking of?" Sasha asks, cheerful as ever.

"Of the weight of sweat," Kyamil says, wiping his forehead. "How many tons do you imagine this sweat weighs?"

"Who do you think I am, the Bureau of Weights and Measures?" Sasha pleads.

"Forward," Kyamil says, changing the subject.

One last effort remains for them to overcome the "sentinel".

Beyond the crest sparkle the ice fields of Garlydag.

The summit itself is still enveloped in mist like in a dense smoke.

The wind blows stronger, sweeping fine powdered ice across the slope.

The climbers sit down around Faramaz on a circular plateau with thermoses and bars of chocolate in their hands.

Tofik coughs hoarsely and Kyamil turns to him.

Tofik tries to quell the fit, but the cough gets more harrowing. He turns away.

Kyamil grips Tofik's scarf and turns the lad back.

"Did your nose bleed?" Kyamil asks with a frown.

"Whose, mine?" Tofik feigns incomprehension as he hastily wipes his cheeks and nose. "Oh, there was a pimple...."

Sasha lays a hand on his brow. "He's running a fever."

"It's a pity, of course," Kyamil says, "but you'll have to stay behind."

"All right," Sasha sighs. "I didn't like the idea down below, I care even less for it here.... But I'll stay with him."

"As a matter of fact," Kyamil starts, but falls silent, pulls out a cigarette and lights it.

His companions understand that he wants to say something important.

"As a matter of fact," Kyamil drawls, blowing out smoke, "I think the best thing would be for the guide to remain with you. I don't need him, I can reach the top myself."

"No one can," Faramaz says suddenly. "It's hiding."

247

"Let it spew fire and brimstone," Kyamil growls. "I said so before the 'sentinel', and I say so now when the summit is straight ahead.... Why, I'll get there dead or alive. Sasha."

"Yes," Sasha says bleakly.

"We'll find a shelter and you'll remain with the sick man."

"Who's sick?" Tofik rises to his feet. "You mean to say I'm sick?"

He demonstratively pulls out his flask, swallows a large gulp from it and picks up his alpenstock.

"You call me a poor sick thing?" He even tries to guffaw.

Headlong, he shambles stumblingly in the direction of the summit.

"He'll last for no more than quarter of an hour, and we have four hundred metres of ice and snow before us," Sasha muses outloud.

"Stop!" he cries. "Stop, Tofik!"

In response Tofik strikes up the familiar students' song about the professor and the student. He not so much sings it as shouts the words in a frenzy, and it doesn't sound at all gay.

"There's no stopping him," Kyamil mutters.

"But he's really ill," Sasha says worriedly. "He was ill even yesterday, and now...."

"Forward!" Kyamil interrupts.

They hurry after Tofik: a dark shape in an opalescent haze.

They approach it, but the shadow turns out to be Faramaz, who somehow got there ahead of them.

Faramaz overtakes Tofik and takes his place at the head of the file.

The wind grows stronger, a blizzard begins.

The four start the climb to the summit.

Three times the white haze shrouds them completely.

...They have to cross a bottomless chasm in the ice.

...They have to dive under a ledge to seek shelter from a sudden thundering ice-fall.

...Finally they are forced to ascend facing the sky, their backs to the steep crest, hacking steps with an ice-ax, finding a foothold, and hacking new steps.... All the while their backs to the summit....

Suddenly, as if by magic, the blizzard subsides.

Absolute stillness sets in.

We see the mountaineers in the midst of a primordial kingdom of snow: they are on the highest point of Garlydag, next to the cairn erected by previous climbers; the blinding sun shines above them.

Only three of them are standing: Faramaz, Kyamil and Sasha.

Tofik lies by the cairn. It was his last spurt, after which he collapsed and is gasping like a fish pulled out of water.

One would have expected the conquerors to laugh, shout, dance. But it was a hard-won victory, and Kyamil and Sasha stand stock-still, only a blissful smile reveals their triumph.

"Garlydag, top difficulty," Kyamil says, whispering for some reason, as though hardly believing himself.

"Up here you feel like thinking in music and poetry," Sasha whispers like one entranced and begins to quote from different poems. "Up here I see how torrents are born, how clouds assembly and dash for a storm.... Or: Your mountains have tresses whiter than milk, surrounded by veils softer than silk.... Or: Cliffs and glaciers and mountain streams, sun and sky and clouds like dreams.... Oh, boys, I'm overwhelmed."

He switches on the radio on his chest, striking music at once.

"Can you see it all?" Kyamil asks Sasha.

Lifting his glasses he spreads his arms wide as though he would embrace the whole world.

The sun blazes and glitters, and a remarkable scene lies before them: the fanciful silhouettes of formidable peaks, the blackness of precipices and gorges, billowing clouds over valleys.

"I see it," Sasha whispers. "The ridge, the spurs, even an eagle hovering yonder."

"And, beyond the mountains, the main vestibule of the Institute," Kyamil adds irrelevantly.

"What has the vestibule got to do with this?" Sasha asks incomprehendingly.

"There's a list of students' arrears hung up there, but now it's not important," Kyamil whispers. "Now pictures of the most distinguished alumni of the Institute will hang on the façade wall."

"Is that what you climbed up here for?" Sasha asked, switching off the radio.

"What else," Kyamil says, blinking—and not suspecting why. "To recite poetry, and that in a whisper? But why in a whisper?"

"What people say loudly down below, they say quietly on the summit," Faramaz suddenly says, speaking from under his hood completely closing his face. "We must go down, it'll start blowing again."

Kyamil stoops to place the traditional note in the cairn and suddenly just realises that all this time Tofik has been lying motionless at its foot.

"He's unconscious!" Sasha exclaims, taking out a vial with some medicine.

Faramaz hurries over to the cairn.

Sasha tries to pour the contents of the vial into Tofik's mouth, the old man helps raise him.

Kyamil keeps blinking furiously, not understanding what has happened.

In the excitement no one noticed when he had lifted his snow glasses.

As Tofik regains consciousness a nebulous dark spot gradually grows clearer until it becomes Kyamil.

In Kyamil's eyes his three clearly visible companions gradually turn into nebulous shadows. They condense and merge into a dark spot.

"Your glasses, how could you take off your glasses!" Sasha moans. "In this glare!"

"That's why our guide pulled his hood so low," Kyamil says, continuing to blink perplexedly. With belated haste he pulls the glasses over his eyes.

"Do they ache?" Sasha asks, peering into his face.

249

"Points.... Hot, prickly points ... a sheaf of glittering points..." Kyamil describes his sensations.

"You can't see anything?" Sasha asks intensely. He looks about as the wind begins to swirl ice powder again.

"Nothing," Kyamil confesses.

"Can you stand up?" Faramaz asks Tofik.

"Yes," says Tofik trying to get up. "But I can't walk," he adds hopelessly.

"I'll carry him," Faramaz says, approaching Sasha.

"In your arms?" Sasha mutters in baffled wonder.

"In my arms or on my back — depending on the situation," Faramaz explains.

"What about Kyamil?" Sasha asks after a pause. "He can't see."

"I'll remain," Kyamil's voice says behind them.

Faramaz and Sasha turn together.

"Remain where?" Sasha asks.

"Find a shelter, leave the thermoses, preserves," Kyamil says, feeling the wall of the cairn like a blind man.

"You're crazy!" Sasha shouts at him.

"It's only my eyes. It'll pass," Kyamil says, clenching his teeth stubbornly.

"Don't be a fool, Kyamil," Sasha says, grabbing him by the shoulders.

Kyamil shrugs off his hands.

"No one's to blame for my taking off the glasses," he says bitterly. "No one but myself. Get that?"

"No," Sasha says firmly.

"Go away," Kyamil says imperatively. "Three men don't wait for one."

"Leave me too," Tofik says suddenly. "The storm is starting. You two go away."

Completely at a loss, not knowing what to do, Sasha stands between Tofik and Kyamil.

"All four," Faramaz says curtly. "Four came up, four will go down."

"Three!" Kyamil shouts frenziedly.

Faramaz presses his arm with such strength that he cringes with pain.

"Four," the old man repeats stubbornly.

The moaning of the wind drowns his voice.

...A strange train races down the snow-covered slope, through the moaning of the wind, through the gusts of the storm: using their rucksacks as sleds the mountaineers slide down two and two: Faramaz mith Tofik gripping him by the neck from behind, and Sasha with Kyamil sitting severely and rigidly in front of him.

Faramaz uses his stick to steer and brake the improvised sled, Sasha uses his alpenstock. They race down the slope.

Faramaz slows down at an ice crest, swerving sharply to the right.

Sasha repeats his manoeuvre.

Again the sleds glide down. It is like a breath-taking slalom.

Faramaz stops at the top of a steep slope and waits for the other sled to catch up.

"You ought to make out a patent for the invention," Sasha says, catching his breath as he comes to a halt. "World stunt, reality verging on fantasy, free of charge.... Pretty hard?" he turns to Faramaz.

"It'll be easier now," Faramaz says evasively.

Gradually gathering speed, the rucksacks slide down the snow-covered field.

Faster and faster, the turns sharper and sharper.

"And now?" Sasha asks Faramaz again.

Faramaz is silent.

He tosses Sasha one end of the climbing rope, ties Tofik and takes the other end in his hands.

Helping each other, all four crawl over the snow-covered crest.

...The exhausted climbers get beneath an overhanging rock and stop to catch their breath.

The blizzard moans about them. One is blind. The other ill. Sasha, too, is near the end of his tether.

Faramaz sits alone, hunched like an old bird.

"Is today the twentieth?" Faramaz asks suddenly.

"Hell knows. I've forgotten," Tofik says through clenched teeth.

"The twentieth," Faramaz says confidently.

Immersed in his thoughts, he removes one bead from his rosary and stealthily drops it into a fissure at his side.

Kyamil could have seen nothing even if he wanted to, Tofik has his head tilted back, drinking juice from his flask, but Sasha notices the old man's movement.

"What's that, a superstition?" he inquires.

"A law," the old man corrects him.

"But you won't say anything," Sasha sighs with regret.

"Yes, I will," Faramaz suddenly agrees, fingering the rosary absently.

Kyamil cannot see them, only a scintillating curtain of darkness stands before his eyes. He does not understand what they are talking about, but he hears the phlegmatic voice of the old highlander.

"They belonged to Fatma, I gave them to her on the day she became my wife. We agreed that the hundred beads meant a hundred years of life together. Each year she removed one bead. But when we had led the scouts through and were returning a bullet whined by.... It was a nazi sniper.... Fatma fell, but she was able to give me this.... There were thirty-eight left. 'Remember our agreement,

Faramaz,' she said. That agreement is my law.... I'm obeying it.... Today is one more year.... And there are seventeen left."

"How old are you, old man?" Tofik asks wonderingly.

"Ninety-two," says Faramaz.

"What's that you're talking about?" Kyamil asks.

"Rosaries," says Tofik. "And love in the mountains."

Kyamil starts and fumbles for something in his pocket.

"Lost something?" Sasha leans over to him.

"I forgot to put a thing ... in the cairn up there...."

...Not far from the base camp stands a group of people headed by Kurbanov: boy and girl students, workers of the base.

"*Salam*," the freckled girl waves her hand.

"*Hi ... Bon jour ... Guten Morgen....*" the voices rise in a babble.

But the gay exclamations die down.

Four people advance down the moraine field: Faramaz leading Kyamil like a blind man, Sasha supporting Tofik, barely dragging his feet.

Kurbanov stares at the four: then he mutely asks Faramaz what happened.

Faramaz shakes his head vigorously as though to say: It's nothing, it's nothing.

Kurbanov again asks mutely: What happened to the boys?

Faramaz nodds again: Nothing terrible.

Kurbanov then points upward: Did you get there?

Faramaz points his battered stick back and up, to the very Garlydag....

And again Garlydag lies on the surface of the lake, its white snowcap reaching into the sky.

A little lower is Kyamil's head with a white bandage on the eyes.

Next to it is Sevda's head.

"What happened, Kyamil?" she asks anxiously. "The eyes will cure in a week or two. But you *did* reach the summit?"

"We climbed very high, Sevda," Kyamil says softly. "Much higher than I had thought.... Where are the boys?"

"Over there, at the pavilion," Sevda points towards the camp. "Probably singing again or showing tricks."

"Forward," Kyamil says rising. "I can't stand being alone. Got used to being tied together these days."

They walk from the lake towards the pavilion from which voices and laughter can be heard.

Subdued, Sevda leads Kyamil. She peers shyly into this changed, matured face, trying to read his thoughts.

As they walk, Kyamil pulls the beads out of his breast pocket and fingers them like a rosary.

"There are too few here," he muses. "When we return to Baku I'll buy you another string so's there'll be one hundred.... Or at least eighty...."

Yusif Azimzade (b. 1917)

The prosaist and playwright Yusif Azimzade began writing during the Second World War.
His prose and dramatic works are characterised by romanticism and lyricism. This explains why Azimzade often writes prose poems, as exemplified in the cycle Songs of the Khazar. *The songs express a fervent boundless love for the Caspian Sea. His beloved Caspian is also the subject on which the story "The Little Captain" is based. Here Azimzade shows how a young boy comes of age.*

The Little Captain

Nusrat loved the sea. This may have been because his father was considered one of the most experienced older captains on the Caspian. Or perhaps there was some other reason. In any case, Nusrat's love of the sea was quite natural and arose from a great wish that possessed his whole being. He wanted to be a captain, like his father, and to pilot ships.

Everyone at home, and especially Imran-kishi, Nusrat's father, sensed the young boy's dream. Nusrat had spoken to no one of this dream. But it was enough to watch how in winter Nusrat returned from school and after preparing his homework for the next day sat down and drew steamboats, sailboats, and seascapes. In summer when they had moved to the cottage, he spent long hours sitting on the cliffs and admiring the sea.

When the first glow of dawn appeared on the horizon Nusrat rose, dressed and went out into the courtyard. All was quiet. The leaves of the tall mulberry tree that grew in front of their home rustled quietly. Carefully making his way across the dewy ground Nusrat went up to the pond, bent over, washed himself with cold water, and went back inside. He wiped his hands and face with a towel, took a tall reed from the corner where it had been left and a military mess-tin that his brother had brought back from the army, and, taking care not to wake anyone, exited from the room and headed for the gates.

It was still early. A gentle breeze blew from the sea. This pleasant morning, typical for Baku cottages, made Nusrat's heart throb with joy. He hurried to the shore toward the boats. His feet left small tracks in the wet earth. Soon the sun would warm the earth and dry the dew, and the small footprints so clearly visible now would vanish.

Nusrat reaches the cliffs at the shoreline. Crossing over the small rocks, he climbs to the very top of a tall cliff. This cliff is called *Aslan gayasy*. The Lion's cliff. Nusrat had his own name for it: *Gozbel gaya*. The humped cliff. And in fact *Aslan gayasy* seems to stoop like some enormous animal that has bent its back and lowered its head to the sea to get a drink of water.

Nusrat descends carefully along the uneven surface of the cliff toward the water until he reaches a small flat area where he always sits, sets down his reed, fills his mess-tin with water, finds a comfortable position, baits his line, and casts it into the water. The actual spectacle begins only after all this has been accomplished.

Below, between small cliffs covered with moss and very slippery, the water seethes. Now from his vantage point, Nusrat clearly sees the unfolding seascape.

Suddenly Nusrat glimpses a ship in the distance at the very edge of the horizon. The ship seems to shift along the line of the horizon. It is as though there is no sea beyond the ship and if it deviates the slightest bit from its course, it will plunge into a bottomless abyss. But he knew quite well that this only seemed to be the case. If he climbed higher than *Aslan gayasy* the line of the horizon would still be behind the ship. For the earth is round. Therefore the higher a man climbs, the broader his field of vision becomes. Everything in the distance, not visible from below, suddenly comes into sight and grows clearer.

The steamship gradually disappeared beyond the line of the horizon. Soon even its steam was out of sight.

Nusrat thought to himself: "Ah, if only I could be on that ship," and sighed deeply.

Before his eyes a picture came to life, born of his daydream.

Nusrat is navigating an enormous ship. The ship moves forward, piercing the calm mirror-like surface of the sea. Smoke rises from the steamship's great, tall smokestacks into the sky and vanishes into thin air. Nusrat stands on the bridge and clasps his hands behind his back, just like his father. He gazes attentively around him. Sometimes he gestures to a sailor standing at the helm, sometimes he lifts the binoculars hanging around his neck and looks into the distance....

Suddenly the "guard" on the line plunges into the water. The line itself bends toward the water. Tearing himself away from his daydream, Nusrat jerks the fishing line up. A silvery fish glistens in the air. Nusrat takes it off the hook and tosses it into his mess-tin. Then he casts the hook into the sea again.

The long shadow cast by *Aslan gayasy* on the sea grew gradually shorter and then disappeared entirely. The sun had already passed its zenith. At this time Nusrat realised that he was hungry and tired. Although it was hard for Nusrat to bid farewell to the magnificent seascape, he took up his tin, full of fish, and fishing line, climbed the cliff and headed for home....

Nusrat liked to admire the sea only on calm days. There were days when Nusrat did not stir from the house, but sat at the window, reading books or listening to his brother's tales of the front, turning from time to time to gaze sadly at the black clouds that covered the sky.

The wind howls endlessly, spraying sand into the air and sweeping up fallen leaves in its path. In such weather the slapping and roar of the waves can be heard from the sea. In such weather when Nusrat imagines himself on his favourite patch of ground at the foot of the cliff he shudders. Probably the horizon is invisible there too. Whitecaps beat against the cliffs and scatter in the air like tiny beads. It is as though the sky has merged with the earth....

"Why don't you go fishing?" asked Nusrat's brother smiling.

Nusrat sensed the gentle irony in his brother's words but tried to show that he was indifferent as he answered: "Nobody goes fishing in such weather."

"Then why don't you go and admire the sea?"

Nusrat was embarrassed to utter the words "I'm afraid." He answered curtly, hoping to end the conversation: "There's nothing to look at now."

His brother pressed him. "But you so love the sea."

Nusrat fell silent.

His brother laughed heartily and slapped Nusrat on the shoulders. "No, brother, I'm afraid they'll never make a fisherman out of you, much less a captain. Cowards can't go to sea. That's why our father won't take you with him. A man who loves the sea, who dreams of being a captain, has to be able to face the waves without flinching, eye to eye. If a wave comes toward him, he shouldn't even blink. But you...."

His brother broke off in mid-sentence, gestured to make his point, rose and went off about his own affairs.

Such conversations between the brothers were frequent. Nusrat had never gone into the open sea on a ship. He knew of storms and gales only from his father's tales.

His father spoke of the most terrifying things calmly, as though recounting a normal occurrence.

Once, Nusrat was allowed to go with his father on a long voyage. At first his mother forbade him, but at the insistence of his father and brother, and at Nusrat own request, she agreed.

How did it happen that Nusrat, who so feared waves and gales, accompanied his father on that voyage?

There were two reasons. His brother's words—"Cowards can't go to sea"—wounded Nusrat's pride. He looked for a chance to show his brother that he was not a coward. Nusrat always thought: "Sooner or later I'll go to sea because I have decided once and for all to be a captain. Let them see that I'm no coward. Although I am a little worried about mama...."

The second reason was that Nusrat wanted to see his uncle, his mother's brother, whom he had not seen for a long time. His uncle worked in Krasnovodsk. He often received letters and presents from him and looked forward to the meeting. But he never thought he would go to visit his uncle on a steamship.

When the enormous steamship, emitting thick smoke from its large smoke-stacks, sailed from the estuary of Baku, the sun was already setting. The shore gradually moved farther into the distance, the houses disappeared. Soon the shore could no longer be seen. There was only water all around.

The weather was clear. There was not a cloud in the sky.

Standing on the upper deck, Nusrat surveyed the sea. His father paced from right to left along the captain's bridge. Passengers strolled along the foreward deck, then congregated and conversed.

As the sun moved towards the horizon, a chilly spring evening descended on the mirror-like surface of the sea. Soon the lights were turned on in the cabins. The moon rose, and the sky was strewn with stars.

The image of the moon and stars could be seen mirrored in the sea. The steamship seemed to move along an enormous mirror. A gentle breeze from the sea stroked Nusrat's face. Slowly his eyes closed....

Nusrat went into his father's cabin and lay down. He did not know how long he slept. He was awakened by an unfamiliar rumbling. When he opened his eyes, he felt giddy. He sat up in bed. The room gently rocked.

Holding onto the walls so that he wouldn't fall, Nusrat got out of bed and went to the door. As soon as he had opened it, a cold wind whipped into the cabin. He turned back, put on his coat and then left the cabin, climbing up to the bridge where his father was.

Imran-kishi, dressed in a long, black overcoat, stood on the bridge. As usual his expression was calm. The helmsman listened attentively to his curt orders. Without taking his eyes from the compass, he turned the wheel to the right, then to the left. Catching sight of his son, Imran-kishi asked, "What are you doing here?"

"I can't sleep," replied Nusrat.

"Well, come in then. There's going to be a gale."

"You mean it hasn't begun yet?" thought Nusrat anxiously, as he entered the pilot's cabin. He looked out at the sea.

Gradually the waves grew larger. There was not the slightest sign of the earlier calm. It seemed as though the thick clouds covering the sky would shatter into pieces and fall into the sea where, blending with the waves, they would cover the whole world.

Nusrat could not tear his eyes from the raging sea. His heart beat as he was gripped by strange feelings.

The ponderous, gigantic steamship now rose on the crests of the waves, now sunk into the "abyss" opening beneath it. Then it seemed to Nusrat that the steamship would plunge into the water and instantly sink into the depths of the sea, the waves closing over it.

Nusrat held tightly to the handle of the window, involuntarily clenching his hands. His eyes closed. Then after a little while he opened them and saw that the steamship continued along its course, stubbornly passing through the enormous waves.

At times Nusrat turned to look at the helmsman, a man of forty or forty-five. Beneath the seaman's cap pulled over his eyes were streaks of gray. A serious expression was fixed on his sunburnt face. The calm eyes beneath heavy brows did not notice the waves or the clouds that grew denser on the horizon. He turned the wheel quickly according to the captain's orders.

Nusrat wanted to be like the helmsman. He tried to stand firmly in place and look at the waves as he did. Not looking back, his father continued to give commands. Sometimes he lifted a megaphone to his lips and called something to the sailors below. Only once did he glance back at his son, smile and ask gently: "You aren't afraid, are you, son? Do you feel sick?" Without waiting for an answer, he continued, "Don't worry. This is your first time. You'll get used to it."

The helmsman looked at Nusrat and said: "He thinks that's a gale? He'll be seeing a lot more."

The gale continued all night. Nusrat had stopped being afraid. Now his eyes expressed interest and amazement. Now the waves which beat against the side of the ship and sprayed onto the deck inspired Nusrat with pride, instead of fear, although this feeling was mingled with some anxiety.

It seemed to Nusrat that some huge animal lying at the bottom of the sea was trying to rise and grab him with its terrible paws. But it couldn't do this. It was as though the ship, directed by his father, was running over the beast, forcing it to the bottom and smothering it.

Nusrat felt that he was stronger than the sea, the wind, the black clouds and the waves. When he returned home he would know how to answer his brother. Let his brother see once and for all that Nusrat could be a captain and would be!

Now Nusrat loved the sea even more. He resolved that when he returned from this voyage he would go to the sea in the stormiest weather, he would sit on the Lion's cliff and gaze on the sea, and he would go out often with his father on long voyages. Next year he would enter the school for navigators.

He would stay with his uncle in Krasnovodsk for a whole week and then return with his father. Naturally during this time his father would come home without Nusrat and would tell his brother and mother about Nusrat. This didn't seem enough to the boy. It was good that he remembered that. Together with his uncle he would write a letter to his mother and brother and tell them exactly how the voyage went. His mother would read it and rejoice, and his brother would understand that he had been wrong....

Toward morning the weather grew calm. The waves subsided and the clouds were scattered into pieces. Individual stars could be seen in the sky. Imran-kishi turned the steamship over to his assistant and went to his cabin with Nusrat. Sitting at the table, he began to write in a thick book.

Nusrat lay down in bed. The ship rocked slowly. When Nusrat looked through the porthole he saw that the eastern side of the sky, the very edge, was growing light. The stormy night was followed by a calm, clear day. Whether from exhaustion or because the ship rocked him like a cradle or for some other reason, Nusrat felt asleep.

And his dreams were sweet indeed.

There are his mother and brother sitting in the courtyard, in the shade of the mulberry tree, drinking tea. The postman comes with the mail. His brother looks at the envelope and exclaiming "From Nusrat!" opens the letter and reads it, stopping from time to time to repeat, "What a fine fellow! What a fine fellow!"

His proud mother says to her eldest son: "I knew that Nusrat wouldn't be afraid. That's why I allowed him to go out to sea before any of the rest of you."

Nusrat smiles in his sleep. It is strange how his mother reasons. After all she had not at all wanted to let Nusrat go on this voyage. His brother laughs at his mother. But neither of them dare to insult her.

Let her be proud of her eldest son who showed his heroism at the front, and let her, looking at the "little captain"— Nusrat —also rejoice.

Salam Kadyrzade
(b. 1923)

Salam Kadyrzade was born in Baku. Upon completing a secondary education he left for the front at the outbreak of the Second World War. After being demobilised from the army, Kadyrzade began to write. In the postwar years he graduated the Gorky Literary Institute in Moscow.
He has authored some twenty books and several plays; the latter have been successfully produced in Azerbaijanian theatres. His novel A Winter's Night *deals with life in modern-day Baku.*
Salam Kadyrzade's story "Roses in the Snow" was written out of sincere agitation and sympathy for the characters.

Roses
in the Snow

Parviz-kishi, who had woken up earlier than usual this morning, leaned his elbows against a pillow and watched the expanses of countryside recede into the distance through the window of his train compartment. For two days now he had been melancholy because there was no fellow traveller with whom he might converse. He was eager to reach his destination as quickly as possible.

The landscape beyond the window gradually changed according to the movement of the train: country homes whose roofs, courtyards and flues were covered with snow, small knoll-like ricks. The naked trees were covered with hoar-frost. One telegraph pole after another was left behind. The water of rivers and small lakes had frozen. Icicles hung from awnings. The asphalt road gleamed like glass. In some courtyards, hens and chickens dug in the snow, searching for something. All around things were peaceful, clean and white. Winter, like a malicious artist who envied the green and yellow patterns drawn by Spring and Autumn on nature covered everything with a thick coat of its favourite white colour and hid it all.

The fiery-coloured sun quietly peeked out from the invisible ends of the fields. The horizon, adorned by the red dawn, burst into flames and burned.

Along the country road that ran parallel to the permanent way rode a motorcyclist; behind him sat a girl.

261

The young man was wearing a gray cap on his head and a warm jacket. He was shod in high boots. The red-cheeked girl holding onto him with both arms wore a white fur coat and was very gay. Despite the speed of the train, the motorcyclist tried to keep pace with it. From time to time the youth would look back, laughing, and say something to his companion. The girl would throw back her head and laugh loudly or beat him on the back with her hands hidden in mittens.

When they reached a large bridge, the country road swerved to the right. The young people could no longer be seen as they traversed a narrow avenue of tall trees covered with thick snow....

Parviz-kishi who had followed them all this time sighed with regret and went away from the window. He silently thirsted to regain his youth and relive those years again. Crossing his arms above his head, the old man stared at the ceiling. He was transported far into the past on the wings of his daydreams.

There was a cautious knock at the door of the compartment.

Parviz-kishi got out of bed and sat down on the berth. "Come in," he said.

He had not noticed that the train had stopped. The compartment door opened and there stood the conductor with a woman at his side.

"Uncle," said the conductor, "for two days you've been lonely and sad. I've brought you a companion."

A woman of fifty-five or sixty in a black scarf and coat entered the compartment, greeted him and set her small suitcase down.

"Hello! Welcome!" said Parviz-kishi showing his new companion the seat across from him. "Please sit down," he added.

The woman took off her coat, hung it up, shifted her black shawl from her head to her shoulders and smoothed her hair.

"It's very cold outside!" she said.

Parviz-kishi thought for a moment. He pressed the button by the door. Shortly thereafter the very conductor who had brought him this travelling companion appeared anew.

"Please bring us two glasses of freshly brewed tea."

"Yes, sir."

Parviz-kishi took up his towel and soap. He went out to wash up, calling to the conductor ahead of him: "Listen, son. Leave room for our lips on those glasses. Don't fill them up to the brim like you did yesterday. That won't do."

About fifteen minutes later he returned and, noticing that the compartment was closed, stopped. He coughed deliberately several times, so that his new companion would permit him to enter the compartment.

"Please come in."

Parviz-kishi entered the compartment.

"Once again, hello!"

When the woman, having glanced at him, smiled, hollows appeared in both cheeks. "Hello," she answered.

The small table by the window had been cleaned and set. Two glasses of tea steamed in the centre of the table. Parviz-kishi shut the compartment door and looked in the mirror fastened to it. Taking his comb from his pocket, he ran it through his thinning hair. He smoothed his broad gray brows and short white moustache. "Moscow climate suits me," he thought. "I've put on a little weight." He passed his hand down his newly sprouted beard. "But I should have shaved this morning. Now I don't feel at ease doing it in the presence of a woman...."

262

Buttoning the collar of his woollen barberry-coloured shirt he walked over and sat opposite the woman.

"I see you too are going to Baku."

"Yes."

"Marvellous. That means you will be my companion until evening...." He moved one glass closer to the woman. "It seems to me we ought to introduce ourselves. My name is Parviz-kishi."

"My name is Reikhan."

"Oh, then please drink your tea before it gets cold. What a lovely name!" The old man held out one of the two pillows beside him to the woman. "Please, put it under your elbow and you will be more comfortable."

"Please don't trouble yourself about me. I'm quite comfortable. Please."

Not wishing to annoy him, Reikhan reluctantly obeyed. The railway cars rocked with the motion of the train; the tea, splashing in the glasses, spilled onto the table cloth. Parviz-kishi noticed this for the first time and shaking his head with dissatisfaction observed: "It's easier to find a needle in a haystack than to explain something to a dunderhead! The most important thing is that I warned him not to fill those glasses to the brim. But he did it his way."

After a little while a sincere, warm conversation started up between the two occupants of the compartment. Reikhan explained that she had studied in a gymnasium and then taught, that her husband had died at the front in World War II, that since that time she had not remarried. While she spoke, Parviz-kishi gazed at her neatly combed black hair, streaked with gray, at her open round face, her thin delicate brows, her brown eyes bordered with shadows, her gentle, thin lips that had lost their red colour. It seemed to him that her trembling voice was telling the story of a person dear to him and it touched him greatly....

Noticing that Reikhan had fallen silent, her companion solicitously asked: "And what are you doing now?"

It seemed that the woman didn't want to answer this question. Then she thought of something and reluctantly began to speak: "Now I'm old and on a pension. But if I had my way I would teach for several more years."

Parviz-kishi looked out of the window. The train was approaching Derbent.

"Reikhan-khanum, why have we met thirty years too late," the old man began to speak regretfully. "Although my arms and legs are still strong...." Parviz-kishi broke off in mid-sentence. His leg touched his walking stick which he had left under the table, propped against the wall and the stick fell.

Reikhan, smiling gently, picked up the stick and set it in its former place. The old man pretended he hadn't noticed.

"Hm.... What was I saying? Ah yes. My arms and legs are still strong, but the problem is that I've reached the age of seventy. I regret my lost youth. Then we went hungry, we bore all sorts of burdens, we met with all sort of difficulties and endured them all. My deceased father, complaining about the burden of time, said: 'I've lived a long time in this world and still don't know what it is like. Now it's time to enter the other world and discover what is over there.'

Now a man wants to live longer. And why not? Take me, for instance, I have an apartment, furniture ... sons, daughters, grandchildren.... Each has a name and a claim to respect. Why, sixty or seventy years is nothing to me or you!" Parviz-kishi fell silent for a moment, deep in thought. Then shifting to a more comfortable position, he added: "When this government came to Azerbaijan I

263

was working as a stone mason. My buildings were so beautiful that you had to have more than two eyes to gaze to your heart's content! Now each month I receive a pension, quite a round sum. The main difficulty is that I have nothing to spend this money on. I can't imagine what I should spend it on. And I can't help but thinking, if only mother of my children was still alive and could witness our times and rejoice."

Reikhan's voice broke the long silence.

"Why are you travelling in such cold weather?"

"My grandson is studying in Moscow. I just wanted to see him. So I decided, I'll go and pay him a visit. I stayed a week and then received a telegram from Baku. My sons sent it: 'Father we expect you in Baku for New Year Eve!'"

The elderly passengers' conversation had not yet run dry when the train had reached its final destination. Parviz-kishi much regretted that he hadn't met Reikhan if only two days earlier.

"How true the proverb: conversation makes time fly. Look how swiftly the time passed." He looked at the lights of the city twinkling in the distance.

When Reikhan pulled her shawl over her head, Parviz-kishi rose and held her coat for her. The old man dressed and put his fur cap. The woman handed him his cane....

* * *

Next day, after lunch, the weather cleared somewhat. Noticing this, Parviz-kishi left his home and slowly went toward the boulevard by the seashore. The sun was blinding and snow crunched under his feet. Parviz-kishi got great pleasure out of this.

The old man sat on a bench along the boulevard. Propping his elbows on his cane and his hands under his chin, he admired nature. The sky was cloudless. The Caspian was calm. The city was peaceful. The music coming from the ship anchored in the estuary caressed the ear like a cool breeze in the burning summer heat.

"You could give up your soul for Baku," whispered Parviz-kishi to himself, admiring the beautiful landscape that spread before his eyes. Involuntarily he compared winter's attire with old age.

Weighed down with snow, the firs along the shore bent their branches low like trees burdened with fruit. Along the avenues hurried women holding their children in their arms; girls walked arm-in-arm. But there were more men. From time to time, elderly people moved on slowly and carefully. Children, who never tired, ran around, laughing with loud ringing laughter, and throwing snowballs at each other. Now they would fall down, now stand up again.

Parviz-kishi lingered on the boulevard by the sea. When he rose and headed toward home, he saw the smiling Reikhan approaching him. Seeing this the old man pressed his cane firmly into the earth and stopped.

"Why, I was just having a conversation with you in my thoughts," said the woman, slipping off her glove and extending her hand. They greeted each other. "Then as I passed by, I saw you sitting alone. I recognised you from a distance."

"It's a sin to sit at home in such beautiful weather."

264

"You're right. A person feels that a burden has been lifted from him when he breathes this air." Reikhan did not speak for a few moments, then asked: "I see you are getting ready to leave. Where are you headed?"

Parviz-kishi pointed with his cane. "I live over there, close to the Garden of Sabir. But all the time I've been sitting here, I've been thinking, if I go home so early I'll never get a moment's rest. Everyone is preparing for New Year's Eve. You can't move for tables and chairs." The old man took from his pocket two candies wrapped in silver paper and offered them to Reikhan. "Please take these. May you have a sweet taste in your mouth. I brought them from Moscow."

The woman took the candies. "Thank you. May you always enjoy many sweets."

Conversing together they headed toward home taking small slow steps. Stepping down from the sidewalk, Parviz-kishi stumbled and almost fell. Reikhan saw this and took his arm. Then for some reason the old man stopped and began to laugh uncontrollably. Turning to the woman with tears streaming from his eyes, he said: "Reikhan-khanum, it just struck me that if I had fallen, my two legs and my cane would rise in the air and to a bystander this would all seem very funny. Ha-ha!"

The laughter was contagious. Reikhan-khanum too stopped in the middle of the street and began to laugh heartily. Passers-by turned and looked at her in amazement.

They continued to walk.

Reikhan's cheeks turned red from the cold, as did the tip of Parviz-kishi's nose. It seemed to the old man that he had never walked so peacefully and comfortably along that street in snowy weather. Since Reikhan had taken his arm, he didn't even need his cane. On the contrary, now the cane was a nuisance.

"Do you have a telephone?" asked Parviz-kishi who had thought of something.

"Yes. Why do you ask?"

"I thought we might let each other know when we plan to go for walks on such pleasant days. It's dreary being alone. A person needs someone to talk to...."

They had gone a good distance beyond the Garden of Sabir. Reikhan asked: "Where is your house?"

Parviz-kishi stopped: "We've passed it. I'm seeing you home now."

The woman smiled gently: "Don't trouble yourself. I have to go back the way we came. I did't want to leave you alone."

"That's a good one!... And to think all this time I've been convinced that I was seeing you home."

They went back. When they reached the gates, Parviz-kishi took the woman's arm and suggested: "Listen ... I'm speaking to you from the heart. Come by and visit us."

Reikhan expressed her gratitude and they took leave of each other.

* * *

Toward evening the weather unexpectedly turned bad, like a gay, coquettish woman who has suddenly been addressed with a caustic remark which angers and exasperates her. The sun which had been gradually losing its warmth hid beyond

265

the horizon, the sky turned gray as though covered with lead. The fine snow was driven by the wind with all its might along the streets of the city.

Fearing that the cold might kill the wild, perennial rose that he had planted in a large pot on the balcony and carefully tended through several winters and summers, Parviz-kishi brought his old raincoat and covered it. Then the old man tightly closed the balcony door and returned to his room. The noise of the guests gathered to celebrate the New Year and the music in the large room made it impossible to hear conversation.

Parviz-kishi put on the suit which his daughter-in-law had pressed and prepared for him that afternoon and a white shirt, tie; finishing his toilet, he went out to greet the guests.

When the old man entered the room, everyone rose to show their respect for him and came up to shake hands and ask how he was doing.... These were Parviz-kishi's relatives, his son — the engineer, his friends and the friends of his daughter-in-law, and their co-workers. It had become customary to celebrate the New Year in this home in this way. Each time the host would make the first toast, then choose a toast-master and, sitting down in a corner, listen to the jokes of the young people, and watch them enjoying themselves.

Tonight was no exception. The long table in the dining room was laden with tasty dishes, greens, and all sorts of fruit.

Girls who had come alone to the celebration playfully caught Parviz-kishi's arms and pulled him, each in her own direction. "Uncle wants to sit by me!" cried each refusing to give him any peace.

Eventually the guests were seated, the goblets were filled and emptied, and the air rang with gay stories and loud laughter.... Although Parviz-kishi, sitting in the place of honour at the head of the table noticed that the girl sitting beside him was exchanging winks with a young man, he pretended he didn't see this, thinking: "I see that I am in their way. I must think of some excuse to change seats so that they can chat freely."

As he mused on this, the music began to play and the dancing started. The young man, as though he had been waiting for just this moment, went up to the girl seated next to Parviz-kishi and asked her to dance. The old man took advantage of this and immediately sat down in the young man's place. "That's more like it!" he thought to himself. "Now I can relax and so can they...." Having thus justified himself, he sighed in relief. When the young man returned to his place after dancing, Parviz-kishi quietly told him: "Please excuse me, son. I didn't want to be sitting in a draught, so I took your seat."

This was exactly what the youth had wanted: "No matter, Uncle, dear. Sit wherever you're most comfortable. I'm used to sitting in a cool place and like it." He was so happy that he nearly embraced the old man....

When the gaiety was in full swing and everyone was talking and enjoying themselves, the old man remembered something and went back into his room. At first he sat by the window for some time and looked out at the street. Then he went to the telephone, lifted the receiver, and dialled: "Hello. Reikhan-khanum? Good evening.... Parviz-kishi speaking. I want to wish you health and much happiness in the coming year...."

"I wish you the same!" answered the woman. "I wish you long life and happiness."

"The funny thing is that when we met this afternoon I quite forgot to congratulate you."

"But you did remember my telephone number. That's quite a lot."

Reikhan's joke pleased the old man. "I suppose you have guests now?" asked the old man.

"No. I'm all by myself."

"Alone?"

The old man thought for a time. "That's not right. Why should she sit home and be sad and lonely?"

"Reikhan-khanum," he said, "to tell the truth, although our home is filled with guests I also feel lonely, and you know, that is ... if you refuse me I will be hurt. You know I'm very quick to take offense.... You get dressed right now ... and come here by taxi...."

The woman demurred, but Parviz-kishi would not give in.

"I've said what I have to say and that's all there is to it. I'm going out right now to meet you."

After long deliberation they agreed to meet in the Garden of Sabir. Parviz-kishi felt calm and relieved. He felt as though he had lighted a cold, dark apartment and kindled the hearth, warming its walls.

The old man went to the window and looked out. The snow storm had picked up force.

Snow swept howling along the streets this way and that, then rose back into the sky and whirled in the air. As though chilled by the cold, the naked wires on their poles groaned tremulously.

Parviz-kishi went back to the telephone and called Reikhan: "When you leave be sure you are dressed warmly," he said. "It's very cold. And don't forget to put on galoshes. It's slippery out there!"

* * *

The old man looked at his watch. Not much time was left, but he didn't hurry. "It's only about a hundred paces off. Better to leave on time than to have to stand and wait in the cold."

Suddenly Parviz-kishi recalled how he had carried his grandson in his arms and gone for so many strolls in that garden. Then he had sharp eyes and a brisk gait. The child had hardly time to blink before his grandfather set him down in the garden among the trees and in the pure air. How quickly the years fly past!... Now his grandson was past twenty.

"Time!" he said as he rose and prepared to leave the house. He put on his coat and fur hat, and tied his woollen muffler above the fur collar. Then he went out to the balcony, picked one rose from his bush and neatly wrapped it in paper. "This is for Reikhan," thought the old man. He took up his cane, put on his gloves, and slowly descended the marble staircase.

As he started to go through the gates onto the street the wind began to rise, resisting his will and driving him back. So as not to fall, the old man held onto the wall. "I should have asked one of the young folks to accompany me," he thought and turning his side to the wind made his way down the slope with difficulty.

267

It was difficult to get to the garden this way. The blizzard seemed to be playing with him like a small boy; it could drive him in any direction. Now the old man was more worried about Reikhan and began to think about her.

When he reached the street corner, he stopped and considered how to cross the street. Suddenly someone took his arm from behind: "Uncle, what urgent matter made you come out in this weather?"

The old man turned his head back and saw the unknown young man standing behind him.

"Thanks, son. If you lead me to that garden I'll be convinced that you are young."

The young man grasped the old man's waist with a strong arm. Parviz-kishi's legs seemed to be whisked up from the ground. Suddenly he felt himself in the place of his grandson whom he, in his time, had carried in his arms.

"To tell the truth it isn't all that cold. But for folks like you it's a bit slippery," said the young man, who reckoned that he had completed his mission and went off.

Parviz-kishi squeezed his way into a cosy place so that he would be sheltered from the wind. He took his watch from his pocket. It was five minutes later than the time they had agreed upon. That meant that he had not been able to cover the distance in the time that he had supposed he could. He waited, staring at each passing car and taxi. Not one stopped. Each galloped past him....

The snow fell thickly. A wild wind blew, rattling at the doors and windows of the buildings. The old man still held the flower in his right hand; he felt his fingers growing numb inside his gloves. His shoulder-blades were cold and his legs seemed frozen.

"Too bad about the flower. The cold will kill it." Parviz-kishi tucked the flower under his coat and, hanging the cane on his arm, stuffed both hands into his pockets. Unvoluntarily he recalled the words of the young man who had accompanied him here: "To tell the truth it isn't all that cold. But for folks like you it's a bit slippery."

Half an hour passed and Reikhan didn't come. "The weather must have frightened her off," thought Parviz-kishi. He went over to a nearby telephone booth and called her. "It's me again, Reikhan.... I see you couldn't come because of the weather." The old man marvelled when he heard her answer.

"I waited for you a long time...."

"What? You mean you came?"

"Yes. I was there right on time. I waited fifteen minutes, then couldn't stand there any more and went off."

Parviz-kishi sighed deeply and bitterly: "It's my fault, Reikhan-khanum. Or to be precise, I'm not at fault. Blame old age. I was a little late."

Laughter rang from the receiver. "Then our meeting will have to wait until next year," she teased him.

The old man left the telephone booth and hanging his head went home.

"Ah, youth, youth! If I were still in my prime I would never have been late! Late for a rendezvous! Why, even in a storm I would have come an hour earlier and waited!" When he reached his building the flower that he had tucked into his bosom slipped out and fell to the ground.

The old man bent over intending to retrieve it. But he couldn't. The wind picked up the bud like a prized trophy and carried it off in its claws like a bird of prey.... Parviz-kishi regretted deeply that he had lost this flower; he had cared for it and nurtured it for a long time and it reminded him of his lost youth. He crossed the threshold, entered the building and then turned back once more to look. The rose lying on the white snow seemed to burn and illuminated everything around it. But he was far from the bud. So far that he could not reach it....

Gyulhussein
Husseinogly
(b. 1923)

Novelist Gyulhussein's prose is distinguished for its lyricism and emotionalism. His favourite genre is poetic prose; each line is imbued with great humanism, but cut to the limit.
The writer makes it a principle to think over each word.
Gyulhussein's poetic prose (including the piece presented here) praised the best, most noble feelings: faith in the power and beauty of man, in his good will and creative impulses.

Prose Poems
Man

The sea, the forest and the mountain. All three are one.

I stand in the forest. The sea lies below me. Above is the mountain.

The sea laps at the shore, washing over the amber sand. Every sea wishes its shore to be clean.

The leaves rustle. The leaves whisper among themselves. The wind, that fine conductor, brings all the trees into motion at once, evincing their song of the woods.

The water of seven springs flows between the singing trees, glittering in the greenness. The water is as cold as the snowcap on the mountain and as clear as crystal. It flows along, whispering gently to the breeze, that fine conductor, saying, "I also exist. Here I am. Don't forget about me and my running waters when you caress the leaves, making them rustle and sing." And the breeze did not.

The forest breathes. The forest is at rest. As it rests, it listens to the nightingale's song, to the rustling leaves, to the running water of the seven springs.

A waterfall cascades from a high cliff. It thunders and foams. And the mountain gazes down. At the swift flight of the eagle, at the thrashing of the foaming water.

The sun sets behind the mountain. Ever so slowly. It sets in order to rise again the next morning. It tints everything in sight a dull red. As it sets, it becomes an intense yellow.

271

Everything changes colour. The mountain, that haven of eagles, and the thundering waterfall. The forest, home to the seven springs. The trees with their trembling leaves and nightingales. The sea and its flocks of gulls. The polished amber sand, and the clean shore.

I stand gazing at the sea, the forest and the mountain. I cannot take my eyes from them. One is more breathtaking than the other. All are exactly as they should be. Exactly!

But are they? Why then do I feel that something is lacking in this beautiful landscape? Indeed, something is lacking.

I ponder over this. I gaze at the sea. I gaze at the forest and the mountain. I try to find the answer. Suddenly, I see two figures on the crest.

My fellow-humans! Where were you all this time? With you as a part of the scene, everything I so admire becomes better still, and still more beautiful. Everything. The mountain, the forest and the sea.

Earth and mother

The babe drank of his mother's milk. His sleep was her sleeplessness. She did not spare the light of her eyes, the blood of her heart or the strength of her hands for him. She gave her all for him, her son, her light. She spared nothing. She gave everything she had to him, every last drop and bit. She nurtured him. Set him on his feet. Stood him firmly on the ground.

The earth fed and clothed him. It was gentle towards him. It cared for him as a mother. It spared nothing, giving him its all.

The boy grew up. He took his place in life. Soon word of his fine deeds spread far and wide. He became famous. And he discovered he had many relatives. He had never heard of many of them before. He had hardly seen any of the others. And those he had had made him shiver from cold. He wondered now at their great numbers.

As soon as a candle begins to burn brightly, moths will flock to it. So did he discover ever new relatives. Their passions flamed. Some were intent on proving they were his close relatives. Others wished to impress him with their own fame, while still others noted, as if in passing, that they had helped him, or put in a good word for him at some step along the way. Each tried to put his best foot forward. And all talked on and on.

Only his mother and the earth were silent. Nature had created them thus. A mother and the earth.

The train was leaving

The train was leaving.

So many trains passed their village. Every single day.

She recalled the days of her childhood, when she and the other little girls had run up the embankment and waved to the passing trains. To the trains? No, to the people in them. Grown-ups and children had looked out of the windows. She had waved to them.

There had been no special reason for waving to them. She had not then known what it meant to wave to a train that was leaving.

Meeting and waving to the trains became a game. She had liked the game when she was small.

When she grew older she forgot about the childish game. She did not know when she actually forgot about it, but when she later recalled it it seemed a foolish game.

And now a train was leaving, and she was waving goodbye. It was not the train, no, not the train, it was a part of her heart that was going farther and farther away.

The train was leaving. Stop! Don't vanish! But it was leaving.

She was helpless to stop it.

Her eyes tried to draw it back, to hold it still, to stop it, if only for a moment.

But the train kept on moving. She waved, and waved again.

The train was leaving.

Hussein Abbaszade

(b. 1922)

A participant in World War II, this poet and prosaist authored the documentary novel The General *which brought him renown in Azerbaijan; the novel is about Hero of the Soviet Union Azi Aslanov. Abbaszade is editor-in-chief of the Azerbaijanian literary journal.*

He draws his inspiration from the brighter side of life, the noble deeds of his contemporaries. Fascinating plots and colourful characters have guaranteed the success of Abbaszade's books. The story "A Man's Name" presented here is about a meeting of an old photographer with a hero of the first five-year plan. The reader is given a glimpse of these characters' troubled youth.

A Man's Name　　Pirverdi got off the bus at Vagif Street. He took a piece of paper from his pocket, looked at the address on it, then at the number of the nearest house. Yes, he was on the right street. He would cross over and walk down a bit until he reached Fatulla's house.

Old Pirverdi set off slowly along the narrow sidewalk, limping slightly. He was in no hurry. Pensioners had all the time in the world. Actually, he had not intended to go to see a protographer whom he did not even know. He only knew the name from having seen it often in the photo credits which appeared in the Baku papers: "Photo by Fatulla Chemberekendli". However, they had been missing for quite some time. For a very long time, in fact. As he had taken his usual walk along the seaside boulevard the previous day, he had chanced upon a poster announcing a one-man show of photographs by Fatulla Chemberekendli, the city's honoured news photographer, to be held on the occasion of his 80th birthday. It was sponsored by the local branch of the Journalists' Union. Pirverdi had decided to drop in and see the exhibition.

Enlarged and mounted photographs lined the walls of the two small rooms. These were moments of time long past and now a part of history, captured by the lens for all time. There was a photograph of the inauguration ceremony for the country's first electric railway between Baku and Sabunchi settlement, the oldest oil-producing district. That was back in 1926. The people at the sunlit railway station were all poorly-dressed, but they were smiling and carried flowers and posters. The first electric train was about to pull out of the station. Next was a portrait of the revered bard, Djabbar Karyagdy. His head was slightly inclined towards his tambourine. As Pirverdi looked at the picture he imagined he could hear once again the clear, high-pitched voice singing the familiar "Hcirati". Here was another photo of the 20's. It showed a group of women flinging away their heavy veils. He had never forgotten the picture, which had been reprinted in many newspapers and magazines at the time. Three young girls wearing mini-skirts stood arguing in front of the picture.

Pirverdi walked slowly from photograph to photograph. But what was this? He stopped short and stared at a photograph by the door. It was a panorama of a construction site on the waterfront. Barges by the breakwater were loaded with huge rocks. Here and there he could see the old-fashioned steam-driven excavators. The shore was crowded with men wielding shovels and picks, and sawing and hammering. Two young men pushing wheelbarrows laden with sand along a plank-walk were in the forefront. You could make out their faces, especially the one on the left. It was Rizvan, his childhood friend and fellow-villager. Pirverdi's heart beat faster. They had come to Baku together very long ago, and this had been their first job, filling up Bibi-Eibat Bay, which was now Ilyich Bay. And wasn't this second fellow Abdulla? Yes, it was. Abdulla was so strong he could pick up the biggest rocks and astonish all the other men. That, at least, was what Pirverdi had thought in those far-off days. Ah, Ilyich Bay! He would never forget it. He thought he could again hear the creaking barrow wheels, the pounding pile-drivers and the incessant hum of the pumps. Once again the stinging north wind whipped at his face. He recalled the blind man who had been in charge of operations, an engineer named Pototsky.

Later oil derricks were raised here on land reclaimed from the sea. That was when Pirverdi had begun his long working career. He had sunk wells in Ilyich Bay, then in Lok-Batan and, shortly before the war, when he had gained experience and was a well-known drilling foreman, at the new oilfields on the northern shore of Apsheron.

Pirverdi could not take his eyes from the photograph and the faces of his old friends. Rizvan had been killed in action during the war. Abdulla had died long ago, when some ailment had claimed the strongman. Pirverdi leaned closer to read the caption: "Builders of a new life." Indeed! He was furious.

"See that?" he said to the young man standing next to him. "You'd think they had no names!" The young fellow looked at him, said nothing and moved on to the next photo.

"I could kill that photographer," Pirverdi muttered as his anger rose. "You'd think since they're both dead no one's even expected to remember their names."

When he had worked himself into a fine state he stalked off to find someone in charge.

"Please don't get excited," the director of the exhibition, a middle-aged woman, said after she had heard his complaint. "I can give you Chemberekendli's telephone number and you can phone him if you wish."

He did just that, right there and then. The voice on the other end of the line was very polite, and though Pirverdi had been prepared for an argument, he soon cooled off. The photographer invited him over, saying he was not well and was confined to the house. "I'd very much like to talk to you," he said in conclusion.

And here Pirverdi was now, trudging down the steep and narrow street instead of sitting on a bench on the boulevard like any self-respecting pensioner. He checked the number again and entered the yard of an old house. There were lines of washing hanging in the sun. A youth in a blue sweatshirt was puttering around a dismantled motorcycle. His arms up to the elbows were full of axle grease. His audience consisted of several boys sitting around on their haunches.

"Where does the photographer Fatulla live, boys?"

The youth glanced up and then said: "Take him up to our place", to one of the boys.

When they reached the third floor the boy pointed to a glassed-in gallery and raced back down the stairs, taking them two at a time.

Pirverdi wondered why boys were always on the go, forever running. What was all the rush about?

He rang the bell. A middle-aged woman opened the door. Pirverdi hung up his raincoat and his old karakule hat, worn in all weather, then followed her into a dimly-lit room. A shrivelled little man wearing eyeglasses was sitting on an old oilskin-covered divan. There was nothing to him but skin and bones. Could this wizened old man be the famous photographer? Pirverdi had imagined him to be tall and robust, with several cameras slung on straps over his shoulders.

Fatulla smiled and rose to greet his visitor. His black corduroy suit hung on him. "I'm sorry you had to come all this way," he said in a frail voice, "but I don't go out any more. I don't have the strength to. I keep up with things on TV."

"What time does to a man!" Pirverdi was thinking. "There was a time when this news photographer was here, there and everywhere."

Aloud he said, "No bother at all, my dear Fatulla", and sank down beside him on the divan. "I'm glad to have the chance to meet you. You know the old saying: to hear the brave man's name is more important than seeing him. I would put it this way: if you know the name, try to see the man."

"Well, you have now, but there's not much to look at, is there?" Fatulla chuckled.

"We're a good pair. I'm over seventy myself, you know."

"Ah, no one can stop time. After your angry call yesterday, my dear Pirverdi, I phoned the people at the exhibition hall and asked them to change the caption. It now reads: 'Ilyich Bay, 1923. (Foreground): Rizvan Ismailov and Abdulla Abdullayev.'"

"Yes, that's much better. A man isn't given a name just to have it vanish when he dies."

"You're right. Absolutely right." Fatulla nodded. "I never published that photo before. You know, a news photographer accumulates a regular mountain of pictures in his lifetime. Only a small part ever appears in print. After the people from the Journalists' Union spoke to me about having an exhibition, we went through thousands of photographs together. Naturally, all the ones that had appeared in the papers had captions. But not the others. That's why we gave it a rather general caption when we chose it for the show. I'm very glad you saw it and called my attention to it."

"I'm glad I was of help. I might have sounded a bit harsh...."

"No, no, not at all. What you said was very true. There's something else I'd like to ask you about, my friend Pirverdi. They're going to put out an album of my photographs. The editors chose a hundred prints for it, and there are several I took at Ilyich Bay. That's what I wanted to ask you about. Maybe you still remember the names of some of the people on the pictures "

"Let's have a look."

Fatulla padded over to a filing cabinet, his felt slippers shuffling across the floor. He removed several snapshots from a folder and laid them out on the table. "The editor likes this one best. He wants to put it on the cover."

The photograph portrayed a tall youth working a crowbar under a rock. He was engrossed in his job and unaware of the photographer. The camera had caught him at a moment of great exertion. One could actually feel the muscles bulging under his shirt.

Pirverdi squinted as he gazed at the picture.

"I'll tell you about this one," Fatulla continued. "After I'd snapped it I went over to another section of the site. Suddenly I heard people shouting. There had been an accident. I ran back to where I'd just been. The foreman told me a wagon-load of rocks had been unloaded, and some of them had fallen on one of the workers and broken his leg. I may be wrong on several points, but that's how I remember it. Anyway, I do remember a stretcher going by, and the young fellow whose picture I'd just taken lying on it. I can't tell you how bad I felt. The picture came out fine, but I couldn't hand it in to my paper. I didn't know what had happened to the fellow. It wouldn't have been right to put the picture in the paper when he may have been on his deathbed. Well, it's been in my files for half a century. Do you think you might know who the fellow was?"

Pirverdi said nothing.

"I understand. So many years have gone by. I know it's impossible to remember a name after all this time. I've gone through all my old notebooks looking for it. It's a shame, really." Fatulla sighed.

He went on speaking, but Pirverdi did not hear what he was saying. He rubbed his leg that had suddenly begun to ache and gazed at the photograph which brought back the wind of yesteryear, the biting north wind that sweeps across Ilyich Bay.

Aleviya Babaeva
(b. 1922)

Aleviya Babaeva was born in Baku. She graduated from Azerbaijan's Kirov State University with a degree in Philology. She began to write when still a student. Her first collection of stories was published in 1950. Since that time she has published several books, primarily collections of short stories.

The story presented in this anthology "That One Was Sweeter" is not a long one, but it offers the reader a vivid sampling of the authoress' unique style. Her prose is laconic, but at the same time rich in fresh, accurate details; she takes great pains to reveal the psychological complexities of her characters.

That One Was Sweeter

1

I pressed my son's curly head to my breast and said, "Happy Birthday, dear. Grow big and strong."

Eldjan, as in the days of his childhood, embraced me. His eyes beneath the fine arched brows gleamed like two dark olives. His full lips turned up in a smile, making his sparse moustache bristle.

"Grow big, Mother? Not really?"

"Dearest, I still think you're as little as you were before. Would I have put away such a special present for your birthday if I didn't?"

Eldjan untied the package with boyish curiosity, went through the contents hastily and then, coming upon a tiny packet, unwrapped it. It contained a lump of sugar which he popped into his mouth, sucking it loudly as he had twenty years before. I laughed.

His dark eyes laughed, too. Then he raised his hand and said: "But that lump was sweeter!"

I will tell you the story of that lump of sugar.

Twenty years ago to a day, as I was going off to work in the morning, I stroked Eldjan's curly head and said: "What would you like me to get you, dear?"

Eldjan turned over in his warm bed, gazed at me sleepily and was silent for a long moment. He was probably thinking of what he might ask for. Then he put his arm around my neck and said: "Buy me a lump of sugar, Mamma."

281

"All right," I promised. But then I was sorry I had, because I might not be able to find any sugar. This was wartime. People were dying at the front lines. Death notices were reaching out for many houses, now knocking at one door, now at another. The children would often be put to bed hungry, and the last thing they would ask their mothers before falling asleep would be:

"Will you bring us some bread tomorrow, Mamma?"

"Will you give me a lump of sugar tomorrow, Mamma?"

That was a time when the bright and happy dreams that always fill a child's heart took on the shape of chunks of bread and lumps of sugar.

As I was returning home from work that evening I took the road past the army hospital, for I had noticed that the wounded soldiers sometimes traded a part of their rations for extra tobacco.

A cold north wind was blowing the stinging sand into the faces of the lone passers-by. A blond sergeant stood by the hospital fence, leaning against the iron rail. One of his sleeves was empty. It hung limply by his side. A gust of wind blew into it and it moved suddenly, raising up angrily as if threatening someone.

I came closer. The sergeant was holding a little packet in his hand, which only had three fingers left. Pointing, I asked: "Is that sugar, Brother?"

The sergeant blushed and offered it to me, never raising his eyes from the ground. "Yes. Here. I'm out of tobacco."

I looked at the sugar, fingered the single three-ruble bill in my pocket and, knowing that it was not enough, I said: "I don't need that much. I only want a couple of lumps."

The sergeant did not reply. I sighed and found myself saying, "You see, it's my boy's birthday today. He said he wanted a lump of sugar for a present. But I'm afraid I don't have enough to pay for so much." ·

He looked at me closely and then asked in a muffled voice: "How old is he?"

"Three."

He stared at the ground again, as if he were searching for something in the cracked pavement. As I turned to go he said, "Wait! Come back." He offered me the packet, holding it awkwardly in his three fingers. "Here. Take it to your boy." I quickly removed two lumps and stuffed the bill into his pocket.

The sergeant turned sideways and, indicating his pocket with his elbow, said sternly: "Take back the money." He did not wait for me to do as he asked, or, rather, commanded. He stuck his hand into his pocket, took out the bill and shoved it into my purse.

I looked at him. He smiled suddenly. It was a broad, boyish grin, so unexpected on his stern face. "Give this to your son. Tell him it's a present from the sergeant."

"But what about your tobacco?"

"Ah, I wish it were never invented. The doctors don't want me to smoke anyway. They get mad if I do."

My son and I sat at the table drinking tea that evening. Eldjan popped the little cubes of sugar into his mouth and sucked them loudly. "The sergeant's sugar is so sweet," he said, repeating the phrase over and over.

Twenty years have passed since then. No matter what I gave him for his birthday, I never once forget to enclose a lump of sugar in a little packet. There is always a sugarbowl on the table, but Eldjan always eats this lump and says:

"Ah, but that sugar was sweeter!"

Vidadi Babanly
(b.1927)

Babanly began his career as a poet; he is the author of many verses and a series of narrative poems. In 1954 he wrote the novella The Daughter-in-Law; *it was well received by readers. Subsequent novellas and novels confirmed Babanly's talent as a prose writer.*

In recent years he has been working on a major novel about Azerbaijanian scholars of chemistry: When Conscience Falls Silent.

The characters of his realistic works are obliged to surmount many difficulties to prove themselves. The story "The Wounded Heart" deals with ethical questions; it depicts people who have gone through the harsh trials of the last war.

The Wounded Heart

Old Khalyg-kishi had been lying on the narrow divan for several hours, puffing on his chibouk as he reclined against the pillows. Evening was creeping slowly into the room.

Someone knocked. Although the old man had been expecting this knock for many hours, he started visibly, as if it had come unexpectedly. The mouthpiece slipped from his lips that were brown and puffy from age. Bright sparks fell through the open collar of his shirt, singeing the grey hair on his chest. He rose, muttered as he brushed away the ashes, and shouted angrily into the darkness: "Hey! Isn't anyone at home? Where is everybody? Can't you hear them? Someone's knocking!"

The door of the adjoining room opened and a tall, well-built young woman appeared on the threshold. The old man immediately changed his tone of voice, saying gently: "May Allah bless you, my daughter. Go and see who's there."

The woman pulled the woollen shawl that had gathered about her shoulders over her head with a graceful movement and flipped the switch. The room immediately became bright and attractive, and the autumn gloom outside still more impenetrable. She went to the front hall quickly.

Khalyg-kishi heard the large bolt slide back and the heavy door creak open. A gust of cold air swept into the

285

house, bringing two elderly men in its wake. The wind tore at the door, and as the woman was unable to close it, the two men came to her aid. They appeared in the doorway of the room where Khalyg-kishi awaited them. They were both grey-haired and of the same height, and were probably of an age as well. The bright light made them halt and squint for a moment, then both cleared their throats, entered the room sedately, greeted their host and sat down without waiting for him to offer them a seat.

The door of the adjoining room opened again and old Gulistan's head, swathed in a large black veil, appeared in the crack. Recognising the visitors, she came out to greet them. She was small and slim, and her body was like that of a youth. "Hello, Gummet-gardash," she said pleasantly to the old man with the bushy white beard that seemed made of cotton. "How are your children? And you wife?" Then she turned to his companion and said: "May your visit bring us happiness, Bilal-kishi. Is your family well?"

"Allah protect you, Gulistan-badji. They are all well and remember and love you. And how are you? Are you well? Khalyg-kishi goes out for a walk in the village every now and then, but we haven't seen you in ages."

She sighed. "What's the use of talking about me? Old age is a curse. I'm up and around one day and flat on my back the next." She shook her head, which seemed weighted down and immobilised in its black covering. "Ah, the years fly and time is a cruel companion. Gummet, remember the way you used to prance about on your dappled grey charger? You were both so young and full of fire then. It seems like yesterday...."

"Yes, Gulistan. We are but visitors on this earth, all fated to gallop down a single road. But there is no one so great as to have come back after he has once traversed it."

"You're right. You're right, Gummet! Life is like a window. After you've come up and had your look, it's time to move aside." There was a sadness in her words that seemed to rise up from the very depths of her soul, making her small eyes large and moist.

"For the sake of my deceased father, Gulistan, I beg you to be still! Let's speak of the business at hand," Khalyg-kishi said irritably.

"What's the matter with you today, Khalyg? You're not at all like your usual self. You came home and lay down and haven't uttered a word all day. Has something happened that I don't know about?"

"Be still, woman!" he snapped. Then, speaking gently, he addressed the younger woman: "Take your mother-in-law's arm, my dear, and escort her to the other room. She's onto the same old song again and won't let us talk of our business."

This time his wife did not protest. She pursed her pale lips and left the room hastily. Her daughter-in-law followed respectfully. Khalyg-kishi rose and shut the door tightly behind them.

The conversation that followed was short. The old men left without even having had any tea. The moment the heavy front door banged shut Gulistan reappeared. She sounded both hurt and timid: "Our daughter just set the table, Khalyg. Why have the guests gone?"

"I don't know!"

"Why did they come?"

"It wasn't about anything important."

"Gummet would never have come for nothing." She looked at her husband suspiciously. Her voice was reproachful.

"Stop questioning me. I said it wasn't important. For the sake of Allah, woman, leave me alone!"

"What's the matter with you today?"

He did not reply, but looked at her furiously. She sobbed aloud like a child, lowered her head and shuffled out.

The old couple did not sleep that night. Gulistan tossed and turned, unable to sleep because of her husband's harsh words. Khalyg-kishi stared into the darkness in silence, fearfully awaiting the dawning day.

For forty-five years Khalyg-kishi and his Gulistan, a woman as slim as a girl, had laid their heads side by side on the large pillow each night, and in all those long years Khalyg-kishi had not once reproached her, had not once argued with her. Khalyg-kishi was known as a stern, taciturn man in the village. But at home he was gentle and thoughtful, and his greatest joy was to fulfil his little Gulistan's every wish. Many wondered at how a man could have two such different sides to his nature.

In the years following their marriage Gulistan had born him eight children, but all had died in infancy. She had grieved, tossed about at night and become withdrawn. Grief had wiped the rosebuds from her cheeks and tears clouded her eyes. Khalyg-kishi comforted his wife as best he could, trying to cheer her up and distract her from her terrible sorrow, but in his heart he grieved with her and yearned as she did for a child.

Their youth was behind them when fate finally took pity on them and gave them two sons. The boys were sturdy, good-natured, high-spirited children. Their laughter and running feet warmed the old house, banishing its stillness and sorrow. Gulistan and Khalyg-kishi were happy once again. It seemed that misfortune had forever forgotten the way to their home.

But grief comes after happiness just as happiness comes after grief. War broke out. Their elder son, who had been called up just before the war, was immediately sent to the front lines. Weeks passed, then months, but still there was no word from him. The parents now lavished all their love and hopes upon their youngest son, Madat. As soon as the boy graduated from school his father found him a bride, a beautiful, intelligent girl named Sanubar. "There's a war on," the old man said to himself, "and who knows, they may soon call up Madat, too. I only hope there is a grandchild." He knew that this was not a time for merry-making, as anxiety and sorrow were knocking at all the doors. Still, they had a proper wedding. His fellow-villagers understood and did not censure him. Everyone in the village came to the wedding: old men and women, young women and girls. Many came with hearts that were heavy and had tears in their eyes, but they all wished the young couple happiness.

The thunder of war was drawing ever closer. One bright spring morning Madat embraced his parents, kissed his young wife of but several days and went off. A year had not passed when the mailman brought the terrible news that he, too, was missing in action.

Gulistan was unable to bear another blow. She took to her bed, spoke to no one, would not eat and began wasting away. Khalyg-kishi became bent under the burden of his grief, for it was twice as heavy, since he has lost his two sons and was now about to lose his beloved wife as well. Gulistan was melting away like a burning candle.

And yet, human endurance is boundless! Khalyg did everything humanly possible to save his wife. He carried her in his arms and on his back like a child, taking her from city to city to see all the best doctors and every great professor, obtaining every medicine that might be of help. He became still more gentle and patient, repeating over and over again that it was too soon to give themselves up to despair.

"Don't grieve so, Gulistan," he would say, not really believing what he said. "You'll see, everything will turn out well in the end. After all, it says they're missing in action. They're alive. What if we wake up one fine morning and see that our boys have come home again? We must be patient and wait."

And the old couple waited. The war ended. Month after month slipped by. Many of the village men returned, but no one came back to their house.

The love Khalyg-kishi had had for his sons was now transferred to his daughter-in-law. He accompanied her to the city and helped her get settled when she entered a teacher's college. Every month he would send her money and food parcels, for those were still hard times after the war.

Sanubar was grateful to them and did not leave the old couple after she had graduated. She returned to the village to teach at school, living with her in-laws, caring for them, always treating them with patience and kindness. They, in turn, loved her as a daughter.

The years passed. Many young men tried to court Sanubar, careful not to let Khalyg-kishi learn of their intentions. They sent match-makers to her on the sly who would tell her it was high time she stopped shedding widow's tears and began thinking of a home of her own and children of her own.

But Sanubar would have nothing to do with them, and in time the young men desisted. One, however, was more persistent than the rest. He followed her like a shadow for three years, and wrote to her of his love. He was the same age as Sanubar. He was the collective farm's senior agronomist, liked and respected by everyone in the village. Sanubar was attracted to him and would have probably married him, but felt she could not abandon the old couple. After all, they had no one except her to look to in the whole world. If she left it would mean laying bare the old wounds that had just begun drawing over. The young man understood this. He decided he must first have Khalyg-kishi's consent, and so persuaded Gummet and Bilal, the two most revered old men in the village, to act as his sponsors and ask for Sanubar's hand. When they came upon Khalyg-kishi on the square outside the farm office, the old men each took one of his arms gently, led him aside and spoke cautiously of the agronomist's intentions, trying not to hurt their friend's feelings. Khalyg-kishi listened to what they said in silence. When he spoke his voice was calm and sad, and he did not raise his eyes to look at them.

"It's up to her to decide."

"She's been living under your roof for ten years," Gummet said. "Everyone knows you've been a father to her. It's up to you."

Khalyg-kishi said nothing. The old men did not insist, for they knew this was not something that could be decided on the spur of the moment.

All this had happened several months before. At first, Khalyg-kishi had been restless and depressed, though he did not say a word about it to his wife. Days passed. No one spoke of the wedding again and the old man calmed down. Perhaps the agronomist had changed his mind? Then that morning Gummet and Bilal had approached him again.

"We'll come to speak to you this evening," they had said.

And they had come. The conversation had been short. Everything was decided quickly. The following morning Khalyg-kishi was to send Sanubar's things to her new home, and that evening she would leave his house forever.

How was he to tell Gulistan of this?

That morning, as always, Sanubar was the first one up. She made the fire, boiled the water in the samovar, set the table and called the old couple to breakfast. They usually came right out, as if they had been waiting for her to call, but not today. They did not even reply. When she called to them again, Khalyg-kishi rose from the bed reluctantly, took a long time in washing and finally entered the room in silence. He did not touch a thing and did not even have any tea, but lit his pipe and sat there smoking in silence.

Sanubar, too, was not her usual self that morning. Her pleasant smile was missing. She was pale and sad, and her eyes were red-rimmed from crying and from a sleepless night. She tried not to look at her father-in-law, as if she were guilty in some way. She forced herself to swallow the hot tea and hurried off to the schoolhouse.

"I'll go outside with you, daughter," he said.

They walked to the gate in silence. When they were out on the street the old man stopped, puffed mightily on his pipe, coughed and suddenly said in a voice that was husky with tears: "My dear, you know how much we both love you. I want you to be happy...." He began coughing, gave up speaking, embraced his daughter-in-law and kissed her on the forehead.

Sanubar said nothing. She wiped her eyes with the corner of her fringed silk kerchief.

"Go, dear," Khalyg-kishi whispered, trying to force a smile.

Sanubar walked quickly down the path. He stood looking after her for a long time. When she finally disappeared beyond the bend, he called to the neighbour's boy and said, "Run over to the farm office and say that Grandpa Khalyg wants to know if he can have the use of a horse and cart. If they give it to you, drive it back here."

Gulistan was still in bed when Khalyg-kishi returned to the house. He did not go to her and did not say a word. In silence he opened the chest and took out the dowry that Sanubar had once brought from her father's house. Then he collected everything he himself had given her through the years. Gulistan watched him as he went about packing everything methodically. Soon a cart rumbled over and stopped by the gate. Khalyg-kishi began carrying out the bundles. At this Gulistan jumped out of bed.

"What's the matter, Khalyg? Are you mad? Where are you taking our daughter's things?" she cried, blocking the way.

"Let me pass, Gulistan. Don't stand in the doorway."

He spoke to her gently, as always.

"No, I won't. Are you crazy?" she shouted and pulled at the bundle he was carrying. "Give it to me!"

He did not become angry. All he said was: "Don't scold, Gulistan. It's not my fault. Our daughter is getting married."

"Married?" Her hands began to tremble, her knees gave way and she fainted.

It was a merry wedding. The table groaned from all the food and drink. There was music, and fine toasts, and the young couple were wished much happiness. The grey-bearded bard, strumming his gleaming *saz*, inlaid with mother-of-pearl, sang of love. When the song ended he slipped the instrument over his shoulder like a rifle and, passing among the seated guests, began reciting a hauntingly beautiful legend of true love.

At the height of the wedding feast the door opened. All eyes turned to the newcomer. In a moment the music was stilled, and the bard cut short his recitation. A tall, grey-haired old man stood stiffly in the doorway. The eyes in his proud head were stern and sad. It was Khalyg-kishi.

Everyone rose in silence to greet him.

He, in turn, greeted them with dignity and walked slowly to the table. He was given the place of honour. A dish of fragrant, steaming pilau was set before him and his glass was filled with wine. The old man touched neither food nor drink, but asked for a glass of tea. As custom demanded, he sent the bard a generous gift and asked him to resume his song. Once again the room was filled with music, and the bard sang with greater gusto then before.

Khalyg-kishi did not stay long. He congratulated the bride and groom and wished them many years of happiness. Then he left, walking as proudly as before.

Gulistan awaited him at home. She sat all hunched up on the bed and had been weeping. He sat down wearily beside her and put his arm around her. "Wipe your tears, Gulistan. She's young. How much longer should she have sat here beside us? We don't have much left. Our caravan is nearing the end of its journey. I only hope that she is happy. Offer your blessings to your daughter-in-law, Gulistan."

She did not reply. Instead, she pressed close to him and sobbed bitterly.

Isa Husseinov
(b. 1928)

This talented prosaist represents the postwar generation of Azerbaijanian writers.

Isa Husseinov's prose is severely realistic; he delves into the psychological complexities of his characters and strives to analyse the complex world of modern man.

His novellas and novels have witty, dramatic plots reflecting life in the modern Azerbaijanian countryside and the most vital problems of our times.

A Fervent Heart, Native and Alien, Saz, The Telegramme, *and* The Sound of the Pipe *are among his well-known novellas and novels. Isa Husseinov is also famous for his film scenarios including scripts for the films* Twenty-six Commissars from Baku, The Stars Can't Be Extinguished and Nasimi.

The story presented here "A Village Wedding", reflects the author's profound knowledge of the life and customs of his people.

A Village Wedding

There was a wedding in the village.

They had come for the bride.

In olden times horse-drawn carts covered with rugs would have pulled up outside the bride's house. The horses whinnied and reared at the loud music. And there would always be horse racing as a special event.

Now automobiles crowded the yard of the bride's house, and the air was full of the loud honking of horns instead of the neighing of yore.

The caravan of cars drove slowly out of the yard.

Although the houses of the bride and groom were adjacent, fashion called for the wedding party to drive down the village streets and even through the fields, to demonstrate the joy and triumph of those who had been joined in matrimony as well as of all their friends and relations.

The hood of the first car was covered with a length of red cloth. The toibabasy*, a stately man with a heavy black moustache, the groom and his best man rode in it.

Next came an open truck carrying the bride's dowry: a chiffonier, a wardrobe and other household articles. A group of musicians sat on a set of chairs, squeezed in among the furniture. The tambourine player was enthroned on top of the wardrobe. Two tipsy young men

* *Toibabasy*—Master of ceremonies at a wedding.— *Ed.*

293

were clutching the wardrobe and the tambourine player to keep him from flying out of the truck at the turns.

The chrome deer on the hood of the car following the truck was wearing a garland of fresh roses. The bride, the matron of honour and the matchmaker were in this car.

All the other cars were adorned with flowers, too.

When they had all left the yard they formed a cortège and set off on their journey, with every single horn blaring.

The groom was a physics teacher at the village school. He was a tall, slim, swarthy, rather shy, intelligent young man. He would shake his head every time his brother fired his gun.

The bride buried her face in the matron of honour's shoulder and wept.

"Everybody will think you're being married against your will," the matchmaker said and laughed. "If you don't want to go through with it, tell me now. May I not be my father's daughter if I don't turn the car back at once."

The bride peeped out from behind her veil and looked at the matchmaker. Her pretty face appeared for just a moment. She realised that the woman was joking and smiled through her tears. "I really don't know why I'm crying."

The matchmaker kissed her cheek. "You're acting like a baby. It's from happiness. You're crying from joy, my lamb, from joy."

The matron of honour kissed her other cheek. "Look at the wedding your brother-in-law's arranged. Lucky you. Open your eyes and look around."

The bride's long lashes trembled. She lifted the edge of her veil with her henna-painted fingers and peeked out. Then she smiled again and covered her face once more.

Seven or eight young men were crowded into the third car. These were friends of the groom, young teachers, tractor drivers and two militiamen. They jostled each other and made crude jokes, roaring loudly at each one.

The *zurna* players were playing "Vagzaly". The tambourine player was now balancing on his knees on the wardrobe, hitting the tambourine for all he was worth. The groom's brother kept reloading his pistol and firing shot after shot into the air as the cortège proceeded along its triumphal route.

Naturally, none of them had an inkling of what lay ahead.

The brakes of the first car screeched so unexpectedly it startled everyone. All the cars immediately drew to a stop, nearly colliding in the middle of the village, right outside the community centre.

The large, menacing eyes of the toibabasy in the lead car opened wide as he stared ahead. The groom looked up in surprise. His best man grabbed the handle of the door angrily.

The *zurna* players stopped playing. The tambourine player tumbled off the wardrobe. The two tipsy youths reached quickly for him and his tambourine. Then they gaped.

The groom's brother, forgetting he was inside a car, stood up on the seat, cracked his head against the inside of the roof and gazed dazedly at the driver. "What's the matter? Why'd you stop?"

"Go on! What's the matter?" the people in the rear cars shouted. Horns honked impatiently.

The cortège was stalled.

A stocky, broad-shouldered young man was standing in front of the lead car.

He was wearing a faded, grease-spotted army shirt that was open at the collar, over a pair of black riding-breeches, and a pair of old army boots. Locks of dark-brown hair covered his forehead, making his handsome, large-featured face with its high cheekbones appear harsh.

Car doors began slamming. People stuck their heads out of the car windows. A whisper ran down the line.

"It's Shamil! Shamil!"

"Shamil's blocking the way!"

"No!"

"There he is. See how cocky he looks!"

"How awful!"

"Shameless son of a shameless man!"

"He must be crazy. What's the matter?"

"Tell him to get out of the way!"

"You tell him, since you're so brave. He doesn't look like he's going to move."

The guests poured out of the vehicles and ran to the lead car, towards the man who was standing there with his legs so firmly planted on the road and his work-hardened hands, as heavy as any sledge-hammers and covered with black axle grease, on his hips. He was looking at them calmly, yet defiantly. They stopped and stood around in a cluster.

"What's the meaning of this? Why'd you stop the cars?"

The toibabasy approached. He laid his hand on the shoulder of the groom's brother and said: "Pardon me for saying so, but don't you think I'm in charge of this today? Come on, back up! A little more now! Fine! Hey, boys, bring me something nice to pay him off!"

The toibabasy ran his finger over his heavy moustache and waited patiently. The matchmaker dug into one of the bundles in the car and after some time came up with a long, tassled white shawl. The toibabasy shook it out solemnly and laid it over Shamil's shoulder. "Here's your ransom, my brave man."

An ironic smile touched Shamil's lips. His narrow, oriental eyes flashed. He removed the shawl slowly and returned it to the toibabasy just as solemnly.

"Let someone come forward from your side first," he said.

"What if we don't find a contender to wrestle with you?"

"Try looking."

The toibabasy ran his hand over his moustache again, went back to the car, stood there silently for a moment as he looked over the wedding guests. They were whispering as before.

"Well? Isn't there one brave man among you?"

The mysterious whispering continued. The guests seemed excited about something else entirely. Some peered with ill-concealed curiosity at the bride's car. They could not see her, as her face was covered with a white veil. Now, however, she bent her head still lower in order to be completely hidden behind the front seat.

The groom's face was flaming. His best man turned pale. The *zurna* players in the truck behind them stared. People began coming out of the community centre. Others came running from all over the village. The small square was filling up. Dozens, perhaps even hundreds of eyes were trained on Shamil. He stood there nonchalantly, as before, with his fists on his hips.

"I'm staying here until you set up a contender," he said.

A car door slammed and a fat blond fellow, the best man, emerged. He was very pale. "Didn't you hear him say we have nobody to tackle a lout like you? And we offered you the ransom. What else do you want?"

Shamil turned grey under his tan, though his oriental eyes still glinted ironically. He glanced into the bride's car, then quickly averted his gaze. "It's not a matter of who gets the upper hand. As far back as anyone remembers, it's been a custom to set up contender from the wedding party to wrestle anyone who blocks the way."

At this, one of the groom's friends, a tall, thin, pock-marked teacher of literature, came forth. "He thinks he's Don Quixote! This isn't the time of epic heroes, you know!"

Shamil did not hear what the teacher said, because the best man, whose breath smelled of sour liquor, was leaning into his ear, saying:

"Be a sport, Shamil! You've made everyone feel bad. What's the use of wrestling and proving you're stronger than anybody else?"

"You were a tankman in the army," the toibabasy was whispering into his other ear. "Everybody knows you're our best tractor driver. Stop acting like a child. The chief is beside himself. Don't make a scandal. Don't ruin the wedding, son."

Caught between the two whispering men, Shamil seemed not to hear either of them. He could only think of Zakhra. She was not in love with the teacher. She'd been overwhelmed by his rich and highly-placed relatives, by the two-storey house and its fine furnishings that belonged to his father, who was in charge of the dairy farm. Shamil was as certain of this as of anything. That was why he had decided to seek revenge for his lost love. He had no clear idea of what he would do. Should he remind Zakhra that she had loved him for many years? No, that was not enough.

He planted his legs still more firmly apart and looked around. Then he spotted two of his friends among the wedding party. They were both tractor drivers and knew he loved Zakhra, yet they had accepted the invitation from the chief of the militia. He forced himself to smile and was about to say something to the toibabasy when his gaze came to rest on the groom. Shamil straightened up. He seemed to grow taller. "Well if that's the case, I'll wrestle with the groom."

The literature teacher clutched his head with such force he lost his balance. The groom's brother cursed and then lunged at Shamil, but was led away and shoved back into the car.

The crowd was restless. Voices were heard saying:

"Get back into the cars, everybody!"

"Come on, let's go!"

"Get out of the way, you louse!"

The two tractor drivers approached Shamil.

"Listen, what's the use of breaking up the wedding?"

"It's not going to make you any happier, and you're spoiling everything."

A third tractor driver who stood off to a side, not being a member of the wedding party, said: "It's not his fault. He can't help himself." No one was listening.

The horns began blaring again.

The lead car moved. It was heading directly into Shamil, and stopped when the bumper touched his legs. He did not budge.

The toibabasy's large eyes glittered through the windshield. The best man's bloodless face seemed white beside him. Both men stared at Shamil, who had eyes for the groom alone.

Suddenly he moved aside, not really conscious of what he was doing. He left the square. When he saw some of his friends he said: "He knows what I feel like now."

"Who?"

Shamil did not reply. He did not say he meant the groom, or that he had seen such despair and sadness in the innocent fellow's sensitive eyes.

He left the village and crossed the fields to the tents of the farm's summer field camp in the distance. The two tractor drivers walked along in silence.

The wedding party continued on its way.

The groom was chain-smoking. The best man had not yet regained his natural colour. The toibabasy kept opening the door, sticking his head out of the car and glaring at the *zurna* players and the tambourine player who had climbed off the wardrobe and was sitting beside them. "Well? What are you so unhappy about?" he shouted.

The players tried to show some life, but became silent again after a few moments.

The bride, meanwhile, was cringing under her large veil and weeping. Neither the matchmaker nor the matron of honour said a word.

The groom's brother in the third car was also chain-smoking.

The cortège drove past the cotton fields, past groups of girls and young women standing by the roadside, it circled the neighbouring village and returned. The festive spirit had been regained. Once again the triumphant blaring of the horns announced the arrival of the wedding party. The cars drove into the yard.

As the lead car drew up, the toibabasy got out. He was about to stroke his moustache, but his hand stopped in mid-air. All but the second and third cars were empty.

"When did everybody get out?"

No one replied.

The groom's brother stared at the militiamen. "Well, say something. Why'd you let everybody go?"

They did not raise their eyes. The groom and the best man were speechless. A dead silence enveloped the yard.

The toibabasy gazed at the ground thoughtfully. Some time elapsed before he turned to the musicians and said wearily, "Go on, play something!"

After all, they were supposed to be playing. This was a wedding, after all, and that meant the *zurna* players were supposed to play.

Sabir Akhmedov
(b. 1930)

"He is ready to burn if this will help people," says one character in Sabir Akhmedov's novel Aran, *describing another hero.*

Akhmedov's stories and novels reveal new, remarkable traits, the noble impulses of working people in the socialist countryside.

Akhmedov is observant and able to penetrate into the inner world of other people. His prose is charged with emotional, figurative language.

In the Story "A Puzzling Night", Akhmedov, who began his literary career in the postwar years, deals with moral questions, showing the complex interrelationships of a family.

A Puzzling Night

A pile of notebooks held together by a thin rubber band lay before the teacher. She checked each pupil's work sometimes marking it with a ball-point pen. It was an interminable task. She patiently continued to work at it.

A brother and sister sat at the other side of the table. While their mother corrected notebooks, they posed each other riddles, some in writing, others in pictures. The television set stood on a small table in one corner, to the right of the door leading to the balcony. It had become a member of the household and independently managed its own affairs.

The children's father was sitting on the balcony. As the five-storey buildings, all in a row, began to wallow in their own illumination, one could see the milk-white tulle that covered the Shuban mountains and lingered more than an hour after sunset. It seemed to be daylight beyond the mountains, as though they marked the other side of the globe.

To the right two buildings darkled like enormous passageways. A small piece of the city gleamed beyond them. Further yet an eternal torch burned over the oil refinery day and night.

Father sat on the balcony and watched the mountains melt and vanish in the twilight. At times he could hear the children's voices and the television.

299

The woman spoke. She was asking him something. Noticing that his father had not heard, the son answered:

"Yes, there is."

A little while later there was a second question:

"Is there a café 'Sadko' on the boulevard by the sea?"

This time the children were silent. The father, waiting for a moment, responded: "Yes."

"Where?"

"At the very end of the dike that leads from the boulevard into the sea. I might add that it's as lovely and mysterious as the dancing of Sea Princes. They don't allow smoking or alcoholic beverages."

Some time passed and then the teacher asked yet another question: "Are there fruit trees, apple and pear trees, on the boulevard by the sea?"

"They planted an orchard."

The children's father hesitated. He did not understand what these questions were leading up to and why they had been posed in the first place.

"And where is 'Venice'?"

The man stood up, went into the room and walked over to the table.

The teacher lifted her pencil from the notebooks and explained: "I assigned a composition on the seaside."

The father extended his arm and took the notebook that lay before her. He looked at it: "I suppose there are mistakes here."

"I haven't finished correcting it."

"What do these lines mean?"

"That is where the text must be changed. We underline the mistakes in red so that the student will notice them." She stared in perplexity at the notebooks. Instead of asking another question, she said, as if to complain: "It's impossible to make sense of what they write. I can't tell what's correct and what's a mistake."

The teacher sat over a mountain of notebooks every evening. She would take one notebook from the pile, leaf through it, find the most recent assignment and then carefully examine the letters and words of each uncertain line; each was like an untrodden, unformed mountain pathway. The letters drawn in violet ink on the white paper were as near and dear to her as her dear children who lived in that building. But reading the compositions wearied the teacher. As she corrected the work and set the notebooks and papers to one side, she grew more and more exhausted. At times the pen would fall from her hand and her heavy eyelids would close.

Sometimes the father wanted to help her. He too was frightened by the large pile of notebooks, and waited impatiently even nervously for the last notebook to be corrected.

But the teacher had to finish everything herself. The mere fact that her husband realised what hard work this entailed gave her some aid and comfort.

Or perhaps this was not the case. When the lights had dwindled one by one from the five-storey buildings, and the balconies looked like sleepy railway cars at a silent, obscure station, a strange miracle should have occurred in the mute solitude of that night. The children's compositions that lay before the teacher would be transformed into green forests, dewy aromatic glades; and when her head leans over the table, filled with sweet dreams, the sonorous voices of children and the songs of birds would ring in her ears. And perhaps these would be the most precious days of her life.

The daughter, dark as a starling, gazed tenderly at her father: "I have a riddle for you. Can you guess it?"

Suddenly the father was seized by a heartfelt respect for the notebook that he held in his hands, for the person who took care of those notebooks, for his daughter who had only taken the first steps toward reading and writing, for his son who gazed at him together with his daughter; this made them dearer and closer to his heart.

"Just let me read this composition and then I'll guess."

"Guess first. Later you can read it." Seeing that her father was listening to her, the girl began to draw picture puzzles on paper and to read the puzzles aloud. "Here is a tree. An apple tree. People have come to gather the apples. At the very tip of the tree sits a monkey who is preventing the people from gathering the apples. How can they gather the fruit?"

The father stared at the paper. His son laughed. He enjoyed seeing his father puzzled by the drawing. Of course when one knows the answer to a puzzle it seems very simple.

"Think it over well!" The boy had the answer at the tip of his tongue. Laughing, he chided his father to hurry up and answer.

The girl thought that her father had not listened carefully to the riddle. Like a teacher explaining a lesson to her pupils, she took pains to speak loudly and distinctly: "Couldn't guess? Then I'll tell you." Both laughed. The boy blushed. For the first time in their young life, they were embarrassed.

"The people pick up a stone and throw it at the monkey. The monkey plucks apples from the tree and throws them right back at the people, hoping to hit them. Then the people gather up the apples and begin throwing stones again. The monkey plucks more apples and throws them down. The people gather them all up and leave. Understand? Shall I give you another puzzle to solve?"

"That's quite enough." He began to read aloud from a notebook.

"The seashore is beautiful. People take walks there and relax. They go sailing along 'Venice'. If you look down from the bridge above the canals, the canals seem like rivers and the boats like steamships. The bushes and other plants look very much like a forest...."

"Is he a good student?"

"Yes, a good student."

"He has a good eye for description. Everything is as it should be."

"The children know the boulevard better than I do."

Father went back out on the balcony. The private homes that stood close to the high, densely constructed buildings of the settlement threw light into the earth. Beyond them there were no buildings. The quarter gleamed like an island in the midst of an enormous haze. "The children know the boulevard better that I do." She had not meant to reproach him or to hint at something. She had spoken without an ulterior motive, spontaneously. Had she deliberately chosen that theme? The pupils would write their compositions; she would bring their notebooks home, lay them on the table that evening and begin to correct them; then there would be a question that would astound the children and their father.... No, it couldn't be. The teacher would never work in such a devious way. She was not a master of manoeuvring. Or perhaps the theme that she had assigned her students had simply come to her involuntarily like some past sadness, folded in four like a piece of paper, that had slumbered in the depths of her heart.... The teacher had never realised that things might end up like this.

Both children joined him on the balcony. They were enjoying themselves. The girl held a pencil and piece of paper. She wanted to draw another puzzle for her father to guess. But her brother outstripped her, taking the paper from her. Their father switched on the balcony light. The boy put the paper on a table and began to draw. "Here are three lines. Can you make an ox out of them?"

The father froze as he gazed at the paper. He simply could not force himself to think this evening.

The boy pulled the paper back. He drew a large "A". Then he raised his head and gazed at his father. His father was astonished and looked at his son in a way that might have even implied a threat. They boy had used all the lines, but there were three letters left. How was he going to make them? Of course it was interesting to pose riddles to each other. It made a person thoughtful and clever. One was allowed the subterfuge of fantasy, but deceit and inconsistencies were not allowed!

"What about 'nox'?"

The boy put the ends of three fingers together, extended his hand in a familiar way and tapped his father's forehead gently. The sound was delicate and almost imperceptible, like a needle.

"There's your knocks."

The children went back inside. He followed them and sat down. He took both corrected and uncorrected notebooks, leafing through them and examining the latest assignments. Each student had described everything he had seen and heard on the boulevard by the sea so as to complete the assignment. But the educated teacher whom they loved like a mother had been confused by these essays, although she had corrected such notebooks for many years now, because she did not know enough about the subject.

"You assigned a theme that you aren't familiar with and had a hard time yourself."

The woman did not look up. How attentive she was to her work! If someone were to ignore a small detail in his work, if a small mistake slipped past him — the world might come crashing down; cities might perish. If another person made a mistake it might merely mean the loss of a letter or a comma. But perhaps that too could lead to unhappiness. Something indiscernible might vanish. Isn't that so, teacher?

He was touched, but tried to keep his tone light as he asked: "Did you chose that theme purposely?"

"No."

She was terribly embarrassed, as though she had never seen the sea and was not familiar with the shore; as though fifteen years ago when she was a student at the institute she had not sat on a bench by the yacht club together with him. And someone else had gazed at the transparent water of the sea; a girl who had spoken two or three words during earlier meetings; a girl whose tongue had accidentally loosened this one time. And she had said: "The waves that reach the shore remain there forever. They never return to the sea." Then the waters had darkened. The splash and quivering of a wave rang out in the vast darkness of the sea. She got up. He walked her to the dormitory. She recognised the existence of only one sea, the sea of her pupils' notebooks. She knew only one shore, the last pages of those notebooks.

The children had turned off the television and gone off to bed.

The father went out on the balcony. He sat down and turned off the light. A light breeze passed over the balcony. The tall poplars that grew in front of the balconies rustled their leaves. The other side of the Shuban mountains which had gleamed white as dawn some time ago, the side that he called "the other side of the world," had long ago dissolved in darkness. To the east of the torch that burned from factory waste products, clouds of smoke rose and disappeared to the north.

One of the nights that followed each day after the peaks of the Shuban mountains dimmed was transformed into a puzzle. Perhaps the answer to the puzzle was so simple that a child could get it. Someone had to simply tap on his head: "Knock, Knock."

Chinghiz Husseinov (b. 1929)

Husseinov is a prominent prosaist, literary scholar and critic, and a Candidate in Philology.

His stories, novels and poetic prose deal largely with problems of ethics. Husseinov strives for purity in human relations, for noble thoughts, and opposes hypocrisy and vulgarity however these may be manifested or concealed. His plots are simple and uncontrived. Events develop evenly and calmly. Passions are confined to the subtext; the conflict is hidden between the lines. The author is mainly concerned with creating a mood and attempts to convey his thoughts and feelings to the reader. "The Islands" is a moving story about a wartime childhood of the author and his mother.

*For my mother, Makhfirat
Melik-Mamed-kyzy*

The Islands

The first cry. Everyone knows this—the cry of a newborn child. Mine and yours. The first tears. Who remembers them, those tears? They flow without reason. The first laughter—we forget even this. These form my prehistorical epoch.

The islands of memory.... I suppress the first things I remember about myself because such things don't happen. Nobody will believe me and I don't believe myself. It's contrary to nature and unscientific.

But I'll tell about it anyway since I remember it clearly.

My mother and father lay in the shade of an old fig tree slumbering on the rug. Beside them slept a child in a bamboo cradle. When my mother awoke she saw me on the sand. I was eating sand. I eat and eat, and the sand is fresh and crunchy, although I have no teeth yet—before cutting one's teeth one has to pass through the whole historical stage of crawling.

And what, after all, was first? Something else was first.

I was five, or almost five: father brought me a lamb from the country; cousin Enver—our leader and indefatigable ring leader who, I am sorry to say, prematurely left the world of the living—and I push our way through the iron fence surrounding the large, slightly sloping meadow in whose centre towers the gold-domed church of Alexander Nevsky. Enver helps me drag the soft white lamb with trusting round eyes. The meadow around the church is an island of greenery in dusty Baku. I tie the lamb to the fence with a long rope and Enver and I plunge into the cool, tall, green grass.

...Or perhaps this.

A black disk spins. It seems to me that musicians are inside the box which emits sounds. I sit on a stool, my legs hardly reaching the cross-piece between its legs. I'm in the workers' and peasants' militia station No.3, a single-storeyed pisé building with barred windows. Here are only men. A record spins on the gramophone—the *lezghinka*! The men—grown-up and large—dance on the small area across from the table. Brown, resilient straps and gun-belts crackle; breeches billow out; polished boots gleam as though they had been varnished. Father loves to dance, and the other militiamen are no less enthusiastic, rising on their toes like real dancers. Everyone dances, only I watch. Their faces break into smiles. I am glad, I am thrilled by their dance, the dance of grown men.... What happened on that distant day? A gramophone played in the militia station. Who brought it? These questions haunt me now, but then.... Grown-ups were dancing! Grown-ups? They were twenty, twenty-five. They were much younger than I am now, mere youths. But for me they are still giants.

...The first joy that I remember....

I am at the cottage in Pirshagi. Behind the building is a hill of sand thrown against the rear wall by the north wind that often blows on Apsheron. We jump from the flat roof, covered with oily earth, onto the hill, drowning ourselves in the soft sand which runs in rivulets from our bare feet.

Although no one said anything, suddenly I heard that Mama had arrived. I ran out onto the dusty country road. I ran as fast as I could to meet her first. She had just returned from the sanatorium. It was the first and last time she had gone to a health resort. Skimming along the street, I could already see her face, smiling and pleased that I had seen her.

There she was! I jumped into her arms, encircling her with my dust-whitened legs and arms and, clasping my bare heels around her back, pressed close to her. She caught me up and carried me. How dear she was, *my* mama!

Or perhaps this was my first joy.

I remain alone at the cottage, but my aunt finally decides to send me back to the city. My aunt, heavy but agile and quick, gives me over to a driver who is going to the bazaar in the city. Our cart jolts along the dusty road for a long, long time; evening comes and it seems we will never arrive. Suburban trains dash past us with a warm, extended whistle; nearby and in the distance are innumerable derricks; the air smells of oil, an odour that is an indelible part of my childhood and my life today, for in it are my roads, the city where I was born, the sea and everything connected with my country.

Here are the last hillocks; a road paved with cobblestones begins. Through a chink in the cart I can see the large, swollen, smooth cobblestones. I pull myself above a basket filled with gleaming purple eggplants and see the city.

The cart rumbles along narrow streets, past flat-roofed houses. Suddenly it stops on our street. "Can you find your house?" asks the driver with the dark, unshaven face. How could I not find my house! There it is right close by. I jump from the cart and without saying goodbye or thank you—since I don't understand that I should thank the man—I run to the gates. I have already forgotten the cottage in the country, the driver, and I run home where I haven't been for what seems like an eternity. Of course I had no idea of what eternity was then and I have no idea of it now....

There are the gates!

I stop for a moment. Our two rooms on the second floor and the whole gallery are flooded with the brilliant, blinding electric fire of big lamps.

Everyone is alive, both my father and my mother. They are young. How happy they are! They have no premonition of the war that will soon extinguish that brilliant light. They do not realise that not very much time has been allotted them—a little over a year for Father, six years for Mother.

...The first grief that I recall....

A cry pierces the hot August Baku day. All the doors and windows in the gallery have been thrown wide open in the hope that the interminably cloudless sky will have mercy on us and send us the smallest breeze, or something like a draught.

This was the cry of our neighbour who lived at the very end of the gallery, the owner of the only telephone in the building.

More than anything on this earth that cry was aimed at me. I trembled all over. The neighbour, lame from birth and today the mother of eight grown sons, hobbled over to me. On her white lips I read: "She is dead!"

My mother had died. She was younger than I am now and it had seemed that life had only begun, that everything lay ahead of her.

...My first act of cowardice. Oh, how I remember it!

My mother's sister, her eyes swollen with tears and her voice somehow strange and deep, said: "Come right over to the hospital! Your mother wants to see you."

I knew they had taken her from the ward into a partitioned area in the hall so that the other patients would not see her dying.

In my aunt's words I heard: "She is dying, she wants to bid farewell to you."

But I didn't go. I was afraid.

I was afraid to see a person dying.

I won't go!

I was stubborn and silent, like a stone.

I saw it with sharp grabbing claws, that death that circled round my mother.

Suppose it caught hold of me (Who caught hold of me? Death? My mother? They had blended into one being for me in my fear.) and ordered me: "You come too!"

But I don't want to!

I'm afraid.
Dull, animal fear.
Stupefaction.

...My first cares.... It lasted for a year, that first anxiety.

It became difficult for my mother to accomplish the steep ascent up our street when she returned home from work. It was dark, there were no lights because of the war. One could be injured, or attacked on the street. But the main thing was the defect in her heart. I heard the heart when I walked beside my mother and even imagined it — large, filling her whole chest, hungry for air and space, tired.

My mother came out of the maternity home where she worked as a midwife. I met her at the door. She immediately took me by the hand and leaned on me, and we slowly went along the gardens in front of the two-story building of the maternity home, and right up to the tram stop on narrow Basin Street we could smell the iodine.

The tram took us only two stops. We got out on noisy, crowded, dusty Bazarny Street and ascended for a long time, agonizingly long for mother, along the steeply rising street that used to be called Staraya Pochtovaya, past single-story buildings with dark windows, almost touching the walls because the sidewalk was so narrow. With great joy we crossed Kasum-Izmailov Street and stopped at a large, old-fashioned house. Mother wanted to say something with her blue lips but couldn't, she hadn't enough air and so she stood, hanging her head and holding onto the chipped stone wall. I stepped away so as not to impede the flow of air, so that it wouldn't be stuffy for her, so that my nearness would not weigh on her breast where the heart beat and knocked in feverish tempo. We were almost there. There remained only the final stage, one block. She raised her head and I sensed that she was telling herself that she had enough spirit to go on; she was calming her heart, reminding it of the time when it had obeyed her and could have easily managed the short climb that hardly demanded any work from the heart.

Once again we walked slowly and I deliberately slowed each step; during that year I perfected the art of walking slower and slower. Let mother think that it is she who hurries.

We cross one more street, Polukhin Street. There is our building with the semi-circular balcony hanging over the street, our tall iron gates — how much iron there is in Baku! I know all the projections and dents along the short path from the gates to the stairs; I know where water can collect, dripping from the faucet if it has not been tightly closed; I know where to lengthen my stride and where to shorten it so as not to stumble on the round cover of the sewer which protrudes in one place close to the window beneath the balcony.... I could follow this segment of the path with my eyes closed.

And here are the railings that shake when you touch them. Mother clutches at them and once again stands still, trying to gather her breath for the final assault on thirty stone steps, worn and almost concave.

At home, mother quickly recovered. Home is home. She sat down on her favourite couch to let her heart calm down, so that it would go back in place and stop trying to break free of her chest.

308

...My first anger....

I see him sometimes, my mother's uncle Abdula.

He is dried out with age, a dry cough shakes his frame. I feel sorry for the old man, so weak and sickly. He's already past eighty. My mother's uncle rarely comes to the city. He lives in his cottage in the environs of Baku, in one of the buildings of a former estates that at one time covered half the village. In the garden is an enormous mulberry tree, a century-and-a-half old and probably the largest in the area. The black mulberries are large, juicy, and shaggy like bumble-bees.

We greet each other politely, speaking of this and that until the next meeting; the shorter the meeting, the better, and the less often we meet, the more peaceful things are. And already my heart stirs, not with anger, but with regret and thoughts of one of the weaknesses of human nature.

With the advent of summer it became oppressively hot in Baku. In that year the war ended, and mother was granted her first leave. But where can one go with an ailing heart?

We went to pay our respects to Abdula.

No, no we have no pretensions to a room on the second floor. We won't eat grapes without paying for them. All we want is the small room, you remember, in the wing close to the well; it is isolated, no one lives there and the household tools that are stored there could easily be moved to the barn: a spade, a crow-bar, a saw, a barrel. Uncle frowns and glances at his wife, who looks at those with whom she speaks with a sour expression as though they were eating a lemon or some pickled eggplant in front of her.

Fearing a refusal, mother begins to speak about money, although money.... And uncle says that they promised to rent this room to a "holy" man who once went to Kerbela to pay his respects to Imam Gusein; there is a long account of this journey and of Imam Gusein's father Imam Ali, and the advance payment for the room, a sum in three figures, "Not a lot money," says Uncle, "but we've already spent it...."

And Mama promises to pay this amount.

With a tearful, complaining voice, uncle's wife explains that they are not only worried about the advance; they had counted on the whole amount, to hire a gardener, because the grapes that you want to buy have to be grown after all.... Mama promises to pay this too. Where will she get it all, I wonder. We haven't a penny to our names. I look at Abdula with fierce hatred, hoping he will sense my stare. But I remain silent. It's not proper to interfere in the conversations of one's elders. He doesn't even look in my direction.

To pay for the cottage, mother had to sell the fringed silk shawl — father's first present to her — and a string of pearls, part of her dowry.

That summer, her last summer, she felt better. Once clinging to the projecting stones of the wall, carefully calculating the distance and setting her feet down on them, she climbed to the railings of the balcony on the second floor and stepped over them. On the balcony, she straightened up, threw back the hair from her forehead, and for a long time fixed her gaze on the sea. Then she looked down at me with a calm, almost amazed expression on her face.

In a few days there was another attack; we returned to the city and she was back at the hospital....

I gave Abdula his money before our arrival at the cottage. Their home is in the

Fortress, on one of old Baku's narrow streets. They still come back here for the winter from the dacha; the eighty-year-old man and his wife, the same as ever, with a sour expression on her face even when she talks about fig jam, the sweetest of all jams.

...I was first insulted by my father.... My throat smarted. It was painful to swallow. The insult was so great it could not be overlooked.

We were walking along the street, my mother, our neighbour and myself. Suddenly mother turned pale and stopped. Our neighbour, a regional activist, was well known for her loud voice. Now I felt like the whole street could hear her as she said: "You fool! It isn't worth suffering because of a tramp like that! You look terrible!"

As though she had not heard, mother looked straight ahead.

The neighbour did not stop. "If you want, I'll go right up and give her a good kick in the behind! Shall I? Say the word."

Mother silently pressed her hand to her chest. From that ill-starred day on, her heart called attention to itself....

Father did not come home that night. Recently he had been coming home late, and was irritated by the slightest thing. Nothing satisfied him. Someone whispered that he had been seen with a blonde, and then they told us the address where she lived.

At dawn, mother left the house. She opened the door without knocking.

Father, his legs hanging over the edge of the bed, pulled on his boots. The blonde stood by a table set for breakfast.... This was the first time that my mother's heart lurched.

...It was she, the blonde, who walked in front of us. She walked and I imagined how our neighbour would steal up to her and give her a good kick.

It is as though I myself watch my father pulling his boots over his breeches. And my throat smarts. The lump has to be dissolved before I can swallow freely. But how can it dissolve if there are no tears?

This was my first insult. Already it has ceased to exist. Only the sadness remains, for the hearth has long been extinguished, the coals have long died away....

...No, no! It is cruelty. You can't get around it. How could you be silent?

— How could I avoid speaking of my first cruelty?

— Well, tell about it, then!

I don't understand how those words were wrested from me on that distant day. How much time has passed and yet the words still burn.

Mother ate a small piece of the black, heavy bread, the sort we ate during the war years, on the way home. When I saw the loaf with one piece gone, I cried out loudly: "You ate bread on the way home! Bread must be divided!"

Mother looked at me, her eyes filled with horror. Her whitened lips moved soundlessly from agitation. Our room filled with a silence that terrified me. Mother bent under the weight of my words. I saw profound anguish in her eyes. Quietly, she said: "If we begin to divide the bread, my heart will stop."

"I don't want that to happen either," I mumbled. But on that day, mother divided the bread all the same and gave me half of her share. You know, I didn't touch a piece of it....
— Bravo!
— I returned the bread to her....
— Loud applause!
— In the name of my late father I forced her to eat that piece.
— But the words were uttered.
— She forgave me.
— But I don't forgive myself!

...That's all from my childhood. What was the first thing in my adult life? Many things. But these are different songs, a different motif. And all the same....
I will tell of my first feeling of envy. Time and again it wells up inside me anew.
I envy my son. He has a mother, with a clear ringing voice, young, well-built. Like my mother. But not mine!...

**Altai Mamedov
(b. 1930)**

Prosaist and playwright Mamedov is the author of Countrymen *and* Men, *comedies well-known in Azerbaijan.*

Altai Mamedov is primarily a writer of humorous short stories. With a kindly smile he depicts men at labour; such is the hero of "The Eighth Son", the story selected for this anthology.

Mamedov has also successfully tried his hand at writing psychological short stories.

The Eighth Son   The ninth son blew up the bellows. Uncle Mursal straightened the red-hot horseshoe and turned to his assistant: "Geibaly!..."

"Yes, Master."

"Geibaly, Allah might better send a man a blind daughter than an unskilful son...."

"?"

"Why don't you say something, Geibaly?"

"You are right, Master."

"Geibaly, I want to tell you that instead of a good-for-nothing son, Allah would do better to give a man a stone! That would be much better."

"Once again, Master, you...."

The ninth son squeezed the bellows. But they spoke of the eighth son. It was a familiar topic. Geibaly had heard such conversations from time to time during his apprenticeship to the blacksmith. The blacksmith complained about his eighth son if not every day, then in any case once a week. There was a time when Mursal had great hopes for this son. And what had come of them? Misfortune. That eighth son had raked his father over hot coals.

The eighth son had become a football player and was known as number seven. Mursal could not forgive this. All over the world people were studying and picking out respectable occupations, but his eighth son Tofik was rolling a ball around a football field while people watched him, whistling and shouting.

"Seven of my sons have found their place in the world," thought Mursal. "Only the eighth turned out to be a blockhead...."

When Mursal thought about his son as he stood before the fiery forge, he would turn as scarlet as red-hot iron. At such moments he would recall his father who had spent his life in poverty, carrying burdens on his back. He had been a porter. Mursal also recalled how his father had apprenticed him to Ramazan. At the time, many people thought that Mursal would also become a porter. But his father had taken him by the hand and brought him to Ramazan, now deceased.

"Make him a man, Ramazan! I could never become a real person, no matter how hard I tried. At least let him be a person," said Mursal's father, taking a grey change purse from his pocket with trembling hands and extracting ten golden coins.

Mursal had never seen so much money in his father's possession. "If father has so much money," he thought, "why doesn't he buy a new shawl for mother? Why do we go to sleep hungry?... Why?"

Mursal asked himself these questions and could not answer them. Meanwhile Master Ramazan gladly accepted the golden coins, tucked them away in his change purse and said: "My father also paid such a price once...." He said this as though he felt guilty about something.

Mursal worked for Master Ramazan two years and then opened up his own smithy next to him. When he became a blacksmith his father's joy was boundless.

"My dreams have come true, son! I can die content. This trade is like a golden bracelet. Wear it and you will always be strong.... Your children should also master this trade. My son, in this world nothing is more precious than a trade...."

Those were the days of bullock carts, horses, donkeys. A blacksmith was always busy. Involuntarily, Mursal compared his life with that of his father. Naturally, he rejoiced. He could not help but rejoice. At last Mursal had broken free of poverty. He was also grateful to Master Ramazan who had given him this blessing.

Mursal married. His first son was born. Then another son was born. Mursal lost himself in a sweet boundless dream: "Let God give me fifteen sons, I will make each one a person."

Mursal wanted his first son to become a blacksmith. The second should be a barber and set up shop by the gates of Serche Bazaar. The third son would set up a tailoring shop next door. And the remaining sons would be respectively a watchmaker, a shoemaker and a jeweller. Thus Mursal's sons would take over the entire Serche Bazaar. Mursal sighed as he gazed upon the schoolboys, the young *beks* and merchants' sons; he never dared even to dream that his sons might obtain an education. He knew that for him this was unobtainable.

But he dreamed and even swore an oath that he would make his sons tradesmen. As he beat the red-hot iron with his sledge hammer, it seemed to him that his dreams would come true! He believed that he could realise them. But it seems that dreams are not all that easy to deal with; sometimes you just can't catch hold of them.

The world changed.... New people came in khaki-coloured shirts and riding-breeches and enrolled all the children in school. It was a miracle! But

Mursal worried that someone would grab him by the collar and make him pay for his sons' schooling or throw them out of school in disgrace. So inspite of the fact that his sons were going to school, Mursal quietly taught them blacksmith's trade. After they had learned their lessons, his sons were obliged to join their father in the smithy. Allah be praised, Mursal's children were good students. But when someone praised them, Mursal said with amazement: "Why shouldn't they do well in school? The school is free! How could they dare to do poorly in such a school?..."

Whenever money became the topic of conversation, Mursal grew anxious. He feared that someone might still demand payment for his sons' education. But this never happened. Both he and his wife were enrolled in courses under a state programme for the liquidation of illiteracy and began to study. This too was free. The eldest son, Ziraddin, studied hard: 10 years in Gyandzha, 5 years in Baku, then 5 more years in Moscow.

And a miracle happened. Mursal's eldest son was sent to work in the embassy in an Eastern country. Mursal could not believe that his son could hold a responsible diplomatic post. "My son a consul? No, it's a miracle, not my son but a child sent from on high."

Farrukh, the second son, remained in Moscow at the Atomic Institute. Salakh, the third son, also never returned to Gyandzha. He graduated from a construction institute and became an engineer. Now he lived in Bratsk. Two of Mursal's sons worked as physicians in Baku. The sixth son was the director of a village school. The seventh taught in a university. The youngest son, the ninth, was still in school....

"But that eighth son, the one that broke my back, is rolling a ball around a field!"

When Tofik, who was an all "A" student, would come to his father's smithy and beat the anvil with his hammer, Mursal, scrutinising him distrustfully, was speechless with joy. The red-hot iron yielded to Tofik's deftly aimed hammer like soft wax.

"That son will be smarter than all of them. Except, of course, for my son, the consul. He's intelligent, perceptive... " thought Mursal looking at his son's bulging muscles. "Or maybe his arms are strong but his brain is weak, Allah forbid."

From time to time Master Mursal would lay his hammer down and wipe away the sweat that streamed down his brow. He would think about something and stare into the red fire.... Yes, his skilful son had finished the tenth class and decided not to enroll in an institute. He found work and brought a goodly sum to his mother each month. Mursal marvelled at this and began to grumble to himself: "Am I dead that Tofik shouldn't get a higher education. But what kind of work is he doing? Rolls a ball around a field! People must be getting feebleminded to give him so much money for that. It's not right. It can't be...."

Often Tofik would be gone for three or four days. Mursal would ask his wife: "Where's your son?"

"He's in training."

"What do you mean?"

The youngest son joined the conversation: "Before a match he has to train for a few days...."

"Accursed evil!"

315

Sometimes the eighth son would disappear for fifteen days or even a whole month. And Mursal would ask the ninth son: "Where's your brother?"

"In Karaganda."

"And what did he lose there?"

"That's where he's playing."

"Accursed evil!"

Days would pass and Mursal would ask again: "Where's your brother?"

"In Samarkand...."

"Now where is he?"

"Now he's in Ashkhabad."

"What's the good-for-nothing doing there?"

"Playing."

"Accursed evil!"

Sometimes Geibaly's mother would fall ill six times in one month. Long before sunset he would disappear with a very plausible excuse: to find the necessary medicines at the chemist's. As ill luck would have it, on such days the ninth son would always be occupied with something.... The barbershops, stores, and stands all closed towards evening on those days to Mursal's great astonishment. What was going on?

"Where is everyone?" he would ask.

"At the football game."

"Accursed evil!..."

On such days the town was deserted. People vanished and silence reigned. From time to time one could hear distant voices: "Hit it!"

This all struck Mursal as very strange. Sometimes a barber would come up to Mursal and say: "Mursal! Yesterday your son scored two goals."

"I'd rather he beat his head against a stone...."

"What a master!"

"The devil take your master."

It would not be out of place to remind the reader that Mursal had never once beaten any of his sons. He had never even threatened them.... He dared only one serious punishment; he did not speak with his eighth son.... When Tofik was at home during the evening meal, Mursal would address his wife rather than his son: "You teach some sense. Let him grow wise."

Then Tofik would also address his mother, without looking at his father: "Tell him my wits are in working order."

His father would not relent: "Tell him that the mind is in the head, not the feet...."

Tofik did not fail to give an answer: "Tell him that if you're fast on your feet it doesn't necessarily harm your mind."

"Tell him not to be stubborn and to go enroll in an institute."

"And you tell him, Mama, that I'm enrolled in a correspondence course at an institute of physical education."

"Tell him that no one in this town would give his daughter away in marriage to such a person."

"Tell him I'll marry the daughter of a fan."

"Accursed evil!..."

Mursal was overcome with bitter thoughts about his son. His hopes were pinned on his eldest son, the consul. If that son would speak with Tofik, the latter

316

would surely come to his senses. The consul knew the ways of the world. He knew everything worth knowing on this earth and above it.

"Soon my son the consul will come. In his last letter he promised to come for a month's visit."

Mursal pictured how Ziraddin would open the door and come in. Mursal would throw the sacrificial lamb to the ground and slit its throat at his son's feet. "If only he would come...."

"Geibaly!"

"Yes, Master!"

"Geibaly, why does Allah do everything backwards?"

"Yes, Master, yes."

Mursal blew up the bellows himself; a spark flew from the hearth and fell at Geibaly's feet, burning his toes. The boy took his foot in his hand and began to leap around on the remaining foot.

"What happened, Geibaly?"

"I got burned, Master!"

"Well you shouldn't wear sandals to work in a smithy! Accursed evil!"

His assistant calmed down and begged Mursal: "Master, I have to leave early today. To buy medicine for my mother."

"What, you mean she's still not feeling better?"

"No, Master, no."

"Well, go on then.... May Allah give her back her health!"

At that moment the ninth son came barreling into the smithy like a bullet: "Papa! Give me a present! Ziraddin is here."

"Whatever you want! Geibaly, I'm leaving. Set the place in order and then you're free to go buy your medicine."

Mursal untied his apron and threw it in a corner. "Get a taxi!" he said to his son.

"Father, we'll never get a taxi now."

"Why not?"

"Simple! Today there's a football game."

"Accursed evil! I'll tell Ziraddin everything. He'll give your football-playing brother what for!"

The ninth son smiled.

They walked along the street. Mursal hurried. He wanted to see his son as quickly as possible. On his way home, he thought to himself: "I'll enter the courtyard by the back entrance. I'll take the sheep by the horns and slit its throat at my son's feet. Then we'll talk for a whole month."

A blue "Volga" stopped and its powerful driver leaned from the cab: "Climb in, Uncle Mursal, if you're going to the football game!"

"Football be damned! Give us a lift home if you can."

The driver looked at his watch: "I see there's no persuading you. Climb in. After all, you are Tofik's father...."

Had he heard these words at any other time, Mursal would not have entered the truck. But he was eager to see Ziraddin as quickly as possible.

"Master, if your son scores one goal, I'll win a handsome bet."

"I wish it were his last goal!"

"Why so?"

"From this day on, you'll never see him with a ball in his hands. The trap is set."

"What sort of trap, Master?"

"If Allah so wills, you'll see."

When they reached their home, Mursal came in the back way. Ziraddin was taking a stroll about the garden. When he saw his father he ran to meet him. They embraced each other. Then Mursal tore himself away to slaughter the sheep. Ziraddin wouldn't permit it.

"Don't do that, Papa. Change your clothes and let's go."

"Where?"

"To the football game."

"Where?"

"To the football game, Father. I was supposed to come two or three days later. But I arranged to fly here earlier so I could see this match. I want to see how my brother plays."

Mursal did not believe his ears. He stared blankly.

"Don't just stand there, Father. Go change your clothes...."

"If everyone's gone crazy, you go too," thought old Mursal. "Wife! Bring my suit!"

"What! A suit in this heat?"

"Bring it here. I must wear it."

"You're going to wear a suit that is thirty years old?"

"Give it to me!"

His wife pulled a suit smelling of mothballs from a trunk. While she ironed it, Mursal washed his hands, scraping them against a stone. He put on a white shirt. The suit, with its dashingly tapered trousers, was becoming to Mursal.

"Father! What a stylish suit!" joked his son, the consul.

Looking around to make certain that his wife was not in the vicinity, Mursal winked at his son: "That suit has quite a history. The late Meshadi sewed it for me.... The late Kabla Yakub took me with him to Tiflis a few times, to parade. This suit was only for trips to Tiflis.... I'm ready, son."

They got into the taxi summoned by the ninth son....

Mursal thought that even though he was going to the football game, he would speak with his son, the consul, about Tofik later that evening.

They had to wait in a long line to enter the stadium. Mursal was astonished: "Oh, Allah! What a crowd! The doctors are here. The barbers are here. The store managers are here and so is the entire militia force!" Then Mursal glimpsed Geibaly in the crowd; he was trying to get into the stadium without waiting in line.

"Geibaly!"

"Yes, Master."

"Geibaly! I suppose this is a chemist's! I suppose they sell medicine here!"

Geibaly looked with amazement at the master's full dress suit: "Master! Mama isn't sick. I am and so is everyone here. With the help of Allah you will be too!"

"Come with us, Geibaly. Just shut up!"

"Master, as soon as you enter that stadium you'll see how catching the sickness is!"

The stadium was so full there was hardly room to move. Everyone invited Mursal and his son to sit by them. The ninth son pointed to some people sitting higher up: "Look, Papa. Even the city leaders are fans!"

318

The father and his sons sat close to the central stand. There was not much time before the match would start.

Twenty-two fellows in blue and red jerseys came onto the field and began to limber up.

"There's Tofik!" The ninth son showed his father jersey number seven.

"And you call that a game?"

"No, Papa. These are only warm-up exercises."

"And what does that mean?"

"You know how a person stretches himself after waking up. Warm-up exercises are the same thing."

"Accursed evil."

The elder son explained the rules of the game to his father. There was a whistle from the umpire and the game began. Everyone but Mursal followed the play. Mursal did not understand why twenty-two players all concentrated on the ball. The blacksmith tried to question his sons, but they were caught up in the game and didn't answer. Since there was no one to talk with, he also began to watch the players.

When the players in the red jerseys carried the ball toward the opposing team's goal posts, people began to shout:

"Hit it!"

"Hit it!"

Mursal heard the people around him calling: "Hurry, Tofik!"

"Tofik, score!"

"Hit it, you son of a blacksmith!"

This encouraged Mursal to concentrate all the harder on the progress of the ball. Neither team had scored yet. From all sides came shouts:

"Our boys aren't even playing today!"

"Until our team gets a goal, they always play badly!"

"That son of a blacksmith is sloughing off!"

"They should have thrown him out of the game long ago!"

Mursal turned to ask the man who had called out why Tofik should be thrown from the game. But another man answered first: "You're out of your mind! Tofik's our best player. Watch him go!"

Mursal calmed down. The visiting team kicked the ball almost before the umpire's whistle.

"Now we'll see some real playing," said someone.

The umpire blew his whistle and the sweating team went off the field.

"You won't benefit from Gyandzha's bread!" cried someone.

Mursal looked at his sons: both were despondent.

"Why are you so glum?"

319

"Why not? We're losing."

"Show me where your brother is. Go tell him to score a couple goals. Just let him try and not score after I've told him to."

His sons' faces brightened.

In the second half, the game picked up. The ball was passed more often to Tofik. He would get up to the goal posts and pass it to his comrades, but they couldn't make a goal.

"Hit it yourself!"

"Hit it yourself!" Mursal cried suddenly, unable to hold back. Then as though he had suddenly woken up, terrified that people were laughing at him, he looked to either side. No one was paying any attention.

Tofik ran toward the goal once again.

"Hit it yourself!"

Tofik kicked the ball. It passed over the bar.

"Break a leg!" screamed Mursal. "You ought to have your feet shoed!" Once again Tofik had the ball. He took it around one man....

"Watch him go!"

Suddenly Tofik got up to the goal.

"Hit it!"

"Score!"

"Kick it yourself!" screamed Mursal. "If you score I'll slaughter a sheep at your feet."

Mursal forgot everything else. Tofik, the ball and the goal posts swam before his eyes.... A hit! The goalkeeper falls. Too late! The ball has passed through the goal. The whole stadium rises to its feet:

"That-a-boy! You son of a blacksmith!"

"May you live a thousand years!"

"I'll slaughter a sheep...."

The second goal was scored after Tofik passed it. He scored the third goal himself....

Mursal's joy had no limits. If he'd had wings he would have soared above the stadium and descended on the field to embrace his son. The game was finished. Everyone was smiling. A stream of people poured through the streets. Mursal had never been so happy. He wanted to see his eighth son.

"You can't, Father. You'll see him at home."

"Tell me, are there a lot of these matches?" the old man asked.

"Yes."

"Why didn't anyone tell me about them? Accursed evil!... Such an interesting game and I sit at home.... Geibaly!"

"Yes, Master."

"Your mother isn't sick any more?"

"No, Master, no."

"Geibaly!"

"Yes, Master."

"Next time you go for medicine, take me with you."

"All right, Master...."

"Geibaly! How many men on a team?"

"Eleven."

"If I had eleven sons I would make them all football players."

Akram Ailisli
(b. 1937)

Akram Ailisli belongs to the generation of young writers who grew up in the harsh years of the Second World War. With pride and pain these writers recreate their troubled childhood and the trials borne by their parents. Such is the theme of Ailisli's story "Granny's Pouch".

The prose of this young writer combines a profound grasp of psychological complexities with warm humour. Some of his novellas are written in the form of confessions made by a sensitive, observant boy who matures during the harsh wartime years and the first postwar years when the economy is being restored.

His novella Tales of Aunt Medine *won the Azerbaijanian Komsomol Prize in 1968.*

Granny's Pouch

When Granny ran out of tobacco she always used to ask me not to leave the house. "Sit with me a while, sonny!" she would say. "There's a mighty fine smell of baccy coming off you." I would shake out my pockets and turn my shirt inside out, but never could find even a grain of tobacco. I also could not smell the tobacco. How could I, when I had never lit up a cigarette in my life. Why then, did Granny hug me so tightly and say I smelt of tobacco?

This was beyond me: I would start crying, shouting and imploring her to let go of me. I indignantly tried to prove to the old dear that she was wrong, and that I did not smell of anything. "It's you who reeks of baccy!" I would shriek. "Your mouth, scarf, everything reeks of it! I don't want to sit with you! Leave me alone!"

Granny did not take offence. She quietly moved away, sighed and stared me in the face for a long time. Feeling her gaze on me, I couldn't help but glower at her. How wrinkled and thin she was!... And she had no baccy left.... I began to feel so sorry for her that I promised that I would definitely sleep in her bed that night. She began kissing and cuddling me again, and crying and saying that I was just like my daddy. She always said this when she cried.

Sometimes when Granny was sobbing she would whisper to me to cry also. Perhaps my father would hear my sobs....

When she had cried her heart out, Granny would suddenly grow silent and then immediately begin cursing herself: "See what you've done, old woman, you've brought him to tears! Why ever did you start snivelling? Just so you could break the little one's heart!"

She would quickly wipe her eyes and try her best to smile. She had to see me cheer up at once. "Cheer up, Sonny," she would insist. "Cheer up, just to make your father's spirit happy!"

"She does understand really that I couldn't smell of tobacco," I sometimes thought. "She knows I never pinch tobacco or pick up butts like Azer does. But why then does it happen? Why, as soon as she's run out of baccy, does she not let me budge an inch, shove her face in mine and keep nattering that I smell of baccy?"

Tobacco meant the whole world to Granny. Once her tobacco pouch was empty, hard times fell upon the house. Mummy was then gloomier than usual and would try to be at home as little as possible. As soon as she had washed up the tea things she would go out somewhere. "No tobacco again!" she would mutter angrily at me as if I were to blame that Granny had nothing left to smoke.

I was well aware that the pouch in which Granny kept her tobacco had belonged to my father. I also knew that Granny never used to smoke. She began smoking soon after my father left for the front. She often used to say that my father could not stand women who smoked and that as soon as he returned she would give it up. She really wanted to, but just could not, although she loved my father so much that whenever his name was mentioned she would always begin to cry.

At times like this my mother's eyes would also well up with tears and my aunt, father's sister, would start crying, and even uncle Karash would wipe his eyes on the sly. But somehow I was the only one who could not cry.

And how I sometimes wanted to! Cry bitterly, with all my heart, like Granny! But I just couldn't. This was dreadful, worse than when Granny's tobacco ran out or when Sevil took offence and stopped talking to me.

I asked Mummy and Granny many times why I could not cry like everyone else. Granny usually only sighed and wiped her eyes with the borders of her scarf, and Mother would explain away my dry eyes by saying I had cried too much when I was a baby and simply had no tears left.

True, I hoped that when I grew up I would really come to love my father, and that I, like every other normal person, would feel a lump in my throat at the mention of his name.

But time went by and Granny's pouch got filled up, and then hung empty on the wall again, and Granny became more and more shrivelled and Mummy's hair became noticeably greyer, and I still had not learnt to cry.

* * *

Then Granny passed away. She died on a peaceful summer evening when the sun had just set and the samovar was humming under the awning.... Many people came to her funeral but none cried. "She's gone to a better world," they said, "may the Lord rest her soul." Rumour had it that Granny had died before her time and the doctor, who had looked after her, said that tobacco had been the cause of her death. After the funeral, when she was putting Granny's bed away behind the trunk, Mother heaved a sigh and said: "Tobacco killed the poor old dear."

Did really none besides me understand why Granny had died? Her sorrow had killed her! It was sorrow that made her smoke! And she would definitely have given up the wretched stuff if my father had returned home. She was really afraid that he would arrive one day, look in his pouch and become furious when he heard that his mother smoked. It was not that Granny was frightened of my father — a mother can never fear her own son — but she was terribly afraid of making him sad.

The day before she died Granny beckoned to me and, when Mother was out of earshot, told me that as soon as she died I simply had to buy some tobacco at the market and fill the pouch up to the brim. "Just as it was, full up to the strings, do you hear? Hang it in the niche over there on that large nail."

She showed me the niche and the nail. She showed me them several times....

No, it wasn't tobacco that killed Granny.

The door opens and my father walks in. I want to race over and throw my arms around him, kiss him and cry on his shoulder. But I can not even get up, let alone run over to him: it is as if someone was holding me back.

Then suddenly I remember the empty pouch. I must jump up, tear it off the wall and hide it as quickly as possible. But how can I, when I cannot even move an inch.

My father strolls up to me and bends down: I can see his shaded, stubbly chin as he kisses me on the forehead with his warm, full lips. I throw my arms around his neck and kiss his hard black moustaches, which smell distinctly of tobacco, over and over again.

My father will then go over to his red suitcase, open it and find the suit he had brought for me. I will put it on....

Why don't I run through the streets shouting: "Father's arrived! My father's arrived! I'm no longer an orphan!" Oh, if only I could push Father away, remove his strong hands, grab the suit, put it on and run along the streets, stopping everyone and telling them the news! The whole world has to know that I've now got a father! "Listen, everybody! My father's arrived! I have got a father! Hey, people! Why don't you ask me about him? Why don't you want to talk about him? He really has arrived, returned, come home!"

But I am helpless: I can not tear myself out of my father's arms, nor put on the suit, nor run shouting into the street. I woke up: my father had bent down to kiss me on the forehead and had woken me up. I opened my eyes and saw Mother.

The dream was so vivid that if I had dreamed it for the first time I should definitely have asked where my father was, but I was already used to this dream.... Those hard moustaches smelling of tobacco, the fine new suit, the fountain pen, I had seen them all so often that even while I was still asleep I realised I was only dreaming.

I awoke and immediately remembered my previous day's conversation with Mummy. Today I had to go to the regional centre and find out about the pension. I would have to present myself to uncle Gadji, take off my hat and respectfully greet him. If he let me enter, I had to say to him politely, in a clear voice: "For some reason or other our pension has been held back this month. If it's not too much trouble for you (I definitely had to say that!) could you clear up the matter for us. Mummy's ill.... She couldn't come. Perhaps there isn't any money for us at the moment? If so, don't worry, we'll make do without...."

Uncle Gadji would open the register and see at once that no money had come through for a long time simply because Zarifa had lost our form. He would send me to Zarifa who would find the form and send me to uncle Salim. I would sign and he would give me a hundred and forty rubles.

"One hundred and forty-four" was written in the register, but that did not matter, the four rubles did not count...,

When I had received the money I would have to go to the shop, buy three pounds of sugar and two packets of tea and then get a half pound of peas and a pound of meat at the market.

I took special care over washing. The sun had not yet risen and the room was still dark. The samovar was humming on the table. Mother was in a very bad mood, probably because she had had to wake me up so early.

She had boiled four eggs in the samovar and told me to eat two of them. She wrapped up the others for me. When I had finished two cups of tea she repeated, word for word, everything she had told me the day before.

"If you're hungry, sit down and have something to eat. Eat some of the flatcake. Just you be careful you don't spill the salt when you're unwrapping the bundle. If you see a car on the way, ask for a lift. Mind you don't drink any water at the market. If I find out you have, don't you dare show up at home. If you're thirsty, go to the tea house and have a cup, or better still, don't drink it there but have as much as you need here." And she poured me a third cup, although there wasn't a grain of sugar left in the bowl.

"What's your surname, sonny?"

"Selimov."

"Selimov? You aren't due for any more money."

"Why not?"

"Because you're not. You're already an adult, so you've got to earn your own living and that's that."

My breath got stuck. I stared in horror at uncle Gadji. Never in all my days as an orphan had I felt so terribly helpless. "Daddy!" I wanted to shout. "How can this be true, Daddy?"

How had it happened? I was already an adult but had still not come to love my father?! I had never cried about him? I still had not filled Granny's pouch with tobacco. And it was not because I did not have the money. We received the pension many times after Granny had died. I had not bought the tobacco because I no longer believed that my father was going to return. I had not only lost hope, I had already began to believe that he had never even really existed.

...I dragged myself down the road, seeing nothing before me. Then, for some reason or other, I turned round and went back into town. I walked along thinking of only one thing—about Father's money. "Daddy's money has arrived...." "Take some out of Daddy's money...." "Daddy's money has finished...." "Daddy's money." We had lived on this money for several years. Out of it we bought bread, sugar and tobacco for Granny. It was sent in my name. I bought paper, books and pencils out of it. I had studied for ten years on my father's money, but what "father" meant, I still had not discovered.

I walked along thinking the whole time about something I had never thought about before.... But perhaps nothing had really happened and everything was the same as before: I had simply dreamed up the whole affair? No, this was no dream — no more money was going to be sent, but then why had I gone back into town?

I stopped, wiped my eyes as if I had just awoken from a deep sleep and saw a two-storey yellow building with a sign saying: "Social Security Department". What would I say to uncle Gadji if he spotted me?

I walked past.

...I greeted the man in the most unconventional manner, not even raising my furhat and quite boldly walked into the manager's office. Only when I was already inside the door did my courage leave me. The manager noticed my confusion.

"Come in, my boy, come in!" he said, smiling welcomingly. "Sit yourself down!"

I sat down.

"Well, son, what can we do for you?"

I kept silent, not daring to say a word.

"You've probably come about work?"

I felt a little more confident and looked hopefully at him.

"Ye-es ... I.... Couldn't you take me on at the factory?"

"Why, of course. Work at the factory can always be found for a sensible lad like yourself. Where are you from?"

"Soyudla."

"Whose son are you?"

"Selima's."

The manager's lips quivered into a smile and then he began to laugh.

"Selima's son! Ha, you are a marvel!" He chuckled, but seeing that I was genuinely confused, he turned with a smile towards the window. "Don't get flustered, sonny, it's not you I'm laughing at. But do bear this in mind in the future: when you're asked whose son you are, you must name your father."

"My father? But you don't know my father." I struggled to get the words out. Again I would have to say that I was an orphan....

"He's dead.... He was killed in the war...."

The manager looked carefully at me. The smile vanished from his face, it seemed to me that he wanted to say something but kept quiet. And then I said loudly and clearly:

"I'm Nadjaf's son."

"The surgeon's assistant?"

"Yes.... Mother told me that's what he was."

The manager lit up a cigarette and walked around the office. Then he came up to me.

"Your father was a good man."

I kept quiet, not knowing what to say. Perhaps I should have simply got up and left? But how could I when I had achieved nothing? What would I say to Mother?

"You couldn't advance...."

I could not say any more. And the manager did not seem to have heard me.

"You couldn't give me an advance ... a hundred rubles or so.... And when I get my pay, I'll have it deducted."

And I stared tearfully at the manager, taken aback by my own impertinence. He walked up to the table and stopped pensively in front of it, tapping with his pencil.

"Would you like me to leave? Can I start in the morning?"

"Yes, yes, of course," he replied absent-mindedly.

I stood up and went straight for the door. I was sure he would call after me. I was right. I had hardly reached for the door handle when he suddenly loudly exclaimed:

"Where are you off to, sonny? You said something, I think, about money."

"An advance ... about a hundred rubles...."

I was certain that the manager would call the cashier and order him to write out an advance and then I would have to run around dozens of departments to get the cash. But he simply took a hundred ruble note out of his pocket and handed it to me. I rushed for the door to run straight to the market.

"We'll put you as Kerim's apprentice!" he shouted after me. "Five hundred a month."

I spent the hundred rubles in just half an hour. Now I could go home. Beside myself with joy, I began whistling, skipping and breaking out into a run. "That manager's a good man!" I thought. "A wage of five hundred rubles. And he knows my father!"

Remembering my father, I automatically slowed down. Why was it that the manager knew and admired him, and I didn't know him at all....

I didn't notice how I reached my village. Night was falling. The herd was being driven home and the cows going to be milked were bellowing. I went past the cemetery, and for the first time in my life, did not feel in the slightest afraid. I even stopped by Granny's grave, so I could talk to her a while.

Soon I would arrive home. I would open the door and slowly, as befits a man, stroll into the room and put the bag of meat on the trunk. Mother would immediately notice that there was more than a pound and would, of course, fly into a temper. It would be interesting to hear what she said when I told her everything in detail. For after my father had left home, no one had brought her home five hundred a month.

But things did not turn out as I imagined. I spotted my mother when I was still outside. She had probably already been waiting for a long time because she greeted me coldly.

"Where have you been all this time?" she snapped.

The light was burning in the room and the samovar was bubbling; Mother had probably already warmed it up several times. She poured me out a cup of tea. I felt excited, as at an examination, and impatiently waited for her finally to look inside the bag.

At last she picked it up. I turned round, trying to look as natural as possible. She would soon ask me why there was so much meat.

"What have you gone and done this for, you wretched boy?!" she exclaimed angrily. "Where did you get the tobacco from?"

I raced over and grabbed the bag. The sugar, peas and meat—there was tobacco spilling everywhere. Mummy looked at me carefully and repeated:

"Where did you get the tobacco from? Who gave it you?"

I was silent.

Mother asked no more questions. We sat quietly facing one another. Someone was singing softly. Mother silently watched me as I looked at Granny's pouch which still hung empty.

Isi Melikzade
(b. 1934)

Melikzade was educated as an engineer in the oil industry. He began his literary career a few years ago. But his published novellas and novels, among them Someone Else's Mother, *and* Weak Wings, *already show great talent. Melikzade writes traditional narratives. His works are distinguished mainly for their depiction of typical aspects of life. His story "The Son" touches upon a problem of concern to many readers: the succession of generations.*

The Son

"I wonder where he can be so late?"

His wife did not reply. She merely sighed. Farrukh threw back the covers and moved his legs over the side of the bed. After a few moments of silence he turned to his wife, who lay beside him, and repeated:

"Don't you know where the boy hangs out at night, Amina?"

Amina shrank away, then turned on her side. "No. How should I know?"

"Didn't you ask him?"

"He said he's studying with a friend, preparing for his exams."

Farrukh shook his head. His face, illuminated by the dull moonlight, was a sickly yellow. He braced himself and rose heavily. Then he limped over to the window, dragging his left leg. As he leaned his forehead against the pane and looked out at the deserted street, he said to himself: "If not for my leg, I'd go out and look for Tair. But this sickness has come so suddenly. Maybe Tair's become so bold and brazen because he knows I'm paralysed and helpless?" A bitter smile touched his lips. Indeed, he felt he was an ailing, helpless old man, of no use to anyone.

He began feeling sorry for himself and very upset. Then he remembered the doctor saying: "You must try not to worry about anything. Try to be calm, no matter what."

331

That was easier said than done. Farrukh attempted to get his emotions under control. "Tair never used to be like this," he said to himself. "He never used to come home this late. He never used to leave the house without permission. What's happened? He's been coming home late every single night for the past month. Can't he realise I'm sick and that he's making me worry?" He limped away from the window. "See what time it is," he said to his wife.

Amina rose and turned on the lamp. "It's ten past two," she replied in a voice hoarse from insomnia.

"I can't talk to him, Amina," he said brokenly. "After all, he's no baby. He's a grown boy. You're his mother. It's easier for you. Tell him this is no way to live. Tell him to be home on time or his studies will suffer. After all, he still has two more years till he graduates from college."

"Maybe he really is studying for his exams. Let's wait a little longer. I'm sure he'll be home soon".

"You think I don't know where he's hanging out? I do, but I can't bring myself to say it. I know the kind of crowd he's running around with."

"Tair's not that kind of a boy."

"Who knows?"

"You probably think he has a girl-friend."

"I'd be glad if he did. This is a dangerous age, and he's hot-blooded."

"I'll never believe that." After a few moments his anxiety affected her. "You think he...."

"What else can I think? Tell me honestly: what nice girl will stay out till dawn every night? I don't believe a word about his studying for his exams. When did he ever study like this?"

"Don't accuse him yet."

"Well, don't make me lose my temper. If you don't talk to him...."

"Calm down. Wait a bit. You're jumping to conclusions."

"What's there to wait for? And how much longer? He's still too young to be having his own way. He doesn't care what we think, or how much we worry." The anger that had welled up in him as he had stood by the window now boiled over. He smacked his fist against his knee and cried: "He doesn't have any respect left! Well, I'll show him who's the master of this house."

They heard a key turn in the lock. Farrukh tensed.

Amina jumped out of bed.

"Stay where you are!" he hissed and dragged himself into the foyer. He turned on the light and opened the door. Tair was standing there. Farrukh raised his long, bony arm and slapped his son's smiling face. The smile vanished in an instant. It was replaced by a hurt, surprised look. Farrukh lost his balance and swayed. Tair caught his father in his arms and steadied him. Amina rushed out at the sound of the commotion.

"What's the matter, Farrukh?"

Farrukh brushed aside his son's arm and hobbled back into the bedroom, holding on to the wall for support. Then his strength failed him and he collapsed onto the bed. Once again the doctor's words of caution came back to him: "You must avoid stress at all costs."

"That's impossible, Doctor," he replied now, speaking to himself. He could hear the whispering in the kitchen and the sounds of plates clinking. A short while later his wife came over to the bed.

332

"Why did you hit him, Farrukh? How could you?" Her voice trembled. He sensed rather than heard the tears that were choking her. "He's been working. He didn't tell us".

"What?"

There was a sound of paper rustling. "This is his first pay. He got a night job soon after you became ill." She was unable to go on, and so got back into bed and pulled the covers over her head.

Farrukh was overcome by repentance born of joy. He lay there, looking up at the ceiling.

**Anar Rzaev
(b. 1938)**

*One of the most talented members of the postwar generation of
Azerbaijanian writers. His fascinating, distinctive stories and novellas
quickly brought him national acclaim.*

*His style is rich and flexible. Anar weaves together lyrical, romantic
motifs and realistic themes.*

*He is most inspired by the feelings, thoughts, and outlook of people who
work at the most varied professions. Anar Rzaev's eye for subtle,
revealing details results in a complex depiction of life. The story "The
Last Night of the Year" selected for this anthology is typical of the
writer's work.*

Anar is an active critic, publicist and film scenarist.

The Last Night of the Year

It was nearly nine o'clock, on the last evening of the year. Gamida-hala* was busy in the kitchen. Tofik kept dashing between telephone and kitchen with the latest snippets of news.

"Mum, Seiran's coming, too!"

"Who's Seiran, dear?"

"Don't you remember? You liked him, you said he was always so neat — you know who I mean?"

"A-a-ah! That boy. Well, that's good."

Tofik was dancing with excitement; what boy wouldn't be, before a real New Year party, a grown-up one, at midnight, the first in his fourteen years? All his school friends were coming. They had started talking about seeing in the New Year in style three months ago.

"Come to my place," Tofik suggested. "There won't be anyone but mum, and she always goes to bed early."

"What about your elder brother and sister?"

"Oh, they go out somewhere."

Tofik confided the big secret to his mother: there would be girls, too, their parents had given permission.

"And Vasif's sister may come. She isn't in our form, but she can come with her brother, can't she?"

"Of course she can, and welcome," said mum, hiding a smile.

"Will there be enough to eat?" Tofik worried.

* *Hala* — aunt. A term of courtesy not implying relationship. — *Ed.*

"Enough and plenty for all, and a dozen more. Don't worry, nobody's going to go hungry."

Tofik ran back to the telephone, rang up one, rang up another, argued hotly with someone else for a long time. Then someone rang up and again there was a lot of talk. To get everyone together really was a job. One wanted to come earlier, another later, a third lived a long way off, a fourth didn't know the address, and a fifth had changed his mind about coming. But the girls were the worst of all.

"Oh darn, mum, Franghiz says she isn't coming."

"But why not, son?"

"She said she'd thought it'd be just us, but now, she says, there'll be your grown-up brother and sister and they'll spoil it all."

"Well, what can we do about it, dear?" Gamida-hala spread out her hands in resignation.

Tofik glowered at the door of the room where Dilyara and Rustam sat and sat and just wouldn't get up and go.

"They never stop at home, and now they have to choose just this evening to love their family," Tofik grumbled, with angry sarcasm.

"Well, we can't drive them out," his mother said pacifically.

Tofik flung out of the kitchen and seized the telephone again.

"Hi, don't you hang onto the telephone all evening," Dilyara called, opening the door. "Someone might want to call us."

It really was queer, Dilyara being home on New Year's Eve. It hadn't happened for years. And Rustam? Queerer still. He'd never seen the New Year in at home since dad died.

Yes, those had been real New Year celebrations, when Gazanfar was alive. A full house bursting with noise and laughter.... For some few years after his death the New Year had come into this house very quietly. Gyulyara and Rustam had joined parties of friends, and Gamida-hala, Dilyara and Tofik had gone to bed early. Then Dilyara began going out. And now it seemed to be Tofik's turn.

At the moment, however, the whole family was at home. No, not all. There was no Gazanfar. He had died seven years ago. And Gyulyara wasn't there, either, she and her husband were going to his parents. It never seemed possible to get them all together. There was always someone missing.

The clock on the wall struck ten. Tofik finished his diplomatic negotiations, came back into the kitchen and stood shifting uncomfortably from foot to foot.

"What's the matter, Tofik, can't you collect your guests yet?" Gamida-hala asked sympathetically.

"No, that is—I mean—" Tofik seemed to be stuck; then with an effort he blurted out, "You see, mum, Rauf wants us to go to him. His parents are going away somewhere.... So there won't be anyone but us. Just us."

"Very well, dear," said Gamida-hala and passed a warm hand over her son's hair. "If that's the way you all want it, go to Rauf's place. Why not?"

Tofik's eyes sparkled. Mum didn't mind, then!

"Only what are you going to eat there?"

"Oh, we'll find something," Tofik answered gaily. There'll be tinned stuff or something...."

"Tinned stuff, indeed!" said Gamida-hala indignantly. "Take some pilau with you."

"Oh no, no, mum, we don't need it, really. And if I turn up with a pot under my arm they'll all laugh at me."

Gamida-hala smiled faintly.

"Very well, go along."

After all, what did they need with pilau? They would open tins and feel free and independent. Here they would have eaten excellent pilau but felt hampered, restricted. Pilau and tins, the past and the future, age and youth.... Those were Gamida-hala's thoughts.

Tofik hugged his mother and charged out of the house.

Rustam was asleep in his own room. At least, this was the intention he had announced: "I'm going to have a sleep, don't wake me." Gamida-hala knew all about that. Rustam had quarrelled with his girl-friend, they hadn't spoken for a week—a matter of principle, if you please!

Dilyara fretted restlessly, walked from chair to table, leafed through old magazines, switched on the TV, and kept eyeing the telephone. But the telephone was silent.

Gamida-hala went on cooking.

The bell. Gamida-hala went to the door. Gyulyara and her husband came in, carrying Vagif.

"Now, isn't this nice!" cried Gamida-hala. "Go on into the room, I'll be with you in a second."

And if only they'd come a moment earlier, she'd have had all the children together, she thought. Even if Tofik had gone away later....

Gamida-hala washed her hands and hurried to her daughter.

"This is unexpected—what's brought you—it's not that I'm not glad to see you."

"We've come to wish you a Happy New Year," said Gyulyara.

The bell again. Dilyara's friend Leila dashed in breathlessly.

"Oh, Dilyara—pooh, I can't speak!"

"Stay quiet a moment, dear, till you get your breath back," said Gamida-hala comfortably. "Has something happened?"

"No, nothing special," Leila gasped. "It's just that I ran all the way. The director said, 'I don't care how you do it, but you've got to find Dilyara, we can't have a concert without her!' So I just ran...."

For a moment Dilyara's face lighted up, then she assumed a mask of indifference.

"Oh, really? No, thank you! So they want Dilyara all of a sudden. They could have put me in the programme at the start. But now.... I suppose someone's let them down, so they think I'll do as a stop-gap."

"No, it isn't like that at all, honest!" Leila cried. "The director hadn't an idea you weren't in the programme, and when he found out he was hopping mad!"

So that was why Dilyara was at home!

"Go and get your things on, and hurry up," said Gamida-hala. "It's no time now to be capricious. They've sent for you specially—so go along."

Dilyara shook her head—no, not for anything. But Gamida-hala knew her daughter, and she made no mistake. In a few minutes the two girls went racing off with noisy goodbyes.

Gamida-hala excused herself—she had to go to the kitchen. Gyulyara followed her.

"Look, mum, we're invited to one of Suleiman's friends. But there's Vagif. Could he stop here with you?"

"Of course, daughter, let him stay."

Gyulyara quickly put Vagif to bed.

"We'll have to be going now, mum. To tell the truth, I'm not so keen on those people, I'd much rather stop here with you, but—well, I don't want to offend them. Come here, I want to kiss you.... Best of luck for the New Year."

"All happiness to you, Gamida-hala," said Suleiman.

"Thank you, my dears. Goodbye, and all the very best."

The door slammed. Gamida-hala returned to the kitchen, and repeating under her breath, "all the very best", went on preparing pilau for fifteen. Suddenly she remembered: Rustam! She went into her son's room and called him.

"Rustam! Rustam!"

"Yes?"

"Get up, you'll sleep the year away!"

"Oh mum, do leave me alone—please!"

"Now then, young man, you do as I tell you, get up this minute!"

"What's up, mum? Let me sleep."

"Get up, you hear me? I need you. Come here."

"Why, what's up?"

"Come and help me."

Reluctantly Rustam got up off the bed. Gamida-hala took his hand and pulled him into the entry.

"You take that telephone and ring up."

"Where?"

"You know very well!"

"I won't!"

"Oh yes, you will! None of my children, including you, have ever crossed me. And if you don't do as I ask today, I'll remember it as long as I live!"

"But mum...."

"Ring up! And no more talk."

"But—"

"If you don't want to offend me."

Rustam, shuffled unhappily.

"Well?"

"All right—just to please you."

Gamida-hala went into the bedroom where little Vagif was snuffling in his sleep. She could hear the whirring of the telephone disk and then Rustam's voice, not very loud.

"Yes ... it's me."

Seconds of chilly silence, then a cool "As you see."

Silence again. A voice ironically toned: "No, really?"

She must have said something prickly, thought Gamida-hala.

"And me too. You can be a hundred per cent sure of that," said Rustam in a tone to freeze the ears.

No, why do they have to be like that? They do love each other, thought Gamida-hala sadly.

Suddenly Rustam's voice sank to a whisper. Gamida-hala could not distinguish the words, but the chill and the irony had gone. Then Rustam began to talk more loudly again but now it was the son she knew, kind and affectionate. He laughed, then silence again. But it wasn't that icy silence, it was warm and alive.

A yawn, a quiet, untroubled yawn and a question.

"But what'll I do there at your place?"

She wants him to go there....

"I can't, you see, I told mum I'd be at home tonight."

Gamida-hala wanted to get up and tell him to go, but she remained sitting where she was.

"Oh, I don't know — really. Who's going to be there?"

No need to say anything. He'll go.

"No, somehow I don't feel like it. If it had been just you and the family...."

Or perhaps he won't?

"Honest, I'm not playing hard to get. It's just that I don't like them."

He won't go, then.

"Well, a Happy New Year and all that, and I wish you lots and lots...."

So he won't go.

"You really want me to come — really?"

Looks as if he will, after all.

"No, better tomorrow morning."

He isn't going.

"Oh, all right, all right, don't start it all over again. Maybe I'll come."

He will.

"What? What time is it? Twenty past eleven? I'll come right away!"

Rustam hung up and went to his mother.

"Mum — you see —"

Seven years difference between Rustam and Tofik, but when they feel awkward they act just the same. Got it from Gazanfar. His little finger always twitched, too, when he was nervous or embarrassed.

"Go along, dear, go. And don't forget to give her my love."

As Rustam pulled on his coat he asked, "Where've our small fry gone?"

"Dilyara's gone to school, she's going to sing at the concert, and Tofik's with his friends, a New Year party."

"Tofik seeing the New Year in! We're coming to something...."

"Why not? The boy's growing up."

"And you'll be all alone — ?"

"Not a bit of it! Look, Vagif's here."

Rustam smiled.

"A grand boy-friend, eh?" His smile faded. "If I'd known you'd be alone — "

"Why alone? She and I'll keep each other company. We'll talk."

"She — who?" Rustam asked, surprised.

"The girl on the telly screen," said Gamida-hala. Rustam laughed. "Besides," she went on, "you know I always go to bed early. I'll just sit here a little and then.... Give a good loud ring when you come, or I may not hear you."

"Yes, I know, mum, you don't like sitting up late, even on the New Year night."

Rustam had forgotten, of course, that in his father's time they'd kept it up till morning. He said goodbye to his mother and went.

The table was laid for twelve. It looked strange in the empty room. But it was still stranger when Gamida-hala filled a great dish with pilau and placed it in the middle, saying under her breath:

"You sit here, and Ragim and Nazifa at that end, and you, usta, here.... Teimur, come and sit by your wife, and you, children, move up a bit. Sultan, that's your place, you'll be the master of ceremonies...."

Gamida-hala laughed silently. "My wits must be going!" She went out onto the balcony. Silence, emptiness. Could there possibly be anyone out in the street now? She hardly had time to think about this, when she saw two, they came out of a shop, hands full of parcels, and hurried away somewhere, shivering, with loud laughter and talk. Gamida-hala went back into the room. She switched on the TV. A girl appeared on the screen.

She moved a chair closer to the TV set and sat down.

"Let's have a chat, dear. You must be tired of all these broadcasts, aren't you? Everyone's celebrating, and you're here!"

"One of the most important cultural achievements of the passing year was the ballet by the young composer Yusifov," said the girl on the screen.

The young composer Yusifov, thought Gamida-hala. That young composer's laughing and joking with his friends and not even listening to you. I don't suppose there'll be many people watching TV now.... And to the girl she said, "You go home too, dear. You can tell everyone about our cultural achievements tomorrow. They won't vanish in the night."

"Many fine works of art have been painted," the girl continued.

"It's twenty to twelve, if you can catch a taxi you'll just manage it. They're waiting for you.... You have someone to wait for you. You're young and pretty.

You must have a boy-friend, he'll be feeling blue, all alone. You know I'm right, dear."

"Fazilov's work dedicated to herdsmen is extremely original and natural...."

"All right, let it be as original and natural as you like, but you hurry, dear. How pleased that young man will be! He'll kiss your hair. You have such pretty hair. Even if all Baku were looking at you now, you'd much rather be with him, wouldn't you?"

"Among the new films...."

"I understand, dear. This is your job. You can't just get up and leave it. But it's a shame, just this evening...."

Who else is all alone this evening, she asked herself, and remembered: the telephone operator at the information desk.

Gamida-hala went to the telephone and dialled 09. A high-pitched pip-pip. Engaged. She dialled again. A woman's voice answered: "Information."

"Good evening, dear."

"What number?"

"I said good evening. A Happy New Year."

"Thanks!"

"You're all alone, you must be feeling dull, aren't you?"

"Who's speaking?"

"Just a woman."

"Ah, Raya! I didn't know you. Is everything all right? Where are you? Who are you with?"

"No, it isn't Raya. You don't know me."

"What do you want, then?"

"Nothing. I just wanted to give you good wishes and ask how you feel this night."

"Thanks," the operator said brusquely and added, "Please don't occupy the line. The New Year hasn't begun yet, but you seem ... already...."

Gamida-hala laughed and hung up.

The girl had left the screen. The TV programme had ended. By Baku time the New Year had already come. Gamida-hala felt a slight melancholy, with the girl on the screen gone. Now she was quite alone. But soon Rustam rang up with good wishes, then a little later Tofik, then Gyulyara, and asked about the boy. Dilyara didn't ring up, it would be hard to get anywhere near the telephone at school.

Gamida-hala switched on the radio, but the light music didn't fit her mood. She dearly loved listening to the singer Byul-Byul and they had some excellent tapes of his songs. Gamida-hala switched on the tape recorder.

Why is it that at the end of life you are left all alone with only machines?... But she drove away the melancholy thought. No, I'm wrong. I'm not alone with only machines. I've got splendid children. And they all love me.... Suddenly a strange

341

idea seized her. She wanted to hear Gazanfar's voice. She tried to shake it off, but it was no good. The point was that Gazanfar had once recorded his voice on tape. After his death nobody could bear to listen to it. Now she felt a deep longing to hear it.

Unable to resist, Gamida-hala took out the precious tape and put it on.

Laughter, exclamations; she recognised her own voice and those of the children. Then a sudden silence, and Gazanfar's velvety bass.

"Listen, Gamida...."

Her breath stopped, a chill ran down her. It was as though Gazanfar were talking to her from another world.

"I'm not a poet and not a philosopher. I'm an ordinary worker. Of course, I have made a name in a way, if you got five people together one of them at least would know me. But all the same, I'm an ordinary man and I don't intend to come out with any wisdom or philosophy. But I do know a bit about life. I've seen it inside and out, so to speak, and there's one thing I want to say.... The day will come when I won't be here any more...."

Gamida's voice filled with protest, rejection.

"Stop! For God's sake stop! I wouldn't want to live a single day without you!"

How natural those words were then, they seemed a plain, indisputable truth.

Gazanfar's laughter.

"Well, all right, wife, let it be in forty years—or fifty.... But the day will come when I go...."

"Gazanfar!"

"Don't interrupt! Let me finish my eloquent speech." Gazanfar laughed again. "Well, then I shall leave to you our only treasure, our children. Of course, if death doesn't get in first I'll bring them up myself. But if it does, then you will do it. They don't absolutely have to be doctors or engineers or scientists. Let them be what they wish, so long as they are real people, the right kind of people.

"And then, Gamida, the day will come when they grow up and fly off like birds from the nest. Don't think of them as lost, gone. Remember, wherever they are, in whatever surroundings, whatever family, they will take with them something of yours and mine, just as we brought with us something of our fathers and mothers.

"You say Gazanfar's philosophising after all? But this is the truth, nothing in life ever ends or is lost, nobody ever dies. What one begins, others continue. Good and bad pass on from generation to generation. You and I, Gamida, have always lived a good kind of life, we have earned our bread with our own hands.

All that is good and kindly in our lives, let our children take with them into their new lives...."

The end of the tape.... The end of the recording.... The end of Gazanfar. Of course, she could listen to it again, but however many times Gamida-hala listened, Gazanfar would say no more. She did not mourn for it. She looked at the table but left it as it was. She lay down beside Vagif, gently stroked his pitch-black hair and laid her lips against his warm forehead.

Elchin
(b.1943)

Elchin's first story was published in 1959 when the writer was still a schoolboy. His first collection of stories came out in 1966. He is the author of many stories published in both central and republican press; two novellas have been put out separately.

Elchin writes about our contemporaries. He is keenly interested in his characters' inner world, observant, and attentive to social and moral problems.

Elchin also gives serious attention to criticism. He has written books and articles dealing with the most varied aspects of contemporary and classical literature.

The Telegramme

I felt I was being very witty in my efforts to cheer her up, but nothing was coming of it. Finally, I asked: "Will you say anything at all today, or will you go on being silent?"

Her blue eyes glanced at me and smiled gently, but I was troubled, for though there was a smile on her face, her heart was weeping.

"What's the matter?" I grasped her arm above the elbow and turned her to face me.

The answer came from the loudspeaker in the metro car announcing the next station, which was Moscow University.

"It's a good thing they announce the stations or we would have missed our stop," I said.

But she was still gazing sadly ahead of her. I had teased her about missing our stop. Actually, we would not, for we had been taking the same route and getting off here for the past three years, the young husband, a promising young scientist (that was me), and his young wife, who was another promising young scientist, otherwise known as Blueyes. When our day as graduate students came to a close we would return to our room in the dormitory which I had occupied as a bachelor for only two short months.

Blueyes and I had come to Moscow as graduate

students. Having become acquainted and known each other for all of two months, we had decided to get married one fine day.

"What can I do to cheer you up?"

She smiled. "Do you know Kantaria?"

"Who?"

"Kantaria."

"I don't seem to remember the name."

"He was one of the boys who raised our flag over the Reichstag."

The following day was Victory Day, May 9th. In my mind's eye I saw the young soldier whose photograph hung in our room and said: "I toast you on this day!" He smiled in reply, a wonderful, warm-hearted smile.

"Yes, certainly. The Hero of the Soviet Union."

"There's the streetcar. Hurry!"

It stopped by the graduate students' dormitory on Dmitry Ulyanov Street. Now, as always, we would get off, enter the house, take the elevator up and enter the cosiest room on earth. I looked at her. "I know what you're thinking about. You just said to yourself: 'Kantaria risked his life to hoist our flag over the Reichstag, and my fine, mustachioed husband didn't even remember his name.' Am I right?"

"Rather."

I looked at her again, and in my mind I again spoke to the young soldier: "Thanks. At least she's said something."

The young soldier was her father. "Was", because the young soldier was no more. No, he had not aged and died, but had been killed by a tiny bit of lead when he had still been so very young.

That was in 1944. He became a father after he was killed. Thus, he died first and became a father after. A tiny bit of lead had ripped through his heart. Some time later a blue-eyed girl was born. From the very first day of her life this blue-eyed infant had no father. The blue-eyed girl grew and grew, and on a very ordinary Moscow night it became apparent that she had been growing all this time for me, just as I had been growing for her, just as I had been waiting to meet her all of my life.

My life. So much depends on a person himself, as to whether his life will have meaning or not. How true were the words of the sage who said that one's life is not measured by the number of his days, but by those days which are of significance and are remembered. Everything is relative, even one's age. For instance, I simply could not make myself feel that this young man was my father-in-law. Why, we were both now older than he. He was twenty-three on the picture, and we are more. Some day we will be in our seventies, while he will forever be twenty-three.

We have been married for three years. I feel that I know everything there is to know about her: her ways, her tastes, her weaknesses. Often and unexpectedly I am startled to realise I don't know her. At times her mood changes quickly and without apparent provocation. Actually, there always is a reason. As it later turns out, I was unaware of it. The simplest occurrence in life, one which no one ever pays attention to, can suddenly make her happy, overjoyed in fact, or sometimes as unhappy as if something terrible had happened. I have often noticed that the person who shares my life is not content to worry about herself and me. She is worried about the whole world. She's pretending to be looking at the buildings

346

through the streetcar window now, but I know she's thinking about the young soldier and seeing nothing and no one, save him. She's thinking that he was not alone, that there were thousands upon thousands of young soldiers like him who were never fated to grow old, and her heart bleeds for them, for that is the kind of heart she has.

May 9th is, first and foremost, Victory Day, the day the war ended. May 9th is a testimony to the strength and justice of our fathers and grandfathers. May 9th is also a day of remembering.

Blueyes looked at me. I saw a shadow of fear cloud her face for an instant. I realised she was afraid that I, too, might become a soldier who would never grow old.

Hadji Murad, a future outstanding physicist of Daghestan, joined us in the elevator. He was carrying two bottles of champagne which he would open the following day. He got off on the fourth floor. I breathed in deeply, for the smell was tantalising. The Uzbek students who lived on the fourth floor were cooking pilau again. I took several more breaths and said: "If God wants me to believe in Him, this is the time to prove it. Imagine: we get home and see two dishes of steaming *duishbari* on the table and ten flatcakes, all put there by the loving hands of Aunt Bika."

She finally laughed. "All you ever think of is food!"

Aunt Bika, as I call her, is my mother-in-law. Blueyes always cheers up at the mention of her mother's name. Naturally, I try not to miss a chance to mention it.

Aunt Bika had been married for only three months.

She had been married for three months, and for the next twenty-odd years she had been both a mother and a father to her child.

When we entered the room it became evident that God wished me to remain an atheist for the rest of my life, because the table was piled high, as always, with books, instead of steaming *duishbari*.

Our room looked as it always did. There was the photograph of the young soldier on the wall. He was looking at us and smiling. She stood there gazing at him, while I looked at her. At that moment Blueyes and the young soldier might have been twins.

"You know, sometimes I feel as if he were my brother," she said softly.

Many a time I think of something and then she says it aloud.

She continued: "My younger brother. I feel as if I want to protect him, to shield him. I feel anxious about him. And sometimes I feel like taking his hand and going to see Mother together. As if she were his mother, too."

I went over to the window. Many windows across the street were dark. The people who lived there had gone to bed. But there was one, no, there were three, five, seven, yes, seven windows where the people were still up. These were very ordinary windows. I wondered how many young soldiers' daughters beyond those windows had now become their sisters, and how many sons had become their brothers. There are windows like that in Moscow, and in Baku, and in so many other places.

She came over to me. "At the concert this evening I suddenly felt so uneasy. I felt afraid. Do you know why?"

"Yes."

She seemed surprised.

"You felt uneasy thinking there might be another war, and afraid when you wondered how all those people could be sitting there so calmly and looking at the stage."

She seemed still more surprised.

"Are you wondering how I know what you were thinking? Because I get these thoughts, too, sometimes. Just like the people in the audience do. But they all have faith."

"In what?"

"They all believe that even if this will be so, there will still be a Victory Day in the end."

"At the price of human sacrifice?"

"Well, Victory Day is not New Year's, you know. But in the future there will always be a Victory Day for us, otherwise life would be black. Everything would lose its meaning. The Vietnamese will have a day of victory ahead, and the Arabs, too, and every other people whose cause is just." I looked up at the young soldier on the photograph. "You see, we do have talks like this once in a while," I said to him.

"Wait, I'll be right back," I said aloud.

I went down to the fourth floor and knocked on Hadji Murad's door.

"Who the hell is it? I'm sleeping." After a while Hadji Murad opened the door and stood there sleepy-eyed.

"Listen, we all know you're going to be the most famous physicist in Daghestan! Rasul Gamzatov will dedicate an ode to you! And we all know you have two bottles of champagne. You've got to give me one."

"What?"

I could see the bottles on the table. I snatched one and dashed out. When I entered our room Blueyes was sitting on the bed. She understood me at a glance.

"Poor Hadji Murad."

"He'll survive. We'll buy him two bottles tomorrow, but meanwhile...." I got out two glasses and sat down beside her. A loud pop, as loud as a pistol shot, filled our little room.

"If not for this young soldier, you wouldn't be here, and my life would be dull and senseless. If not for this young soldier, there wouldn't be a Victory Day

348

celebration tomorrow. Let's drink to him and to all young soldiers! Let's drink to there never being any shots other than the one that was just fired here!"

The next morning I went down to the post office and sent off the following telegramme:

"Kantaria, Georgian Republic. GREETINGS ON VICTORY DAY STOP THANK YOU AND ALL OUR HEROES STOP WISH YOU HAPPINESS."

And the girl accepted it, even though there was no definite address on it.

Maksud Ibragimbekov (b. 1935)

One of the most gifted young Azerbaijanian writers, Ibragimbekov, was born in Baku. He was trained as a construction engineer and began writing in the nineteen sixties. In 1964 he completed advanced studies in scenario writing in Moscow.

Maksud Ibragimbekov's novellas and stories deal with the people of Soviet Azerbaijan, moral problems, and family relations. He is well known to readers throughout the Soviet Union. Central publishing houses have put out collections of his stories, including "A Cosy Place in the Square", "A Little Spring Holiday", and "An Unfamiliar Song". Several films have been made from his scenarios. His play, A Mesozoic Story was produced by Moscow's Maly Theatre.

A Cosy Place in the Square

"Clean up!" cried Agasaf-aga in a stentorian voice as he seated his next visitor in the chair. This steady customer had dutifully waited a good two hours for the attentions of "his" barber.

"I expected you last Friday," said Agasaf-aga (he addressed all his clients with the familiar "thou" form). "I think to myself, what's going on here? Where is he?"

"I went to Kirovabad on business."

"In Kirovabad they serve good *khash*,* the real stuff," said Agasaf-aga dreamily. "It's yellow, fatty, and translucent — and they put chopped lamb stomach into it. Throughout all of Azerbaijan the only place where they know how to make *khash* is Kirovabad.... Hurt? You won't find anything edible in Baku anymore. A while ago I ordered *khash* at that place by the station. They brought it all right. But I told the manager: 'Look here, you ought to be ashamed of yourself! This ins't *khash*!' So I spit on it and left...."

"*Khash* has to be prepared at home," said the client.

"My wife gets a headache from the smell of garlic," lamented Agasaf-aga. "She's high-strung.... Will you be wanting a shampoo?"

Agasaf-aga thrust his client's head under the shower. In preparation he shook the bottle of shampoo and, pouring a

---

* *Khash* — traditional rich meat soup. — *Ed.*

351

little of the fragrant liquid onto his palm, sniffed at it with great pleasure.

The nylon brush made circles in the lather on the head. The barber lathered the thick hair several times. He always washed his clients' hair with great fastidiousness and groaned with satisfaction as he worked.

"Compress! Razor!" cried Agasaf-aga, once again tucking a towel under his client's collar. He bent down and examined the man's face. "Ay-yay-yay!" said Agasaf-aga. "What kind of irritation did you make here?... You have delicate, good skin. One person in ten thousand has that kind of skin, but you have to spoil yours.... You probably use an electric shaver. Aha! I thought so. Nothing good can come of an electric shaver. Now it's fashionable, but you'll see in two-three years people will start shaving the old way again. Does it hurt? I know it doesn't hurt. I'm asking just in case.... Yesterday I read the papers.... They're writing about Kennedy again. Despite all the time that's passed, they're still writing.... You think those reporters get money for that every time? Ah? If that's so I wouldn't mind doing a little writing myself. What do you think? Who killed him?"

"I would tell you," answered his client, carefully moving his lips, covered with lather, "but I'm afraid they'll put him in jail."

"Who? They'll never arrest him...." Agasaf-aga wiped his razor on the towel and took a brief rest from shaving his client. "You know where I lived before? Before, I lived on Chetvyortaya Parallelnaya, it was later that I got an apartment on Montino. Anyway, my neighbour there was named Daud. They put him in jail three times. His relatives got together, lead him into a mosque, and forced him to swear on the Koran that he would stop his bad ways. Daud swore an oath. And, sure enough, he was a different man. He opened up a little shop and worked as a shoemaker.... How do you want the temples, straight or at an angle? Whatever you say, but straight temples are more becoming to you. Straight or at an angle? Ha.... From morning to night, Daud repairs shoes. Everyone is happy.... Then one day I drop by on my way home from work. 'They've arrested Daud,' says someone. What? Arrested him?! He stabbed someone. There was a trial. Turns out that a customer came into his shop and made some trouble. Daud said the customer did it on purpose, the customer swore it was an accident. They gave Daud three years.... You understand, sooner or later a guy like Daud will do something.... Now he's back repairing shoes, but I know that sooner or later he'll pull something. Nothing good can come of people like Daud...." Agasaf-aga directed a thin stream of Eau-de-Cologne from an atomizer onto the smoothly shaven face of his client. "I don't recommend powder. Let your skin breathe." Without looking he stuffed the money into the pocket of his smock. "Stop by more often. I'm always glad to see you."

At the doors stood a line of five or six men, who ignored the calls of "Next!" and the gestures that the other barbers made with their towels to attract customers. The line was composed of Agasaf-aga's steady clients.

"There'll be a five or six minute intermission," announced Agasaf-aga cheerfully to the line. He vanished behind a door, curtained in red velvet, leading into a neighbouring room. Here, he sat on a chair and, lifting his legs, supported them on a shelf, specially nailed to the wall for just this purpose. He had varicose veins which bothered him after working for two hours or so. Agasaf-aga pictured the blood flooding from his swollen legs back into his trunk and quietly moaned with pleasure. He opened his eyes in displeasure when the barber who worked at the chair next to his entered the room. He was a young barber who had recently been discharged from the army. He lived in the same building as Agasaf-aga and for that reason the master considered it his obligation to teach the younger barber the trade and a little common sense.

"I don't like you today, Gazanfar," said Agasaf-aga impressively, not turning his head. "My heart bled when you shaved that doctor.... You didn't notice how coarse his facial hair is? You did? You should have lathered his face, then put a hot compress over it, then lathered it again.... You know what kind of sound there was when you shaved him? Like a file scraping over iron. I suppose you're proud of yourself. What is he to you? Your mortal enemy? Or does he pay in forged currency?"

"He was quiet," answered the abashed Gazanfar. "He never said that the razor irritated him...."

"And he won't say so," Agasaf-aga snapped back. "Why should he say anything? He'll go to another barber next time. He won't sit in your chair. And at your age I already had steady customers. It's about time you did too."

"You're different," said Gazanfar. "You have talent. Every barber in Baku knows that. It's a gift of God."

"There's only one kind of talent that a barber needs," said the flattered Agasaf-aga in a voice expressing great displeasure. "Diligence. And attention. If you remember which Eau-de-Cologne pleases a client, and whether he likes a hot or a cold compress after his shave, then that client will stand in line for two hours just to sit in your chair.... The main thing is that the client doesn't feel that you're hurrying when you work on him. That's insulting. Then you have to talk to him, to ask if the razor is irritating him.... And you tell me, 'I shave him, he doesn't say a word.' Maybe he's shy...."

Agasaf-aga entered the room, passing Gazanfar who stood respectfully at the door, and walked over to his chair where a young man with a splendid coiffure "a la Beatles" waited patiently.

"Only trim the back today," he told Agasaf-aga, "and give me a shave."

"What about the moustache?"

"All right," said the youth overcoming a certain inner reluctance, "trim the very tips, over my lips...."

Agasaf-aga nodded and began with great ceremony. After his first passes, the boy's face assumed a beatific expression and he relaxed.

After work Agasaf-aga and Gazanfar usually left the barber shop together. In good weather they would walk to the metro station. Agasaf-aga explained once and for all to Gazanfar that walking could prevent such unpleasant things as diabetes.

"Yesterday I saw well-to-do people walking along the boulevard. You think they don't have their own cars? They do. Their own personal cars. Then why do you think they walk every evening? Because they want to live. They don't want to come down with diabetes, they don't want a stroke. It's understandable. Such people have everything — money, an apartment, a car — but they're not healthy. He-he."

Gazanfar listened respectfully and nodded. He had great reverence for Agasaf-aga.

353

They stopped by a small café close to the station. Agasaf-aga opined that a clever man should always dine before coming home. "You never know," said Agasaf-aga, "what's awaiting you at home. If my wife has prepared a good supper I'll eat it after any shashlik. But if she hasn't prepared anything for her husband?" Gazanfar knew that there was a good possibility that Agasaf-aga would not have supper waiting for him at home.

They went into the basement room of the café. The waiter came out from behind the counter and respectfully shook their hands.

"I don't recommend the shashlik," he whispered to Agasaf-aga, "the meat's tough. The *khinkal** is better today...."

"Two *khinkals*," said Agasaf-aga. "Bring us two, and keep two hot and waiting for us. We'll tell you when we're ready for them. And a carafe of vodka."

They each consumed two portions of excellent *khinkal* and drank a good glass of vodka each. They washed the vodka down with beer. Agasaf-aga insisted that if vodka or cognac was immediately chased down with water or beer, you would not get cancer of the esophagus. Agasaf-aga knew a thing or two about medicine.

"I had wanted to become a doctor," he told Gazanfar. "But I realised that I am a master barber. You understand," said the intoxicated Agasaf-aga. "I have a wonderful trade. I am Agasaf-aga, a master barber. Everyone knows me and I respect myself, and I don't give a fig for the rest."

Gazanfar knew that for Agasaf-aga "the rest" meant his wife whom he feared greatly.

Gazanfar attempted to pay, but Agasaf-aga stared at him with threatening eyes and said to the waiter: "How many times do I have to tell you that when this boy's with me, you shouldn't take his money." He slipped the waiter his money and reeling with satisfaction from food and vodka, went outside respectfully supported by the waiter.

In the courtyard, Agasaf-aga invited Gazanfar up to his apartment. When he tried to refuse, Agasaf-aga angrily grumbled that he ought to listen to his elders, and Gazanfar relented and followed him up to the third floor.

Agasaf-aga lived in a large apartment with three rooms together with his wife and two children—Samid and Fasil. The apartment was well and expensively furnished. Agasaf-aga had picked out the furniture himself.

Agasaf-aga opened the door with his key. They went into the dining room. The table had not been cleared. Evidently five or six people had recently dined there. Agasaf-aga went to the bookcase and took down his *nardy*.**

"Let's see how you play," he told Gazanfar.

While he set up the pieces, Agasaf-aga entered the kitchen. "Give us tea," he said to his wife. "Did you have guests?"

"My colleagues from school," said his wife. "What, are you playing *nardy* again? Disgusting!"

Gazanfar knew that Agasaf-aga's wife invited guests only when she knew he would not be at home. She obviously was embarrassed by his presence. She had finished a course at an institute by correspondence. While she studied, Agasaf-aga had hired a girl to help with the housework and every evening he took

* *Khinkal*—a local sort of pasta.— *Ed.*
** *Nardy*—a table game played with checkers and dice popular in Middle Eastern countries.— *Ed.*

the children for a walk about the neighbouring square. Upon graduating, she changed remarkably. She changed her tone; this was particularly evident when she conversed with her husband. She taught English. Gazanfar could not understand how this was possible, since in his opinion she made mistakes when she spoke Azerbaijanian and Russian, not to mention English. One of Agasaf-aga's steady customers had arranged a job for her in the school downtown.

Gazanfar and Agasaf-aga played *nardy* in silence. Agasaf-aga usually fell silent at home. His wife brought two glasses of tea and set them down with a clatter. Agasaf-aga measured her with a lengthy stare, but his wife, ignoring this entirely, walked into the other room and made a phone call.

"You're right, my dear," she said to the receiver, "of course it isn't seal, not the right kind of piles. Probably it's fake mare."

"Not piles, pile," said her fifteen-year-old son Samid.

"I've told you a thousand times," said mother, covering the receiver with her hand, "not to correct me."

"Well, it's pile all the same," Samid would not stop. "And this morning you said 'I bought a kilo of sheep when you should have said 'mutton'....'"

"Who's going to bring sugar for our tea?" cried the martyred voice of Agasaf-aga. "*I've* just come home from work!"

"Can't you hear that I'm talking on the phone?" said his wife glancing into the dining room. "Get it yourself if you need it. I'm not a hired maid!"

Agasaf-aga banged on the table with all his might.

The checkers and dice on the board leaped up and rolled onto the parquet floor.

"Who's house is this?" cried Agasaf-aga in a fury. "How dare you talk to me like this? What am I, a thief, a murderer? Why are you talking to me like this, I ask you?"

Gazanfar rose and left the apartment on tiptoe. On the landing of the first floor he could hear: "I've told you a thousand times. That barber has no business in my home. Don't bring him here!"

"This is not your home, but mine! I'll bring home whoever I please."

This was a typical row and subsided as suddenly as it had begun. Agasaf-aga went into the bedroom and, putting on his pyjamas, hopped into bed with pleasure. He lay there, feeling the blood pulse in his swollen veins, and found it terrifically pleasant. His thoughts flowed familiarly and smoothly. "As though I don't earn more than anyone in the building. I give her everything. Summer in Kislovodsk, you want to? Go right ahead. Go for three months, for four. Invite your colleagues over? Go ahead. Every day if you like. She has everything. What else could she want? What should a man do? Earn his keep! No one earns more than I do in this building! The trouble is with her family — her deceased mother was a bitch too. That's the problem here."

This thought brought back his mental equilibrium. Agasaf-aga turned over on his right side and was ready to doze off when he felt Samid's hand.

"What is it dear one?" said Agasaf-aga. "What is it, son?" He was crazy about his children and the blackest of his moods vanished as soon as he caught sight of them.

"Papa," said Samid. "I need some money."

"How much?" asked Agasaf-aga.

"To tell the truth," said Samid, "I need five rubles. But I would be happy if you gave me three."

"Why three?" marvelled his father. "I'll give you five." He dug in his pocket and handed his son a five-ruble bill. "What do you need the money for?"

"Oh," said Samid. "Well we want to buy a real soccer ball."

"And why are you so glum today?" said Agasaf-aga to the eight-year-old Fazil, standing silently by. "Here's a ruble for you. Buy yourself some ice cream. How are things in school?" asked Agasaf-aga as he drifted off to sleep.

"All right," answered Samid cheerfully.

"Mama said you got a 'D' in ... what is it.... I can't remember what that subject's called ... trip ... or is it trap...."

"Trigonometry," laughed his son. "It's all right. Don't worry, Papa."

Agasaf-aga ended this instructive talk, kissed both boys and would have finally gone to sleep had his wife not entered the bedroom.

"We're going to the cinema tonight," she told her husband.

"What showing?" asked Agasaf-aga catching his breath.

"The nine o'clock showing."

"Then there's still time," rejoiced Agasaf-aga. "I'll sleep for an hour and then we'll go. Thank God, the theatre's close by."

"Oh no!" snapped his wife. "We're going downtown to the 'Azerbaijan'. So you just get up, shave, and put yourself in order."

"Look here," begged Agasaf-aga. "I'm tired. My legs hurt. Can't we go to the cinema on my day off?"

"I want to see this film like anyone else — on the first day it's showing."

"Well, I'm not going!" shouted Agasaf-aga. "I'm going to die in this building and you don't give a fig."

"That's enough!" said Samid entering the bedroom. "I'm sick and tired of this. Stop it. The neighbours are laughing at you...."

"You see?" said his wife to their son. "I'm guilty. I'm trying to drag this man to the cinema! And it's my fault that he works in a barbershop. My fault!"

Samid gestured hopelessly and exited.

Agasaf-aga put on his best suit and new brown mackintosh. His wife examined him critically and forced him to change his shoes. Then she made him change his cuff-links. Finally she was satisfied. She dragged her own coat from the chiffonier and asked her husband to hold it. Recently she had taken to asking her husband to help with her coat each time she left the house.

They had good seats in the ninth row on the aisle. Agasaf-aga was already glad that they had come. He examined his wife with great satisfaction. She was very well dressed, with diamond earings and rings and bracelets on her well-groomed hands. These were no imitation stones, but genuine. And that was as it should be. Agasaf-aga loved to give his wife valuable things, and he earned enough to do this almost every year.

"Of course it's good that we came to this cinema. The sound is good here and the audience is always respectable." Agasaf-aga indicated a couple making their way to their seats.

"That's the Vice President of the Academy of Sciences," he whispered in his wife's ear.

The Vice President, coming up alongside them, greeted Agasaf-aga affably.

"That's General Mamedov," said Agasaf-aga, shaking the hand of his next acquaintance. It turned out he had many acquaintances and they all greeted him warmly.

"How do you know all these people?" asked his wife.

"I know them all. They respect me."

His wife shrugged her shoulders disdainfully.

As soon as the film started, Agasaf-aga took his wife's coat so that she would be more comfortable as she watched it and, having bought two ices, commenced biting at the crunchy cone with gusto. He was enjoying himself, his legs didn't hurt, the film was apparently interesting, and the ice cream cooled his tongue.

Some people behind him burst out laughing.

"Stop champing!" whispered his wife.

Now Agasaf-aga ate without a sound, but he had stopped watching the screen.

When they arrived home, the children were asleep. Agasaf-aga went into their bedroom. Hardly breathing he looked at the children, and as always a wave of tenderness passed over him at the sight of "his flesh". He covered the youngest who had kicked off the bedclothes and kissing them both left the room. He didn't feel like sleeping, so Agasaf-aga slipped on his mackintosh and went out onto the street.

On the square in front of his building, Agasaf-aga sat down in his usual place. Generally he came here after a row with his wife. A couple sat on a neighbouring bench, kissing abandonedly; they took no interest in the impression this made on Agasaf-aga. Agasaf-aga looked away from the girl's bare knees and thighs with embarrassment. The hem of her short skirt was riding up even without that, and Agasaf-aga caught himself wanting to go up to the boy and say: "Listen, the hem of your girl-friend's skirt is riding up." But he'd be offended, Agasaf-aga decided and changed his mind.

"Now they're kissing," thought Agasaf-aga with a sudden rush of bitterness. "I'll see what happens when they get married, whether they still want to kiss each other in the square. I used to kiss girls myself," Agasaf-aga thought of his wife and grew very sad.

He rejoiced at the arrival of Gazanfar, who sat down beside him.

"Can't sleep?" asked Gazanfar.

"Don't be offended by her," said Agasaf-aga. "She's not a bad person, just very high-strung."

"I'm not offended," said Gazanfar. "I feel bad for you. Excuse me, but you're such a master barber that the whole city knows about you. Everyone respects you. On the other hand, even though you earn more than anyone in the building, you live worse. She doesn't respect you, yells at you in front of other people. Just think — she graduated from an institute. On your money. What would she be without you!"

For a moment Agasaf-aga was struck dumb by Gazanfar's boldness.

"Look here, don't forget who you're speaking to.... I swear, if I didn't think of you as a son, I would never forgive you.... You're still young, you don't understand. A wife doesn't mean anything. The most important thing in life are children. I have two sons.... They'll grow up and be my friends. They'll understand everything, they'll love me and consult with me about everything. Right now they're closer to their mother. That's natural. She's bringing them up. But when they grow up.... Understand?"

357

Gazanfar shrugged his shoulders sceptically.

"You believe me ... I'm enduring everything for their sake...."

"Life is passing by...." said Gazanfar.

"Life is still ahead of me.... Oh, well. It's late already. Let's go home. Tomorrow we have to get up early."

Taking a break for a moment, the couple on the neighbouring bench watched the friends walk away.

In the morning, as always, Agasaf-aga was up earlier than the rest. Quietly he went into the kitchen and conscientiously went through his morning exercises. He made a few movements with his elder son's 2 lb barbells. Then, having toasted a few chunks of bread and brewed strong, genuine Ceylon tea, he breakfasted with a hearty appetite. Agasaf-aga, already dressed, went into the bedroom. His wife was awake.

"You know that today is Samid's sixteenth birthday."

"Ay-yay-yay," said Agasaf-aga and went into the children's bedroom. "Congratulations! I wish you the greatest happiness and wisdom so that I, gazing upon you, will have cause to rejoice. Are you having company?"

Samid nodded.

"Good boy! A good man should always have plenty of company. There's room for everyone in our home."

Agasaf-aga was in an excellent mood as he descended to the courtyard. Gazanfar was waiting for him.

Pleasantly excited, Agasaf-aga told Gazanfar, as they walked: "It seems you have no knowledge of life.... 'Your wife respects you, your wife doesn't respect you....' Listen, what difference does it make whether mine respects me or not.... I don't give a fig for anything but my wonderful children ... my future friends. That's the main thing. Does your wife respect you?"

"She respects me," said Gazanfar. "And she'll respect me all her life. I'm the most important person in the world to her...."

Agasaf-aga gazed upon him with pity and, laughing, gave it up for lost: "Young! You're so young!"

During his break, Agasaf-aga did not go off to breakfast in a café. He used the time to buy six bottles of champagne. The breakfast that Gazanfar had brought from home sufficed for the two of them. They sat in the room reserved for the employees and ate *dolma** with gusto, pouring *matsoni* over it from a bottle which Gazanfar pulled from a small suitcase.

"Does your wife make you a breakfast like this every day?" asked Agasaf-aga.

Gazanfar proudly nodded.

* *Dolma*—grape-vine leaves stuffed with meat and rice.—*Ed.*

"She's a good cook," said Agasaf-aga. "Better watch out or you'll put on weight. Well, time for work. Thank you."

Agasaf-aga told almost every client that today was his eldest son's sixteenth birthday, that almost the entire class was coming over to celebrate, that at first he hadn't wanted to buy wine for them, but then decided that it wouldn't do any harm if they each had a glass of champagne and that was much better than forcing them to drink on the sly. The clients congratulated him and said that it really wouldn't do any harm, and that it was marvellous that Agasaf-aga had such a grown-up son.

"There are good kids in his class, from good families. Today they'll all coming to our place," announced Agasaf-aga to the whole barbershop.

On the radio was a recording of a concert by Zeinab Khanlarova. The conversations died away. At such a time it was not customary to talk in the barbershop.

"How she can sing!" sighed Agasaf-aga. When she sang a *tesnif*, a tear or two even slipped from his eyes. Agasaf-aga was sentimental. "Who knows if she's married?" he asked.

No one in the barbershop could say.

"What do you care if she's married?" asked a client.

"I want to wish her good children. She brings people happiness. She should be happy too."

At that the conversation about art ended. Agasaf-aga looked at his watch and began to hurry. He waited impatiently while Gazanfar finished shaving a fat colonel and, throwing off his smock, went out onto the street.

Early spring would already be sensed in Baku. It was twilight. A fleeting aroma of acacia hung in the evening air. Agasaf-aga gave his bag with the champagne to Gazanfar to carry and walked along slowly, sniffing the air with pleasure.

"A man doesn't really need very much," he said to Gazanfar. "If all at home are well, everything else is unimportant. Look, spring is here again. I wonder how many more there'll be."

In the courtyard, Gazanfar congratulated Agasaf-aga on his son's birthday.

"Thank you," said Agasaf-aga. "God grant that we drink to the health of your sons. It's about time."

Agasaf-aga opened the door with his key and entered the apartment. The dining room had been cleaned and everything put in order for the guests' arrival. In the kitchen, Samid was beating lumps of sugar with a mortar and pestle. His wife busied herself at the stove.

"Why should I tell your father? You're already grown-up. Tell him yourself. There's nothing wrong with it."

"What's that?" asked Agasaf-aga, appearing in the kitchen doors.

359

"Nothing," said his wife.

Agasaf-aga ate in the kitchen. He ate pilau, good pilau! His wife had prepared it specially for his son's birthday. It was cooked properly; each grain of rice was separated from the others; it had been flooded with suet with yellow streaks of saffron. Agasaf-aga poured himself half a glass of cognac, and drank to the health of his son and the happiness of his family.

"I'm going to lie down for a while," he said, "until the guests come." Entering the bedroom, he noticed that the beds had been removed.

"The children are going to dance here. We put the beds in the children's room," said his wife. "Listen, Samid wanted to ask you something, but he's embarrassed...."

"Why should he be embarrassed?" said Agasaf-aga. "We shouldn't be ashamed to tell each other anything. What do you want, son?"

"Papa, you understand, I invited almost our whole class, you said I could, the boys and the girls.... But they're shy in front of you. Couldn't you go somewhere until twelve o'clock.... Don't be offended...."

"There's nothing to be offended about," said his mother. "I'll serve everyone and then go into the kitchen or over to the neighbours' place.... Everyone does it.... There's nothing to be offended about."

"What are you trying to persuade me for?" said Agasaf-aga. "I understand. I won't embarrass your guests. You have your interests and I have mine. I was getting ready to go for a walk anyway...."

The square in front of the building was gently illuminated by neon lights. A pleasant spring breeze was blowing, the same breeze of spring that compels poets to write verses, good or bad, and lovers to say words which they will finally understand in autumn or not at all. Agasaf-aga sat in his usual place. It was pleasant to sit and watch the children play.... Then the children went off and young couples appeared. Generally they were occupied in kissing. Only the bench where Agasaf-aga sat remained unoccupied. Nobody paid attention to this heavy, homely man with the indifferent, puffed-up face.... Or perhaps it was not Agasaf-aga at all. In spring, people on squares are generally preoccupied with themselves....

Then Gazanfar came. He did not say a word, simply came and silently sat beside his friend. But if someone had watched them he would have seen how these two men rejoiced in each other's company.... But be so good as to tell me who needs to watch someone on such a marvelous spring evening....

"I'm happy," said Agasaf-aga. "Today is my son's sixteenth birthday.... God grant you, Gazanfar, to experience the same.... You know I have a piece of land at Pirshagi, on the sea. For many years now I've dreamed of building a home there. I swear to you that I'll do it in the next few years. You'll come and see....

My sons will grow up and we'll go hunting and fishing together. Each night I'll talk with my sons about life, politics.... You know how I love to talk about politics.... And each night I'll have a table full of guests.... And my sons and I will have a pleasant word for everyone, a piece of bread, and a soft bed...." Agasaf-aga talked and talked. Gazanfar listened, but did not interrupt because he sensed that Agasaf-aga believed strongly in what he was saying and one must not dissuade a man when he believes in something strongly, for that is truly a sin.

**Rustam
Ibragimbekov
(b. 1939)**

*A talented prosaist, scenarist and playwright. He was born and raised in
Baku. He is a trained electrician. In 1967 he completed advanced studies
in scenario writing in Moscow. Many films have been based on his
scenarios, the most popular being* The White Sun of the Desert. *Rustam
Ibragimbekov's plays*—The Woman Behind the Green Door, The Man
Who Looked Like a Lion, Along My Own Road—*are currently being
produced throughout the Soviet Union.*
His novella In that Southern City, *in the collection* Forgotten August,
won him national acclaim as a prosaist.
*Rustam Ibragimbekov has a profound grasp of psychology and is
interested in the moral problems of our times.*

A Cottage by the Sea Shore

He had to get to Mashtagi by 8 o'clock in the morning, hire a workman there and take him out to the cottage at Bilgya.

"Why should I have to do it?" he thought pulling on his trousers. "And what's the point of it anyway?"

He was thirty years old. By Monday he had to finish an article on the possibilities of applying certain methods of the theory of stability in economic management systems. For the last few years he had not so much as banged in a nail in his own bachelor's flat, and therefore the necessity of going to Mashtagi for a workman and taking him out to put a roof on his mother's country cottage irked him by its very injustice.

His mother, a plump, stout, short-winded woman, worked simply as an administrator although she had been trained as an engineer, and drew a pension as an invalid — she had pains around the heart and something wrong with her legs. Some three years ago she had suddenly decided that she needed a "piece of land", which she was going to cultivate herself. She had never before felt a yearning for the soil; an energetic and business-like person, she had borne with assurance the economic burdens of any institution into which her employment had cast her and had never had time for anything else.

But then suddenly, on announcing her decision one day, she had set about translating it into reality with such determination that one would have thought she had been nurturing this ambition all her life. To her credit, she managed, in the early days, to infect her sons with her own enthusiasm. At that time they all still lived together in an old flat on Baku's Fourth Parallel Street, a nice old place with one window looking out upon over the cracked earth-bitumen roof of the neignbouring house, a creaking wooden balcony, a Mülback piano and a large political map of the world extending the entire length of the long corridor. He was then 27 years old and his elder brother—who was quite a well-known urologist—was 30.

Mother came home agitated and resolute, sat on the wooden trunk under the map of the world, and, without waiting to get her breath back and periodically interrupting her announcement with her sharp bronchial coughing, informed them of her intention to build a cottage in the country.

For several weeks afterwards, while she was acquiring a section on the Apsheron peninsula not far from Novkhany through the special trust which handled such transactions, the subject of the cottage—"a cosy little white house with a veranda and a grape-vine around it"—arose in their family conversation every day. In the mornings, before dispersing to go about their various business, and in the evenings, after dinner, they got a lot of pleasure out of sharing their ideas for their cottage by the sea shore. Mother went into details about the construction of the house, about the well which would have to be dug and fitted with a motor, the chicks for whom a coop would have to be built. They worked out the design for the house down to the last particular and dreamed of arriving there on a hot summer day, devouring a chicken each and hurriedly undressing and running down to the sea.

But when summer arrived, it became clear that for their family the construction of a country cottage was an utterly utopian enterprise. They had greatly overexaggerated their potentialities: quite apart from the fact that there was a lot that they didn't know and couldn't do, none of them except for mother could find enough time to work on the project; they were all continually distracted by their own affairs. The first to throw in the towel was his elder brother. This happened when most of the stone and cement had already been carted out to the section.

The truck carrying a load of stone blocks got stuck in the sand some 300 metres from the section. After several hours of fussing around under the stupefying rays of a parching sun they managed to pull it out. Then, without a break—so as to finish the job before nightfall—they lugged the blocks over the building site. Everyone took two blocks each—it was impossible to take more—and, bathed in sweat, carried them across the scorching sand, which sucked their legs down as they struggled along. Mother, who was suffering from shortage of breath and heart pains, also did her bit. She had strength enough for one block and she could only move slowly with frequent stops, but nobody in the world could have forced her to abandon that stone. At times she sank down onto the sand under the strain, panting heavily and hoarsely....

It was on this day that his elder brother announced that over the next few weeks he would be very busy with his dissertation and unable to come out to the section.

Mother wept that night—he and his father lay a few metres away from her and heard her sobs muffled by the blanket—but in the morning she picked up another two blocks without saying a word and began to carry them over to the building site....

364

And on the following day she hired an old stone mason who lived nearby and began to build. The old man's 12-year-old grandson transported the water and stone on a little grey donkey, mother mixed the cement herself, the stone mason layed the blocks, and father — a philosopher by profession — prepared meals for them. Father would not take part in the work in any other capacity — neither his frame of mind nor his health would allow him.

Continually interrupted by lack of money, shortage of materials and, for an even longer period, by the bad roads, the construction of the cottage went slowly ahead: a fence was put around the section, a well was dug, in which several buckets of water accumulated over the course of a day, and the walls rose up....

And now Mansur — for so he had been named, in honour of his late grandfather — had to get to Mashtagi by 8 o'clock, hire a workman and take him out to put the roof on....

He pulled on his trousers, went over to the writing desk and read the last sentence — of the article composed yesterday. He immediately took a strong dislike to the phrase. "Why does it have to be me?" he thought again depressed by the prospect ahead. It was about 7 o'clock. He had ten minutes left for shaving.

He brought a hand mirror out of the bathroom, took a seat by the window and, before plugging the shaver in, swore to himself for the umpteenth time that tomorrow he would buy a wall mirror.

When he had finished shaving, Mansur telephoned his elder brother, who was still asleep, of course, and asked him to wait for him until two o'clock.

"I'll just take the man out there and be back. I'm fed up with it all too...." Mansur told his brother about the state of affairs at the section and agreed with him that mother's health would not allow her to live there alone, and it was no use relying on father — once he got in to town, you wouldn't get him back out to the cottage in less than a week.

"A completely senseless waste of time and energy," his brother summed it up, "so much trouble over that cottage and in the end she won't be able to live there anyway...."

Mansur hung up and thought what a lucky fellow his brother was; he got away with everything. Even after he had run away from the section mother very quickly restored him to her good graces, and now he only came out very rarely; he would appear round about the end of the day for five minutes with some ridiculous present, kiss her, tell her he was terribly busy, and shoot off back to town. Yes, he certainly knew how to put himself across!

Mansur made the journey to Mashtagi by bus — one just happened to come along. And he had no trouble finding a workman.

The sun was burning down from the side, right into his ear. The workman trotted beside him, bobbing up and down comically and halting now and then to shake the sand out of his shoes, which were white with dust. Mansur would stop and wait till the other could continue on his way again. The long overgrown toenails on the workman's short, wide feet were thick and almost square and their colour resembled the dark horn frame of Mansur's glasses.

Mansur was thinking about his own affairs. He had to make it back to town by two o'clock without fail. His brother had arranged to go with some friends to visit Sattar-zade, who had long been promising him one of his latest works. His brother was not interested in painting and Mansur had to go along with him to remind him there on the spot about Sattar-zade's promise. He would never

365

remember himself, and the opportunity to acquire a work by this artist would not be repeated....

Mother was digging around the grape-vine when they arrived.

"Ah, so you've come," she said not very affably, critically scrutinising the workman; it was clear she was out of sorts again.

Father was lying under the temporary wooden shelter reading a book. He had the ability to read one and the same book a number of times if there were no others at hand. A small, lean man, who remained unquestioningly subordinate to his wife in everything and had already forgotten the day when he had an opinion of his own if only on the most trivial questions, he was inflexible in one thing — he could not be made to work here. The only thing he did was to prepare meals and wash the dishes.

With a tired moan Mansur dropped onto one of the two iron bedsteads under the shelter. Here in the shade he suddenly felt how much his journey under the sun from Mashtagi to Bilgya had exhausted him.

Mother had already climbed up onto the roof with the workman.

"First you lay these," mother was crossly explaining — such was her way of dealing with workmen, "then the tarred felt goes down on top of it, you secure it with nails, and then you cover it with cement. Got it?"

"Why? What's so difficult about it, as if I haven't done roofs like this before."

"I don't know what kind of roofs you've done before, but this one has to be done properly. Don't try using sand instead of gravel. I'll check everything myself."

"What do you mean sand?" he asked in surprise.

"I know you lot," answered mother and began to climb down from the roof.

No workman could stick her out for more than a day. Three weeks before Mansur had arrived at the section in the evening only to see the husky labourer he had brought out from Mashtagi standing behind the house and pleading with hands raised heavenwards: "O Allah, rid me of this woman!"

"Well, I'll be off then," said Mansur.

"Where to?" asked his father in surprise.

A tiny sunbeam was shining through a crack in the shelter onto his bald skull, which reflected it like polished bone. They both looked in the direction of the house. Mother was handing some boards up to the workman, who was leaning over from the roof too, pulling them up and laying them, beside him.

"Just the time to clear out," thought Mansur.

"Here comes Useyn-bala," his father informed him; for all his myopia he had a good eye, "there'll be trouble now."

"Why?"

"The hammer's gone missing."

Useyn-bala was the watchman for all the cottages in the neighbourhood.

"Greetings!" he shouted on reaching the wire fence.

Mother did not reply. Father pretended that he had not heard and buried his nose in his book again.

"Greetings to you!" shouted Mansur in reply.

Useyn-bala stood by the fence for a while, then, without waiting for an invitation, crawled through the wires. On reaching the house he repeated his greeting. Mother carried on handing the shingles up without saying a word and didn't give him a glance.

366

"Sit down," Mansur moved his legs so that Useyn-bala could sit on the edge of the bed.

Father, realising that the storm would break any time now, kept his nose in his book.

"What an interesting dream I had last night," said Useyn-bala, apparently not suspecting anything, "I dreamt that I was sleeping at home alone, and suddenly someone began waking me. When I woke up, I saw it was Satan. He was shaking me by the shoulder. 'Get up,' he says. 'That's enough snoozing, Useyn-bala. You're coming with me. You've overstayed your welcome in this world.' My heart sank into my boots. Well, I thought, it's all over — your end has come, Useyn-bala. My arms and legs were paralysed. I lay like a corpse. And then, suddenly, I don't know myself where I got the strength from, I began shouting loudly — right into his face. He leapt up and made straight for the door — flew out like a bullet. He was in such a hurry that he bumped his head against the lintel. There was such a loud thud!... And then I woke up...."

"...And after that he calmly turns up here, sits himself down as if nothing were the matter and babbles all kind of nonsense," said mother turning to father.

"Mother!" said Mansur reproachfully. "That's enough."

But mother had already begun a decisive offensive. Changing over from Russian into Azerbaijanian, she proceeded to accuse Useyn-bala of stealing the hammer and boards.

"On your feet!" she shouted at him. "And don't let me set eyes on you here again till you give them back."

"You do me wrong, Dilyara-khanum," Useyn-bala protested, "I didn't take your hammer. May my children starve if I knew who took it."

He looked to be telling the truth. Even mother began to have doubts about the justice of her accusation, but there was no going back now, and as the distressed Useyn-bala departed, she proceeded — as if to convince herself — to adduce some very dubious arguments confirming the watchman's dishonesty.

The incident with Useyn-bala finally catalysed Mansur's intentions to leave. His mother had become completely impossible. For a whole year she had been friends with this man, drunk tea with him, shared her woes with him, arranged jobs for his children — and now because of one wretched hammer she had rendered all this null and void.

"Mother, you'll strain yourself!" cried Mansur suddenly, running up to his mother. He almost pushed her away and with a jerk which caused him a sharp stab of pain in the small of his back, handed the massive board up to the workman.

"I would have coped with it very well myself," said his mother obstinately and grabbed hold of another board.

"What do you think you're doing, specially trying to exasperate me?" asked Mansur.

"Why?" she replied in surprise. "What am I doing to you?"

And she looked at him with her obstinate hazel eyes, which effused from their depths a kind of pathological conviction, completely unfounded, of the righteousness and impunity of everything she did. It was only through an immense effort to control himself that Mansur refrained from swearing; he hated his mother at that moment....

367

Unhurried by nature, Useyn-bala had grown quite sluggish after the host of nonsense to which he had been subjected and had not managed to get very far. Seeing Mansur catching him up, he left the road and ran a few steps away to side of it.

"I swear by my life that I didn't take the hammer," he said stretching his arms out before him in desperation.

Mansur reassured him as best he could and begged him to excuse his mother's behaviour. He firmly decided at that moment to go back to town immediately and not to come out here any more. Once again he went over all his arguments in his head: the construction of the cottage had definitely driven his mother out of her mind; the fanaticism, the obsession with which she engaged in work beyond her strength could not be explained in any other way. After all, she knew perfectly well that no one — neither her husband, nor her sons — would live here with her, and her health made it dangerous for her to stay here alone; this had been repeated over and over again by her doctors and everyone around her. And yet despite this she was building and building. She was straining herself to the limit, sinking into debt, stubbornly, even ostentatiously, continuing to build this confounded house, which would ruin her in the end. He had to summon up resolution and act like his brother — avoid involvement in an enterprise which would be his mother's ruin. If only he could avoid being involved!

Father carried on reading. Mother was sitting on the sand with a hammer in her hand trying to smash a big grey stone into little pieces. She was all covered in dust. The sweat-soaked grime on her face had turned into a dark-grey glue and diffused into a variety of patterns.

Mansur went into the house. The workman had already managed to cover the roof with boards. In places he had even laid the tar felt down, covering up the cracks. Mansur found his old trousers among some things piled in the corner by the gas stove and wrapped them up in some newspapers. Father peeped into the room.

"What on earth are you doing?"

"I'm leaving."

"Aren't you going to help her?"

"No."

Father smiled sadly. Mansur tied some string around the bundle containing his trousers.

"Aren't you hungry?" his father asked.

"No. You don't know where my sandshoes are, do you?"

"On the veranda."

Father went for the slippers. Mansur walked over to the window. Mother was still fiercely banging the stone.

"What, is he leaving?" she asked father.

"He has urgent business in town," father explained.

She said nothing, only gave the stone an extra hard blow. Then another one not so hard. The stone was half buried in the sand. She didn't think to put another stone under it. But maybe she wasn't interested in whether it smashed or not. Maybe she simply enjoyed hitting the stone. Or maybe she didn't enjoy it but felt the necessity of it. She was breathing heavily and after several blows she would sag back, her corpulent body bulging out of her smock, her mouth gaping widely, trying to suck in a bit more air. Three years ago Mansur had seen her lying on her

368

side, dragging a heavy stone along as she crawled. He had got very frightened then: "What's the matter, mother? Why are you lying on the ground?" "It's easier that way," she had explained, "my legs don't ache." For the first time in her life she had made a confession of weakness. He had almost wept then. Now his pity for her was not so strong. But all the same it was painful to look at her banging away at the stone in order to hide her weakness and her resentment at her children.

"Mother," Mansur called through the window, "You're doing it the wrong way. You should put another stone underneath."

He realised that he should not have said that if he really wanted that picture from Sattar-zade.

"I tried that," she said after a pause, as if deliberating whether to reply or not, "it slips out."

Mansur went out of the house and walked up to her. She stopped banging the stone but maintained a guarded silence, not letting the hammer out of her hands. She was waiting to hear what he would say. "You can do what you like," her whole appearance was telling him, "I'm ready for anything from my children...." Mansur also kept silent. Again the thought crossed his mind that if he really wanted to leave he would have to say so now, this very minute, or else it would be too late.

"What's the man doing up there?" he asked without looking at her.

"I don't even know," she replied wearily, again after a pause, "I'll just climb up and have a look...."

"I had a look from down below. He's laid the boards quite well."

"The main thing is to make sure that he doesn't use sand instead of gravel."

"Oh, go on! He doesn't look that type...."

Mansur began smashing the stones into little pieces — it turned out that at least 50 bucketfuls would be needed — then carried the sand for mixing the cement, and then, already late in the evening, passed the mix up to the roof. Slinging several shovelfulls into the bucket, he climbed up the wooden ladder against the wall and handed it over to the workman, who upturned the mix onto a flat layer of gravel. Mansur only had to stop and his mother would grab a bucket or shovel so that there would be no interruptions in the work.

The sun was still high and its burning rays beat down heavily. The workman had wrapped his shirt around his head to protect himself against them.

"The sun can be very dangerous out here on Apsheron," he told Mansur, wielding his shovel, "it can drive you mad. I remember a local man from Gheradil telling me what happened when he was carting sand from a quarry on a truck. He used to do 20 or 30 trips a day under the hot sun. One day he came home — his mother wasn't there and the door was locked. He parked the truck in the street and sat in the shade of the fence. The sun was really sweltering. It was quiet all around.... There was no one about — only the neighbour's mule across the road standing tied to the gate and looking at him. He sat and sat. Then suddenly, for no reason at all, he got up, put the mule in the back of his truck and drove off. He'd completely lost his head and didn't realise what he was doing. The owner ran after him but he stepped on the gas.... Straight to the bazaar in Mashtagi he went. Sold the mule for a big sum. To this day he can't understand why he did it.... The sun had got him in the head."

369

Towards evening, when the sun had already descended more than half-way down towards the sea, the handle of one of the buckets broke. Mansur was working on the roof at the time and while the man was fitting the handle on again he got the chance to rest up a bit. He lay on his stomach on the new stone ledge with his face on the very edge of the roof where the unevenly cut strips of felt overlapped. His face burned with weariness and he pressed it to the rough surface of the stone, which had already had time to cool. Actually, it would be truer to say that his enfeebled neck could not support his head any more and his face was pressed to the stone by its own weight.

Below the workman was still fiddling around with the bucket. Mother sat beside him on the sand, keeping a watch on the work. From above she looked very much like his late grandmother. The workman was having trouble with the bucket handle and spent quite a long time fixing it. Gradually Mansur's torpor of weariness left him. Looking at his mother, he remembered the time many years ago when they had lived with grandmother in Pirshagi, in just such a house without a roof. It was wartime. Mother used to come from town every night and bring them food. When she didn't make it, grandmother would clean off the crumbs that had stuck to the bread-knife and he and his brother divided them between them....

Grandmother had died fairly recently, but for some reason she had stuck in the memory just as she was during that wartime summer in Pirshagi. Mother had now become very like her. In those years mother was good-looking. Or maybe that was just how she seemed to him then.

She loved to read to them. Mansur now realised that she was not in fact a very well-read person. But they did not know this then. She had several favourite books: *Rob Roy*, *The Little Tramp*, *Oliver Twist* and *The Little Lady of the Big House*.

...They would sit on the long open balcony of their flat on the first floor, from which a staircase led down and with great effort he managed to find room for himself on a small wooden platform on the balcony, which joined onto the staircase and listened for hours on end to the story of poor Oliver Twist....

He must have dropped off to sleep for a little while, because when he opened his eyes he saw his mother beside him. She was also sitting on the edge of the roof.

"What's the matter?" she asked. "Does something ache?"

"No," he said, "I just nodded off."

She fell silent for a little while and then, without looking at him, asked in a not very confident voice:

"Does your head ache?"

"A little."

She was probably embarrassed and therefore hesitated as if making up her mind before suddenly lifting his head up from the stone ledge and placing it on her lap.

"I'll massage your head if you like?" Once again she hesitated before speaking and again she asked without looking at him.

"Do," said Mansur.

She began carefully stroking his temples and forehead. The skin on the ends of her fingers was rough. Mansur just lay with the eyes shut. His mother's breathing was hoarse and her big loose stomach, which rested against the crown of his head, rose and fell in time with it. She had aged considerably in the last few years and somehow all at once and imperceptibly, he thought.

"Mother, do you remember how you used to read 'Oliver Twist' to me?" asked Mansur without opening his eyes.

"I remember."

She continued carefully stroking Mansur's temples and forehead and he lay with his eyes closed, thinking. Of course, it was good to have a firm character, as some people have, he thought, but it's not so bad to be kind as well. Each to his own, as they say and, after all, it was not absolutely essential that everything person did should be rational and directed towards a goal which he considered proper. There are situations when you do something that has long lost its sense for you but you continue to do it because people whom you love believe in this thing and do not realise what you have already realised. They are mistaken, from your viewpoint, and their sufferings are pointless, but it is impossible to abandon them if you love them, and how can one not love them....

What wonderful thoughts come to a man when he is lying on the roof of his own house with his head on his mother's lap and the treacherous Apsheron sun has already descended far beyond the sea!

Request to Readers

Progress Publishers would be glad to have your opinion of this book, its translation and design and any suggestions you may have for future publications.

Please send all your comments to 21, Zubovsky Boulevard, Moscow, USSR.

Progress Publishers

Put out recently

Short Stories by Modern Moldavian Writers

This collection acquaints the reader with stories by modern Moldavian writers.

Among the authors of the collection are Y. Burgiu, M. Chibotaru, I. Drutse, N. Esinenku, V. Iovitse, R. Lungu, A. Lupan, G. Menok, A. Shalar, S. Shlyakhu, A. Strymbianu, V. Vasilake, V. Beshliage, writers of different styles and manners. An acute perception of life in present-day Moldavia is combined in their work with the posing of profound social and philosophical problems, with an original national form, which is carefully preserved and developed by Moldavian authors.

The book is supplied with a preface about the development of the Moldavian short story and also with the authors' portraits and short biographical notes.

Progress Publishers

Put out recently

ISSAHAKIAN A. *Selected Works* (Poetry and Prose)

The work of Avetik Issahakian (1875-1957) is one of the most vivid and significant phenomena in the history of modern Armenian poetry.

Alexander Blok wrote in 1916, when he was working on translations of Issahakian's poetry: "Issahakian is a first-class poet. The whole of Europe may not have such a spontaneous talent."

This small collection of Issahakian's poetry, tales, stories and legends was translated into English by Misha Kudian and is being published to mark the centenary of the birth of this great Armenian poet.

The well-known Soviet poet Nikolai Tikhonov has written the foreword to the book.

Progress Publishers

Put out recently

DANGULOV S. *Lenin in Conversation with America*

"Lenin is a whole world," writes Dangulov in the foreword to his book, "a world that is vast and wonderful, and I have set myself the modest task of illuminating one small corner of that world: Lenin in conversation with America. It all began with my story about Lenin and Raymond Robins, who came to the Soviet Union an enemy and left a friend. Is not this an example of how Lenin could conquer a man's heart and mind, of how he sought and found friends everywhere?" Savva Dangulov's masterfully written documentary histories are widely known in the USSR and have been translated into many foreign languages.

Lenin in Conversation with America is based on little known documents and eye-witness accounts, and opens new pages of Lenin's life for a wide circle of readers.

The book is illustrated with documentary photographs.